Cenw

Rachael Treasure lives in southern rural Tasmania with her two young children and an extended family of Kelpies, chooks, horses, sheep and a time-share Jack Russell. She is passionate about encouraging non-readers to read, as well as inspiring farmers to consider regenerative agricultural practices and animal handlers to better understand their dogs and livestock. Rachael has been the proud patron of Agfest, Tasmania's world-class agricultural field day run by Rural Youth volunteers.

Rachael's first novel, *Jillaroo*, published in 2002, was a bestseller and has become one of Australia's iconic works of fiction, inspiring other country women to contribute to the genre of contemporary rural literature. She has gone on to write three other bestselling novels, two collections of short stories, a TV drama and a country song with The Wolfe Brothers.

**RT.** rachaeltreasure.com

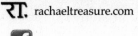 Rachael Treasure

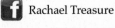

D1334056

2 1 JUN 2018
06. 11. 19

8 OCT 2018
02 FEB 18
9 APR 2018

Also by Rachael Treasure

*Jillaroo*
*The Stockmen*
*The Rouseabout*
*The Cattleman's Daughter*
*The Girl and the Ghost-grey Mare*

*Fifty Bales of Hay* (ebook short story collection)
*Fifty More Bales of Hay* (ebook short story collection)

# Rachael Treasure

*The Farmer's Wife*

HARPER

This novel is entirely a work of fiction. The names, characters and
incidents portrayed in it are the work of the author's imagination.
Any resemblance to actual persons, living or dead,
events or localities is entirely coincidental.

*Harper*
An imprint of HarperCollins*Publishers*
77–85 Fulham Palace Road,
Hammersmith, London W6 8JB

www.harpercollins.co.uk

A Paperback Original 2013
2

Copyright © Rachael Treasure 2013

Rachael Treasure asserts the moral right to
be identified as the author of this work

A catalogue record for this book is available from the British Library

ISBN: 9780007509829

All rights reserved. No part of this publication may be reproduced,
stored in a retrieval system, or transmitted, in any form or by any means,
electronic, mechanical, photocopying, recording or otherwise,
without the prior permission of the publishers.

This book is sold subject to the condition that it shall not,
by way of trade or otherwise, be lent, re-sold, hired out or
otherwise circulated without the publisher's prior consent
in any form of binding or cover other than that in which it
is published and without a similar condition including this
condition being imposed on the subsequent purchaser.

MIX
Paper from
responsible sources
FSC° C007454

FSC™ is a non-profit international organisation established
to promote the responsible management of the world's forests.
Products carrying the FSC label are independently certified
to assure consumers that they come from forests that are
managed to meet the social, economic and ecological needs
of present and future generations, and other controlled sources.

Find out more about HarperCollins and the environment at
**www.harpercollins.co.uk/green**

*For Luella Meaburn, my true earth angel*

*and Colin Seis, a quiet grassroots revolutionary*

*and my children and my guides,*
*Rosie and Charlie Treasure*

*and in memory of Dreams,*
*now in the clouds with Pegasus*

*An environmentalist once asked a wise guru,
'What use is your praying and meditating when you
are not really doing anything to stop the destruction all
around us?'
The guru replied calmly, 'Even if you managed
to clean up the rivers, oceans, soils and the sky,
the pollution will all come back, unless you cleanse the
human heart.'*

**Retold by Bhavani Prakash**


*What we are today comes from our thoughts of
yesterday, and our present thoughts build our life of
tomorrow; our life is the creation of our mind.*

**Buddha**


*The eternal feminine draws us upward.*

**Goethe**

Part One

# *One*

'You told me it was a Tupperware party!'

Rebecca Lewis folded her arms across her chest as best she could with two shaggy terriers sitting on her lap. She scowled at Gabs, who was swinging on the wheel of the Cruiser like an army commando. Gabs aimed cigarette smoke towards the Landy's window and puffed out a cloud, then delivered a wide, wry smile from her unusually lip-glossed lips.

'Get over it.'

The women were lumping their way over the wheel-scarred track, once a quagmire during a severely wet winter, but now a summer-baked road of deep jolting ruts. As they wound over shallow creek crossings and valley-side rises, Rebecca shifted under the weight of Gabs's dogs and hunched her shoulders. She looked out at the dry bushland around them that ticked with insects in the evening heat.

'I thought it would cheer you up,' Gabs offered.

'Cheer me up? Do I look like I need cheering up?' Rebecca frowned at her own reflection in the dusty side mirror. There were deep worry lines on her forehead. Her blonde hair, dry and brittle on the ends, was carelessly caught up in a knot as if she was about to take a shower. Hair that looks as coarse as the terriers' fur, she thought. Bags of puffy skin sat beneath her blue eyes like tiny pillows. She prodded them with her cracked fingertips. Her mouth was turned down at the corners.

Could she actually be a bitter old woman at thirty-eight? She closed her eyes and told herself to breathe.

'How can you *not* be cheered up by that?' asked Gabs, thrusting an invitation at her. Bec looked down to the silhouette of a woman naked save for her towering stilettos. The woman sported a tail and tiny horns like a weaner lamb. *Horny Little Devils*, the text read. *Making the World a Hornier Place. Australia's Number One Party Plan.*

'Tupperware party, my arse,' Rebecca said, rolling her eyes. The tiniest smirk found its way to her lips. She looked ahead on the road to Doreen and Dennis's farmhouse, tucked into the next valley. Maybe this party could be a turning point for me and Charlie, she thought hopefully. Ten years of marriage, two baby boys, the death of her father and a farm that failed to function. Charlie blaming the weather; Rebecca knowing different. Then there was her family, distant in the city. Her mother, Frankie, who seemed to not notice her, and big brother Mick, still treating her as if she was ten. And always, always, there was the memory of Tom. She sighed and pushed Amber and Muppet off her lap onto the floor and grabbed for Gabs's cigarettes.

Gabs glanced over with concern as Bec fumbled with the slim rolls of tobacco. Hands shaking, she put the smoke to her lips and swore as her thumb ineffectively ran over the coarse metal cog of the lighter, creating feeble sparks but no flame. She hadn't felt this down for years. Not since the years soon after her brother Tom's death.

'Oh, for god's sake!' she said, throwing the lighter on the dash and stuffing the cigarette back in the packet.

'Are you *right*? Since when did you take up smoking?'

Bec shrugged.

'Here,' said Gabs, passing her a bottle of Bundy, 'forget the ciggies, forget the Coke. Just cut to the chase.'

'But we've got crutching and jetting tomorrow. And I've got to get the boys to the Saturday bush-nurse clinic. It's Dental Day,' she said, still taking the square bottle of rum from Gabs.

'Dental Day! Again? Thank god Ted doesn't have teeth yet and Kylie had hers checked last month when we were in the city. C'mon, ya bloody sook! Listen to you!' Gabs made whining noises — a parody of the complaints that Rebecca repeatedly made, about Charlie, about the farm, about the weather.

'For god's sake, Bec, go have your period and jump in a shark tank! You need to make the best of your lot so suck it up, princess.'

Rebecca looked out through the heat-wilted wattles towards a stand of white-trunked gums and cracked the yellow top off the bottle. From where she sat, Amber sniffed at the rum and wagged her feathery terrier tail.

'None for you,' Rebecca said gently. She swigged deeply and grimaced at the rawness of the alcohol on the back of her throat.

Gabs looked across at her, softening now. 'I know it's been tough, with the mixed-up seasons and … you know … but build a bridge! You'll have fun tonight. And I didn't suck my tits dry with a pump for Ted's bottle just for you to pike out on me.'

Her friend's tone was humorous, but Bec wished it was harsh. She wanted a kick up the arse. She was used to harshness. She thought of Charlie again and the sight of his broad back as he'd slammed the door of the kitchen that afternoon, taking his fury with him into the yellow-and-green cab of the dual-wheel John Deere. She pictured him going round and round now in the dying light of the hot day, the big wheels crushing a track through the dust of the paddock. A paddock she'd begged him not to plough.

Once Rebecca had liked tractors, loved them in fact. And had loved Charlie within them. During the early summers of their marriage at Waters Meeting, she remembered the sweet smell of freshly baled hay. The big roundies bouncing out the back of the

New Holland and rolling to a stop on the green meadows. The way the cab door would open and Charlie would appear like a Bullrush-clothing-catalogue, sun-kissed god. His boots landing solidly on the steps of the cab, socks covered by canvas gaiters, the golden hair on his tanned legs covered in a fine film of dust. His teeth glistening white in the sun as he smiled, stooping to kiss her. She remembered him taking the smoko basket from her and dropping it into the fresh-cut pasture, and how he'd pressed her back up against the giant tractor wheel, kissing her harder, putting his strong hand up under her shirt, the smell of the hot sun on the rubber tyre making the moment even sexier. His hands urging between her legs, which were smooth and honey brown in ripped denim shorts. Summer love. Newlywed love. Tractor love.

Rebecca shook away the memory. Long gone now. The farm and the river that had run through it and fed her soul had dried up — and so had that magic between her and Charlie. Nothing seemed to lift her out of a stupor that had only deepened when her second son had arrived. Nothing, except for meeting Andrew Travis. After that her whole world had begun to shift. Everything felt changed. She crushed her back teeth together till her jaw ached. 'Maybe I should go on anti-depressants.'

Gabs butted out her cigarette in an already overflowing ashtray. 'Or maybe you should go on a ten-inch dildo!'

With the Bundy now starting to warm her, Rebecca couldn't stop a sudden jolt of laughter spluttering up, just as Muppet and Amber nosed their way back onto the seat and sat like a pair of Ugg boots on her lap. Reaching over the dogs, she picked up the hot pink Horny Little Devils catalogue from the dash and flicked through it. 'So what *is* a jelly butt plug and a Gliterous-G anyway?' she asked, her head tilted quizzically to one side, her freckled nose wrinkled.

Gabs shrugged. 'Dunno, but I'm sure we're about to find out!' And with that she floored the LandCruiser, setting it sailing over a culvert drain. They shrieked as the wheels spun mid-air. The

Cruiser landed with a bone-jarring thud, tyres hitting the rims, smokes falling from the dash, dogs' claws digging into Bec's thighs, two-way radio handpiece falling down. Then on the women drove, their laughter drifting up to the sky along with the dust.

'Fuckerware party, here we come!' Rebecca yelled.

# Two

Charlie Lewis took a swig of his stubby, then set it down in the drink holder beside him, belching out a puff of beer-soaked breath. He adjusted the revs on the tractor, feeling smugly satisfied with his choice. Why should he settle for a 224-horsepower tractor when he could go all the way to the top with a 300-horsepower one? Plus, as he'd told Rebecca several times, he could get a bonus diesel voucher from the dealer if he bought it before the end of January. And it came with not just one but *two* free iPhones!

'One for the missus,' the dealer had said brightly.

Charlie checked his phone to see if he was in range. It'd be good to call Murray to have a bit of a skite about the new Deere.

There was better mobile service at the top of the riverside block so he'd have to wait another round to make the call. The digital clock in the tractor was glowing 8.36 pm, exactly matching the time on his phone. He patted the tractor dash.

'Legend,' he said to it.

Murray, who had finished shearing at Clarksons' today, would by now be taking the cut-out party of his rouseabouts and shed hands to the Dingo Trapper Hotel. Charlie wished he was going too, but he thought back to this afternoon and identified a foreboding conviction not to push his wife on the issue. She was still snaky with him for coming home at two in the morning after cricket training on Thursday.

Charlie recalled the sight of Rebecca's jean-clad backside, which looked surprisingly broad from his angle, as she rummaged around in a kitchen cupboard.

'Why can't I find any fucking lids?' Rebecca had said, jumbling through the clutter. 'No matter what I do, there are never any complete sets of containers. And why is every bloody party organised round here "bring a plate"? I don't know how many of my effing containers are scattered about the district! And now they want me to buy more at a bloody Tupperware party tonight! It does my head in.'

Charlie wanted to say, 'Everything does your head in these days.' Instead he bit his tongue.

In her exasperation, Rebecca began to crash things about a little too roughly for Charlie's liking. He knew the plastic container cupboard was dangerous territory. It was the place where he had seen his wife lose her shit the worst. Particularly when it was school-bus time and Ben's lunch wasn't quite packed and ready to go. Best not to offer help at this stage, he thought, just in case. Charlie leaned on the bench, hands thrust deep in his pockets, looking down to the front of his blue checked flannelette shirt, where the buttons strained. He tried not to look at Bec, who was now kneeling on the floor holding a blue ice-cream container in her lap, staring at its lidless form. Her shoulders were hunched forwards, shaking.

Oh shit, Charlie thought, is she crying? Over lidless containers? Or is she laughing? He bit his lip and rolled his eyes, sauntering forwards, knowing he'd have to do *something* now.

'C'mon, Bec, it'll do you good to go to Doreen's. You could get a new set of containers. Get a bit more organised. It'll help you spend less on groceries.'

Bec swivelled around and delivered him a flash of fury so strong it was like a kick to the head. Charlie held up his hands as if surrendering to a firing squad. 'I was only trying to help.'

Bec got to her sock-clad feet. 'Help? You reckon *help*? Patronise me more like.'

'I … I …' he stammered.

'When the fuck did my life become all about Tupperware and messy cupboards, Charlie?' Tears welled in her sky-blue eyes, her face scrunched with emotional pain. She thrust the container violently at him and he received it like a mid-field rugby pass, clutching it to his stomach.

Charlie stared blankly at her, his mouth open. 'What do I deserve that for? I work my arse off on *your* farm for *you*.'

'You just don't get it, do you?'

'What's there to get, Bec? You're always mad. You're always sad. Not much I can do about it.'

'Do you ever wonder *why*?'

Charlie shrugged.

'Maybe it could be something to do with a two-hundred-thousand-dollar tractor we can't afford,' Bec said. 'Geez, Charlie! A tractor we didn't need. And then you went and got a brand-new fucking plough. And the fact that I'm stuck here! Stuck in this fucking house!'

'Someone's gotta do the house stuff. And you might think we don't need the machinery, but *I* do!'

'Why does the house stuff have to be done by *me*? That was never the deal! And you know how I feel about ploughing. Have you not listened to a word I've said on soils and no-till cropping? Since learning Andrew's stuff, I never wanted to plough a patch of dirt again on this place!'

Charlie, who had tolerated her surly mood till now, turned his head to one side and shut his eyes for a moment. Then he opened them, glaring at her. The anger rose. 'Oh yes! That's right! Andrew, Andrew, Andrew … your god of agricultural change!'

he said sarcastically. 'Just because I'm not into your bloody New Age farming guff, don't take it out on me! You're just upping me because you like bollocking the crap out of me over nothing.'

'That's not true!'

Charlie thrust the ice-cream container back at her. 'Put a lid on it, Rebecca,' he spat. 'Find another babysitter for the boys. I'm going ploughing.' As he pushed past her, he made sure his shoulder collided solidly with hers. Then he walked out, slamming the door.

Now, in the dying light of the evening, crows with wings like vampire cloaks were haunting the plough, trawling the clods of earth for grubs and arguing with the white cockatoos, who screeched and flapped with indignation at their dark companions. Charlie sighed and glanced at his green eyes in the rear-vision mirror, noticing the lines around the edges of them and the way his once thick brown hair was now thinning on either side of his forehead. Where had the years gone?

And why did his time feel so wasted here? Here on a farm that had never been his. Waters Meeting. Rebecca's place.

He ran his grease-stained fingertips over his rotund belly and scratched it through the fabric of his bluey singlet. So what if he had a bit of a gut? What was the harm in a few beers? He thought of Rebecca and the way she constantly badgered him on his diet too, while she dished up salad for the kids that she had grown in her vegetable garden. He would glower at her and defiantly toss shoestring chips from a plastic bag into the deep-fryer, along with a handful of dim sims.

'What's wrong with only wanting to eat peas, corn, carrots and spuds?' he asked one night as he pushed aside her dish of cauliflower cheese.

'The boys,' she said. 'Eating all types of good food is the most important thing for them to learn at this stage.'

He twisted the lid off a Coke bottle, relishing the loud fizzing sound, and eyed her as he gulped straight from the bottle.

She rolled her eyes in anger and turned away. She was so easy to bait like that. But bugger her, he thought. She could be so fucking self-righteous about everything.

For the first few years of their marriage it had been fun, and it was never about the fact that he ate mostly meat and spuds with a small side of peas, corn and carrot. She'd not minded then. She'd been a good chick and their days at Agricultural College had cemented their relationship into one of deep friendship. When he first moved to Waters Meeting, he'd felt a sense of relief that he'd escaped his own family tangles on their farm out west.

After Bec and he were married, Bec's father, Harry, had been an all-right sort of fella to share the space of the farm with. One-armed since a posthole-digger accident, the old man had mostly kept out of Charlie's way, badgering Rebecca about what should or shouldn't happen on the farm. For the last few years Harry'd been too sick to do much anyway and stuck to himself in his log cabin. But since he'd died, Charlie had noticed a shift in Rebecca. A restless frustration. Some days her moods were too much to bear.

Then bloody Andrew Travis and his no-till cropping ideas and holistic grazing management seminars had got into Rebecca's head and she had completely gone off the dial about how he should run the place from now on. She was chucking out over ten years of his good management all because of some Queensland guru who kept banging on about regenerative agriculture and all the profits to be gained from low inputs.

Even though Charlie knew there wasn't much profit at the end of the day on Waters Meeting, couldn't Bec see their *production* was better than the other farms in the district? He remembered their shared passion in the early days when she'd brought him in as 'cropping manager' and, of course, her boyfriend.

For the first few years the business had hummed, exporting hay that was cut from the rich lucerne flats to fancy stables in

Japan. They'd even travelled to Tokyo for a month, living it up with fancy-pants racing people who couldn't speak a word of 'Engrish', but could chuck back sake like you wouldn't believe. But five years into the venture the Aussie government had pulled the pin on water rights due to salinity issues hundreds of kilometres downstream from the farm. Charlie knew it had more likely been due to political pressures after a documentary screened on prime-time television about the evils of irrigation. The water was shut off to them. Waters Meeting had become a dryland farming operation overnight. And once again, like when Bec had first returned from her time away at Ag College and jillarooing, they had had to fight to keep the farm afloat.

In the midst of the fight over water rights, Rebecca had fallen pregnant and she'd become annoyingly philosophical about their situation, saying the irrigation ban was 'meant to be'. She'd said over time she'd realised that it didn't sit well with her to be carting hay around the world. It wasn't environmentally sound, she'd said. Bloody women always changing their minds, Charlie thought angrily. They'd busted their guts to set up the operation and now his very own wife was turning green on him like the rest of the wankers on the planet. What was wrong with her? Didn't people realise farmers fed the nation? And so they should be supported accordingly?

Charlie glanced again in the mirror and watched the plough discs cut neat crumbling lines in the dry paddock he'd sprayed last week.

A plume of topsoil eddied in the gentle breeze. He twisted his mouth to the side. It was too dry to be cultivating: Bec was right. There was something in his gut that told him what he was doing was wrong, but he just couldn't help himself. Kicking up dust was better than sitting at home watching Ben and Archie fight. He felt a twinge of guilt, knowing how crapped-off the boys would have been when they found out they were being plonked with Mrs Newton, their elderly neighbour, for the night again. They could've easily fitted in the spacious new cab with him. They'd been so excited about the new tractor.

Charlie swigged his beer and washed away the thoughts, instead choosing to focus on the new dream tractor. He loved everything about it, from the way the giant glass door pulled open, to the wide view from the cab through even more expansive glass. The massive John Deere was so sleek and modern it looked as if it belonged in one of Ben's *Star Wars* animations. It didn't just have a dash; it had a 'command centre display'. There was even a gyroscope that automatically made steering adjustments when Charlie drove fast down the smoother gravel roads of Waters Meeting. He'd love to try it on the newly sealed main road. Plus the GPS, once he'd worked out how to use it, would mean that his furrows would be perfectly even and straight.

He reached for his fourth stubby and popped the top off it, enjoying the gentle bounce the hydraulically sprung seat offered. It's enough to give me a hard-on, he thought wickedly, toasting himself in the mirror and cocking an eyebrow.

As he rounded up to the top of the paddock, his phone beeped a message. Murray, texting to say it was humming at the Fur Trapper, the locals' nickname for the Dingo Trapper Hotel. Charlie sent a text back saying he was on the chain for the night. Cranky wife. But bloody nice tractor.

As the sun dipped, and the fifth beer sank, Charlie settled into feeling a strange mix of boredom and friskiness at the same time. As if on cue, his phone beeped again with a text. He reached into his top pocket.

When he opened the photo up on his phone, he smiled and chuckled. There, on the small screen, was the image of Janine Turner in some rare kind of silky purple number with what looked like a black salami thrusting up from her ample cleavage. *Come get me later, cowboy!* came the message.

Charlie Lewis drained the last of his stubby. He paused for a moment. Knowing he shouldn't, but with the blandness of his life pushing him on, he reached for his belt buckle with a wicked grin on his face. What was wrong with a little bit of play? Janine was always up for it. She was about to get a nice shot of his gear stick. That would fix her.

# *Three*

Doreen and Dennis Groggan's farmhouse was set in an over-grazed paddock in a narrow valley. Etched along that valley was a jagged, eroded tributary that, in times of rain, fed the larger Rebecca River to the east, the river after which Rebecca was named. The Groggans' was a small, poor dirt farm surrounded by a swathe of bushland that swept up and over rocky gullies and ridges. The land and the isolation of the farm made it not so profitable, so as a result, on weekdays Dennis drove the school bus and Doreen worked at the school as the cleaner and groundsman. Judging from the state of the house, Doreen was good at keeping things in order at home too, Rebecca thought.

On their silver wedding anniversary, Dennis had painted the weatherboards yellow-green for Doreen after being inspired by the colours of their budgie. Rebecca looked at the meticulous yet overdone house and garden. The colour reminded her not so much of a budgie as of a pus-filled cheesy gland on a sheep.

'What would have been so wrong with cream or white? That's just downright tacky,' she said, gazing long-faced at the neat-as-a-pin budgie-coloured house. They rounded Doreen's turning circle of conifers, strategically placed bush rocks, wagon wheels and concrete creatures.

'Get over yourself, cranky pants,' Gabs said, this time sternly.

Rebecca almost hung her head in shame. Where had this dark mood descended from? And was it actually a mood? These days it felt more like a way of *being*. As if she had been like it for years.

The notion scared her. She looked out the window again, not wanting to socialise here with these women. Not wanting to be anywhere.

She could see most of the guests had arrived so the brittle yellow front lawn was already filled with a selection of battered dust-buffed country cars and utes. Rebecca rolled her eyes when she saw dark-haired Janine Turner totter forth aboard tarty 'follow-me-home-and-fuck-me' shoes of shining gold. Janine tugged down a purple negligee over ample Nigella-style hips while balancing a bowl of corn chips, her handbag and a purple horse-lunging whip in the other hand. She waved gaily to them as they parked.

'Oh geez! Look at her get-up!' Rebecca grimaced. 'You never told me it was *fancy dress*!'

'You never would've come.' Gabs unclipped her seat belt, swung round to the back and dragged out a Woolies green bag. 'Ta-da!' she said, emptying the contents of the bag onto Bec's lap. Rebecca pulled a face as she held up the items one by one: a sequined silver skirt trimmed with feathers, an orange boob tube, red high heels and a packet of red fishnets.

'So? Do you like your kinky costume? I made the skirt out of one of Kylie's princess dresses from the costume box. Don't tell her. She'll get the shits up. And I got the shoes on eBay. I think they had a bit of Baby Oil or something on them, but I cleaned them.'

'You are joking, right?'

'Shut up and get changed.' Gabs grinned. 'Or you'll be the odd one out.'

'What's new?'

'You could just thank me,' Gabs fired back. 'Where's your attitude of gratitude?'

Rebecca shook her head, knowing her friend was right. What had happened to her life? She used to be so sure of her place in the world. She never went to women's gatherings, preferring to be out in the pub or the paddocks. Sure she'd had to debate every decision every inch of the way in a three-way tussle between herself, her father and Charlie, but they had started out with what she thought was a shared dream. Then the babies had come. And life had changed. She found herself driving off to play group and doctors' appointments and ladies' fundraising lunches while the men punched sheep through yards, their world obscured to her by dust.

She would glance in the mirror at the two little boys in their car seats, Ben with his dark hair and sincere brown eyes and Archie with his wayward blond locks and dimpled cheeks and smiling eyes of blue. She loved them with every cell of her body, but the daily grind of domestics that they created was eroding her very being. Then there was Charlie. Rebecca pulled her thoughts up so they slid to a stop like a reined-in horse. Her thoughts drifted hopefully, involuntarily, to Andrew. But again she put on the brakes. She just couldn't go there. He's just a friend, she told herself.

Keep it shallow. Shallow, like her breathing had become. Shallow like her life.

'Don't just sit there,' Gabs said as she applied a thick layer of blue glitter eye shadow to her heavy lids in the rear-vision mirror, then tried to pluck a solo chin hair out with her thick thumb and forefinger. 'You've got tarting up to do.'

'And what about you?' asked Bec as she began to reluctantly kick off her boots and pull her socks from her hot puffy feet. 'I don't see you wearing a costume.'

Gabs glanced over to her slyly, then with a daredevil grin ripped off her oversized T-shirt.

'Ta-da!' she said again, revealing a black-and-red bustier, her white bosoms spilling up over the top of the lacy cups. Her farmer's singlet tan lines made her look a lot like a paint horse of white and brown.

'Frank goes nuts for me when I dress up. The other night we got pissed on Beam and he told me to get naked except for my cowgirl boots. And I did —'

'Too much information!' Bec said, holding up her hand and smiling. But internally she grimaced. How many years had it been since she and Charlie had mucked around like that? Since Ben was born six years back? Since before then? She couldn't remember. She could only recall the cold wall of his back and the passionless way he grappled at her in the early hours of the morning, when her body was leaden with exhaustion. He entered her with primal thrusts that were absent of care or love. There was an air of aggression within him that had started to cloud his contact with her. Bec could even feel it in his touch. She rubbed at her shoulder that felt bruised from their clash in the kitchen. It wasn't the first time he'd shoved her in a rage.

As she pulled on the fishnets, she felt the shame of leading such a disappointing life hidden within her apparently functional marriage. On the neighbouring farm, there was Gabs, who must be pushing eighty kilos, naked in cowboy boots doing the wild thing with an even beefier Frank after ten years together. Frank and Gabs seemed madly crazy about each other still, apart from telling each other to fuck off every now and then. They had met at Charlie and Rebecca's wedding. Gabs, her best mate from Ag College, was one of the bridesmaids and Frank had been invited along as he was one of the local farmers. A relationship had sparked between Gabs and Frank over a post-wedding-day carton of beer that they shared on the back of a ute by a dam. Soon Rebecca had found her good college buddy moving into her very own district and marrying her neighbour. At the time, both girls had thought they'd each stumbled upon a match made in heaven. Not so now, Rebecca thought. Only one of them had got it right. Here she was, practically a born-again virgin in wedlock. As Rebecca jammed on the red shoes, she noticed the way her lily-white sock marks were still evident through the fishnet stockings, drawing a line on her ankles that ran to summer-brown legs, a bit on the hairy side. Like Gabs, since motherhood, she too had put on weight and with the fishnets hoicked up to her hips, she imagined her thighs might look a bit like Christmas hams.

By the time she dragged on the makeshift sequined skirt and put on the boob tube so her slightly flubbery stomach rolled out, Gabs was doubled over laughing, falling about in her cork-wedge shoes on the lawn, trying, with her weak post-baby bladder, not to wet her G-string.

'You look hot, Bec! Hot. Hot, hot, *hot damn!*'

Bec sucked in her stomach, stood up straight and held her middle finger up at her friend, then went to the back of the four-wheel drive to collect the platter of dips and biscuits that had been inelegantly thrown in a silver takeaway container and covered with cling wrap.

'I'll have you know I could make a lot of money dressed like this down at the Fur Trapper Hotel. *A lot of money.*'

After winding each window down a little for the dogs and finding a water container for them, Gabs came to stand near her. 'You do look hot, seriously. Maybe we both could lose a bit of chunk round the middle, but check out the guns on us!' She flexed her arm muscles. 'Frank loves my guns — they're particularly good since bale carting. We did six hundred little squares for the new racing stables. Said they'd double their order next summer, until they got their own paddocks set up.'

At the mention of Frank loving Gabs's body again, Bec's face fell. Did Charlie even notice her looks any more?

Gabs picked up the plummet in her mate's mood. 'It'll be OK,' she said, moving to give her a rough sort of hug. Bec felt tears well in her eyes. She wanted to see Charlie as a good husband. When she thought about it, he did put up with a lot. But then again, she put up with more! Was it normal to feel this way?

'Hey,' Bec said, extracting herself too soon from the hug, 'people will think we do a lezzo double act with you groping me like that. Now let's get inside and get this so-called Tupperware party over.'

She marched to the gate in her strappy eBay shoes, nearly doing her ankle in the process. Gnomes grinned at her from nests of white pebbles as she walked along a brown-painted concrete path, flanked with solar lights and identical plastic versions of Jamie Durie designer flax. The spiked dark-leafed plants were spaced as evenly and as exactly as soldiers on parade. Gabs and Bec came to stand on a porch enclosed with corrugated green Laserlite, adorned with hanging baskets overflowing with dangling plants of bulbous juice-filled leaves and infrequent drooping purple flowers.

Before Gabs even knocked, Doreen reefed the door open. She was wearing a very short nun's costume, her legs like cottage cheese in her black fishnets and her feet like pig's trotters shoved into black patent leather pumps. So big was her bosom, it looked as though she had an inflatable raft stuffed down the front of her nun's habit. The fringe of her eighties-style bob had extra product in it and looked much like echidna spines as it protruded out from her black-and-white habit.

'Hi, Sister Doreen! Say your prayers, baby! The goddesses are here!' Gabs said.

'Hello, strumpets,' Doreen said. 'How are you?'

'Great, Dors. You look hot!'

'Yeah, fifty going on fifteen,' Doreen said.

'I like your new garden. Those fake plants are pretty cool,' Gabs said.

'Least the fucken possums and wallabies won't eat 'em,' Doreen said proudly. 'And they'll only melt in a bushfire. Come in, come in. We're about to start.'

'Where's Dennis?' Rebecca asked.

'Hiding in the shed,' Doreen said over her shoulder. 'He's set the telly up in there with a couch. He's got a box of beer and a DVD of cricket highlights so he's happy. A bit terrified, but happy.'

They entered the kitchen, where they found Amanda Arnott, wife of the local publican, at the bench, carving a carrot into the shape of a penis. 'Hello, slutties!' she sang. 'Just exhibiting my extensive creative talents!' There was a glint of the knife and her large diamond rings shining beneath the kitchen lights as she waved a carrot at them. 'Might try these as an extra to the side salads at the pub!'

'There'll be more orders for chips and salad than veg. Especially if you serve it up in that outfit,' Rebecca said, nodding at Amanda's skimpy French-maid costume.

They heard a collective shrill of laughter rise up from the gathering of women in the room next door.

'Go through, but take a Cock-sucking Cowboy with you!' Doreen said, handing them each a shot glass full of cream liqueur. Then she went back to putting bright red sausages onto a platter that had every kind of phallic-shaped food imaginable, including battered savs, gherkins and crabsticks.

'Care for a *cock*tail before you go?' Doreen asked, offering up a bowl of 'little boys' and larger saveloys, her grinning teeth framed by patchy bright red lipstick. 'You've got a choice of big ones, or little ones. The little ones I call "disappointments",' she said as she picked up a small cocktail sausage and bit hard through it with her crooked teeth.

'Oh. My. God,' Rebecca breathed as she took up a little boy and dipped it in tomato sauce. 'Tupperware indeed. I can see tonight is going to get messy. Very, *very* messy!'

# Four

When Rebecca and Gabs entered Doreen's lounge room, it was like walking into a teenager's bedroom overflowing with excited hormonal girls. The giggling, chatting women from the surrounding districts were all dressed like hookers, trannies or tarts with feather boas, lace or sequins. Many of them weighed on the large side, to the point where some might even warrant a spot on *The Biggest Loser*.

Together they huddled around Doreen's dining table as if it was half-time at the footy. Doreen's demure lace cloth was covered with glistening folds of black velour, on which sat an array of naughty novelties, romantic remedies and (more disturbingly for Rebecca, who had been expecting lettuce containers and drink bottles) items such as vibrators, 'bullets' and egg-shaped 'marital aids'. There were clear-faced boxes containing fetish and fantasy costumes. Rebecca noticed that Speedo, the Groggans' budgie, whose cage sat beside the dining table, was discreetly covered with a sheet as if the items on the table would upset his avian sensibilities.

'No Tupperware in sight,' said Bec. 'Don't reckon I'll be fixing my lunch-box deficit here.'

'Nah,' Gabs said, 'but you might fix your *box* deficit problem.'

'Hah! You dirty girl!'

'You have to admit some of those things do look like kitchen appliances. You could mix a cake with that one,' she said, pointing to a giant red vibrator.

Bec grinned at Gabs as the women turned to greet them warmly.

Candice Brown from the Bendoorin general store, two hours' drive away, stepped out of the huddle to give Rebecca a quick hug.

'Good to see you, Beccy. It's been ages,' she said. 'You should come in and get your groceries personally, instead of getting them delivered on the school bus! I miss seeing your lovely smile.'

Nicknamed by the locals 'Candy Shop', Candice Brown was anything but the brown her married name suggested. She was as bright and colourful as a licorice allsort in both looks and personality. She had vividly dyed curly crimson hair that tonight was pinned up so that ringlets fell prettily about her friendly round face. At the store, she could always be easily found in the rows of groceries, wearing her vibrant pinks, reds and yellows teamed with black leggings. Tonight she'd opted for an electric blue taffeta number and six-inch heels, topped off with a hot pink boa and a plastic six-shooter held in place by a frilly garter belt on her bare thigh.

'You look great!' Bec said. 'Like a Western gal who hangs out in the rooms above saloons.'

'Brian almost wouldn't let me out the door.' She laughed. 'Dirty old coot! He loves his Westerns.'

'Here's to whiskey and wild women!' Gabs said, passing another Cowboy shooter to Bec and Candice. 'You look good enough to eat, Candy Shop!'

Bec smiled as she thought of Candice's husband, Brian, who also ran the store-cum-post office. He was the opposite of his near namesake, the lean, chiselled actor Bryan Brown. Instead he was tiny, skinny, rarely spoke and always wore beige. Bec couldn't even imagine Brian getting randy. How was it that he and Candy were so different, yet after running the same store together for thirty years and raising a family of three, they seemed so happy together? Bec decided there and then, she really must make more of an effort with Charlie. Focus on his good points, instead of chewing through his bad.

She was about to search for a chair to sit on when she was distracted by the disturbing sight of Ursula Morgan on the lounge. Ursula was testing the seams of her white Lycra kinky nurse's outfit with her giant Jim Beam gut, the indent of her belly button creating a crater like the moon's. She was yelping with seal-like laughter as she took a photo on an iPhone of Janine Turner. Janine was lying back on the couch, stuffing a gigantic black dildo between the long line of her cleavage and pouting in her pose. Once the image was captured, Ursula began frantically texting.

'I'll tell him the blokes have finished fundraising for the moustache-growing month of Mo-vember and now it's our turn. Us girls are now fundraising for Fan-uary! Growing your pubes for a good cause!'

'Fan-uary!' screeched Janine. 'He'll like that! Can I be in charge of *Pubic* Relations?' Her crow-call laughter filled up the room.

'I'll need a whipper snipper for mine when I'm done!' Ursula muttered as she texted. Janine waved the dildo about in the air as she grabbed another slurp of her drink, a satisfied smile on her fake-tanned face. Rebecca smiled wanly at the sight of them, wondering which poor bastard they were tormenting tonight with their text messages and dirty photos. What was it about women who lost all shyness and sensibility when they were on the drink?

The normally ultra reserved and often bitter Ursula was the daughter of a local logging contractor. She had, at the age of twenty-seven, already managed to help keep the tiny school at

Bendoorin open with her brood — not to mention the gene pool nicely mixed for such an isolated region. She had four kids to four different fellas, causing confusion at school craft-making classes in the lead-up to Father's Day.

Ursula still lived at home with her parents and treated them like crap daily because she could. Her Centrelink payments meant life ticked over and was OK, if a little boring. Bec often found it oddly creepy that Ursula's portly father sometimes still referred to her long lustrous black hair, which she could sit on, as his daughter's 'crowning glory'. Because it was the only bit of praise from her father she'd ever received, the woman had never cut her hair. Sadly it was now greying slightly on her high forehead, but still fell way below her backside, which in recent years had expanded to the size of a large beanbag.

Her friend, or more accurately occasional drinking buddy, Janine, was the complete opposite to Ursula. She was one of the few 'graziers' wives' from the larger properties in the district who tried ever-so-hard to be landed gentry. She walked for miles and miles along country roads to keep her body lean. She adorned said body in all the chunky jewellery she could order from the *Country Style* magazine classified section. Janine was great at dressing richly conservative and tossing her highlighted auburn locks with immense snobbery as she walked into sheep shows on the arm of her excessively quiet, red-faced Merino-man husband. But on nights like this, Ursula and her constant flow of Jim Beam were Janine's undoing and all her airs and graces slid down to her ankles.

'Oh, hello, Rebecca!' Ursula said, her tone a little tainted with drunken sarcasm. 'Didn't see you there.'

Janine gave her a wave of the dildo and a wry smile.

In response, Rebecca picked up what she'd read was a Gliterous-G and waved its pink jelly-like eight inches back at the two terrors. 'Hello, girls,' she said, then turned to Gabs. 'I really need another drink.' Before they could make their way back to the kitchen to mix a Bundy, though, Doreen was clapping her hands, shoving two fingers in her mouth and whistling loudly like she'd just called a Kelpie off the stock. The women instantly fell silent.

'Ladies! It's time to start! Welcome to the Horny Little Devils night,' Doreen said in a drawling, twanging voice that made the word 'horny' sound like a motorbike passing. 'This is Tracey and she's our Horny Rep.' Beside her stood a demure girl, dressed all in black, with heavy eye makeup and jet-black hair pulled tightly back in a pony tail.

'Geez, check out the woman-child,' muttered Gabs as she surveyed the sex-toy consultant. 'As if she'd know how to use this stuff. She looks like she's still in grade six.'

Bec stifled a giggle. Tracey stepped forwards. 'Evening, ladies. I'll walk you through the catalogue. We'll start with our lingerie and finish with the boys' toys.'

Rebecca flicked to the first page, where a fake-tanned, breast-enhanced, air-brushed bottle blonde was slipping off the strap of her hot pink, sheer Yvette Babydoll with matching G-string. Bec's eyes meandered over a few more pages of 'flog-me'-style black lace corsets with suspenders for the larger ladies. For the more demure there was the Courtney Gown in elegant duck-egg blue with 'sexy thigh-high splits'. She wondered what Charlie might do if she turned up dressed in some of the clothing. Maybe as the raunchy police officer, complete with gun, baton and hat, whispering to him, 'Frisk me?' He'd probably laugh at her.

As Tracey passed a few samples around, the women began to 'ooh' and 'ahh' at the potential the outfits could bring to their marriages and partnerships.

'Now if Doreen here sells over fifteen hundred dollars' worth, she's in for tonnes of free product.'

'Not used, I hope!' Doreen snorted.

Tracey smiled patiently. 'Which brings us on to cleaning. On page twenty-two, there's a range of play wipes and safe sterilisers for your vibrators.'

'So you don't just wash 'em and hang 'em on the line?' Janine chortled.

'No,' said Tracey, straight-faced.

'Not in the dishwasher?' Janine added.

Tracey gave her an 'I've heard it all before' look and soldiered on, holding up a six-inch iridescent blue Wallbanger complete with 'additional dolphin', flicking the on switch so the thing contorted like Flipper having a seizure. She passed it to Doreen, who shrieked and almost threw it to her daughter-in-law, Bonnie.

'Oh my god,' Bonnie said, blinking from behind her glasses, 'I can't believe my mother-in-law just passed me a vibrator! I'm going to need therapy!'

Rebecca reached for a crabstick, smiling as the other women laughed. Soon the buzzing Wallbanger got to her. 'Here, Gabs, test it on your schnoz,' she said, buzzing the vibrator to Gabs's long, red-from-rum nose.

'Oh my god!' squeaked her friend. 'I think my nose just went off! It's not dripping, is it?'

Laughter erupted from within Rebecca. 'That is *most* disturbing,' she said.

'I'd be gone before I'd even put the batteries in that thing,' Gabs said, taking it from her. 'That's just too much!'

Next Tracey was holding up what looked like a fancy seat belt for a racing-car harness. 'This is part of our Fetish Fantasy range and is the Door Swing. So you attach it to the door frame like this …'

'Looks like a baby's jolly jumper,' Gabs muttered. 'Ted would love a go in that, then once he's in bed, I could let Frank have a crack at it with me in it!'

'That is utterly gross,' Bec said.

From the back row of women, Ursula called out, 'Would it hold me? Reckon I'd bring the supports of the roof down if I got going in it!' Some of the women struggled to stifle their giggles.

'It takes up to one-twenty kilos,' Tracey said.

'That means I'd need a bloody small bloke,' Ursula said.

'You could grab one of those new jockeys from up the road to give it a go,' Gabs suggested. 'Come to think of it, if you weren't in it, you could fit three jockeys in there. They're only about forty kilos each, aren't they?'

The women all laughed. Jockeys had been the focus of jokes lately since the sale of Rivermont. It was the district's second largest farm after Rebecca's Waters Meeting and a bit more sizeable than Janine's husband's Elvern Estate, and had in the past twelve months sold for three million. The new owners, who wanted to expand their racing operation from Scone, had dived in and proceeded to give the entire property and homestead a facelift and transformation that was beyond belief. Within months it had been cultivated into a premier racing training and breeding facility that would rival the Packers' polo place.

It wasn't the only change the locals were dealing with. The previous summer the road from Bendoorin had been sealed right up through the valley so that rich sightseers wanting an easy glimpse of the summertime snow country could now drive their BMWs and Mercedes Benzes through the valley comfortably. There were also mutterings that the mining companies were sniffing about for new leases.

In short, Bendoorin was experiencing a renaissance. So much so that Candice's daughter Larissa had opened a coffee shop that served flat whites and chai lattes to the Rivermont staff, new tourist trade and mining men.

Transition and change were in the air and, even though there were employment benefits (and sexy visiting tradesmen for the women to ogle), most of the locals didn't like it. Particularly Rebecca. Her quiet backwater farm of peace and solitude had now become a thoroughfare for ski-bunnies, bushwalkers and weekend tourists looking to escape the city during holiday periods, along with four-wheel drives packed with workwear-clad men carting geo-equipment and core sample drilling rigs.

And the conversion of Rivermont to a place frequented by pukka big-money corporates and the best racehorses on the planet was just another pain in her arse.

Absolute tossers could now be found at Candy's store, asking for organic sourdough bread and low-fat soy milk for their coffees. And there was often a rowdy queue at the counter when the playful Rivermont staff zoomed into town in their sign-painted work vehicles and bought up all the sausages and steak from the meat section for their pissy barbecues, leaving none for the locals.

'Bugger the Rivermont jockeys and the snobby bastards there,' Ursula said. 'I'm sick of their bloody helicopter flying over and upsetting me pigs!'

'Hear, hear,' said Rebecca, raising her empty glass.

Just as the other women joined them in a toast, in walked a stunning woman, dressed in skinny jeans and knee-high leather boots. A classy blonde pony tail pulled back from her clear vibrant face meant it was difficult to tell her age. She could have been in her late twenties or early thirties. Or she could have been a well-preserved forty. Rebecca looked at her with a tinge of regret. It was how she wanted to look. How she suspected she *had* looked before life had got in her way.

'Sorry I'm late,' the woman said to Doreen, glancing around the room.

'No problems, duck. We've only just started. Everyone, this here's Yasmine Stanton. From Rivermont.'

The ladies eyed her more thoroughly.

'Yazzie, for short,' she said with a big perfect-toothed princess smile. 'Everyone calls me Yazzie.'

'Jazzie Yazzie,' Bec heard Ursula mutter, knowing news of the presence of the leggy blonde in the area had already spread like wildfire among the Bendoorin men. 'More like fucken Barbie.'

If the woman had heard Ursula's comments, she didn't react. She just beamed a smile and graciously accepted a shooter from Doreen, downing it and eagerly grabbing up a second.

An hour later Doreen had Tom Jones blaring from the stereo. Some of the women were gyrating on the specially bought red shag-pile rug. Gabs's terriers, who had now been allowed into the house, were up for some fun too, trying in vain to hump the rug and the leg of anyone who would stand still for long enough. Amanda Arnott was attempting to slide down the half-metre banister on the small stairs that led to the bedrooms and bathroom, getting her bum-crack wedged on the turned wooden knob each and every time before pivoting onto the floor onto her back, snorting laughter. Candice was peeking through Speedo's cage, trying to feed the disgruntled budgie her hand-made 'cheese dicks'.

Bec, who sat at the smorgasbord of sex toys, tried again to focus on her order form and ignore the chaos about her. What on earth should I get? she wondered, flicking through the catalogue, muddled by the rum. She decided to switch to water for the rest of the evening. What would Charlie like? He never even talked to her much about sex these days. It was as if he had shut down from it. It shocked her to realise she no longer knew what her husband liked. As her pen hovered over the order form, she heard a voice beside her. 'Hi, I'm Yazzie.'

Rebecca looked up. 'Rebecca.'

'From Waters Meeting?'

'Yep, the one and the same.'

'I had *so* hoped to meet you!' Yazzie said brightly. 'My father isn't so good at getting out to meet the neighbours. He's never here, and I fear we've made a terrible racket getting the place built.'

'It has been a bit of a whirlwind,' Bec said a little coldly, thinking back to the times when she and Charlie had been furious at the way the workmen drove huge trucks around the middle of the blind corners of the tight-turned mountain roads, and about the chopper unsettling the calving cows and lambing ewes as the rich Stanton man from the city built his Taj Mahal of racing in their once quiet valley.

31

But Yazzie seemed not to notice Rebecca's coolness towards her, or, if she did, she was ignoring it. 'What are you getting?' she asked with the same pretty smile as before.

'I really don't know. Not sure if I need any of this stuff; plus what if my boys found my stash of sex toys?'

'Just tell them they're part of Mummy's lightsaber collection,' Yazzie said.

Bec laughed. 'You're right.'

'Here, allow me,' Yazzie said, taking the pen and the order form from her. 'I'll choose and I'll pay. Think of it as an apology gift. I know what a balls-up my father creates in people's lives. Trust me.'

'No, really. No. That's too much,' Bec said, reaching for the form.

Yazzie pulled it away from her. 'Please. I insist.'

Bec watched, amazed, as Yazzie sat down in the chair next to her. 'You're giving me sex toys? As an apology gift?'

'Why not? And the policewoman's uniform. You and I can go riding in them. That would be a hoot. I'm assuming you do ride, don't you?'

Bec nodded. 'When I can.' But truthfully she couldn't remember the last time she'd been on Ink Jet, her horse, who was so old now Bec felt guilty even leaning against her, let alone chucking a saddle on her high-withered swayback. She'd wanted another horse and pored over the pages of *Horse Deals*, but never felt she could afford it. Or, more to the point, Charlie didn't feel they could afford it.

His interest in horses had waned over the years. He'd ridden the runs with her in the early years of their courtship, holding her hand as they silently rode side by side, Charlie on Tom's old horse, Hank. But as time passed, he would say, 'Easier to take the steel horse,' and he'd rev away in a cloud of blue-grey exhaust fumes. Nowadays, despite the ruggedness of the mountain country, he didn't think it necessary to teach the boys to horseride. Instead he'd got them little four-wheel bikes that buzzed like bumblebees on steroids. Bec thought they looked incredibly dangerous when the boys were taking sharp turns, but Charlie had said no to ponies for them. She sighed.

As she watched Yazzie fill out more and more items on the order form, then pull out her credit card, Bec felt her cheeks redden.

'Stop stressing,' Yazzie said. 'Let someone spoil you for a change.'

Should I be offended by this bright little rich girl sitting beside me? Bec wondered. Or should I soak up the vibrant energy she seems to emit? This Yazzie bird was almost as intoxicating as Doreen's Cowboy shooters. She seemed to buzz.

'While you do that, I'll get us another drink!' Bec said.

'Thanks. This will bump up the party earnings!' Yazzie said, tapping the end of the pen on her teeth. 'Doreen's going to get so much free stuff she could open a shop. And just wait till the parcel arrives! Your husband's gunna love it!'

# Five

By midnight the Dingo Trapper Hotel was fairly humming, thanks to the cut-out crew who, in a bid to shear the last of the wethers, had finished late at the Clarksons' place. After a few beers on the board, the team had eagerly jumped in their utes, collecting some mates along the way, and poured themselves into position at the bar. Hours later, gun shearer Murray was still leading the charge with a huge smile on his boxy butcher's-dog face. His bristly jowls had captured a few tiny locks of wool from the day's shearing and lanolin still coated his clothes and skin. He was steering his men down a river of drinking that had flowed from beer to Bundy — and now several of them were even lighting Sambuca, then dowsing it with Blue Curacao, before throwing it into their gobs.

Billy Arnott, the bar owner, better known as 'Dutchy' (short for Dutch Cream because of his fair European looks and the fact his surname was a biscuit brand), was enjoying the pantomime that was playing out before him. He and his wife, Amanda, had only taken over the pub three years prior, after a 'tree change' from Sydney. The Arnotts had big shoes to fill following the death of the last publican, Dirty Weatherby, and Dutchy knew it.

Dirty Weatherby, who was buried at the church down the road, still had uproarious visits from his clientele, who would bring him a beer and stand and toast him around his gravesite. His old dog, Trollop, who was as fat and wide as a grizzly bear, would lumber along with the pub crowd and dutifully piss on her owner's grave, much to the mirth of Dirty's former clients, who loved him and the dog in equal measure. Tonight Trollop, full of leftover beef schnitzel, fishermen's basket and chips, had settled herself into an armchair beside the pool table and was farting as powerfully as she was snoring, the resulting smell forcing the pool players to evacuate the area from time to time.

Dutchy was grateful the dog had stuck around.

Even though the former city newsagent was used to wooing a crowd, so too was Trollop. She evoked the memory of Dirty so strongly when people looked into her sincere brown canine eyes that when word got around Dutchy was keeping ol' Trollop, even initially suspicious people would stop in at the pub to see her especially. One beer with the dog began to extend to three and four. And then the locals started to come back. Nights like these were now almost weekly at the pub that was nestled in a pretty river bend, almost entirely isolated from the town. Only the lonely hillside church, a few Ks down the road, was anywhere nearby.

As Dutchy ripped open another packet of chips, emptied them into a bowl and set it on the bar, he smiled at being given the chance to start life over in this part of the world. He and Amanda knew this area was about to awaken, thanks to the sealed road and hungry, thirsty, cashed-up travellers. And even though it was dire news for the district, there was talk of mining exploration for coal. The geos and their crews loved a beer and a chicken parma too, so the future looked bright for the pub. Suddenly life seemed more interesting for the local tarts as well, who'd helped the pub get its nickname, the Fur Trapper.

In the off-season, though, Dutchy knew he had to look after the locals. Give them free stuff to keep them feeling warmed and welcomed. Deliver complimentary trays of golden nuggets and sausage rolls to the bar, along with copious quantities of tomato sauce. Keep the wood fire blazing on cold winter nights. He'd also made sure he'd kept the music collection country as much as possible, despite the complaints from travellers. As another twanging Toby Keith song finished and the CD was about to flip to The Wolfe Brothers' new hit song, there was a lull in the raucous pub prattle.

Suddenly a throbbing sound filled the vacant space. Bright lights blazed through the window like searchlights at a prison. At first Dutchy thought it was a helicopter landing on the road. Just at the very moment the first guitar chords from the Wolfies exploded, the pub emptied and the boozers spilled outside.

Dutchy lifted his little bar flap and followed the drinkers out into the cool night to see what the lights and noise were about. 'What the …?'

There, revving a gigantic new tractor in the middle of the road, was Charlie Lewis.

'Basil Lewis, you mad bastard!' Murray called out, using the nickname that had followed Charlie from Ag College, given to him because of the bed-hair that stuck up like a brushy fox tail in the morning. As Charlie Lewis opened the door of the tractor cab, he drank in the smiles of greeting from the pub crowd. In his larrikin way, he gave everyone the thumbs-up and a drunken smile.

He flicked on the rear light, illuminating the business end of the tractor. The new yellow plough was covered with a film of dust, but the edge of the discs that had been corroded clean by soil gleamed in the tractor's bright lights.

'Geez, Basil, you coulda taken the plough off before you drove in! Ya dick.'

Charlie shrugged. 'No time to waste! It's beer o'clock, according to the Tardis controls in here!'

After conducting a guided tour of the tractor and its features, Charlie was ushered into the hotel by the men, where a fresh bar-frenzy exploded. Dutchy, as he frantically poured beer and Bundy and rang the till, found himself wishing his wife, Amanda, would get back from the ladies' party sooner rather than later.

'They must be trying before they buy at this sex-toy party,' Dutchy said as he pushed a Bundy and Coke towards Charlie. 'It's making me nervous.'

'Sex-toy party?' Charlie asked. 'My missus told me it was a *Tupperware* party!'

Murray and his crew erupted into laughter.

'Nah-uh. No Tupperware, mate,' Dutchy said. 'Wonder what she'll bring you home! Or is she gettin' it for someone else and givin' you the lettuce containers?'

'Sex-toy party? Geez!' The penny dropped for Charlie. That would explain Janine's photo earlier this evening. That wasn't a black salami she had between her tits, he realised with utter amusement and a shiver of excitement. He'd not yet heard back from her. Part of him was relieved, but part of him was hoping she'd be lurking out there somewhere, looking to hunt him down.

'If my missus went to one of them parties and came home with one of them sex-toy things, I'd tell her to pack her bags,' Murray said, his stubble-covered jaw jutting out. 'If my tackle's not good enough for her, then that's it. I'm not getting replaced by some made-in-China piece of plastic!'

'No wonder she's cleared out on you then, Muzz,' Duncan, the cheeky board boy with the acne scars, said, wiggling his little pinky at him.

'She did not clear out on me. I cleared out on her.'

'That was only after she found out you were doing the lollipop lady at the Bendoorin high school,' Duncan said, edging stupidly closer to a set of knuckles in the face from Muzz.

Charlie began to laugh. He remembered how word had got around that Muzz had been having a red-hot affair with the lady who held the stop/slow sign at the school. If they knocked off early, the shearers would try to time their travel home from the sheds to get a look at her. A lot of the women on wet-sheep days couldn't work out why their husbands were suddenly interested in dropping their kids to school.

Muzz shook his head. 'She was the one who stopped me!'

'It was her *job* to stop you,' Charlie said, hoping Muzz would again tell the story. Somehow it made him feel better about his own guilt. As if what he was doing with Janine was normal — acceptable in fact. Everyone else did it, didn't they? They all cheated? Muzz had.

'Yeah, well, she did ask me how my day was …' Murray said, swigging his beer '… and I said it had been rough. We'd been shearing rams. Bloody bastards were full of prickles. As I dragged one out, there was a huge patch of fissles in one's topknot. So I ended up with a fissle in me nuts. Painful as!'

'A fissle?' Dutchy asked, cocking an enquiring eyebrow.

'Thistle,' Charlie interpreted.

'Oh,' Dutchy said, pulling a face, then lifting both fair eyebrows.

'So,' Murray continued, 'I told her I was in agony coz I had this fissle in me nuts and she said to me, "Well, I've got a pair of tweezers in me car, darlin', and a certificate in First Aid." Then she looked at me all funny.' Muzz licked his wet beer lips and shook his head at the memory. 'She had a real good body on her, but, by geez, her head was a bit rough.'

By this stage, the men about him were wetting themselves, wheezing and back-slapping.

'So what's a bloke to do when he's in pain like that? Of course he's gunna drop his strides for the lady to help,' Muzz continued, pretending to ignore them, but savouring their mirth.

'Oh, Muzz. You're priceless, mate,' Charlie said.

Muzz shrugged and swigged his beer.

'So did she get it out?' the board boy asked.

Muzz and Charlie looked at him blankly. 'What? Get what out?'

'The fissle.'

'She got more than just me fissle out, Duncan, let me tell you! Stop! S … low! Stop! S … low!' Muzz said, gyrating his hips.

The men laughed with bravado and swigged their beers with smiles still fresh, but Charlie felt his mind drift away from them. He knew this bawdy behaviour from them all was just a cover for the pain they held in each of their lives. Do they all share the same sense of dissatisfaction as me? he wondered. The dissatisfaction with their women? When he thought of Bec, all he felt was a quiet anger towards her. She had been so gutsy and capable when they had been at Ag College together. Sexy and fit too. Now, since the kids, she'd turned into a nag. A surly one at that. And she'd pressured him to have that operation. Like a Jack Russell at a rabbit hole, she'd dug and dug at him until he caved in. Since the vasectomy, he felt like half a man. A gelded stallion. A castrated cat. Emasculated beyond belief. After the op, one testicle had felt like an AFL football and the other a rugby ball and both were competing to see which could be the bigger code. It was agony. It was humiliating. No wonder in recent months Janine had lit a fire within him.

'Least she never got you to cut your nuts out, like my missus,' Charlie wanted to say sulkily, but instead he just downed his rum faster and pushed a ten-dollar note on the bar towards Dutchy. As he did, he noticed the Rural Land Management poster behind the bar advertising yet another no-till cropping and holistic grazing info night at the pub tomorrow. How many of those fuckers does the district need? Charlie thought.

He rolled his eyes. Andrew bloody Travis. Since RLM had been funding Andrew bloody Travis's visits into the area, Rebecca, who had for the past few years gone quiet on the farm, was now hounding Charlie for change. He wasn't sure if her old man's death was what had prompted her sudden, intense concern with the farm's management, or if it was purely that she had a thing for Andrew. She'd been begging Charlie to come along to one of the nights. Then begging him to change how he'd been running Waters Meeting. All the while parroting Andrew Travis's crap.

When Charlie had first come to Waters Meeting to manage the cropping program and to see if he and Bec had a shot at being married, her father, Harry, was hell bent on grubbing out all the willows on the streamsides and fencing out the stock. The hours they'd put in dozing and heaping and burning. Then Bec had got hold of a book by Peter Andrews and she'd ranted at them daily that they should be doing the opposite. She said they ought to be slowing down the water run-off and letting the weeds choke the marshy places on the property. And she was spouting off that the riverbanks were now undergrazed and they should let the sheep, cattle and horses in from time to time. In the ten years he'd been here, the advice dished up to farmers had done an about-turn. And now here was Bec, snubbing the fertiliser reps when they called by with a new calendar and big plans for more business with them, then slamming him for ploughing, all because of this bloody New Age farmer Andrew Travis.

Suddenly Charlie found himself wondering why she hadn't said it was a sex-toy party she was headed to tonight. Maybe there was something going on? He took note of what time the seminar started tomorrow. This time he'd go. Not to find out what the guy was on about, but to keep an eye on what was going on between the soil/grazing expert and Rebecca.

He glanced at his watch and wondered when Bec would be home.

Just then Dutchy's wife, Amanda, sailed through the door with a waft of cold air and perfume. She carried a silver platter over her head with aplomb and her auburn hair, curled by the damp night air, framed her lively face.

'Never fear, gentlemen, I am here!' she called out as she set down the platter on the bar. 'Leftovers from the ladies, for you!'

As she lifted the bar flap and took her position next to her husband, the men began inspecting the carved carrots with creamy dip and carefully constructed penis-shaped hors d'oeuvres made from tiny cocktail onions joined with toothpicks to sausages.

'Not sure I like the look of those, Amanda,' Muzz said, but with his crooked teeth he snapped the end of a carrot and dunked the rest in his beer, using it as a swizzle stick. 'What'd ya bring Dutchy home?'

'I'm saving my show-and-tell for later,' she said coyly, then went to serve ol' Bart, who was propping up the end of the bar. 'It's Charlie who's gunna have the fun,' she called over her shoulder. 'Stanton's shouted her the biggest order.'

But Charlie didn't hear her. His phone had buzzed and there on the screen was a text from Janine: *Where R U?* He wrote back, *Pub.*

*Church, now,* came her reply. For a fleeting moment he baulked at the mention of the church. Tom was buried there. The memory of Rebecca's crippling grief after her brother's death almost stopped Charlie going now to Janine. But as he looked again at the RLM poster and the smiling photo of fit and lean Andrew Travis with his George Clooney salt-and-pepper hair, Charlie felt the quiet anger rise again.

Next he was downing his beer and paying his dues. 'Better get my tractor cranked,' he said to the boys and out he wavered into the night. 'If your missus is home, mine will be soon too. She'll have my nuts. Again.'

'You right to drive that thing?' called Dutchy, but Charlie Lewis was already gone.

'He's keen to get home to try a few toys I reckon,' said Muzz, watching from the window as Charlie turned the tractor and plough around and revved away into the night.

On the bitumen, Charlie hurtled the tractor to maximum speed. With a thrill he felt the steering wheel jump to its own bizarre robotic life as the automated steering function took over. He felt like he was driving a gigantic monster truck at a speedway. Sure he'd chewed up his bonus diesel voucher getting to the pub, but the laughs from the boys had been worth it. And now here was his chance for a quick stop-off with Janine before heading home. He knew Bec would have his balls for real if she found out, but right now he didn't care. Within him lay an insatiable appetite for any excitement at all in his life. There was something eroding him away inside. It was the same gnawing feeling he'd had in the days when he was stuck at home on his family farm, living under the shadow of his father and constant pressure from his mother. He needed something to move him through this porridge of a life he now found himself in again.

Something like Janine. And there she was, standing in the headlights of the tractor beside the church. The breeze blowing her long dark hair, the coat that was wrapped about her flapping open so Charlie glimpsed the shiny purple fabric of a tiny negligee. Tonight she was all curves and wickedness. He didn't care that she was Morris Turner's wife and mother to two painfully shy teenage boys. He just wanted sex with her. And to forget. Charlie swung open the cab of the tractor and hauled her in.

# Six

Rebecca half fell out of Gabs's Landy on the mountainside and instantly felt a deep unseasonal chill in the air. The dark gums above her glistened with night-time dew and the roadside gravel beneath her feet felt damp and cold.

'You sure you're right to drive?' asked Gabs.

Bec nodded as she hitched up her boob tube and wrapped her arms about her body. 'The old girl will get me home,' she said, thumping the roof of the battered Hilux, once a vibrant red, now faded, scratched and dinted. Knowing she had to drive thirty Ks home from the turn-off where she'd met Gabs earlier that night, she'd been drinking water since ten at Doreen's and now felt horribly sober and incredibly tired. While someone thought it had been a good idea to seal the road, some of the bends on the southern slopes on dewy nights like this were sheened in a slippery concoction of oil and water. She intended to take it slow.

'All right. Hoo-roo then. Enjoy Dental Day!' Gabs said, delivering a gigantic toothy smile, folding her lips up above her teeth, before driving away.

Inside the ute, Bec turned the key and waited for the glow light to click off before she chugged the diesel engine over. She clunked the fan on flat-out for warmth, then headed off at a meagre speed, her headlights fanning across the summertime native grasses that bowed their seed heads with the weight of the dew. The roadside grasses prompted thoughts of Andrew Travis and what he had taught her about native grasses in the past twelve months. It was more than she had learned in a lifetime of farming.

At Ag College she'd never been taught the difference between a C3 and a C4 perennial plant that lay dormant at certain times of the year, depending on the warmth or coolness of the season. She hadn't realised, until Andrew had taught her, that modern agriculture favoured annual plants and decimated perennial plants with herbicides and ploughing. Or how superphosphate fertiliser killed crucial fungi that fed plants essential sugars and nutrients. Mind-boggling stuff, especially when she considered how she and Charlie had been managing the place.

Along with Andrew Travis opening up Bec's mind, she felt he was also slowly opening up her heart too. He not only spoke to her without judgement, but with utter respect; he not only praised her intelligence, but he also fed her what was rare to find in her industry — a positivity and hope that there was a bright future in farming.

Bec sighed and, even though she was a non-smoker, she wished she'd nabbed one of Gabs's smokes. She now saw Andrew as a visionary, despite his quiet way. His work was 'change the world' kind of stuff. She admired him more than any man she'd ever met.

'He's nothing but a bloody Greenie tool,' Charlie had said when she'd tried to explain Andrew's ideas. Driving home now, she wondered how she could shift Charlie in his thinking, and make him come along to the seminar tomorrow at the pub, not just to listen. But to *hear* and understand.

What she'd learned from Andrew's seminars was the only thing that got Rebecca excited about life on Waters Meeting these days. To her, it meant a chance to farm profitably and regeneratively … not the way they were farming now.

As she drove on through the winding mountainside, occasionally the eyes of kangaroos and possums gleamed in the headlights. She knew the steel bull bar that wrapped around the front of the ute like a grid-iron helmet protected the vehicle, but she slowed anyway, not wanting to take the life of any animal. In her youth, she'd barely flinched when she'd tumbled a possum on the road or swiped a roo, but these days, since her boys, she had softened. It was difficult to see any living thing harmed. Ironic, she thought, that I farm meat, yet love my animals so passionately.

Bec wondered guiltily how her boys were at old Mrs Newton's place, and if they had settled down to sleep OK. The boys made her think of Charlie, which in turn made her cross again that he couldn't just set one night aside for being with them. She tried to push the thoughts away.

Maybe tonight and the order Yazzie had submitted for them could kick-start everything for her and Charlie. Maybe they could bring back the days when he was a wild but caring party boy and she his happy, determined, capable girl. But something like a thorn still niggled inside her.

As she wound over river crossings and up around mountain turns, she began to long for the warmth of her bed. She imagined pulling Charlie to her. Making love to him until morning. Then the realisation came that she'd have to be up early to collect the boys from the neighbour. Then she needed to make smoko for the crutching and jetting crew, who were coming with their portable unit at nine to treat the ewes. She grimaced with disappointment.

Were Saturday mornings like that in other people's lives? Wouldn't most people be sleeping in? Television cartoons for the kids while the parents lay in bed cuddling, reading newspapers and eating toast and drinking tea?

She loved her farming life, she loved her boys, but some days she wondered how on earth there'd be time for just her and Charlie? Other farming families went camping together, didn't they? Water-skiing in the summer, snow-skiing in the winter, country-music concerts on weekends, dinner parties on Saturday nights with neighbours? But not the Lewises. Charlie was happy with the pub, footy and cricket-training booze-ups and satisfied with his machinery shed and the fridge, bar and potbelly stove he'd installed for himself there. And he had his trips to the mountain hut with Muzz for hunting.

In the ute in the darkness, she spoke out loud. 'What do I do, Tom?' she asked the empty night, wishing her brother was still with her for quiet counsel. Suddenly, thinking back to Tom and his death, she felt like crying.

The old Hilux gave a chug and the engine cut out to silence, wheels crunching over the newly sealed road, rolling to a stop. As she peered out of the window, she guessed she was still about fifteen Ks from home and about fifteen Ks from the nearest farm, which was Rivermont, where newly constructed white fences flanked the roadside.

'What? C'mon, girl!' Bec said to the ute as she tried the ignition again with no luck. She sat dumbfounded. She'd told Charlie the ute needed a service — the oil light was glowing far too often these days. She turned to the passenger seat, where she expected to find the Woolies bag containing her own clothes and boots. 'Bugger!' she said: she'd left the bag in Gabs's Landy. She didn't even bother to look at her phone. She knew she'd be out of range on this part of the mountain.

She fished around in the grubby space behind the seats, looking for the oil container she remembered putting there months ago. All she could find was an old green high-vis vest with a silver reflector strip and the kids' orange 'Fright Night' torch from a Halloween party at Ursula's last October.

Still in her hooker's costume, Rebecca got out of the ute, looked down at herself and laughed. It was rather funny, standing in stilettos as she pulled on the green fluoro vest. It offered small relief from the cold. A shiver shook through her body as she lifted the bonnet. She shone the torch into the engine and cursed Charlie: there was not only no oil, but very little coolant. Was it her job to check these things? Before the kids, yes, it had been, she reasoned; but surely now, how could Charlie expect her to think of every little thing? As she looked about in the ute tray for a water container or even a pair of boots so she could walk comfortably to Rivermont, she accidentally bumped one of the buttons on the 'Fright Night' torch and suddenly a ghoulish voice was echoing into the night. The voice screamed, then moaned, 'Heeelp me! Heelp me!'

'Shut up!' she said, prodding at the buttons, this time causing a witch's cauldron to bubble and a cackle to emanate from the torch. It was giving her the creeps. She didn't know whether to laugh or cry.

Giving up, she got into the cab and tugged the vest about her, trying to snuggle into the grimy seat to catch a wink of sleep before someone came by in the morning or Charlie noticed her missing. Not long after she dozed off, her eyes sprang open to see in the side mirrors the tops of the trees illuminated in the distance behind her. A car was coming. At this time of night? On this road?

She got out of the vehicle, wrapped the vest about her torso and flashed the torch in the direction of the car. A gigantic, shiny black Kluger four-wheel drive pulled up beside her and slowly the window slid down, revealing a classically handsome man, complete with a flattering amount of facial stubble on his olive skin. He was looking her up and down with a slightly amused expression on his rather smug face. The man was wearing a dark woollen coat that was turned up at the collar and Bec thought he looked like a mysterious traveller you'd find on a European train platform in the 1930s, not on a back road to Bendoorin. From the glow of the dash, his dark eyes seemed to mock her a little.

'Broken down, have we?' he said in a rather haughty deep voice that was coloured with an accent that Rebecca thought sounded like Puss in Boots from the *Shrek* films. 'At least I hope you have,' he added, eyeing her tarty shoes and fishnets.

'Well, I'm not looking for business, if that's what you're implying,' Rebecca said snappily. 'I've been to a fancy-dress party and I need to get home to Waters Meeting.'

'That is a relief. You'd better get in then.'

'And you are?' Rebecca asked, trying to sound dignified and not at all insulted that the man thought she wouldn't make a very good lady of the night.

'Sol. Sol Stanton. We've just moved into Rivermont. I can run you home, but I'd better call into Yazzie first and let her know I've arrived. My phone won't operate in these mountains. She'll be worried sick.'

'Fine. That would be great, thank you. I'm Rebecca Lewis.' Just as she said it, she bumped the button on the torch and it promptly gave a werewolf howl. 'Sorry. Kids' torch,' she said, pulling an embarrassed face. 'All I could find.'

Sol Stanton looked again at her with a mix of pity and amusement. 'Just get in.' Then he muttered, 'Mierda.' That might have been Spanish, but she knew, whatever he said, it wasn't good. She wanted to say rudely, 'Only because I have to, Mr "You may have a Kluger, but you haven't got a clue",' but in silence she stomped around to the passenger side and tried as best she could in Gabs's poorly stitched sequined miniskirt, once a six-year-old's dance dress, to look ladylike as she climbed aboard. Instead her thighs in her now laddered fishnets squelched on the real-deal leather interior and she heard the skirt rip noisily along the seams that ran over her backside.

As they turned off the road and drove along the recently renovated drive to Rivermont, Rebecca was awestruck at the changes there. Their power bill for one must've been huge. No wonder the Stantons had installed their own wind tower on the western side of the farm. French Provincial-style lamps lined the driveway, illuminating elegant oak trees and elms at least ten metres tall that had been trucked in. Two dozen of them now lined the wide drive like a welcoming committee for the Royal Family. The understorey beneath them had been laid with instant lawn, which sprawled richly like carpet and was lit by low solar lights. But more incredible was the transformation of the classical old Rivermont homestead. It was how Rebecca's own Waters Meeting could have looked, had the seasons been better and the money flowed. Had Charlie been easier to motivate, she thought bitterly. Or, more likely, she reasoned, if I wasn't so weighted down with my own sorry self. If only, if only ... Why, despite her struggle and hard work, did her lifelong dreams seem to constantly wither and die before they'd even reached the budding stage?

A gasp of admiration almost escaped her when she saw the illuminated homestead extensions helped along warmly from the lights within the home. A glass conservatory had been added, and what looked like an entire wing of rooms flanked by a verandah that perfectly matched the original.

'You've done some work on the place,' she said, trying to make conversation, intimidated by Sol Stanton's silent haughty presence. He didn't answer, his dark eyes fixed on the road ahead. Bec suddenly felt foolish. State the bleedin' obvious, Rebecca, she thought crossly.

As they swung past the box hedges and softly lit fountain complete with elegant bronze racehorse statue, she was met with the lovely vision of a gently floodlit old stone barn that had been decked out and extended into what looked to be state-of-the-art stables. Reflecting the yard light beside that was a brand-new Colorbond shed with giant air-conditioners on the side. The shed stood no chance of remaining at odds with the stables and homestead. It was already getting a makeover with a pretty cladding of freshly planted climbing roses. Rebecca wondered what on earth the shed was for, but looking at the stern face of Sol Stanton, who was not dissimilar in aloofness and grumpiness to Jane Austen's Mr Darcy, she bit her tongue. If he kept on like that, Rebecca decided she was ready to be truly rude. Surely such an excessive display of wealth was distasteful. Some may even find offence in what they had done to the old McDowell property. Marty McDowell would be rolling in his grave, she concluded. He had been a humble farmer and after his wife died and his boys refused to take on the farm, he'd mostly kept to himself. In truth, he had been a stingy old Scotsman who ran wormy cattle, but Bec preferred to side with the memory of him tonight ahead of this dark, stinking-rich stranger, who was now driving his brand-new vehicle into a new-made-to-look-old expansive three-car garage that already contained a Prado and a pristine blue Colorado 'farm' ute.

'Follow me,' he said with his chocolate voice. She was starting to feel as though Antonio Banderas had taken her prisoner.

'I'd prefer to wait here.'

'And I'd prefer you to come,' he said impatiently, as if addressing a wearisome child.

Rebecca raised an eyebrow and mouthed 'OK' as she got out of the car and tottered in her heels, following Sol to the back door. She found herself in a freshly tiled 'mudroom', into which not a skerrick of mud had found its way.

As Sol swung open the kitchen door, Yazzie looked up in surprise from where she stood in a magnificently renovated kitchen in her peacock-blue silk robe, clutching a mug and distractedly flicking through a magazine at an island bench that was large enough to be one of the Maldives. Somewhere in the house Rebecca could hear dogs barking excitedly, clearly overjoyed to know their master had come home. There was a moment of confusion when Yazzie saw Rebecca, but then her expression turned to joy when she saw Sol.

'Rebecca? Sol! Oh! Thank god you're here,' she said, rushing forwards to give him a kiss and hold him at arm's length, surveying him. 'I imagined the plane went down! Where have you been? I left the lights on for you.' Then she looked at Rebecca, puzzlement and concern on her face. 'And what happened to you?'

'I could see that you had illuminated the entire district, and the plane was just delayed,' said Sol. 'Then I found this one on the side of the road broken down.' He looked at Rebecca as if she was roadkill.

'So you had to endure Mr Cranky Pants, did you? He's terrible when he's tired,' Yazzie said, looking at Bec with a glint in her eye.

'I'm very grateful he came along. I would've been very stuck.'

'How could you be *very* stuck? You are either stuck or you are not stuck,' he said pompously.

'Yes, well, now you're stuck here,' Yazzie said to Bec, taking her by the arm. 'I'm not letting you go before you've had a hot chocolate,' Yazzie insisted, 'with a dash of something stronger to warm your cockles, you poor thing.' She smiled and winked, obviously pleased she had company.

Bec shook her head. 'No, thanks, really. I'd rather be getting home.'

'Well, I want a drink. It's been a long journey,' Sol said bluntly.

Rebecca looked at him in surprise. Maybe all exceedingly rich people were this rude? She shrugged. 'Well, I suppose I'll have one too then,' Bec said.

'Great,' said Yazzie, clapping her hands and teasingly tugging on Sol's coat. 'I see you're still an old grump.'

As Yazzie extracted all kinds of café noises from the giant designer coffee machine in heating the milk for the cocoa, Rebecca thought she better at least make polite conversation with the grim but incredible-looking man before her. Before she could open her mouth, though, he was muttering something about getting his bags from the car and saying hello to the dogs and was gone.

'Sorry about him,' Yazzie said, digging out a container of marshmallows before generously splashing Irish whiskey into the cups. 'He's jetlagged. And licking his wounds from missing out on a big gig.'

'Gig?'

'With the Orchestra of Paris. He's a piccolo player.'

Rebecca almost burst out laughing. 'Piccolo? You mean one of those tiny little flutes?' She remembered the sight of his large man's hands gripping the steering wheel. His long strong fingers looked as if they'd more easily hold a rugby ball than a dainty little silver instrument. She internally giggled at the thought of him playing his tin whistle.

'Here,' said Yazzie, handing Rebecca the mug. 'Follow me! Come and see my new toy!'

Rebecca wasn't sure if Yazzie was drunk from the expensive champagne she'd brought to Doreen's party earlier or if she was always this bubbly, but as she followed her down a wide passageway that was freshly painted and carpeted in classy cream, Bec suddenly didn't care. Yazzie seemed so nice. Like a breath of fresh air.

They made their way through what Rebecca thought must be Sol and Yazzie's bedroom, where a gigantic four-poster bed was spread with a gold-and-black quilt. Next she found herself standing in a huge bathroom with the heat lamps blazing.

'Ta-da!' said Yazzie, holding up what looked like a panel beater's spray gun. 'My new spray-tanning machine!'

Rebecca looked blankly at her, wondering if she should mirror her excitement. Was this woman serious?

'C'mon, strip off,' Yazzie said.

'Me?'

'Yep. I'll show you how to do it. Then you can have a go with me. I've had them done in the salons enough, so we'll be right. I kind of know what to do.'

'I'm not —'

'C'mon!'

'But —'

'C'mon. It'll be a hoot.'

'Are you completely pissed off your head?'

'No … I just love having a bit of fun. *This* will be fun. Come on, Rebecca! Don't think I don't see it.' Yazzie narrowed her eyes and suddenly pinched her arm.

'Ouch! See what?'

'That you are a can-do jillaroo. You've forgotten that, haven't you? You're stuck in a rut, sister.'

Rebecca's eyes widened as she stared at Yazzie.

'I only see it because I've been there too.'

'You're too young … to —' Rebecca began.

'Too young! What are you talking about? We're practically the same age!'

Rebecca caught a glimpse of them both in the mirror. They shared the wayward look that came from a night on the grog, but, standing there under the bright dazzle of the heat lamps, Rebecca looked like a beat-up ute parked next to the Porsche-like Yazzie.

'They say never judge a book by its cover …' Yazzie said, following her gaze. 'But we all do. Look, a good friend of mine — Evie; you'd love her, by the way — once said, "If you wake up and do the same things every day and think the same things every day, you'll get the same results. But if you change how you think and what you do each day, then life will change!" So come on, Rebecca, live a little!'

Live a little? Rebecca wondered. By having a spray tan? Was this little rich girl nuts? She pictured Charlie back home in bed, snoring his head off. Scratching his nuts. Gut rumbling with his belly full of beer and deep-fried food, brewing farts for the morning. But then maybe it was her view of him that was the trouble? Maybe if she did change how she thought of him and of herself, life could get better?

'OK. I'm up for it. I'm living a little,' Rebecca said as she began to peel off her clothes. She looked down to her rather daggy black underpants and the hair that curled out from under the elastic. With the Baileys Irish Cream warming her up, she said dryly, 'Cripes, my George W could do with some attention. It's like a bloody national park down there, full of blackberries and suffering from undergrazing!' She looked back up at Yazzie. 'C'mon then, let her rip!'

It was three-thirty in the morning by the time Charlie crept up the big wide wooden stairs of the old homestead at Waters Meeting. In the bedroom, Rebecca had already passed out after devouring a large bottle of Baileys at Yazzie's. His socked feet trod on the worn carpet that ran the length of the stairs. No matter how gently he trod, he still couldn't avoid the creaks from the old steps. Even the solid oak door would not comply with the secrets he was trying to keep from his wife and it moaned loudly as he gently opened it. He quickly shed his clothes onto a pile on the floor and ducked into the bathroom.

Since Tom's death, Bec had been a light sleeper so he made sure the door was shut before he switched on the light. In the bathroom, he cleaned his teeth roughly and swiped his body over with a sodden face washer and soap, hoping to erase the smell of Janine. He caught his image in the mirror. The beer belly, the brown hair receding at the sides. Lines around his once iridescent green eyes and dark circles he knew were from a stressed-out liver. He looked a mess. He felt a mess. As he gingerly opened the bathroom door, a shaft of light speared into the darkness of the bedroom.

There he was met with the sight of his wife lying spread-eagled on the bed. She was wearing a little white G-string and a floaty kind of see-through dress with white fur trim. But what was most unusual was that she was as golden brown as a potato wedge. All over. He crept closer and peered at her skin. In patches, it looked like she was splattered with water from a muddy puddle.

What on earth had she been doing? Something was not quite right. Andrew Travis came to his mind.

As he slid softly into bed beside her, he could smell the booze on her breath.

Phew, he thought. She was drunk and wouldn't wake.

But next thing he knew Rebecca was reaching for him, rubbing her body against his and making sleepy noises of desire. He shut his eyes and sighed, knowing he'd have to oblige. How long had it been since she'd asked for it? Slowly, with a blank, shut-down feeling within him, Charlie began to caress his wife.

# Seven

Only a few hours later that morning, as Rebecca dragged the bent and rusted gate open, she cursed her lack of sleep and the fact that none of the gates on Waters Meeting swung easily. She stooped and dragged a bleached limb that had fallen from the nearby stone-dead gum onto the track to the shearing shed. How many times had she said to Charlie they should fell the tree? It was dangerous. As she got back into the vehicle, she cursed her hangover and the chorus of whingeing from a very disgruntled Ben and Archie in the back seat. They were still sleepy and still crapped-off about being dropped at Mrs Newton's last night.

Rebecca gunned the Toyota four-wheel drive wagon towards the corrugated-iron and timber shearing shed that sat on a flat-top knoll above the river. Knowing she was already pushed for time, she hastily grabbed the smoko basket from the front passenger seat, almost tripping over Charlie's feathery sheepdog, Stripes. The tri-colour collie had been lured from the yards by the enticing scent of hot sausage rolls and party pies and was now wagging his tail frantically, delighted to see both Rebecca and the food. But Rebecca was in no mood for Stripes's enthusiastic welcome.

'Git out of it, Stripes!' she said, just as she stepped in a fresh pile of sheep manure in her good town cowgirl boots.

She glanced up and saw Charlie's broken-down Hilux, still with the tow rope attached to one of the crutching plant crew's cars like a tethered horse. Phew, she thought. Charlie must've called the boys to pick it up on the way. That was one less job on her lengthy to-do list. The sight of the vehicle prompted memories of her bizarre night. Sol and Yazzie Stanton flashed into her mind. What a weird night. What a weird couple.

She looked down at her splotchy tan and grimaced.

'*Mum!*' called Ben from his booster seat. 'Can I get out? Pleeease!'

Rebecca shut her eyes and clenched her teeth. 'No.'

'Why?'

'Because I'll never get you back in and we have to get to the health clinic! We're late as it is.'

'Oh, but Muuum! I want to see the sheep machine! Daddy said I could.'

Ben's little brother, Archie, joined in. 'Mummy! Get out? Pleeeease!'

'No! Enough of the begging! I don't care what Daddy says. He never has to get you anywhere on time! Plus Daddy insists on using nasty chemicals on the sheep. I don't want you near the sprays,' she said as she slammed the door, barged past Stripes and jogged with the basket over to the shearing-shed yards.

As she rounded the side of the galvanised-iron shed, Rebecca baulked at the intensity of the work that met her seedy senses. The contractor and his crew's team of barking dogs were noisily pushing Merino ewes up and into a mobile shearing plant. A diesel generator was adding to the din. Each sheep was unceremoniously tipped upside down on her back into a metal crate for the men to treat. Kelvin the contractor and his workmen stood on the trailer platform, wielding their handpieces through the wool around the startled faces of the ewes, then jabbing through the dags on their rear ends.

When she saw the pile of dirty wool crutchings accumulating in the bins, Rebecca felt another wave of disappointment and frustration. She'd asked Charlie not to put the ewes on the rich monoculture diet of oats, which messed with their digestion and led to shitty dags around their bums. She'd reminded him the animals needed mostly dry feed to fill their gut, with just a bit of green pick.

It would soon be joining time, on Anzac Day, later than most places due to the altitude of Waters Meeting, though Charlie never seemed to manage to meet even that deadline, putting the rams in too late, thereby pushing lambing out too late and missing the feed burst in spring.

'If you don't crutch them before joining,' Rebecca had yelled at him one recent Sunday afternoon, 'the bloody rams won't be able to get their dicks past the shit!'

Charlie had simply looked up at her with annoyance from his football viewing, feet propped up on a stool, a row of empty stubbies beside the chair. He had waited until a goal was kicked and the TV flicked to an ad break, then he'd turned to her. 'Not only are you a screaming banshee in front of the kids, but you've got a filthy mouth,' he'd said to her mildly. He swigged his beer, then turned up the volume some more. Rebecca had quietly taken herself off into the bedroom to cry and fold washing.

She looked down to the river flats now. They seemed exhausted to her. Bare soil that she knew would sprout weeds in between what was left of the oats. She thought of the luscious vibrant feel of the farms she'd visited with Andrew. There, the farmers had waited for the perennial plants to become dormant as they did at certain times of the year. Then when they had grazed the plants down, they had sown the oats directly into the soil, without the need for a single pass of a chemical spray unit or a plough. The farms looked untidy with the long dry grasses and vast variety of plant species, yet as Andrew explained, the grass was simply hay left standing for the animals. The array of plant species offered the animals a banquet of healthy options. She had seen first hand on those farms how the stock thrived. When she suggested to Charlie that they try the same so the animals could self-medicate on herbs, forbs, annuals and perennials, he'd looked at her as though she'd dropped her guts in front of the Queen.

Couldn't he see today that the ewes looked terrible, weighted down with dags from the too rich, too lush oat crop?

Rebecca noted the shorn strips of dull green wool that ran up the backs of many of the ewes. They had been flystruck and maggots had taken hold, eating their flesh away. Charlie's jetting looked to be way too late.

Despite that, he seemed happy with himself, keeping the flow of the wigged and crutched ewes moving through the jet that sprayed anti-fly mix over their bodies. The sheep packed tightly onto the trailer as the frantic commotion of men, dogs, metal yard gates clanging and machinery buzzing rolled on. Some sheep were sinking to their knees in the crush of bodies. Rebecca hated to notice the weak ones among them.

In the let-out yard, the processed ewes stood watching, their faces now bright white. Some occasionally nibbled at the short yard grass while others planted their feet, cast their heads low and shook their bodies, sending any excess of the bitter-smelling jetting-fluid droplets into the air.

'Smoko!' called Charlie when he noticed Bec clearing a place on Kelvin's ute tailgate for the basket. Each shearing plant was pulled out of gear and as the last sheep was dropped from the trapdoor release, the dogs were told to 'siddown!' Soon all that could be heard was water running from the tap at the tankstand as the men washed their hands.

'Better late than never,' Charlie said as he shoved a sausage roll into his mouth, looking pointedly at Rebecca. A simple 'thank you, darling' would be nice, Bec thought bitterly, but she bit her tongue. She was still angry with him for not being at home when she'd arrived back from Yazzie's. He spent more time at the pub than he did at home. Then there was the shameful, embarrassed feeling that had clung to her this morning — when she'd made a move on him to make love, he'd been unable to keep going for her. In the dark in her ridiculous borrowed negligee and even more ludicrous spray tan, she felt humiliated and repulsive as Charlie's penis had withered in her hand. She had cried silently, drowning in misery and the expensive perfume Yazzie had drenched her in.

'And how's Mrs Lewis this mornin'?' Kelvin asked.

Rebecca grimaced internally, displeased to see him back on Waters Meeting. Charlie would've told Kelvin about the humdinger of a fight they'd had the first time he'd come last winter. Charlie was not big on tact, especially if it made Rebecca look foolish. He would've told Kelvin she'd wanted to hire another contractor, George Pickles.

Rebecca knew George had a passion for understanding stock movement and used his brilliant team of Kelpies to shift sheep through the yards quickly but with as little stress as possible. With George came a wicked wit too.

In the early years, before the boys, Bec had loved to work on the plant with George's crew of cheeky, flirtatious young men. For Rebecca it had been a godsend to find a stockman like George after years of butting heads with her father over his motley crew of ill-trained working dogs and his rough, yelling ways around animals.

But it seemed since having children, Rebecca had left more and more of the stock work and decisions up to Charlie. George was ten cents a sheep dearer than Kelvin and so last year Charlie had decided George wouldn't be coming back to Waters Meeting.

Kelvin had arrived last winter for footparing during what had been an incredibly hard time due to days and days of huge rains following three years of drought. With weak stock, muddy yards and a rough team of pushy men who looked as if they belonged in prison, the whole experience had been a disaster for Rebecca.

There were lame sheep everywhere on the property with foot abscesses, foot scald and a bad run of foot rot. Bec had been furious with Charlie for not paying enough attention to rotating the stock around the paddocks properly. Charlie had put sheep in boggy marsh paddocks and let mobs onto pasture that needed resting for regrowth.

There was also the issue of quarantining treated stock from contaminated soils that held intestinal worms and foot rot within them. All the while that winter, Bec had also battled the inconveniences of an ever shabbier house with a leaking roof, the seemingly endless domestics created by two small children and the disquiet in her mind, as the rain fell and fell. She felt guilt for everything. Even the fact she had begun to resent the rain after such a long dry spell.

One very dark afternoon, after dragging yet another weak in-lamb ewe out of a gully wash, she'd drawn up a hundred-day paddock rotation for Charlie to begin, based on Andrew's seminars. With a bit of fencing sub-division, they could push the grazing out to a hundred and fifty days so the paddocks rested for longer. But Charlie hadn't taken a scrap of notice. She knew it wasn't entirely him. Rebecca knew deep down after Archie was born she had been hit with waves of post-baby depression that had never seemed to lift. Too proud to seek help from others, Rebecca had begun to let life on the farm slide on by without her. And with it went Charlie.

Hitting the gin one night after the boys had gone to bed, Rebecca had angrily thrown all the plans in the bottom drawer of the desk in the farm office and left them there. It had all got too hard and she simply didn't have the energy any more to battle with herself, let alone Charlie.

It hadn't rained since that wet winter and now in the dry, Bec was faced with Kelvin again. Grubby, rough and toothless. She glanced at the body of a sheep that had been tipped over the fence. A broken-necked ewe that had hit the railing hard in panic, singled out by dogs not taught to 'steady'. Bec clenched her jaw.

By the end of the day, she knew there would be more ewes piled there, with their glassy-eyed death stare.

Busily she laid out the cakes, biscuits and savouries and tried to ignore that she had just been called 'Mrs Lewis' in a voice that was tainted with the weight of disrespect.

She clamoured to find inside her the young woman of her youth, who had worked alongside the men at the sale yards or in the shearing shed. Instead she attempted a smile for the man who stood before her. Like always, Kelvin was dressed in grimy jeans and an even grimier tractor cap, with brown hair that was almost matted into dreadlocks sticking out from under it.

'I'm feeling pretty ordinary, thanks for asking, Kelvin,' she said.

'Big night?' Kelvin's blue eyes narrowed and his thin smile twisted at one corner as he looked her up and down.

'Yes, it was a bit of a big night. I'm not terribly piss fit at present,' she said. 'Not like Charlie here.' She intended it as a dig, but Charlie seemed to pay no heed as he patted his belly proudly.

'Yep, I've been working on this baby for a long while.'

'Charlie tells me you got some nice Tupperware on order,' Kelvin said slyly.

'You blokes!' Bec said. 'And you say we women gossip! *Really!*' She turned to Charlie. 'I've gotta go. I'll be back well after lunch. There's sandwiches made and could you please switch the slow cooker on for tea? It's ready to roll. I thought we could eat at home rather than the pub. Save the dollars as you say. You are coming to the info night with Andrew, aren't you?'

Charlie seemed to tense up at the mention of it. 'If the boss says so, I suppose I must,' he said, glancing at the men.

'No doubt who wears the trousers round here,' Kelvin said, tucking his tongue cockily inside his cheek and raising his eyebrows at her.

Rebecca felt frustration simmer within. Then Ben arrived at the yard gate, Archie behind him, both little boys looking guilty.

Sheep manure was already squelched into their town shoes, and paw marks, compliments of an overexcited Stripes, now smeared their once clean shirts.

'Get in the car. *Now!*' Rebecca said through clenched teeth.

As she ushered the boys back to their car seats, she heard Kelvin call, 'Nice fake tan, by the way. Next time use something other than molasses.'

As she strapped the boys in again, she didn't know whether to laugh or cry at where she found herself in life. She looked at the beautiful round face of her dark-haired Ben, who was suddenly growing long and lean now he was six. There, next to him, was quiet little Archie, who had the most beautiful sandy hair in ringlets about his fine-featured face, much like her own. They were the dearest little fellas. Her best mates.

Surely while they were this little, hanging in there with Charlie and feeling shut out from the farm was worth it? Things would improve over time. She knew it. She breathed in her resolve and puffed air from her mouth.

As she turned, she saw Charlie walking towards her, sleeves rolled up, his khaki work shirt tucked into brown RM Williams jeans, his Akubra obscuring his face so it was hard to tell what he was thinking.

She thought by the way he approached her he was about to give her a serve over something she had done that he disapproved of. She felt her internals flinch, then she steeled herself.

'About last night,' he said, 'I'm sorry. Y'know, I've been under the pump lately.'

Rebecca wasn't sure if he was alluding to the abysmal love-making that had ended in a flop of failed sex, or the fact that he had been out all hours yet again, or his guilt over the ploughing, but she was relieved that at least he was talking. She waited in silence, hoping for more from him.

'Let's, you know … give it another go. Give it a red-hot shake,' he said.

She searched his face, but he gave her little to go by. 'You know me. I'm up for anything,' she said. And next he was pulling her into his embrace, holding her close to his chest. He smelled strongly of lanolin, dirty-tailed sheep and fly chemicals, but she let her face be pressed against him; starved of his affection, she drank the moment in.

'Yes. Let's give it a go,' she said. ''Specially for the boys' sake.'

As he pulled away from her, he muttered, 'You know I love you, babe.'

And that was all Rebecca needed to hear.

# Eight

As Rebecca drove away from the stockyards and shearing shed, thoughts tumbled in her mind. If Charlie felt that way, surely they could solve anything in their marriage? She took comfort from his hug and those few precious words, as if they were a rope to which she could cling. As she passed her father's now vacant log cabin, she looked at it, suffused with emotion. The dwelling sat low and lonely on a tree-lined rise in the heart of a river flat. She didn't want to be like her parents. Ever. Separated and surly with each other. Surely she and Charlie wouldn't suffer that fate?

When Bec's mother, Frankie, had left, taking with her a carload of her vet equipment, life at Waters Meeting had spun out of control. Frankie thought she was doing the right thing and had waited for years until her children were 'old enough'. Bec, the youngest, was sixteen when her mother left, but the impact had been huge for all of them — even her brothers, Mick and Tom, who were young adults at the time. The three children of Harry were left at Waters Meeting to deal not only with his temper and drinking, but also his hurricane of negativity, which battered them daily. Burdened with memories of parents who no longer cared for each other, Rebecca had keenly felt the struggles of the whole family.

After Harry's death, Bec felt guilty that there were days when she was relieved her dad was no longer on the place. His once green lawn, kept vibrant by the house grey-water, was yellow and bleached. The vegetable garden was now filled with long rank grasses and weeds. Some days it hurt Bec too much to look at it. Let alone go into the place.

Bec had watched age soften her father a little, so that by the time he'd died, most of the bridges between Rebecca and him had been rebuilt, if only cosmetically. Even though her father's love was unspoken, Rebecca tried to believe it was there. Like the river. Sometimes it flowed, sometimes it didn't, but the bed of it, the vein of it, was always there. Deep inside, though, she knew she was telling herself a lie. Her father had resented her. Loathed her tenacity. Her unmovable commitment to remaining on the land, despite the fact he didn't want her there. He wanted his sons.

Bec looked at the verandah and imagined her father sitting there. His one arm resting on the squatter's chair, the stump with the pinned sleeve held close to his chest. His solitary wave as she and Charlie passed his house, both of them busy with the farm. At first he was supportive of her and the plans she and her rural counsellor friend, Sally, had put in place, but then as the seasons stalled and, as she now knew thanks to Andrew, the soils began to decline from their outdated farm practices, Harry's bitterness and disbelief in her ability had returned.

Bec suddenly wanted to find a tenant for the cabin so that new memories could be made there. Charlie had reservations about having strangers in their space. But she was ready to move the memory of her father on.

It was four years ago this summer that Harry had died. On a sweltering day in February, in the same bush clinic she was taking the children to now. His stomach cancer had worsened. Bec had driven him, Harry wincing at each and every pothole.

With the morphine no longer hitting the spot, his face had blanched a deathly grey. She hadn't thought it would be the last time Harry would draw in the fresh Waters Meeting air. Rich clean oxygen, seeping from millions of trees. Instead Harry ended up breathing from a canister, the mask on his face slipping sideways, his inhalations slowly softening until his life was no more.

When Harry's casket was lowered into the grave next to Tom's, it was as if her wounds were torn open again. She didn't want him buried so close to her brother. Now, four years on from Harry's death and over a decade on from Tom's, she still felt wide open and raw. Bec had not a clue how to heal herself.

The minister in his sermon encouraged the sentiment that it was nice that a father would be reunited in Heaven with his son, but Bec thought bitterly that Harry was the last person on the planet Tom would want to see.

Even though she had made peace with her father, the shadow of Tom always sat between them. She still got chills as she passed the spot where the old wooden garage used to be. The rafters on which he had slung the rope, long since burned and blown to the wind, gone since the night she took to the structure with a tractor and a chain, followed by a drum of fuel and a match, in a wild rage of grief.

She often talked about Tom to Ben and Archie, trying to keep the memory of him alive through her words. She rarely spoke of their grandfather. It was sometimes difficult to find positive things to say about him. Ben remembered little of his granddad and Archie had been a baby still being carted about in a front pack by Rebecca when Harry had died. But it was the energy of Tom she wanted to foster in her boys.

'He was so different from your Uncle Mick,' she would say to them, often when she was busy so the little ones couldn't see emotion contort her face. 'He was smaller than Mick, but very, very handsome. And brilliant at art. You know that painting in the dining room? Of his horse, Hank, and the hut? He did that. Before he died.'

When Ben sometimes asked how their Uncle Tom had died, Bec would go quiet. How could she explain suicide to a child?

'The angels called him away because they needed him,' she would eventually say, then change the subject. But the shadows of Tom were all about Waters Meeting and the light of him. Some days she was overjoyed to see the sun paint the mountainside golden and she felt sure he was there, still up at the high-country hut, where he had long ago sheltered from the storms in his own head. Other times, in the half-dark, when her own mind was awash with despair, she felt the torment of his haunting.

As she passed the big double-storey Waters Meeting house on the hill, she wondered why, no matter how much she pushed and worked, she could never seem to transform the place to anything other than a tired old homestead that struggled, alongside a farm and a family that struggled. The visit to Rivermont the night before had made the feeling even more sharp. Bec was failing. Failing life, failing her boys, failing herself. Her dreams were dying before her eyes, yet the reason why was beyond her reach. Did she not pour enthusiasm into everything she did? Did she not try her hardest?

She glanced at the plastic bag on the front seat; it contained Yazzie's freshly washed baby-doll nightie. She must've been so drunk to borrow it and put it on for Charlie! Along with the spray tan! She felt such a fool. Wheels whirring over the grid onto the bitumen, Bec settled into the drive to Bendoorin. Again she reassured herself that things would be OK. Once the parcel from the sex-toy party arrived, she and Charlie would get back on track and she would feel alive again.

As Rebecca drove into town, her bleak mood shifted to one of amusement when she saw the sign that announced the current campaigns of the state police. A wag with a big black Texta had defaced the sign. The formal overzealous state budget font read: *POLICE ARE NOW TARGETING* … And in the space provided some clown had scrawled *CRANKY CHICKS.*

She burst out laughing. That was something she and her college mates would have done in their wild Ag College years.

'Police are now targeting cranky chicks!' she said, giggling again. 'Huh! That's *funny.*'

'What, Mummy?' Ben asked. 'What are you laughing at?'

'Oh, nothing, sweetie. Just a silly sign. Not very politically correct.'

'Not very what?'

She smiled at Ben in the rear-vision mirror, his serious dark eyes looking at her, curious.

'Politically correct. It's when very nerdy people don't get jokes and take life far, far too seriously for their own good.'

She now looked at her own image in the mirror and wondered if she would be considered a 'cranky chick' these days. She suddenly realised she too had become a very serious person. With a start, she wondered when? And how had the seriousness set in? Why didn't she do anything crazy any more, like she had done at Ag College? Where was it in the rule book of life that you had to grow up and be sensible? Even at the sex-toy party, she had barely let herself go. She resolved that she should be more fun, like Yazzie had suggested. Rebecca realised she was in one huge deep rut — she needed Charlie's bloody stupid new big tractor and a chain to pull herself out of it. For herself, for her boys and, of course, for Charlie. With that resolve in mind, she cranked up the CD of The Sunny Cowgirls for the last hundred metres of the main street, rocking to 'Summer' until she turned into the car park of the health clinic.

An hour later, after the dentist, Bec found herself whizzing the boys in a trolley up and down the supermarket aisles of Candy's store, making V8 engine noises. At Ag College they'd had many drunken adventures with the sturdy steel contraptions. Why shouldn't she have fun with them at this age? But even as she whizzed the boys from the canned goods section to the sauces, she felt her mood was forced. Strained. She knew the Who's Who of Bendoorin would be lurking in the aisles to find out the gossip from the scandalous party at Doreen and Dennis's. Luckily Bec managed to avoid too many encounters, making it to the checkout with only one 'Hello, how are you?' from Mrs Newton, who looked equally knackered from minding the boys.

At the checkout they found Candy also looking frazzled from the party. Her bright orange poncho with blue knitted flowers cast a sickly hue across her greenish-grey face.

'What a night! I feel so undone!'

'You're not alone,' Bec said, loading groceries onto the counter.

'Nice tan, by the way,' Candy said, starting to bip the goods past the scanner. 'One of Yazzie's, I'd say. She got me last week when the parcel first arrived. We took the bloody thing upstairs into my shower and she turned me into a Polly Waffle.'

'Hah! Yeah, it's not the best look,' Bec said, holding up the palms of her hands to reveal patches of tanning lotion.

'It'll wash. While you're in town, you should get yourself a coffee and some lunch for the boys. Larissa's new shop is open for business. I know I'm her very proud mother, but she really does make the best coffee. She can give you a double shot. Get you over the line back to Waters Meeting this arvo. There's also the hoodoo guru's new shop next door. You should check it out.'

'Hoodoo guru?'

'Yeah,' Candy said as she bagged a few groceries. 'Some blow-in woman from somewhere opened it this week. Filled with crystals and Buddhas. If you're into that sort of thing. The kids might like it. Loads of colours, fountains and that funny-smelling incest stuff.'

A smile lit Bec's face. 'Don't you mean incense, Candy?'

'Oh my god! Did I actually say *incest*?! I must still be drunk. *Incense* … Oh dear, I've been in this tiny town too long with people like Ursula!'

Bec shook her head, smiling. 'Now I'm intrigued about this shop. I'll have to take a look.'

'She's got clothing in there too. But I can't see you in a kaftan. Bit hard climbing fences in one of those numbers, and the tie-dye colours may scare the sheep. Me though — I bought five of them!'

'Before yesterday, I couldn't see myself in a bondage suit either, but apparently Yazzie's ordered me a Catwoman outfit. Never say never.'

'Look out, Charlie, when the parcel arrives!' Candy laughed. 'He won't be driving his new tractor to the pub! He'll be at home with you.'

A cloud of puzzlement passed across Bec's face. 'He drove the new tractor to the pub?'

'Didn't you know?'

Bec shook her head and felt her cheeks redden in humiliation and anger as she handed Candy some cash and gathered her grocery bags. 'I was asleep when he got home. Then we had the livestock contractors out early, so I've not really seen him much.'

'Sorry,' Candy said, searching for eye contact as she handed Bec the change. 'I thought you would've known. He's a wild boy, your Charlie Lewis. Always was. Always will be.'

'Oh, there's a lot I don't know, I'm sure. It's no biggie. Funny really. The tractor to the pub. What a nong,' she said, forcing a smile and only glancing at Candy.

With the little boys in tow, Bec felt a chill as she stepped out through the brand-new automated sliding doors of the general store, despite the summertime heat.

She glanced at her stern reflection in the window of the shop. 'Wish they sold senses of humour in there too,' she said absently. 'I think I need a new one.'

'What, Mummy?' Ben asked.

She was momentarily distracted by the handsome face of Andrew Travis, who smiled back at her from behind the glass. His picture was on a large RLM poster advertising that night's information seminar at the pub. 'I wish the store sold men like that too.'

'*What*, Mummy?' Ben asked again.

'Nothing, darling. Nothing. C'mon, let's eat.'

A while later, full from Larissa's home-made hamburgers and chips, and Rebecca rejuvenated with a frothy chocolate-dusted cappuccino, they ventured out again onto the now sweltering main street of Bendoorin. Bec was amazed to see on her new iPhone that it was almost two o'clock. She and Larissa had lost themselves talking and laughing about the sex-toy party and who had ordered what. The boys, happy with the toys in the corner and soothed by the air-conditioning, had enjoyed the comings and goings of their other little mates, who had also been dragged in for the half-yearly dental check.

Bec, who was often tetchy about getting back to the farm as there was always so much to do, surrendered to her hangover and the heat of the day. Surely she could let Charlie sweat it out in the yards with the fellas and she could have an hour or two off for lunch once-in-a-Saturday-while?

She found herself outside the brand-new 'guru' shop admiring a lovely display of potted herbs, vibrant and strong despite the heat. *Heaven is Here!* proclaimed the sign on the awning. Pretty prayer flags strung underneath it spoke clearly of peace, and silver and bamboo wind chimes adorned the shopfront with colourful sounds.

The boys and Bec hovered, looking at the display of what Charlie would undoubtedly term 'hippy shit'. Then the boys, holding the strong work-worn hands of their mother, plunged inside.

The smell of sandalwood, gentle light from many candles and drifting piano music engulfed Bec's senses. Peaceful smiling statues of Buddhas, fat and thin, sat or stood in various places all over the shop. Silk lotus flowers floated in small fountains that tinkled silver water. Crystals of all shapes and sizes reflected light and gleamed in glass cabinets.

'Wow!' said Ben while Archie let go of his mother's hand and stood, his little head tipped back, blue eyes wide, gazing about the shop.

'This place is boooootiful!' he said in awe.

'It sure is,' Bec said, feeling too coarse and too undone by her mood and attitude for this place. 'Don't touch anything!' she warned the boys. The serenity of the shop was shattered by an outburst of yapping.

'Jesus Christ!' a woman's voice yelled. 'For god's sake, *Jesus Christ*! Put a sock in it!'

Next thing a little Jack Russell came scampering towards the boys, wagging its entire body and flicking its tongue madly like a monitor lizard.

Out from behind a curtain stepped a woman who had striking white hair, plaited like a Native American's and tied with elastics sporting summer daisies.

'Jesus! That's his name,' she added as explanation. 'I'm so sorry about the dog.'

Despite her white hair, her face was tanned and youthful-looking, even though from the look of her slim strong hands she was definitely old. Her eyes were stunningly green and seemed to see right into Bec. But it was her serene and generous smile that told her all. This woman was utterly alive. How long has it been since I put flowers in my hair? Bec wondered. This woman, whoever she was, looked so energised and above all free from troubles, apart from a crazy dog.

'Can I help you with anything?' the woman asked, scooping up the dog.

'Gosh, where to start?' Bec laughed quietly. 'No, I'm fine. Thanks. Candy from the store said I should come and have a look.'

'Ah, bless her. What about your little ones? Can I help them with anything?' The woman stepped forwards and stood before the boys. 'Hello, I'm Evie,' she said to Ben and Archie, 'and that little cretin you are patting is Jesus Christ. Annoying little mutt.'

Archie tilted his head to the side and looked up at her, clearly fascinated.

'Here, pick a crystal that you'd like to put in your pocket,' she said to the boys.

'Really?' Bec asked. 'Are you sure …?'

The boys hesitated, blocked by their mother's discomfort.

'Go on,' Evie said.

Archie reached out, his small fingers hovering over the counter that had crystals sorted into boxes, then he plucked out a perfectly rounded reddish-brown polished stone with mysterious swirls embedded within.

'Ahh, good choice, my son,' Evie said. 'The carnelian. This little crystal will help you connect with your inner self and give you courage!' She looked directly at Rebecca with those green eyes that could be crystals themselves. 'It also has a reputation for rekindling intimacy within marriage,' she said above the heads of the boys.

Rebecca's eyes slid away. Her cheeks coloured.

Ben, who was normally the more forward of the two boys, reluctantly reached out for a black speckled crystal with blue hues and a dusting of white, like the Milky Way was somehow captured within.

'And you, young man, you've chosen the sodalite. "The longest distance you will ever travel is the journey from your head to your heart." This stone will clear confusion and give inner peace. It can help clear rifts and arguments. Now I know you don't fight with your brother, but this stone has called you. Maybe to help others around you who are arguing?' This time both the boys and Evie looked at Rebecca.

Ben looked back to the palm of his hand where the round polished stone lay. 'But how do they work?' he asked, clearly awed both by the stones and the strangeness of the woman.

'Rocks contain energy. You're from a farm, right?'

Ben nodded, eyes wide with curiosity.

'Well, all that land you walk on and the mountains around you has an intelligence, an energy. A universal intelligence and energy. The same as what is in your body, my body, your mummy's body. You with me?'

Ben nodded. 'It's life,' he said.

'And death and everything in between,' Evie said. 'Science has proven that everything in the universe is in a constant state of vibration. You know vibration?'

'Yes,' said Ben. 'Like when Mum drives on the corrugated road and the things on the dash vibrate off onto the floor.'

'Yes! Good boy! Well, even you hold a vibration. And crystals are the same. If you look at them under an electron microscope, you can see them actually vibrating. Unlike us humans, who waver between good and bad moods, being happy and sad, these crystals are stable and their vibration is steady. Because of this they can help us heal our unsteady vibration.'

Ben closed his hand over the crystal.

'And now for you, Mum? A store-opening gift for you?' Evie asked.

'No, please, really … You have a living to make.'

The woman smiled gently at her. 'You must allow people to give you gifts,' she said.

Just as Bec felt compelled to select a crystal, her phone buzzed. It was Charlie.

'Excuse me,' she said, pulling the phone from her battered old leather handbag, the one her mother had given her for Ag College graduation years back. She flicked the text onto the screen: *Too hot here to work. The crew has knocked off early. They've gone to pub. I'm fixing ute.*

Bec couldn't help herself rolling her eyes. Sure he was fixing the ute. He'd be at the pub. Always the pub. If she could pick up the Fur Trapper Hotel and fling it off the mountainside, she would. How many times had that place kept her husband away for hours and her at home trapped with the babies and the blowflies? Guiltily she looked at Ben and Archie. They were such dear little boys. If only she had time to enjoy them. But everything seemed to be crammed in around running the house and the farm business. And running after Charlie's apathy. This was the first day Bec could remember ever taking it slow with them.

Sensing Bec's mood, Evie had ushered the boys to the largest fountain and had passed them twenty cents each to make a wish. Her kindness made Bec feel obligated to buy something, and this too made her feel a little flushed and annoyed. Charlie counted the pennies she spent.

She cast her eye over the colourful racks of clothing — perfect for Candy, but not at all for her. Come wintertime she knew the summer Indian cottons would be replaced by alpaca beanies and jumpers all looking as if they were made from yak fur. In her mind, she echoed Charlie's sentiments: 'Hippy shit.' She felt rude thinking such thoughts. What if the old woman could read minds?

Instead she wandered to the book section. Her eyes, used to popular fiction and agricultural publications, grappled with the titles: *The Anatomy of Peace, Practical Spirituality, A New Earth, The Children of Now, The Vortex.*

'Anything that catches your eye?' the woman asked.

'I really don't have time to read.'

'You have an iPhone. Perhaps a downloadable CD, then you could listen to it on that. I sell earphones too. Or you can listen when you drive. You must drive a lot.'

Bec was beginning to regret coming into the shop. This seemingly kind shopkeeper was actually a pushy saleswoman. She had to get out of here and back to the farm. She'd call in at the Dingo Trapper Hotel and drag Charlie out by the collar on the way. Surely she couldn't be expected to feed the dogs and dish up tea, along with all the washing to get in off the line, all before the seminar? Especially after his secret trip to the Trapper the night before in the new Deere. If he got back on the booze today, he'd be rotten by tonight and wouldn't take in anything Andrew had to say, let alone be ready to put in a full day's work on Monday on the farm.

Just wanting to get out of the place, she grabbed up a CD titled *The Law of Attraction* by two rather normal-looking Yanks, Esther and Jerry Hicks. 'I'll take this one.'

'Good choice. If you're open to it and ready for it, this book could be the start of you creating a life beyond your wildest dreams. It comes with a booklet. It's out the back. I'll get it for you.'

Before Bec could say 'don't bother', the woman was gone.

Frustrated now, she gazed out the shop window onto the quiet Bendoorin main street. Across the road the service station was adding on a takeaway shop and next to that the motel was receiving a facelift. Then at last the woman was back.

'This book will show you that if you can master your own mind and always seek positive, appreciative thoughts, your whole world will open up to new ways for you. Money, health, relationships. It teaches you that you create your own reality, good and bad, through your thoughts,' Evie said.

'That's nice. OK, well, thank you,' Rebecca said, trying to usher the boys out the door.

'Enjoy your journey — and remember, always follow your bliss!' Evie called after them.

'She was nice,' said Archie as Bec strapped him into his booster seat.

'Kookie more like,' she said.

'No, she wasn't, Mum,' Ben retorted. 'You should think more good thoughts, like the lady said.'

As she shut the car door, Rebecca stood in the sweltering heat. Her son had a point. When she was younger, she had believed she could achieve anything, but the more life had moved on, the more and more she had been steered by others and life no longer lit a fire in her belly. How could she rekindle it? She looked down at the book and CD she had just bought. They said books landed in your lap for a reason, didn't they? This one looked way out of her comfort zone. She flipped open to a page that told her that it might take some time to adjust to the notion that she was creating her life through her thoughts, not her actions.

'Huh?' she said out loud before reefing open her door and throwing the book on the front passenger seat with a huff. The CD slid from the back sleeve of the book and dropped to the floor.

'Bugger it,' Bec said and started the engine.

By the time they'd passed the Cranky Chicks sign, both boys were asleep. The shopping will be almost roasted, she thought. She should've left the groceries until last and she shouldn't have spent thirty bucks on a book and audio she never wanted in the first place.

'Get over yourself, Rebecca,' she muttered crossly to herself. 'Think good thoughts. Not bad ones.'

Maybe she could pass the CD and book onto her city sister-in-law, Trudy, so it wasn't wasted. She glanced at it, taking in the swirling cover art of outer space. There was no way known that Trudy would like it. Maybe her mother, Frankie, would be interested. With all her veterinary science knowledge, she might find something in the pages. Didn't all this New Age spiritual stuff have physics and other science at its heart? She was again distracted by her phone.

There were already two missed calls and two voice mail messages to retrieve and now a video call was coming in from Charlie.

Video call? she wondered, frowning. He'd never made one of those to her. She rolled her eyes again. He was probably trying out things on the new phone that he'd so proudly scored in the tractor deal. Being married to Charlie felt like she was mothering *three* boys, not two, most days!

She pulled over onto a roadside verge, the Cranky Chicks sign still in sight in her side mirrors. Her index finger pressed the answer button. 'Hello,' she said.

There was a rustling noise and Charlie's breath, then the blurred and darkened image of what looked like the inside of his jeans pocket.

'Hello? Charlie!' she yelled at the phone. 'I think you've accidentally called me. Charlie! Char … lie! *Charlie?*' Behind her in the back seat, her boys stirred, but did not wake. She smiled at them. Shearing-shed babies, she thought. They would sleep through a hurricane. She looked back at the phone and called Charlie's name again.

It sounded like he was walking up a hill, his breath coming fast. He must be out ploughing again, she thought irritably, and he'd be out checking the sods of earth, where she knew billions of soil micro-organisms would have been butchered.

She pressed the end button, not wanting to waste money. Not wanting to think of the Waters Meeting soil she knew they were buggering with bad farming practice. He'd been going off lately about the high phone bills. Never mind that he spent bucketloads on fertiliser that she hated and fuel to run the machinery that he brutalised the landscape with. She sighed, glad the no-till cropping and holistic grazing night was tonight and she could get a good dose of Andrew and his positivity. She so badly wanted Charlie to click with Andrew, so that things on Waters Meeting could begin to change.

She was about to pull the vehicle onto the road when a video call came in from Charlie again.

'Hello!' she said, this time crossly.

In the palm of her hand, the iPhone screen lit up, revealing a glimpse of dry grass and again what was the edge of Charlie's jeans pocket. She could now not only hear Charlie's breath, but also his voice.

'Oh yeah,' he half whispered. 'Oh yeah, baby.'

A faint smile arrived on Rebecca's face. After their early morning attempt at love-making and his peace offering in the sheep yards, was he sending her a naughty message? Her heart skipped a beat. She glanced back at the boys to make sure they were asleep. In an instant, she felt elation. The possibility of a rekindled relationship flooded her with hope. A marriage at last back on track. This iPhone could be fun for them …

Then Charlie's phone must have taken a tumble onto the ground and all she could see on the tiny three-inch screen was the tanned dimpled thigh of a woman and what looked like a part of Charlie's backside pumping up and down. Then she heard the woman moan and Bec felt sick. Shock punched pain throughout her body. Winded.

She dragged her eyes from the screen, tears blurring her vision. With the horror of the moment crawling into her mind and body, she turned to take in the sight of her beautiful sleeping boys in the back seat. Their faces unguarded. The perfection and innocence of their youth giving them the aura of angels. All the while she heard the moans of the woman. She looked back at the screen to witness the thrusting of flesh, raw and ugly in the sunlight. Her husband's breath coming fast, the way she'd heard it in her ear in the early hours that morning, before he had withered so quickly with lack of desire. She ended the call and sat for a time, gulping in air, holding the phone in the palm of her hand. Then slowly she steeled herself as she dialled the message bank. The first recording cut out almost instantly, but the second revealed the rustle of clothing and the same moaning of the woman and heavy breathing of her husband. Rebecca shut her eyes and felt her entire life as she believed it to be dissolve. With shaking hands, she pressed the end button.

# Nine

Rebecca stood at the Rivermont front door and rang the brass bell. She barely registered the presence of a blonde Cardigan Corgi and the elegant auburn German Short-haired Pointer sniffing at her weary, just-woken boys, who were standing beside her. She clutched the bag containing the baby-doll nightie, wondering what on earth had possessed her to turn into the Rivermont driveway.

The Stantons were strangers. Having only met Yazzie the previous night, why wasn't she seeking out Gabs as a friend to share her despair? Wouldn't she be better to crumble at Gabs's doorstep with the news of what she had just seen? And heard? Her husband's sex-breath, matched with that of another woman. Something deep within her, a shame, a sense of failure, wanted to keep the grubby knowledge of her husband's infidelity away from Gabs and out of the loop of gossip that permeated the district. Gabs seemed at this time too close to home, whereas Yazzie was virtually a stranger.

Rebecca knew that shock had brought her here to this massive glossy white door, and maybe it was something else too? Maybe it was Yazzie herself. A hope that somewhere left inside her was a way of being, similar to Yazzie's vibrancy and enthusiasm for life. The hope that the young jillaroo she once had been still remained. But that was stupid, Rebecca reasoned. Maybe she should just bottle up all her feelings and shove them deep down inside? Put up and shut up. Get on with it. Thousands of men had done this to thousands of women over the ages. And vice versa. Maybe she was overreacting? And everyone grew old and down and disappointed, didn't they? She could sort this out herself, couldn't she?

She was about to turn away when the door was reefed open by Yazzie, looking gorgeous in a little floral rose-print dress teamed with Ariat work boots. Her loose hair was casting a long straight silky curtain of blonde over her ultra brown, slightly streaky but definitely tanned shoulders.

'Geez! You scared the pants off me! I didn't hear the bell. I thought it was the Rivermont ghost and the dogs were after him. Oh, hello,' Yazzie added when she noticed the boys behind Rebecca. 'Tell Wesley and Ruby to go away if they're annoying you, boys. But they are very friendly dogs! They *love* children.'

She barely glanced up at Rebecca, continuing with her bright monologue. 'Are you as hungover as me? I tried working my horse, but no good. No good. And those tans! Mine is so bad … I look like a caramel slice. Can you believe we did that?' she said, lifting the hem of her already short dress. 'Ah! I see you've brought back my nightie.' She took the bag from Rebecca's hands. 'Thanks. I suppose you washed it,' she giggled, 'I expect you did. There's nothing of it so it takes no time to dry. So tell me, did it work with your Charlie? Will there be another little farmer for Waters Meeting in nine months' time?'

'Yes, I did wash it,' Rebecca said, finally able to get a word in. 'And … no. No babies. Charlie's not capable. You know … he's had the snip …' stammered Rebecca.

Yazzie was about to giggle some more, but her face clouded with concern as she noted the strain in Rebecca's voice, then fully took in the sight of her red-rimmed eyes and hunched shoulders. 'Oh, Rebecca. God, sorry, I'm gibbering. What's up? Tell me. What's happened?'

'It's Charlie … It's …' Rebecca cut herself off, looking at the boys. Sensing their mother's upset, they were sidling closer to her, Archie putting his little hands about her legs and burying his face in her thigh. She stooped and swooped him up in her arms.

'Come in,' Yazzie said gently. 'Boys, would you like a milkshake? Yazzie makes the *best* milkshakes! With blueberries. I'm Yazzie Stanton, by the way. I'm new here. What're your names?' she asked, glancing over her shoulder at them, laying a caring hand on Bec's shoulder as she ushered them into a grand entranceway.

As Yazzie got busy making milkshakes, Ben and Archie gazed at the giant house with gobsmacked expressions on their faces. Their eyes kept tracking back to the beautiful, friendly lady. A huge black-and-white French Provincial clock ticked quietly on a stone wall in the kitchen. Giant white lilies in a clear glass vase sat on a simple wooden dresser. Striking artwork of a galloping horse, created by swathes of black dribbling paint, hung on a pure white wall. A long wooden kitchen table that had enough seats to host the entire Australian cricket team was decorated with summertime flowers arranged *Country Style* in a glass bowl beside a white china bowl filled with lemons. The dogs still hovered, dropping chewed teddy bears and slobbery balls at Archie's and Ben's feet.

Rebecca perched on a stool at the kitchen bench. Yazzie had plonked a box of Kleenex near her and Bec was now gradually making a small pile of scrunched tissues in front of her like a wedding-day meringue as uncontrollable tears silently slid down her cheeks. She fixed what she hoped was a smile on her face so the boys wouldn't notice her distress. The blender roared as blueberries were mushed into milk and ice-cream.

Soon Yazzie settled Ben and Archie outside with their drinks in a shaded, picture-perfect courtyard beside a fenced swimming pool, the dogs lying panting at their feet, waiting for the ball action to commence. Bec watched them sadly from behind the white wooden wall-to-ceiling bi-fold doors that made up one entire side of the kitchen.

Inside, after Bec had hastily sketched out her story, Yazzie ushered her to one end of the monumental table and they both sat staring at the now silent iPhone that lay between them. They eyed it with suspicion, as if the thing would come to life and jump up and bite them. It had already bitten Rebecca today, savagely.

'Are you sure it was him on the video call? Could he have lent his phone to someone else today?'

'I'm sure it was him. He accidentally called me too and the phone went to message bank. Listen.'

Yazzie's eyes lit up. 'No, don't play it!' But it was too late. The kitchen filled with the muffled moanings. Rebecca let the recording play longer and suddenly the voice of Charlie said, 'You wanna play tennis? Do you? Huh?' Then there were some scuffling sounds and a woman began to moan, 'Oh yes. Oh, Charlie!'

'Yuck! Turn it off!' Yazzie said, grappling for the phone. They sat staring at it once more until she eventually spoke again. 'Maybe he was just tossing off. You know, blokes do. They are, after all, most of them, just apes. Wankers, quite literally.'

'Yuck. No. You heard. There was a woman there.'

'Maybe they were actually playing tennis and it was a really hard game?'

Bec shot Yazzie a look.

'Sorry.' She passed Bec another tissue. 'Did you see on the video call what she looked like?'

Bec shrugged and wiped her nose. 'I don't know. Does it matter who?'

'What are you going to do?'

She hunched her shoulders up and down, then hung her head and devastation swamped her. Life as she knew it had just ended forever. 'I don't know. I just don't know.'

Outside Sol Stanton pulled into the garage and collected a giant box of groceries from the back of his Kluger. He whistled to let the dogs know he was home, but already he could hear them barking from the other side of the house. There was a strange vehicle in the drive, and he wondered which local had dropped in with some trivial excuse for a sticky beak. Yazzie had often complained in her emails of the fine balance between building their dream and not offending 'the natives'.

As he went to the back door, Sol almost dropped the box; he swore in Spanish, as was his habit. He was having trouble adjusting to the time zones. He'd woken far too early, his body clock still geared to the Northern Hemisphere, and now the day was dragging. He still had the seminar evening to get through tonight and badly needed a coffee.

He thought briefly of the trouble he'd left behind in Paris. The delicate lead violinist with her shocking English but sexy accent screaming at him and hurling a bunch of flowers. Her extreme Italian behaviour was a parody of itself and even though at the time Sol was laughing on the inside at the clichéd Mediterranean tantrum, he also could feel her pain. Not so much the pain of his leaving, and his going home to Australia, but the pain caused by his indifference to her.

He had bedded so many women like her. Ones he could be indifferent to. Ones who left his heart still closed off and hard like a stone. The European orchestra scene was far too abundant with women who were both beautiful and volatile. Maybe it was time to settle down? He decided there and then, as he leaned the box against the door and grappled for the doorknob, that he ought to go on the fidelity wagon for a time.

Settle back into a domestic existence. Just him and Yazzie. He was looking forward to at least six months in Australia if his workload would allow, mostly based at Bendoorin, working to get the racing stables up and running. It was just the thing he needed.

No more women, he vowed.

Sol at last swung the kitchen door open and walked in juggling the giant box of groceries. He stopped momentarily when he saw a pretty and curvaceous blonde woman at the table. He couldn't stop his eyes running over her tight jeans and the slightly torn, checked blue cowgirl shirt that hugged her curves. Pearl press-stud buttons nearly popped at her breast line and her décolletage was tanned deeply. So different from the thin pale Italian girl he had recently bedded. There was something about her … Then he realised with a start that it was the same woman he'd met the night before.

In the light of the kitchen, even with Yazzie's terrible spray tan blotching the woman's skin and no makeup, she looked prettier than he'd remembered. One of those natural earthy types, he concluded. And such blue eyes! Eyes that had been crying. There was no vanity in her as she stared back at him. A contrast to his Parisian orchestra women, all dolled up, looking stunning, but with ice-cold agendas inside them. Ones who still tried to look attractive even when they cried. He knew the women played him for his wealth and connections ahead of his Spanish-born soul.

Sol realised as he looked at … Rebecca, that was her name … that she still held the same aura of sadness and uncertainty she'd carried with her the night before, only today the sadness seemed deeper. Maybe some teasing to cheer her? Sol thought.

'I see you're a little more clothed than last time I saw you,' he said as he set the box down on the kitchen bench. 'Get any business last night? How's the hangover? As bad as the tan?'

'Leave her alone, Sol,' barked Yazzie.

He shrugged and began unpacking all the contents of the box onto the island bench.

'What are you doing?' Yazzie said, irritated. 'Do you have to do that now, Sol, honey? We're having a very important girls' chat.'

He cast her a dark look with his intense brown eyes. 'I'm sure it's infinitely important. Earth shattering in fact.' Sol steadily laid out flour, eggs, vanilla essence and an array of cookbooks.

'Sol,' Yazzie growled.

'Shush!' he said loudly so that Rebecca started, her nerves frayed. 'I'm on a mission to make a "Man Cake" for the Home Industries section at the Bendoorin Show. I saw a poster at the store.'

'You have got to be kidding,' Yazzie said. 'Spare me.' She put her head in her hands.

'The theme of the show is Prime Lamb, so my plan is to work in and around that theme,' Sol said. 'There is a comedian who promotes Aussie meat who will be judge of the cake competition. It's the first of its kind.' He waved his arms around as if conducting an orchestra.

Bec frowned, momentarily distracted from her plight with Charlie and slightly annoyed by the arrogant man who had burst into the room. No matter how good-looking he was or how endearing his Spanish accent, he still spoke to his wife far too haughtily — and was he serious about the cake cooking? How insensitive and rude! Couldn't he see that she was distressed? Could he do nothing but think of himself and bang on about baking cakes? She concluded Yazzie was married to an arsehole, and all men — no matter what nationality — could be selfish and thick at the worst possible times.

'You do know the show isn't until October,' Bec said coldly.

'Yes, of course I know, but I want to perfect it now,' he said with a theatrical sweep of his hand.

Yazzie let out a frustrated scream while Bec thought, what a pansy! A piccolo-playing pansy!

'He's always like this, Rebecca! Mr Pedantic Pants!' Yazzie turned to him. 'Just because you didn't get your orchestra gig doesn't mean you can slip back into being Mr Slack-arse-I-do-bugger-all around here other than bake cakes for shows. That's bent! You're bent! There's a tonne of work to be done out there. Dad would be livid. Get out of my kitchen.'

'Your kitchen? Shut up, Ms Vocal Velocity. I briefed the staff this morning before I left for town. You seem to forget I'm the one with the jetlag. You are the one with the hangover.' He cast another dark gaze at her and Yazzie poked her tongue out at him like a child.

Rebecca shut her eyes, not wanting to witness the strain in other people's relationships. Yazzie picked up on Bec's discomfort and dropped her tone to one of gentleness. 'Please be nice, Sol. Rebecca's not had a good day.'

'You make your bed, you lie in eet,' he said, his accent thickening with his theatrics.

Rebecca knew Sol was referring to her hangover, but she felt a twinge of deep upset. She had made her bed. She had tried so very hard to create a life on the farm with Charlie. But nothing seemed to work. She had tried to be everything to everyone. A good daughter to her father as his body shut down with illness. A good daughter to her mother, even though she was always absent. A good mum to her boys, tending to their every need with as much grace as she could muster. A good wife to Charlie.

Even when the boys had been tiny babies, she had still summoned all her mental and physical strength to both work the farm and put a meal on the table. She had strived to be a good workman beside Charlie in the paddocks, despite the internal drag of depression within her. She had mixed memories of those times, some of them fond, some of them forlorn, of having to pull up in the paddock or the yard to breastfeed the baby or change a nappy or both, either on the seat of the ute or on a blanket that picked up thistles from the barren paddocks. Sometimes she felt strong and empowered like women of the ages who had worked in the fields, but other times she felt completely uncherished and used up.

There were days when all she wanted to do was fall to her knees and cry with exhaustion. She had been everything to everyone, but nothing to herself. And it had all come to nothing. Or at least not nothing. It had all come to a ten-second vision of Charlie humping into a bare and moaning woman via an iPhone. It was Rebecca who felt stripped bare. Punished as a witness.

At that moment bickering between the boys could be heard coming from the courtyard. Rebecca groaned and stood up.

'Leave it to me,' Yazzie said. 'I'll fix them. Now, Sol, please get out of the kitchen. I'm not used to having you in here, hulking about with icing sugar and food colouring. It's just plain wrong. And take Rebecca with you. Give her a tour. Cheer her up for me.'

'But the information night at the pub with Andrew is on soon,' Sol protested, 'and I've only just got in.'

Bec glanced at Sol. So he knew Andrew Travis? The fact startled her. They were so unalike. From different worlds.

'There's time,' Yazzie said, glancing at the clock. 'Rebecca can come with us. You were going, weren't you, Bec?'

Bec shook her head. 'I'm not sure I can. Not now —'

'Rubbish,' Yazzie interrupted. 'I have a plan. After your tour, give me thirty minutes and I'll transform you into a diva to die for. Charlie won't know what's hit him when he walks into the pub. If he's cheating on you, then he deserves to be shown what he's so carelessly destroying and throwing away.'

Rebecca glanced at Sol, who was still busy unpacking his 'Man Cake' ingredients, his dark eyebrows pulled down over his broody eyes in a frown. Should he also know all her business? 'I really better get going,' she said, trying to block any more involvement with the Stantons, regretting the fact she'd come here. 'The information night starts at six-thirty and I have to get the boys' dinner. It's almost five now!'

'Stay,' Yazzie implored. 'I insist.'

Bec looked at the other woman's pleading blue eyes. She noticed they were not only filled with compassion but also, perhaps, a hint of loneliness. It was too late. She had a brand-new friend. Yazzie was now heavily involved in the grubby secrets of her life. And so too was Sol Stanton, whether she liked it or not.

'Why go back to him right now? Give yourself some space and time for reflection. I'll fix the kids something. After Sol's shown you around, you can go have a soothing bath and then I'll do your hair and makeup. I'll pick out a dress for you to wear.'

'A dress? To the pub? The Dingo Trapper?'

'Yes! A dress. Oh, there's strategy in what I do!' Yazzie said. 'We'll show him. Beauty, if used correctly, is strength. And strong you shall be. Sol, don't just stand there. Take her for a tour. Get her mind back to the place where it should be.'

Sol set down the packet of flour and looked at both women, unimpressed. Just when Bec thought he would refuse, he abruptly said, 'OK. Follow me.'

As uninviting as his tone was, Rebecca followed in the wake of his expensive cologne.

'You have a way of cheering up ladies, don't you, Sol?' Yazzie called after him in a voice that sounded a little too sarcastic for Rebecca's liking. Not at all wanting a farm tour, but not knowing what else to do, she followed him meekly.

# Ten

Sol ate up the distance of the long glass-faced hallway with his stride. He wore classic navy shorts, his legs fit and handsome with skin a delicious-looking milk-chocolate brown. He barely slowed for Rebecca, who had to jog to keep up with him, feeling pummelled by his tail wind. He flung open a door at the end of the wing and held it for her, letting her pass. But then he was off and racing again towards another stone courtyard, this one flanked by rows of beautifully crafted stables of deep red wood, made even more glorious by shining brass latches and hinges.

Giant wine barrels spilled with red and white geraniums, the Rivermont racing colours if the flag flapping in the wind was anything to go by.

At the centre of the yard was a stone horse trough that had a small bronze fountain at its heart. The sound of trickling water soothed the stable courtyard, giving it an aura of tranquillity and opulence. At the other end of the long line of stables, one man was unloading feed bags, another trudging a wheelbarrow filled with stable waste out a side gate and yet another was scraping water from the sides of a deep bay gelding in a washbay. A tiny pasty-faced girl, clearly a trackwork jockey, waved as she carried a saddle pad and disappeared into a stall.

Surprising Rebecca, Sol whistled low, then called out in a deep voice, 'Hello, my beautifuls! Come talk to me!'

Over the tops of the stable doors came the heads of tall thoroughbreds, classy and glossy, their brown eyes bright with curiosity. Some shuddered out a welcoming whicker. Others flicked their ears in Sol's direction, pawing at the doors and tossing their heads.

Rebecca was slightly amazed. This big-wig rich man, who had just barked at her and Yazzie, and behaved like a complete self-absorbed tosser, had the whole stable of horses under his spell. She could tell the horses were drawn to his deep cooing noises and giant peaceful presence. She watched as he tenderly rested his brow on the starred forehead of a black racer and lifted his hands to either side of the horse's face. Just then, as if the gods had flicked a switch, the most beautiful sunset draped golden light across the jet-black hair of the man and the midnight sheen of the horse. Rebecca saw, roaming in the darkness of the horse's coat, a silver light. She took in a hasty breath and goose bumps spread across her skin. She surprised herself by feeling so moved by this moment of tenderness as she watched the big handsome man communicating in silence with the giant horse.

She remembered the woman's words in the shop, how thinking thoughts of positivity and gratitude and living in the moment would allow her life to transform. Suddenly she was grateful something had brought her here. Just this snapshot vision was enough to fill her with hope. Then there was the kindness of Yazzie to be grateful for.

For the first time Bec really understood the true richness of the gift of seeing how life *could* be.

Beauty and bliss *were* everywhere, if you knew how to look.

As she continued to feast on the visuals of Sol and the horse, she suddenly thought how the man before her would make a beautiful lover. Shocked, she stamped the brakes on her thoughts. Where did that come from? she wondered. Her cheeks flushed and she swallowed nervously.

Then Sol was off again, striding down the length of the stable doors. 'We have thirty horses in,' he said over his shoulder to Rebecca, who was still jogging to keep up, 'and only five running at present until we get properly set up. The rest are just young stock we've picked up in our travels. Racing blood from America, Ireland and Japan. All a bit of a gamble, if you'll pardon the pun.'

He walked up to a dark bay horse and laid his hand on its face. The horse dropped its head into the pressure of his hand, half closed its eyes and let out a contented sigh. Bec wondered if his hands on her body would prompt the same reaction.

'This one here is our hope for the Melbourne Cup in a few years. We'll see how we go, won't we, Arthur, boy?'

But the warm stillness and slowness of Sol as he stood with the horses didn't last. Without warning, his aloof, abrupt mood seemed to return. He spun about and was off again, quickly pointing out an enclosed sand roll, a high-fenced round yard for education of horses, the heated indoor horse swimming pool, and the tack room where not a bridle or a lead rope was hung out of place and every bit of metal on the gear threw bright reflections out to the world.

Before she could take it all in, Rebecca was ushered through the door of the staff room.

Around the table sat a collection of fresh-faced girls, an older man and an extremely good-looking young bloke. All of them were downing beers or bottles of brightly coloured lolly-grog drinks.

'I see you're hard at it, you lazy lot!' Sol said in his deep Spanish-draped voice, but the smile in his eyes told Rebecca he spoke in jest. She sensed he was as glad to see them as they were him.

'Just finished the night feed-up, boss,' said the young man, who was showing no signs of discretion in the way he eyed Rebecca's breasts.

'This is our neighbour from Waters Meeting, Rebecca Lewis.'

'Saunders,' Rebecca corrected. It came out of her mouth so suddenly it surprised her. Rebecca Saunders — the name she'd had when she was young. When she was a jillaroo and single. Her days before becoming a farmer's wife. Before she married Charlie. A name, after today, she wanted again.

'Rebecca *Saunders*,' Sol said, sounding slightly irritated once again. 'I'm giving her a tour.' He took a step back and surveyed her. She couldn't tell if his gaze was cold or mocking.

'Rebecca, meet some of the staff who've come with us in the move from Scone. We couldn't get rid of them,' he said, his fond tone returning when he addressed them. 'This is Daisy Peters, our foreman; Kealy Smith, our stablehand; Bill Hill, our everything; Simply Steph, because no one can say her surname; and —'

'Don't introduce her to Joey, boss,' the older man, Bill, said quickly. 'He'll race her off to the sand roll when youse aren't looking.' The girls all sniggered.

Sol Stanton cast them an amused look. 'Yes, well … and this is one of our riders, Joey,' he finished.

'Rider's right,' muttered the pint-sized Daisy cheekily.

'One of?' Joey said. 'Your *best* rider.' He had jet-black curly hair and violet-blue eyes, and he scraped the legs of his chair on the timber floor loudly as he abruptly stood up. He half bowed, reached out and shook Bec's hand. Then he stooped over to kiss the back of it and, as he did, Bec took in the stubble on his chin and the twinkle in the eyes smiling wickedly up at her. His looks set him up to be more like a pretty-boy actor than a jockey.

At the table, the strong-looking, curvy, short-haired girl in the Blue Heeler Hotel singlet, Steph, gave a mock cough behind her hand. '*Man whore*,' she hacked. The girls giggled as Steph 'coughed' again.

And Rebecca smiled with them. She was not used to this sort of attention from men. She had barely thought about herself as sexual at all for years, until she was waiting, pissed, for Charlie to come home after the sex-toy party. She had become a wife, a mother, a slave to the days on the farm. She did of course think often about the lack of sex in her life, but it was always in the context of 'not giving Charlie enough'. God knows he'd made her feel plenty guilty for it.

Now, since the shock of today, she realised she had been longing for sex, but not just sex for the sake of sex. She wanted to feel worshipped. Like a mother goddess. To feel passion again inside herself, on all levels. She realised too she had been longing to feel appreciated by men. In the wake of today, she decided to give herself permission to soak up the pleasure of being in the company of broody handsome Sol and now flirty Joey. Male energy, so different from Charlie's.

Over the years at parties, campdrafts, rodeos and barbecues, Rebecca had shut down any attention from other men to avoid Charlie's jealousy. She'd done that for so long that now when she went out into the world, she had forgotten who she was. Could she still be desirable? If she could, she wondered, what was the harm in flirting with a player like Joey or enjoying the visual erotica dished up by the beautiful (but married) Sol and his horses? Was that being unfaithful as a wife? Certainly it didn't even approach the limits of faithfulness — the ones that Charlie had just shattered so irreparably today.

'Take no notice of them,' Joey said. 'The pleasure is all mine, Miss Rebecca.' He gave a cheeky wink of his now dark blue eyes — they seemed to alter in the light — refusing to drop her hand and eyeing the line of her breasts.

'If she'd like a tour of the staff sleeping quarters, I'd be happy to assist, boss,' he said with a grin, not taking his eyes from her.

'Thank you, Joey, but there's no need,' Sol said. 'Unless of course Miss Rebecca would *like* a tour of the staff bedrooms?' He half turned his face to her, his eyebrow raised a little, a mocking look on his face.

Rebecca felt her cheeks redden. They were taking the piss out of her. 'No,' she said almost crossly, snatching her hand from Joey's, then she tried to cover her reaction with a hasty, 'Thank you.'

Steph snickered behind her fist.

As the conversation drifted to work, with Sol briefing the staff about what jobs needed doing the next day, Rebecca had time to take in the framed photos that hung on the smoko room walls.

There was Sol wearing a polo outfit, holding a giant silver cup and standing next to a little chestnut horse with a zig-zag blaze. She noticed the curve of his strong thighs and tried not to look too closely at what was a fairly nice bulge at the front of his cream jodhpurs. The caption below revealed the picture was taken in Argentina. Another photograph showed a girl on a black horse sailing over a giant jump with yellow daisies at the base in an indoor show ring. The same black horse with the striking white blaze was pictured standing next to a helmet-clad Yazzie, who was also wearing a blue winner's sash and holding a cup. Other shots showed pictures of racehorses placing first all over the globe, noses outstretched to the winning posts. Then there was a picture of Yazzie squatting next to a double pram containing two little babies. She had one hand on the pram and the other on the wide forehead of a giant bay warmblood, who stood meekly beside her, dropping his head. Rebecca wondered whose children they were.

She was startled out of her daydreaming when Sol, done with briefing his staff, was halfway out the door, apparently expecting Rebecca to follow pronto.

'Last stop the fodder shed,' he said after she'd hastily farewelled the team of workers and at last caught up with him.

'The what?'

But Sol was already through the wide stone stable archway and in a parking area formally lined with box hedges. There on the other side was the new Colorbond shed Rebecca had seen the night before. The shed, destined to be covered in climbing roses in a few years, had solar panels on the bulk of the northwest-facing roof and beyond that a wind turbine spun lazily in the heat. At the door Sol stood waiting for Rebecca.

'Thanks,' she said, surprising herself by feeling a little gushy and giddy at passing so near to him. He smelled so expensive — probably wearing some kind of men's fragrance that she was sure she would find advertised in the pages of *Vogue*. He looked so utterly 'movie star' or 'private yacht' that she told herself to get a grip. She'd only ever lusted after boys in farm boots in her younger days. But as she stepped into the silver-lined shed, thoughts of Sol as a sex-bomb dissolved. She felt the blissful ambient temperature of the room wrap over her skin, a relief after the strong heat of the late summertime afternoon. And relief too from the headache she was now experiencing due to Charlie.

'Wow!' she said, taking in what she saw. Racks and racks of long white plastic trays held grain that was shooting to green sprouts in strips that ran for several metres. Some of the racks tumbled with iridescent shoots of lush fodder, ready for harvest.

'I saw something about this system on TV on *Landline*,' Rebecca said. 'It was fascinating.' Sol seemed pleased with her reaction and looked at her openly for the first time, with a white-toothed smile on his face. He probably gets those cosmetically enhanced, thought Rebecca as she looked at his perfect teeth.

'Grain goes in,' he explained, 'nutrients and water goes on in a reticulated system and green feed comes out seven days later. One kilo of grain is converted into eight kilos of highly digestible, alkaline green feed.'

'Amazing.'

'No more gut trouble for our horses,' Sol said. 'No more ploughing our paddocks for grain crops. No need to pour thousands of megalitres of river water onto hot dry soil as irrigation. It's all produced in here. Daily. Two tonnes of grass a day for our animals, so we can allow those tired old soils out there time to recover.'

Rebecca felt her heart flutter. He was talking the Andrew Travis talk! She hadn't realised Sol was heavily involved in managing the Rivermont property, *and* he was using the same methods she was so excited about. Until now she thought the Spaniard was a musician, based in Europe, doing a poncy thing like playing the piccolo.

Before she could push him more on the farm management, Sol continued on about the shed, 'Plus with solar power, wind energy and organic nutrients, we're hoping to put back into the system what we take out.'

'But why sprout the grain and not hard feed?' Rebecca asked, thinking of old Hank and Ink Jet, who ate oats by the bagful, only to crap them out the other end, seeds whole.

'What most Australian farmers don't realise,' Sol said, his accent thickening with passion, 'is that birds are the only creatures in the Animal Kingdom designed to eat grain. Horses, sheep and cattle are not designed to eat whole grains. It's really hard on their gut. It makes their system so acidic. Birds germinate the grain in their crop before it goes to their stomach.' Sol indicated the equivalent area of his own throat. Rebecca imagined kissing him there, just below the line of his freshly shaven jaw. She swallowed nervously at the rampage of her thoughts. It must be the shock of Charlie, she told herself.

'This little baby has saved us a fortune in vet bills and given us an advantage on the track. The horses have never run so well. And as I said before, it frees our paddocks up for rehabilitation. The soils are tired on this property. That's why we're bringing Andrew Travis's farming systems to Rivermont.'

'Fantastic,' Rebecca said, a genuine smile lighting her face, her troubles over Charlie momentarily forgotten.

The smile did not go unnoticed by Sol. He narrowed his eyes and tilted his head enquiringly at her. 'You can clearly see the potential here before you. I like this in you!'

'I get excited about good farming,' Rebecca said, her guard down for the first time.

Sol was impressed. He smiled warmly at her. It was rare to find a person so quick to understand the benefits of the new system. She really is incredibly pretty in a very Australian, earthy way, he thought, despite her reddened nose and eyes brought on from her crying. Despite whatever was going on with her and her husband, Sol suddenly realised he liked her. She was so much more solid in the world than the wishy-washy European women he had spent his time with. She is like an Australian stock horse, he thought, amused at his own analogy. She was pretty but practical. Sturdy and sensible, but with stamina and, he suspected, a cheeky temperament within, once you had her trust.

As Rebecca walked up the centre aisle of the shed, taking in the irrigation poly pipe and computerised watering system, she was too absorbed in the excitement of seeing state-of-the-art farming technology to notice Sol's close appraisal of her. As far as she could see, the system offered solutions for many problems faced when farming in this arid land.

I'd love to show Charlie, she thought excitedly, but then her excitement plummeted. Did she even still have a Charlie to show? Did she even want a Charlie in her life any more? Grief swamped her. Even if she hadn't discovered what she had this afternoon, she'd still be facing the giant wall of his refusal to try anything new or ever think outside the square. She knew if he toured the fodder shed, he'd tear it to shreds, citing all the reasons it wouldn't work, just because he hadn't thought of it himself. And he'd do it in front of Sol, which would be embarrassing for her, and arrogant and rude of him. Not to mention ignorant.

'But the labour?' Rebecca asked; this was one of the issues Charlie would pick on.

Sol shrugged. 'You've seen our staff. We need a cast of thousands anyway, so I'd sooner have them in here, harvesting a crop that is nutritionally consistent and of benefit to the horses, than going around on a tractor sowing grain crops that may or may not succeed depending on rain, and producing feed that will burn a horse's gut, you know? *And* give them laminitis in their hooves so they can't run let alone walk. It all adds up.'

Rebecca turned and practically shone, so broad was her smile at him. 'It's completely amazing.'

'I did all the sums and looked at all the health science. Rivermont comes out in front alongside conventional feeding methods. Old Bill Hill fights to work in here on hot days. And wait till winter. They'll all want to have a go. It's a peaceful place to work.'

Sol walked into the fodder rack aisle and came to stand before her, very near. He looked down at her and said softly, 'You'd like it. You should give it a try one morning. Come and do a shift. It helps you think. I'd like to show you personally how to spread the grain.'

Is there an edge to his voice? Rebecca wondered. One of suggestion? She glanced up at him, suddenly self-conscious, realising his deep dark eyes were looking at her rather more intensely than before. Was he pushing for something? She saw one of his perfectly shaped dark eyebrows lift slightly at the corner. It's definitely an invitation, she thought, and not a pure one.

'Often in hard times, one needs comfort,' he said in a voice far too soft for Rebecca's liking, 'and I know you are going through hard times. Men can be such bastards sometimes … trust me, I have been one … but now is my time to change.' His head tilted slightly, searching her face for a response. 'Maybe we could help each other, yes? In our search.'

She pulled a puzzled face and pushed past him out into the centre aisle of the shed. 'Search?' She shook her head. 'Thanks, but I'm busy enough on my own farm.' She continued in a rather cold voice: 'I think now you'd better get back to Yazzie in the kitchen and to your "Man Cake".'

'Are you mocking me about my cake?' he asked.

'Are you playing me?' she fired back.

'What if I were?' He shrugged.

'It would be rude. And wrong,' she said.

'Are you always this frosty? Even in this god-awful heat?' He smirked at her, amusement playing in his dark eyes.

She stood before him in her cowgirl shirt, torn at the side from a barbed-wire fence, buttons bursting at the boobs, he in his stone-coloured authentic Ralph Lauren polo shirt and creased shorts. He *is* playing me! she realised. Were all men the same? Here was another man just as prepared as Charlie to hurt his wife.

'Me? Frosty? Are you always this forward with your neighbours, when Yazzie is so close by?'

He pulled a 'maybe so' face.

'You are certainly better with animals than you are people,' she snapped.

'And you are certainly very rude and one of the most unhappy women I have ever met.'

Bec felt tears prickle and Sol noticed her pain.

He let out a big breath. 'I'm sorry. But yes,' he continued, 'I do prefer animals to people. Forgive me. Now I must get going. Andrew Travis is expecting me. Please, find your own way back to the house.' And then he was gone.

She stood in the shed, holding in tears, pressing her nails into the palms of her hands so hard they hurt. How could he do that to the beautiful Yazzie? Rebecca felt a wave of guilt because she had actually been excited by his nearness. The way he looked. His smell. His complexity. But she shut out the thoughts. Again her mind ran to the same questions. Were all men the same? Cheats? After one thing?

Her jaw clenched, her headache worsening, Rebecca walked back out into the daylight.

As she passed the stables, she heard a wolf whistle. Turning, she saw Joey standing with a wheelbarrow. He was leaning on a shovel at a pile of sawdust. She noted his tight faded denim jeans, hitched closely to his hips with a brown leather belt. He wore a body-hugging blue singlet and again that wide cheeky smile. The sweat on his brow was trapping dark curls against his skin. From his expression, Rebecca could tell Joey clearly had not missed the fact she looked red-faced and flustered coming from the fodder shed.

'Did you enjoy looking at Sol's assets?' he called to her as he tilted his chin arrogantly upwards and smirked.

She tucked her head down and kept walking.

'You've got a good set of assets yourself, cougar girl,' he said, bending over for another shovel load, 'and I'm liking looking at 'em right now. Later maybe, baby?'

'Huh!' was all Rebecca managed to reply as she stomped off towards the homestead.

# Eleven

Charlie stood at the hollow-log kennels under the pepper trees, the bucket of dog pellets sitting by his worn-out boots. Nervously, with one eye on his master, Stripes wove in and out of his kennel on the end of his chain, saliva dripping to the ground, while Bec's old dog Stubby sat gazing through foggy eyes, beating up mini dust storms with the very tip of her tail. The dog was blind and deaf, but could still miraculously work sheep if they didn't get too much of a run on her. And she always knew when it was dinnertime. Charlie growled at Stripes to settle, then pulled his phone from his pocket. It was getting late. He tipped pellets into an old rusted oil tin for Stubby and watched as the dog got up and shuffled over.

Every night Charlie thought about shooting the old Kelpie, who was these days more black with grey on the points than black and tan. But she was Bec's dog. Yet another one of her links to the past and the glory days of her youth on Waters Meeting with Tom. There were days when the old dog was too disoriented to come out of her kennel. Other days Charlie could tell Stubby suffered from the pain of a long-ago diagnosed tumour that there was no use treating. To Charlie, it seemed pointless to keep

Stubby alive, but Bec had the final say on the matter. She wasn't letting go.

Despite her constant moaning that she wanted another pup, Charlie had refused. When would she have time to train it? He would end up copping the rap for training his way with methods she didn't agree with. And it was always up to him to feed the useless mongrels. Never her. She always just hid in the house.

His fingers slid over the screen of his phone and he began to type a message to Rebecca. *Where the eff are you?* He pressed the send button.

Normally Rebecca would've been onto him several times via the phone: to check dinner was under way; to badger him into going to the Andrew Travis grazing night; to bark orders at him about taking the dead sheep, compliments of Kelvin's rough work crew, away from the yard. But not a word from her all day. Maybe she couldn't, or more likely *wouldn't*, use the new iPhone as a sulky protest over the tractor. Just as he thought this, the phone beeped a message.

*Meet you there,* was all Rebecca replied.

Charlie frowned. Something was up. Was it to do with that bloody greenie farmer bloke Andrew? Charlie realised the no-hoper New Ager would've been travelling through Bendoorin today on his way to the information night at the Dingo Trapper. And Bendoorin was where Bec had been. Had they been meeting up with each other?

But what if he was wrong?

Charlie remembered the brief conversation with Rebecca this morning about getting their marriage back on track. Suddenly guilt over Janine found him. He raised his phone again and typed a row of Xs to his wife and pressed the send button. He knew the token kisses would buy him a load of brownie points. They would also steer Bec away from thinking that he was onto her about Andrew. Charlie thought of Janine again. Today, after her moans of passion had subsided, he remembered with a grimace, she'd suggested they run off somewhere together. He'd assumed she was joking. She'd gone silent when he laughed at the notion. Charlie sighed. It was getting complicated. He had thought Janine understood that it was all just a passing fun fling, to take their minds off the drudgery of their lives. She was getting too clingy.

To keep Janine calm, and quiet, he raised his phone again and forwarded her the same row of kisses. He had learned that you had to be careful with women. They could get hysterical over the smallest things. The kisses would earn him brownie points there too, he concluded.

Satisfied with himself, Charlie threw the last of the dog pellets at Stripes, neglecting to refill the dogs' water, and jogged through the slanted old wooden gate to the side of the homestead, headed for the shower. He needed to wash the scent of Janine from his skin and get himself down to the pub quick smart.

As he kicked off his boots in the mudroom and made his way along the hall to the stairs, he winced, his fingertips meeting with the fresh bright blood-red scratches that Janine's acrylic nails had left on the back of his neck. He smiled. All in all, it had been a good day.

After lunchtime, following a spate of sexting, Janine had turned up at the Waters Meeting machinery shed, telling her husband, Morris, she was off for a hit of tennis with Ursula. *As if* Ursula would play tennis, thought Charlie. Janine wasn't too bright with her alibis. But he had the feeling Morris really didn't care where his wife was. So long as his stud rams were shedded and fed, and there was *The Land* to read and a square meal to eat at the end of the day, Morris wasn't fussed about Janine's whereabouts. Charlie suspected Morris liked the peace when she was gone and was more aroused by the soft crimp of his white-faced Merryville ewes than Janine's black, somewhat coarse hair and overbearing presence.

Charlie had been adjusting the discs on the plough when Janine's little sports Jeep had beetled to a halt. She alighted to the tunes of Dr Hook and stood before him, legs long, mostly toned and deeply tanned in an itty-bitty tennis skirt, wielding a racquet.

'Anyone for tennis?' she said suggestively, then laughed.

At first Charlie had been nervous Bec would arrive back from town, but he knew that time was on his side. She'd be a while yet. It was the scent of Janine's perfume and the way she grabbed directly for his backside that got him.

'I'm addicted,' she had said as she bit at his earlobe. She ran her fingers into his jeans pocket.

'Is that an iPhone or are you just pleased to see me?'

'Both,' he'd said. It was so good to feel truly wanted by a woman, not like Bec who only wanted a bit when she was tipsy. Charlie had pushed Janine up against the Jeep, his hands roving under her skirt, happy to find she wasn't wearing any undies.

'You wanna play tennis? Do you? Huh?' he'd said, shoving his finger deeply and roughly into her.

He'd taken her there and then in the home paddock under the hot sun. It had been great, up until the part Janine had confessed she was falling for him. He'd silenced her with a jovial whack on the arse with the tennis racquet and told her to 'get going' before Bec came home. He'd lied that she was on her way very soon.

As he stripped for his shower, he swivelled to look in the mirror. He even had a touch of sunburn on his glowing white arse cheeks to prove his midday session had really happened.

If Bec asked about the scratches, Charlie decided, he'd tell her he did it getting a wether out of the scrub. Although, as he ran the water hard, he knew Bec wouldn't ask about his neck, let alone his sunburned bum. She barely looked at him these days. Her focus was always on Ben and Archie. Her touches, her cuddles, her kisses and her smiles, when they came, were reserved for the boys. Not him. Not any more. She's as cold as a witch's tit, Charlie thought bitterly. No wonder I'm playing about, he reasoned as he kicked his oily jeans across the bathroom floor to the growing pile of dirty washing and stepped into the shower. With a wife like that, what man wouldn't stray?

An hour later, when Charlie walked through the door of the Dingo Trapper Hotel, the place felt vastly different from the night before. The bar was subdued and the carpet, usually cleaned to within an inch of its life thanks to Amanda Arnott's steam-cleaner machine, smelled of stale grog. The crutching plant crew had been in on a bender that afternoon and had left a wash of spilled beer, torn sodden coasters and chip crumbs scattered in a trail that would confuse even Hansel and Gretel. The reason for the remaining mess was that Amanda, with her post-sex-toy-party hangover, had taken herself upstairs for a nanna nap, leaving Dutchy to run both the kitchen and the bar, with his rather inept young offsider, Lucy, who was on the dopey side of simple.

Charlie cast his eyes about for Kelvin and his crew, but the team must have left, chasing more pub action and a larger selection of women in Bendoorin. Instead Charlie delivered his cheeky grin to the cluster of farmers who had gathered at the bar for the no-till cropping and holistic grazing information night. All the men were clutching beers for security and their stilted farming conversations were peppered with pauses as wide as the Great Dividing Range.

'What crops you putting in?' asked one.

'Oats.'

Then there was a pause.

'Dry. Isn't it?'

'Sure is.'

Pause.

'Who's gunna make the cricket finals this year?'

'Dunno.'

Pause.

'You reckon that knob Andrew Travis knows what he's on about?'

The men shrugged.

All were relieved when they found Charlie in their midst. Their faces brightened and their belted-in personalities loosened a little. Charlie Lewis was always one to liven things up.

'Hear you got a new John Deere that knows its way to the pub already,' said Dennis Groggan.

'Yeah!' beamed Charlie. 'I sure do!'

As he told an embellished version of last night's tale, he glanced about, searching for Rebecca. In the corner of the bar at a wooden table were a handful of government scientists and facilitators, who were polishing off their travel-expense-covered counter meals, all clad in their uniform of baby-blue polo shirts and navy trousers.

Their task was to chaperone Andrew Travis to as many regions and reach as many farmers as they could rally. Not an easy task. Despite their jovial conversation, the RLM men looked slightly nervous to be in the vicinity of the menfolk farmers, who collectively carried with them a brutish judgemental air of scepticism regarding bureaucrats. Particularly when the farmers held the belief that the RLM staff were 'shiny bums', overpaid and underworked. People who wasted their time fluffing and fussing over 'feedback' forms for their 'reports'. To make the RLM's job even harder, Andrew's crucial message about increased carbon sequestration into soil using grasses not trees, and his controversial stance on reducing the use of both fossil fuel and artificial fertiliser, were not liked higher up the chain in the political arenas. Their bosses in upper department levels were loath to spruik too loudly about a system that let the giant corporations down. Corporations that the government backed. There was a lot of money to be made and revenue to be generated in tampering with Mother Nature. Andrew's philosophy was dangerous and the on-the-ground RLM men were junior in the pecking order.

At a slight advantage over the male RLM staff were the female members, who the farmers had a little more time for.

They wore their pony tails pulled back tightly, looking 'sciencey' yet pretty in their manly uniforms. Regional Catchment Co-ordinator Mary was the pick. She had bright smiling blue eyes, lovely long wavy hair and an arse in jeans that the men loved to admire. Charlie was disappointed she was sitting as he looked at her now and made a mental note to have a good look when she stood up.

As he ordered his beer, Charlie glimpsed Andrew in the lounge area setting up a projector and tinkering with a laptop. He was dressed in a cobalt-blue RM Williams shirt and Charlie jealously noticed how flat his stomach sat against his golden belt buckle. A fit bastard, he concluded. Still, he reasoned, he certainly had a bit of age about him. Andrew's once black hair was blended with grey and his life in the sun as a Queensland farmer had deepened the laugh lines around his eyes. Charlie sniffed and sipped at his beer, not taking his eyes off Andrew. He may have been going bald, but so far he had not found one grey hair on his head.

But if Andrew was here, where was Rebecca? Charlie glanced at his phone. No messages. Where was she?

Andrew Travis, satisfied the room was set and ready, strode towards the bar with his long muscled denim-clad legs. His authentic smile of greeting warmed up his yet-to-be-seated audience in an instant. The way he slid past the RLM employees and casually propped himself alongside the farmers at the bar without any hint of self-consciousness and easily slipped into conversation told Charlie that this bloke was one of their kind. There was no faking it with farmers, and Andrew was one of the clan. Charlie felt a little disgruntled.

'And have you met Charlie Lewis?' Dennis Groggan asked. 'Got a big place not far from here. Waters Meeting.'

'Ah, no, we haven't met,' Andrew said, setting down his beer and turning to Charlie. 'But I sure know Rebecca, your wife. What a girl! You're a lucky man. She's been to a few of these. She's keen as buggery to trial a few things. It's nice to see you along.'

Charlie raised his beer to his mouth and his eyebrows at the same time. 'Wouldn't miss it for the world, mate,' he said dryly and swallowed down his beer.

# Twelve

When Rebecca saw Charlie's battered Hilux parked beneath an old gum on the side road outside the pub, her resolution to be strong wavered for a moment. She sat in the Stantons' Kluger and puffed out a big billowing breath. How would she face him? And was the woman he was screwing also sitting inside the pub? She breathed in deeply and blinked quickly, not wanting tears to ruin the eye makeup Yazzie had so carefully applied.

'Daddy's here! I see his ute!' shouted an excited Ben, diving to undo the car door.

'Wait for us, Ben,' Rebecca said snappily, her nerves frayed.

'Mummy said wait, young man,' Sol cautioned kindly. 'So hold your horses.'

Rebecca watched as the big man elegantly unfolded his frame from the driver's side and opened the back door for her. He gently cupped her elbow as she stepped down from the car in Yazzie's high black shoes. For a moment, with Sol's hand on her skin, she felt his touch stirring her shut-down body awake. Looking up at his handsome profile, Rebecca felt as if she could be alighting from a chauffeur-driven vehicle in Paris. He had such grace about him: like Pierce Brosnan, only grittier, sexier, Spanish. Divine. Gabs would be wetting her pants to be even standing near someone like him. She felt a deep breath of desire inflate her lungs. How could she even be thinking like this? Because, she thought, it feels like revenge. Rebecca knew it was dangerous, but she wanted to feed the feeling.

'Yazzie has a way,' Sol said, smiling down at her. 'You look transformed. There is nothing more beautiful than a freshly groomed woman,' he leaned a little closer, 'except for a freshly bedded woman. Provocativo!'

She cast a self-conscious glance at Yazzie, who just shook her head and laughed.

'You're such a dweebazoid, Sol,' the other woman said as she helped Archie down from the car. Rebecca wondered why Yazzie never seemed to show a flinch of jealousy at Sol's ways.

'Sol, why don't you take the boys inside and get them a lemonade?' Yazzie suggested. 'Rebecca and I will be in shortly. We need to get the "girl power" thing happening before we go in.'

Looking like one of his sleek dark racehorses in his cool slate-grey denim jeans and tight black T-shirt, Sol took the hands of the two little boys on either side. Their joyful laughter pealed upwards into the evening sky as he gently lifted them one-armed, carrying them through the air. Yazzie watched him go and Rebecca noticed a hint of emotion cross her face.

'He's gorgeous, really. Once you get past the gruff bit,' Yazzie said.

'He's bloody more tolerant than Charlie. He never complains much that you boss him about. Most men would call you a nag,' said Rebecca.

'Hah! I'm entitled to boss him.'

'You're a lucky girl, Yazzie. I wish Charlie had some of Sol's traits.'

'Me? A lucky girl? God to have a brother like that? All the broken-hearted ex-girlfriends I've had to counsel! He's too much! I just wish he would settle! He's been miserable for years — ever since his first wife left him. They married so young.'

Rebecca frowned. '*Brother?*' she asked. 'Are you for real? I thought he was your *husband*!'

Yazzie threw her hand to her mouth, covering her explosion of laughter. 'Sol? My *husband*?! God! No way! Yuck! How could you think that …? He's my brother, you dork! Well, half-brother — same dad, different mums. Dad's ex-wife is Spanish and went back to live in Spain. She's the musician of the family. That's where Sol gets it from. And our sister Estella was a dancer and pianist. She's my half-sister too. But she's in Venice now. Studying art.'

'Wow. So he's your *brother*! No wonder!' Rebecca wound her thoughts back over the time she had met them both. It all fell into place. 'So you're the youngest?'

'Yes. Mum met Dad when she was being one of those car-bunny models at the Grand Prix in Germany. I think after Sol's mum, Dad wanted someone less complicated. Less creative. Less intelligent. But he certainly judged my mum by her cover. She was doing the Grand Prix job to help pay for her Master's. She's madder than a cut snake and smarter than Stephen Hawking and Leonardo da Vinci combined. Poor Dad. She gives him a run for his money. So Sol's from the first Spanish batch. I'm from the second all-Aussie one. And Dad's parted company with my mum and is onto his third missus. French this time. So, all in all, it's a mad family. Mad.'

Yazzie pulled a silly face, then laughed, her light blue eyes opening wide. 'Now you know Sol's not my husband, you get to perve and flirt with him a whole lot more. I wondered why you weren't falling all over him. Most Australian women do. It's the accent. Makes me wanna puke.'

'Me? Fall all over him? I hadn't even thought of him as hot. And I'm a married woman. I haven't looked sideways at a man in fourteen years — not since I started going out with Charlie at Ag College. Well, maybe I did look once. At Tim McGraw, when he came to Melbourne to play his concert and he was wearing that tight white T-shirt, even tighter jeans and that big black hat.' Bec put her hand to her chest. 'That really got my pulse going. But other than that one time with Tim, I haven't looked.'

'You're either a liar or a fool. You're allowed to look, silly.'

'Charlie would argue differently.'

Rebecca stared down at her freshly painted fingernails glistening in the pub's verandah light and thought of how Charlie had thrown a fit every time a man came near her. It was easier to shut herself down.

'Things change,' Yazzie said, linking her arm in Rebecca's. 'Come on, yummy mummy. It's time you let your inner goddess out again. We warrior women go to war to win!'

And with Yazzie steering her, they crossed the road, Rebecca steeling herself for what was about to come.

# Thirteen

The banter from the pub crowd cut to silence when Yazzie and Rebecca entered the bar. From the back, someone wolf-whistled.

'Geez, Bec, you scrub up all right,' called out Tonka Jones from his bar stool. The men laughed and the conversations resumed, still with a few eyebrows raised. What was going on? some of the local men wondered. First the sex-toy party, then Charlie Lewis's missus arrives dressed like that with the Stantons. Something was out of place.

Ignoring the stares, Bec delivered Tonka and the men a gentle smile, her face a mask on the turmoil that swam within her.

Charlie had already been put off balance by the sight of an incredibly handsome male stranger ushering Ben and Archie, his own children, into the pub! The boys had only run to him briefly to say hello and were soon back talking animatedly to the tall foreign-looking bloke.

Then Rebecca had swanned in, wearing a short tight black dress and incredibly high heels. The blotchy tan had been washed smooth and her limbs looked honey-coloured and edible. Her normally long wavy hair had been straightened, then turned in loose curls at the ends. The blonde sheen of her hair under the pub lights and the way her made-up eyes glinted caused Charlie's jaw to drop and his hackles to rise. What was she up to? He hadn't seen her out of scuffed boots, oversized rugby tops, the same old pony tail and grimy jeans for years. When they did have a 'do', she always dragged out the same dress with the same old complaints about how fat she'd become and how she really should buy new shoes since Ben had spewed on her only good pair when he was two.

And who was the little blonde piece with her? She too wore a body-hugging dress, this one in a stone colour that showed off her long lean brown limbs. She was as pretty as a swimsuit model, but without the large breasts: the ones she had, nonetheless, would have been enough of a handful for Charlie's liking.

Rebecca glanced over to Charlie and caught him eyeing Yazzie's cleavage. She gave a snide smile and mouthed 'hello' before walking straight-backed like a snob to the tall dark-haired man, who passed her a glass of champagne while feeding the kids chips and lemonade. Charlie felt an uneasiness simmer inside when he saw Rebecca's smile warm to that of a cosy winter fire, as she received the champagne from the man and offered him up a stylish 'thank you'. What was with the champagne? Charlie wondered. Since when was Bundy not up to scratch? And who were these people? Surely not the Stantons? Surely she hadn't befriended those rich tossers? After all the grief they'd given them on the roads and with the helicopter while they built their racing empire? She wouldn't dare.

Charlie was about to move from his bar stool when Andrew set down his beer, swivelled off his own bar stool and called out, 'Rebecca!' With a bright smile, he moved over to her. 'Great to see you! You look wonderful. My goodness. You *really* look wonderful! I don't know what's in the water up here. And this must be Yazzie? Sol and I have been on Skype talking through the changes at Rivermont, and he told me you'd at last moved up here.'

Andrew shook Yazzie's hand, then put his hand on Rebecca's waist and leaned down to kiss her on the cheek. Even though the muscles beneath her skin felt like wire from the tension of the day, she welcomed the pressure of Andrew's hand on her and drank in the warm lips brushing her cheek.

'Inner goddess,' she heard Yazzie whisper in her other ear. 'Bring her out to shine.' She smiled back at Yazzie, holding in her emotions. She would not, could not, be crushed by Charlie and what she had witnessed today.

Soon it was time to begin the information evening, so the Stantons and Andrew made their way, still chatting, into the lounge room. The RLM crew were doing their best to round up the farmers from the bar and get them to follow and take their seats.

'Where have you been?' Charlie whispered to Rebecca.

She looked at him, her blue eyes direct and strong. 'Maybe I should ask you the same question?'

Charlie froze for a split second. He grappled to read the expression on her face. She looked utterly different. It wasn't just the makeup. There was an energy to her. A fury.

Maybe she knew? But how could she know?

'Dunno what's up your bum tonight,' he said casually. 'I've been working. As usual. Working.' He sipped his beer, his eyes sliding away from her.

'Working? Have you?' Rebecca delivered another frosty smile, and tears brimmed a little in her eyes. 'Thanks for telling me how nice I look. Thanks, Charlie.' She nodded. 'You're putting in such a fine effort to "get us back on track",' she said sarcastically. She stood looking at him, pain written across her face. 'I have to settle the children,' she said, her voice tight, then she was protectively putting both hands gently on the backs of Ben and Archie and ushering them away from him. As she stooped to speak to the little boys, Charlie caught a glimpse of her full, curved breasts. That dress was dangerously low cut. Far too low cut for the mother of his children. And again, Charlie thought angrily, she's being an utter bitch to me.

In Dutchy and Amanda Arnott's private living room above the bar, Rebecca kissed both boys on the head, her lips meeting first with Archie's blond curls, then the sheen of Ben's dark crown as they settled in front of the DVD. Trollop, the pub dog, knowing children often spilled food, settled herself down at the boys' feet, hoping for a stray corn chip if she could keep herself awake long enough. Bec hovered over her boys and shut her eyes, holding in the scent of their perfection. The boys sensed their mother's nearness and need.

'I love you, Mummy,' said Archie, turning his face to her, his voice light and kind. He put a tiny little hand on her forearm and she felt the glistening of what felt like tiny stars sparkle across her skin.

'I love you too, sweetheart,' she replied. Then the hurt came again like a dark swelling wave … a new knowing that her and the boys' future as a family on the farm hung in a new and frightening space — in the blackness of uncertainty. Then Trollop farted and suddenly they were all undone with laughter. The air waved clear by flapping hands, she settled the boys back down again and left them to twelve episodes of *Ben 10*, hoping they would drift off to sleep before Andrew's talk was through.

At the top of the rickety pub stairs, Rebecca tugged her borrowed black dress over her thighs, then swore as she hoicked it back up over her cleavage. She felt like an overstuffed sausage, the casing not coping with the ooze of meat and fat. She steeled herself, holding tight to the oil-stained banister, gingerly sidestepping downstairs in Yazzie's towering shoes, trying to remember what she had said about walking in them. Something about heel-toe, looking forwards and forgetting you were wearing them.

Yeah, right, Rebecca thought, regretting she'd agreed to Yazzie's makeover. She felt a fool. And it had been Charlie who had turned her into one.

She recalled sitting at a timber laminate desk in a tutorial room at boarding school, flipping through a dog-eared work of Shakespeare. What was the word the teacher kept on with? Cuckold? *Cuckold.* That was it. She had been 'cuckolded' by Charlie, and she suddenly realised that her schoolteacher must have been too, the way she'd coughed up the word and so violently taught the Shakespearean text to Rebecca's English class. Rebecca tried on the word: *cuckold.* She shrugged it over her shoulders and wore it like a grubby coat. It felt hurtful and dirty. But somewhere deep inside, the pride within her — from the days when she was Rebecca Saunders, not Mrs Lewis — swelled. It was enough pride and energy to get her down the stairs and into the room full of people and to where her cuckolding husband would be.

# Fourteen

Rebecca eyed the backs of the crowd of men, who were mostly farmers. They sat squarely on the brown vinyl-covered chairs that oozed foam stuffing from worn corners. Many of the men clustered in the back rows in case the talk became too boring and they needed to escape to the bar. There was only a sprinkling of women; they sat at the front and mostly worked for RLM.

The farmers in the room don't know what they're in for, Rebecca thought smugly. Tonight, with Charlie as a bitter aftertaste, she viewed many of the farmers as cowards, too scared to go into battle against the problems on their land, but mostly too scared of the battles within themselves. She had seen it before, the way the farmers were challenged by Andrew's words and how they sat closed off as they mentally wrestled their own bullish beliefs.

Tonight Rebecca knew many of them would be trapped within their own resistance and simply label Andrew a 'wanker'. But she also knew the more open-minded farmers would be in for paradigm shifts in thinking about themselves and their land. A small percentage would become intrigued and join the growing group who were changing management on their farms. Andrew's methods of grazing, cropping and restoring native grasslands not only solved many of the problems that the media spewed out about global warming, but his methods also provided a quick answer to carbon sequestration from the air into the soils. However, his methods also went against the grain of every complex government program on tree plantations and carbon credits that had been dreamed up by the corporates and bureaucrats. In the past ten years or more, he'd copped a lot of flak. But he always seemed unaffected and brave, despite the storms that people tried to hurl at him.

As Bec ordered herself a beer from Lucy at the bar, she resolved to be brave too. She raised the cold beer to her lips and suddenly thought of the white-haired woman she had met today in the Heaven is Here! hippy shop. What was it she had told her about her thoughts creating her reality?

She realised she was passing all her blame and all her problems to Charlie, instead of getting on with achieving her own wants and needs. It wasn't *him* causing the issues. It was her *thoughts about* Charlie. She suddenly saw clearly how constant her negative thoughts were. A subconscious knowing that she had failed before she had even tried! Just as soon as the clarity came, it folded in on itself. She tried to grapple with what her mind had just so clearly seen, but the distraction of the people in the room blurred what she felt could be the key to unlock her prison.

She sipped her beer, watching Andrew, whose face was illuminated by a computer screen as he prepared to start his slide show of farming photos. She realised now that Andrew spoke a similar language to Evie from Heaven is Here! He had the same quiet, balanced yet passionate energy.

'You reap what you sow,' Andrew had once said to Rebecca in a break at a field day. 'And the most important seed to sow is positivity. I've been to so many farmers' meetings and all we focus on are the problems and the negatives in farming. We need to change our thoughts to positive ones. Life is easier that way. And our farms benefit from it.'

Rebecca realised she was drawn to Andrew for the little gems of wisdom and positivity that sprang so naturally from his Queensland cattle farmer's mouth. He often joked to his audiences that he learned as a small boy in the outback cattle yards not to open his mouth too far or the flies could get in. Everything about Andrew had surprised her and inspired her, because he thought about the world in such a different way from how she and Charlie did.

'You've got the hots for him,' Charlie had said once after Rebecca had failed to deliver dinner to the table on time, her nose so firmly stuck in the gigantic pasture-cropping course manual. She'd sighed. How many times had she fought Charlie with denials about Andrew? Sometimes to the point where she was red in the face with fury and frustration, slopping a careless dinner in front of him.

If the boys hadn't been around, there were nights that she would have dumped the plate on him, wanting the scatterings of burned chops, frothy overcooked spuds and plain cups of iceberg lettuce dotted with cheese, that was supposed to resemble a salad, lying in his lap. But instead, like always, she bit her tongue and set his meal down in front of him. What a good wife, she thought bitterly. Some days she wished she did have the hots for Andrew. It would make the beatings of accusations from Charlie easier to bear.

Andrew was a good ten years older than Rebecca, and although tall and gorgeous-looking in that rangy Queensland horseman way, it was the vision and vitality he had for farming that had her hooked. That and his quiet wisdom. There was nothing sexual about it, Rebecca had decided. But Charlie had pushed and pushed her on it, eventually using his suspicions as an excuse to reject Andrew's farming techniques for Waters Meeting. As Rebecca studied Andrew now, she let the notion bubble to the surface that she *could* be physically attracted to him. The fact that she was married had seemed to put a haze around how she saw men in the world. At this moment she noticed Andrew was actually extremely handsome. In fact, she was stunned to realise he was hot!

She liked the feelings that it raised in her, seeing him that way. She toyed with the idea for a short time, like a prisoner imagining an escape from an apparently inescapable prison. She told herself not to feel an ounce of guilt at the thoughts. After all, hadn't Charlie started all of this? A mix of fiery anger simmered inside her and she felt her cheeks redden. If Charlie thought she had a thing for Andrew, if he badgered her and accused her daily about it, then she might as well *create* a thing for Andrew! She couldn't win either way.

Then she caught herself. Her thoughts! She had just thought, I can't win either way. So that would be her future? Angrily she again realised how that woman, Evie, had unnerved her with her weird words and ways. Bec's mind was a mess. She was starting to hear the words that traipsed through her head, and she didn't like them one bit.

Her eyes bored into the back of Charlie's head. She tried to make her memory see him as the young man she'd fallen in love with, but the crown of his head was shining through his brown hair and his shoulders no longer tapered towards a slim waist. Rather they were rounded down, a mix of muscle and middle-aged fat. She felt a sudden grief for the larger-than-life party boy she had fallen in love with. Somewhere back in time that love was alive, but for Rebecca it felt unreachable in the now. She wished she could find it again. But instead of seeing Charlie sitting on the chair, she now saw his father. His bitter, Bible-bashing, misogynistic father, who sat on the couch expecting dinners to be dished up, washing to be done, cleaning to be performed without complaint and women to put up and shut up.

Waking her from her thoughts, Rebecca realised Yazzie was waving at her from the front row.

'Come and sit here,' Yazzie mouthed and motioned. Bec lifted her head and raised her beer.

On her way, she glanced at Charlie, not noticing the stares from the others in the small crowd.

No one had seen Rebecca Lewis dolled up like that in years. What was on the go? The men had sniffed a change and were intrigued. Charlie didn't let on. He sat amidst the men with his arms folded across his chest and his crossed legs kicked out in front of him. He hadn't even saved a seat for her. Nor was he looking to invite her to join him.

In Rebecca's mind came a flash vision of his white pumping backside and she felt her jaw tense. Betraying bastard. She pushed the thought away and sat, with as much grace as she could muster, between Yazzie and Sol.

Now it was Charlie's turn to bore *his* eyes into *her* from behind. She felt the heat and it took all her willpower not to cry. Instead she chose to focus on Sol's gorgeous hands, clasped in his lap. The beautiful smooth strong hands of a European musician and a gentle horseman. She imagined Sol's hands running along her bare inner thighs. The thought of his hands, like revenge. She shut her eyes and breathed in his Ralph Lauren flavour, leaning slightly towards him. Then, still thinking revenge, Rebecca turned her attention to Andrew, as he began to talk in the beautiful deep, gentle tones of his very manly Queensland-speak. She let the vibration of his voice permeate her body, welcoming him into her. She felt eroticism stir within and with it came a vengeful satisfaction.

'About twenty years ago,' Andrew began, looking out to his audience with clear outback-sky eyes, 'we got burned out by bushfires. No fences left, three thousand sheep dead, all the crops gone and no money left for fuel and fertiliser. Instant broke, I was. I ended up not just psychologically burned by that fire, but also physically. I was in hospital for a time, knowing my life had changed forever. What do you do in a crisis like that?'

With a measured pause, Andrew cast his sincere gaze around his hard-arse audience.

'It's obvious. You get on the piss with your neighbour,' he said with a grin. 'He'd been burned out too. We were both buggered. Up shit creek without a paddle.'

The farmers defrosted slightly with a trickle of laughter underlaid with empathy. All had been through hard times.

'While we were sitting drinking beer, feeling our backs to the wall with nowhere to go, we came up with a really silly idea. We thought, bugger it, we'll just sow the bloody crops straight into the ground … no ploughing. Just one pass over the ground with a direct drill seeder when the perennial pastures were dormant — just to see what would happen. And partly because we had no choice.'

Andrew paced the room and delivered Rebecca a subtle look and a gentle smile. Rebecca bit her lip and Yazzie nudged her.

'We were as shocked as anyone to find it bloody well worked! The yields weren't great that first year, but it worked! And we've been direct-sowing crops into dormant perennial pastures ever since. Not only have we saved eighty thousand bucks a year in fertiliser, but we also use only ten per cent of the amount of fuel we used to need. Plus I've doubled the livestock I carry. The topsoil that was once only about five centimetres deep now goes down over a metre in places and the carbon in the soil has more than doubled. The farm is resilient to drought, to pests and to debt.'

He paused again as he showed slides of rich soil, where root systems like abundant, healthy tributaries of lungs breathed vigour and life deeply into the earth.

'Now I've got Australia's leading soil and climate-change scientists chasing me, saying, "What have you done, Andrew? How did you do this? Can we study it?"' He smiled at his audience. 'Nowadays I leave my manager to the farm while I travel the world, speaking to people like you. People who are struggling. People who are wondering why their land and their farm businesses are bleeding to death. Why they no longer feel happy with farming. Imagine if we farmers were paid to sequester carbon like I've done in my soils. Agriculture would be stabilised and the environment would be regenerated.'

Rebecca half turned to see if Charlie was taking in any of Andrew's words. There he sat, with his body language closed, like most of the men in the room. Arms crossed, ankles crossed, a glazed expression on his face. A chin that had doubled in the past five years, resting on his hairy chest. Why didn't his years at Ag College open him up to new ideas? Rebecca thought. She looked back down the years and realised Charlie hadn't been at college because he had a thirst to learn about agriculture. He'd been there because he had a thirst full stop. For grog. And he had been there to escape his family. To get shit-carted and be a party animal with his peers so as to forget the badgerings of his mother and the demands of his father.

The realisation left Rebecca feeling cheated, not so much by Charlie, but mostly by *herself*. *She* had imagined him to be someone else. She had married him believing he was a totally different person from who he actually was. She realised she had been putting demands on him he simply couldn't meet. She felt suddenly sorry for him. Sorry for both of them.

He caught her looking at him, so she hastily turned away and fixed her eyes on Andrew, who was now saying passionately, 'You don't put a Band-Aid on an arm that has been cut off! You'll bleed to death. But that's exactly what we're doing as a human race ... putting environmental Band-Aids over our problems when we actually need extreme remedies, because this planet is *bleeding to death* and our farms and farming families along with it.'

Rebecca had heard Andrew use this analogy before and she both loved and loathed it. It sparked memories of her father, Harry, and of his severed arm in the posthole-digger accident years back on Waters Meeting. During the years afterwards, he carried himself like a wounded returned soldier. He had turned inwards and softened. But he hadn't changed. He still saw right past Rebecca and each year, no matter how gently insistent her coaching and encouraging, nor how strong her rages of silence, her father and Charlie more and more ignored her. They ordered the fertiliser truck in without consideration for what the land actually needed. Superphosphate nuking the earth. Year in, year out, toxic waste dumped on her beloved Waters Meeting. Because the men said so. Because the men refused to see. Because they would not *listen*.

She felt the sting of years of the men's scoffing scepticism and she felt Harry's and Charlie's relief when the babies came and they had quieted her, getting her off their backs. But recently, with Andrew's work and his words as her wind in her sails, she had begun to make noise again. This time Charlie had no one-armed Harry to back him up. This time Charlie was struggling to quash what was growing within his wife. A return to self. A return to the passions she had held as a younger woman.

And now, cheated and cuckolded, Rebecca felt the barbed wire snap and the fence that held her within break. She felt the urge to bolt. To run. If yesterday she'd felt old and washed up, today she could choose to feel alive, powerful and full of energy. She could now see that she was no longer who she was meant to be. It was time to get mad and to get even. Not just for herself, but for the land. For their bank balance and for her sanity. And most of all, for her boys. The new generation of men, who she knew she had to guide to see the world differently.

She realised it all pivoted on what was within her, and the myriad negative thoughts that ran rampant in her head from the moment she woke to the moment she slept. She shifted a little in her seat, feeling a bit woozy. She knew it wasn't the hangover or tiredness that was making her giddy. She knew it was the revelation: her whole being had shifted.

'Agriculture is crashing all over the world due to the misapplication of technology,' Andrew continued. 'I'm here to tell you that the cost of fertiliser and fuel is going to go through the roof.

It'll be reserved in the future for the military and the governments. You as farmers need to learn how to work with what you've got and let nature move us forwards in our own "quiet revolution" — so you don't have to depend on the thieving bastards who take our money. But first you need to open your mind.

'Did you know that there are six billion living organisms in just one teaspoon of healthy soil? That's almost equivalent to the entire world population of humans on the planet today. Each time you plough you are killing those organisms. When you think it's possible to have that much life in such a small amount of soil, it really does blow your mind at what we've been doing to our soils.'

Despite trying very hard, Rebecca couldn't keep her own mind still. She glanced about the room, looking for the woman Charlie had been with. The only other local women in the room were Lucy the barmaid, Amanda, Yazzie and old Mrs Huxley. None of them would be the culprits, Rebecca thought. Unless Charlie was into octogenarians in Mrs Huxley's case. God, she thought, how can I think such flippant things right now? But then she realised there was almost a sense of relief about today's discovery. She was being forced to change, whether she liked it or not.

'Change!' Andrew said, eerily echoing her thoughts. 'We've all heard we need to embrace it, but the methods we inherited from our British past and our pattern of not being connected with animals, plants and landscapes has to change. We need to see that industrial agriculture has failed us. Often we need a crisis to force us to change. That's what we all face. A crisis is not necessarily a negative thing. It may feel that way at the time, but it is the best catalyst for positive change. That fire was the best thing to happen to me. Didn't feel like it at the time, but it was!'

Bec noticed how lively Andrew's eyes were. He was unafraid. He paced up and down, his tones confident yet soothing, as if he was talking the farmers down from a high ledge.

'We need to ask ourselves, why do we do the things we do? Why? But we don't ever question these things. Farmers who see their pastures getting worse put more superphosphate fertiliser on. Then, the next year, the rainfall is down so they ring the fertiliser company and put *more on*. Then the year after that, even though things aren't improving, they put *more on*. It's what I call the *"moron principle"*.'

A scattering of laughter rose from the group.

Andrew opened up his palms to them and widened his eyes. 'But when you think about it, it *is* moronic! I'll tell you why … It's the phosphate fertilisers and the overgrazing that're ruining the soil. It's not the lack of rain! Later, when we get into the science end of the business, I'll show you how phosphates actually lock essential sugars up so the plants can't use them.'

How many times had Rebecca told Charlie this fact? How many times? She had felt like bashing her forehead with a closed fist as he shut his body language down and turned his sulky face away from her. She daren't look at him right now. She couldn't. There was a she-bear in her that wanted to roar.

'So as you go on with your recreational ploughing, round and round in ever diminishing circles, take that time on the tractor to think. Think *why* am I doing this? Is it working?' His voice was gentle like a warm breeze. People could feel his sincerity. Feel his genuineness. But even once he had their trust, Bec knew the listeners would waver as he delivered more information that brought home just how misguided they'd been all along.

His voice got stronger, louder. Sometimes he became brutal and uncomfortable to the crowd, like a cold blast of wind.

His words made the farmers prickle within and fold their arms across their bodies in defence of their own outdated beliefs — though they could not help but like him. He was one of their kind. He would flick up images of his own farm. The way it was when his grandfather had it. The proud family portrait of the new tractor in the 1930s. Then he showed slides of how the farm had diminished in vitality by the seventies, tapering off to the barren wasteland of the eighties. And then his photographs showed the turnaround after the fire, with the new management. The gleam of the coats of the fat cattle. The tall grasslands that brushed the curving skyline. One of the most striking slides — and one Rebecca could feel convincing the room — was a photograph of a fenceline dividing his brother's conventional farm from Andrew's own pasture-cropped and properly grazed paddock. His brother's paddock looked like a desert; Andrew's looked like an oasis.

The first time she'd seen Andrew talk she'd been the same as the men in the room now. She'd felt her hackles rise against him. He was direct. He was firm in his opinions and he wasted no time in pointing out how foolish and mindless some farmers were in land management ... but he also had a knack of including himself in it all. How he too had made mistakes on his farm, and how, by acknowledging he'd got it wrong, it also meant forgiving his father and grandfather, who had also got it wrong.

Rebecca thought of her granddad and his quiet ways with stock. He'd been somehow more in touch with the cycles of the grass and animals on Waters Meeting and, while he was proud of the very first tractor he bought, he used it sparingly, preferring to ride about his stock on his old mare to turning clods of soil with a noisy hard steel horse. He was not a fan of the 'new manure' that the men spread on the pastures, believing the phosphates would poison the soil. It had been her father, Harry, who spent day and night on the tractor and who had turned wholeheartedly to modern technological agriculture.

'We bang on about the destruction of the environment by the introduction of rabbits, of cane toads, of feral cats, donkeys and camels, but the most destructive thing introduced to this country, by far, is the disc plough,' Andrew said determinedly. 'One day I want it to be socially unacceptable to create bare ground — so that it is viewed as worse than smoking over a baby. I want to revolutionise how you walk on the land. I want you to wake up and realise it is not about rainfall ... or the lack of it ... it is about *management*.'

Just as Rebecca felt the men pull away from Andrew, he softened his tone.

'C'mon, fellas. We all know it — I used to do it too — we talk about our stocking rates as if we're talking about our manhood. What's your DSE versus the next bloke's? As if we're lesser men if we run fewer sheep or cattle! But it's been proven: high-risk farming loses over time. The lower the stocking rate, the slower the business, but the *less risk*. It's better business; and I can tell you now, it's a better lifestyle. Instead of being on the tractor, I can be at home with my family.'

Rebecca almost snorted with cynicism. Charlie would never choose to be at home with her and the boys. He'd create work to avoid it. When had he even been to any of the early learning days for fathers and sons at Ben's school and Archie's littlies group?

Andrew soldiered on, though the energy in the room was flagging. He'd have to raise it or slam the message home soon. 'At first, with these methods, I suffered guilt if I was enjoying a beer on the verandah — I felt I "should've been working". But the reality is I have two hundred per cent more soil on my property. I am the cause of it. I built it. And my business is more profitable. But the best thing is I'm not giving all my money to the giant multinational seed and fertiliser companies. *They* are the culprits of poor farm practice.'

He had them back again. Rebecca could feel the audience mood shift again. Now off the hook for their lack of awareness, they stirred in unison, knowing each of them had been bound and led by multinational monopolies and oligopolies that increased prices every year and slanted science to suit sales to farmers.

'We are fed bullshit by the companies. It's time to say NO!'

Yazzie leaned towards Bec. 'Oh, he is good! Way good! Hot too,' she added and Sol rolled his eyes while Rebecca felt a warmth spread across her cheeks. Was this a first-flush feeling for a man other than Charlie after all this time, or was it her first feeling of freedom?

# Fifteen

Charlie joined the applause that thundered throughout the room when Andrew was done, although his clapping was less enthusiastic than the others'. There was an energy of empowerment amidst the farmers that charged the air as the men talked loudly and animatedly on their way to the bar.

Charlie stood too and stretched so that his flannel shirt pulled out from his jeans, exposing the skin on his belly. He tugged it down, feeling annoyed.

'Time for another beer,' he said to Dennis Groggan, who, unlike the rumpled-looking Charlie, had his stiffly ironed work shirt, compliments of Doreen, tucked into both his undies and his King Gees, the waist of which was pulled up practically to his armpits by an old leather belt. He wasn't known as Harry Highpants in the district for nothing.

'That Andrew Travis fella wasn't too bad,' Dennis said. 'The guy had a point.'

'Yeah, but some of it is bullshit,' said Charlie, 'especially when you try it in this bloody hard-to-fence and rocky goat country. We've got too many rocks on Waters for the direct sowing to work.'

'Yeah?' said Dennis. 'You think your place is rocky? Try mine! Still, I'm goin' to give it a whirl on my thousand-acre quarry. And, after hearing him, I'm gunna shut up all my north-facing hills for the spring. And try the grazing. He's got a point.'

'I suppose.'

Charlie let the flow of the crowd draw him away from Dennis. He realised he was still, after all this time, struggling to call the country that he worked on every day his home. He thought of his own family farm out west. The black soil plains and stilted scrub running for hundreds of miles in every direction. Windmills and turkeys' nests. Country cut by irrigation channels with square swathes of grain and cotton crops shooting in regimented rows. The opportunity to drive tractors morning, noon and night. The buzz of harvest time. The sweltering, shimmering, oven-dry heat. And above all the big clear sky. He suddenly longed to see the place again. Even to taste his mother's cooking and feel the comfort that her orderly home brought.

His brother, Garry, had abruptly left the farm last year to get married to a tubby stuck-up bird from Mudgee who wasn't prepared to budge out west. Since Garry's departure, the phone calls from his parents had become more frequent. They often invited Charlie out for visits, but he always told them getting away from Waters Meeting was difficult. He endured his mother's silence on the end of the phone that followed his decline of their invitations. It was a silence that shouted hurt and disappointment and even abandonment at the selfish hands of her eldest son.

'We're not getting any younger, you know,' she would say, and Charlie would feel the guilty tug that had been implanted since the first days in his cot. Each time he asked his father how he was getting on, the old man would reply, 'I'm getting too old for this.' Again the fizz of parental disapproval would linger with him. He felt like a deserter. And what was worse, he felt like he faced the firing squad every day for doing it, from the moment he woke up and saw the sullen mountain mist and the steeply pitched fencelines of Waters Meeting. And, more recently, the sad, vacant look of a woman he no longer knew. Rebecca. Once a vibrant, denim-clad goddess with a shoal of Kelpies swimming around her legs and a quick and ready wit. She was now distant and sad. And there was nothing he could do.

He knew he should try to make it work. He should load the boys into the family wagon with Bec and make a holiday of it, visiting his mum and dad, stopping for burgers and inland-river swims along the way. But he also knew he couldn't stomach the hours in the car with them all. Her and the kids. He'd put himself on the periphery of it all. Child-rearing was a woman's world. At least, that's what his father had always said.

As he propped himself at the bar and fished out a five-dollar note to buy a beer, Charlie thought maybe it was time to put a bit of effort in and pack up for a while with the family. Get Dennis and Doreen or Gabs and Frank to help oversee things on Waters Meeting, so he and Bec could take off. It might just fix things.

His hopefulness fizzled when Charlie spotted Yazzie and Rebecca in the huddle of RLM staff, along with Andrew and who he now knew was Sol Stanton. Rebecca had both men's undivided attention. It wasn't only the words she was speaking that they were paying attention to, he realised. Charlie felt amazed that his wife of ten years could in the space of an afternoon chuck on some makeup, get a tan, stick on a dress and heels and suddenly have the world treat her differently. He didn't know whether to feel insulted or flattered that other men were paying his wife such close attention. Confused and suspicious, he turned his back on her when she looked over to him.

'What can I get you, mate?' Dutchy asked as he moved swiftly behind the bar, stacking ten-ounce glasses in the washer.

'I was going to get another hair of the dog, but come to think of it I'm done. I'm going to push off.'

Dutchy nodded and went to serve the next customer.

Charlie shoved the five-dollar note deep into his jeans pocket. He turned from the bar, avoiding eye contact with the crush of men. His last vision in the pub that night was both Sol and Andrew ushering Rebecca towards the bar. As they did, Rebecca caught Charlie's eye. She gave him a cold look, one of disdain, then continued laughing at something Sol had said.

It was enough to make Charlie see red.

When he got to his ute, there were two text messages on his phone.

One was from Ursula. *Who's been a naughty boy then?* she taunted. The other was from Janine: *When can I see you again?*

He threw the phone on the dash. 'Fuck,' he said and cranked up the old Hilux, reaching across for the hip flask he knew he'd stashed in the glovebox. With all thoughts of his holiday plans gone from his head, Charlie gunned it back up the mountain road to Waters Meeting.

In the mudroom, he fumbled with the lock on the gun safe. He took from the cabinet the .22 and shoved a box of bullets into his pocket. The night was breezy now and the wind stirred the trees. Stripes gave a nervous bark seeing the dark figure approach.

Charlie growled at the dog to settle. Old Stubby hadn't heard him coming in the torment of the wind, so the dog was startled awake when Charlie dragged her by the chain out of her hollow log. Stubby whimpered. She could smell the gun. Charlie put the barrel to the dome-shaped area of skull at the back of the old dog's head, shut his eyes and pulled the trigger. The shot rang out above the hills. Stubby slumped to the ground.

Stripes hit the back of his kennel and stayed there, his body shaking uncontrollably, urine soaking into his fur. Then Charlie unclipped the chain and lifted up Rebecca's dead dog. Fluids began to run from her body; her eyes were still yet to glaze. Blood spilling on the dust. It took Charlie some time to realise he was crying. He swiped the back of his hand across his face as he carried the lifeless body of the dog. He wished in that moment that someone would be kind enough to put him out of *his* misery.

Bec should have let the past go a long time ago. Walking to the shed, Charlie hurled Stubby into the back of the ute. He'd take her to the offal pit in the morning.

# Sixteen

Wearily Rebecca shut the boys' bedroom doors and trod quietly along the hall to her own room, hoping Charlie would be asleep. She had seen him leave the pub hours before, and was disgruntled that he hadn't offered to take the kids home when he left. She knew she should put a load of washing on and she should keep the fire smouldering over night — despite the late summer heat, the kitchen was always chilled in the morning this time of year. But all Rebecca wanted to do was fall into bed. With her high-heeled shoes hooked over an index finger and handbag on her shoulder, she quietly pushed open the bedroom door.

Instead of being asleep, Charlie was standing in his boxer shorts. Beyond him as a backdrop was the rumpled unmade bed from the previous night, hideously streaked with fake tan, the sheets looking shit-stained. As she looked at him, Rebecca saw the tragic naked truth of her husband, his lily-white potbelly and deep-tanned arms, the ingrown hairs on his thighs clustering in tiny red pinpoints of angry infection on his pale skin. The haunted look he held in his eyes. She walked past him without a word to the bathroom.

'What's wrong with you?' he spat. Rebecca felt raw under his gaze as she peeled off the black dress in the bathroom and cast it over the back of a chair.

As he watched her undress, his expression became tainted with distaste. Underneath the dress was her everyday drab underwear. Without the dress, she felt unarmed. Just a humiliated frumpy woman.

'Well? Spit it out?' His voice with its harsh edges jangled her nerves. She realised that, little by little, over the years, she had become scared of him.

He'd been rough with her lately. A shove here as he passed her angrily. A slammed door there. The hammer of a clenched fist banging on the tabletop at mealtimes. The boys starting with nervous twitches as if surprised by a gunshot. The outbursts were building, like a storm. Earlier tonight at the pub his mood had just been a rumble. Rebecca knew the worst of the storm was about to hit.

Gazing back at him, Rebecca slammed the bathroom door in his face, then stooped to retrieve her old flannel PJs from the pile of wilted clothes on the lino. She glanced at her image in the bathroom mirror. The woman who had earlier been transformed by Yazzie's makeup was now back to her bleak, dowdy self. Mocking her imagination, she buttoned her pyjamas up to her neck and stuck out her gut. Where had the young girl with a work-fit body gone? The one who smiled and partied? And was frisky for life? Tonight she had felt that girl return temporarily, with the glimmer of fun reflected in Sol's and Andrew's eyes. But even that small victory felt hollow. There was still Charlie to face and the dirty secret she had discovered today.

As she cleaned her teeth, she looked into her own weary blue eyes. 'Get a grip,' she told herself.

Rebecca pulled on her polar fleece jacket over her pyjamas and hugged it around her body. She shivered against the chill. She had begun to hate this house. Its broken woodheater, the leaky roof. Since their wedding, there'd been talk of renovation. A new firebox and heat pumps, solar and skylights, but ten years on it had never happened. There'd only been money for tractors and fertilisers and new machinery. Bec was a farm girl. She knew the drill. The farm had to come first. Not herself; not the kids. And certainly not the grand old dame of a homestead. Hadn't she tried her hardest? For her father and for Charlie? Hadn't she given all of herself? Now with Charlie's affair, Bec felt she had utterly failed.

She moved into the bedroom, grabbing up her pillow. 'I'll sleep in with Arch,' she said quietly.

'Why?' he asked. 'Why are you acting like this towards me?'

She didn't answer.

'Tell me,' he pushed aggressively.

She swallowed hard. Her eyes narrowed, her mouth set in a firm angry line.

'For fuck's sake, Rebecca! You're being a surly bitch! Talk to me!' He grabbed her so hard she winced. She tried to wrestle away, but he was too strong. The anger of seeing her dolled up with the two men rose and swelled in him like a tsunami. For a moment they struggled, his hands locked onto her skin, Bec using the full strength of her farm woman's body to try to reef herself free. Teeth gritted, jaws locked, both their bodies shaking from effort and rage in a silent desperate tussle. Neither of them wanting to be like this, not wanting the boys to hear, yet each so bound by the other's bitterness.

'Let. Go. Of. Me. Bastard!'

At last Charlie relented and threw her back against the bed. She lay for a moment, her chest rising and falling, tears sliding down the sides of her temples. Her wrists where he had grabbed her pounding. She rolled over and dragged her bag towards her.

'I don't need to talk to you … it's all here … I saved your delightful voice mail … and I saw your accidental video call …'

It felt as if she was watching herself in that moment. The grappling in her bag for the iPhone. The way she stabbed at the screen, like a hysterical actress in *Home and Away*. The ridiculous drama of it all as she tossed the phone onto their bed. The phone filling the room with its sordid soundtrack. Charlie's sex talk, then the woman's moaning. Rebecca got up off the bed and stood before him, the hurt contorting her face, the tears blurring her vision. And she left him there, standing in his checked boxers, his beer belly with its trail of hair protruding over the elastic, his mouth hanging open, mute, as the phone played back the sounds of the hideous scene.

# Part Two

# Seventeen

From where she lay on the couch in the bay window of the lounge room, Rebecca could hear the sounds of the Last Post playing on the alarm-clock radio upstairs in Charlie's bedroom. She knew he was not there to turn it off. He would already be over in the machinery shed, avoiding her. In her sleepy state, she wondered if she could get up and face the day. The boys would soon stir, then she would have no choice.

It had been two months of war at Waters Meeting. A silent, cold war since she'd found out about Charlie's affair. Along with mental wrestling with herself, of cold-shouldering Charlie. Of midnight talks and tears. Suggestions of counselling from Bec, agreement from Charlie to go, but never an appointment made. There had been last night's emotionally hurtful sex, where Rebecca had longed to have her husband back and she had tearfully climbed the stairs at midnight to find him. But as she felt his body heat near her, and smelled his coarse odour, the nausea flooded her senses. The knowledge that he had been with another woman seemed to strip everything away. Rebecca had lain beneath him as he humped into her. She'd stared at the blackness, feeling dormant both emotionally and physically. Scrunching her eyes tight, all she could think of was how he had done this very thing to Janine Turner too. She had prised the information out of him as to 'who'. It was like squeezing a boil and had taken a week to extract from him. The information burst out only to leave a gaping, weeping emotional wound in her. Janine Turner. She was there with them in the room with every angry thrust from Charlie. After Charlie had come inside Rebecca with a groan and a sigh, then tried to hold her, Bec had pulled away from him and begun to cry.

'For fuck's sake,' was all Charlie had said, and Bec had slipped out of bed, moving silently back downstairs like a ghost of herself. Back to what had become her regular night-time place on the couch.

His confession that it was Janine had sparked many nights of raging fights. They shouted in whispers, but soon one of them would roar at the other, the boys' welfare shamefully forgotten in those moments.

The packages of sex toys and lingerie ordered by Yazzie were still untouched, shoved to the back of the cupboard. Her life in tatters.

And of course there had been two months of business as usual on the farm to endure. In the lounge room on the couch, Rebecca combed her fingers through her knotted long hair and rolled over, streaking her fingertips across the cool pane of glass. Upstairs the Last Post continued to play. A blackness had settled inside her soul. She and Charlie were at a stalemate.

In the mist outside, Bec could see two dark shapes. The curved ridges of the horses' deep old spines and hummocky old withers echoing the hills beyond. Hank and Ink Jet, Tom's and her old horses, like old Waler horses, put out to pasture after the war, never to be used again. Charlie always commented that their bony bodies were even too far gone for dog tucker now, their teeth blunt and worn down to yellow stumps. Too weak to tear at grasses. Bec fed them daily with chaff, oats and Completo, and Charlie threatened daily to shoot them both, like he had her old dog.

She thought of dear old Stubby now and wished for the comfort of the old dog's head that fitted so perfectly under the cupped palm of her hand. Charlie had told her he'd found the dog after a fit, froth in her jaws.

'Snake or a seizure,' he'd lied. 'So I shot her. You shouldn't have hung onto her for so long.'

Rebecca winced, knowing what he said was true. But she was still shaking mad with Charlie. If only he'd had the courtesy to bury Stubby in the garden, so at least she could sit beside the dog's grave and say goodbye. But Charlie being Charlie hadn't thought. Rebecca couldn't bring herself to go near the offal pit, knowing her dearest old Kelpie had been dumped there.

Now all she had were the horses. They were the last link to Tom and the days when Bec was free to ride the mountains alongside him. Ink Jet and Hank moved eerily past in the white mist. She heard them snort and watched the silhouettes of their lifted heads.

Upstairs in the vacant bedroom, the final heart-wrenching bugle strains echoed throughout the house, then silence. She thought of the fallen Anzacs. The men forever young, hooked dead upon the wire. She thought of the ones who lived, but were maimed in their bodies and in their souls. Her brother Tom was like an Anzac to her. A fallen young man. But now, sitting in the space of her suffering, she wondered, what if Tom had been able to endure life, with all its grotesqueness and harshness? What kind of a man would he be now? One scarred by life's battles? Or, like her, forced on paths he never intended to take, battling what was within and raging at what was outside himself. Was she grieving the loss of Tom and the Anzacs, or was she grieving the loss of her own youth? Was that what she was grieving of Charlie and herself? The loss of his youth? The romance of him?

As he had aged, his face had become more steely. An expression of disdain towards Rebecca and her ideas seemed to drag his expression downwards when he looked at her. She thought of him now as the young man she had once loved and suddenly she was grieving him. And angry at what she had allowed him to do to her. Now she could see the brutality of his passively aggressive ways with her. Now she could see she had let him scar her so deeply that the wounds were carried within her, from the inside out.

Getting up, she dragged on yesterday's clothes — work jeans, old grey bra, red T-shirt with the tear in the shoulder and a faded flannelette shirt — then slowly she went to the kitchen.

At the sink she ran the water so it was boiling hot and shoved her hands in so they were reddened and stinging. Her head pounded from clenching her jaw tightly in her sleep. Too many thoughts swam in her mind. Most of them negative. All of them hurtful.

She watched the steam curl its way up the windowpane pressing against the cool misty morning air outside. The house was so quiet she could hear the detergent bubbles pop. Rebecca swiped her nose with the back of her hand.

She thought of her boys.

Some nights she slept with one of them just to ease her loneliness, feeling guilt that she was relying on such young beings for solace. She found comfort in turning back the tumble of the tractor-print quilt cover and snuggle rugs, pulling the warm sleeping body of Archie or Ben to her. She pressed her face against the skin of their necks, breathing in their sleepy little boy smell, as sweet as fresh-mown hay, as divine as chocolate. On nights like that, she watched her whole life unravelling behind the dark canopy of her closed eyelids.

Should she ask Charlie to leave? Could she make a go of it, just her and the boys? She'd run the farm on her own in the past, years back. Surely she could do it again? But her body felt old and busted now. Who could she call on to help? She thought of leaning on her rural financial counsellor friend, Sally, as she had done years before. Even though Sally was busy with twins, she'd pulled her out of a mess before, not long after her dad had had the accident, but could they do it a second time now they were both mothers? Rebecca realised, disturbed, that history was repeating the messes of her life.

She wondered how to protect Archie and Ben from what was unfolding around her. Should she even be making such a big deal? Surely couples went through infidelities all the time and their marriages survived. Didn't they? But Rebecca knew it was more than that. Charlie had left her as a friend and lover a long time before Janine. The sting of hurt came again and she pulled the image of her boys to her, knowing they were part of the jigsaw puzzle as to why Charlie and she had drifted apart.

Now, at the sink, she wondered how long she could stand this silent, unshifting stand-off between them. There was no remorse in him. His anger was hovering in his space like a shroud over him. And he was blaming her. Blaming her for all the miseries he carried inside himself. And she, to a point, had been blaming him for all her failed dreams. Today she resolved she would make some changes. Move things along. Today she resolved she would ask him to leave. It was her farm. It was her Waters Meeting.

She heard the familiar noise of the boys creaking their way sleepily down the stairs in search of her. In the mornings, Archie was always cuddly, Ben hungry. She stripped the little one out of his junior pull-up, throwing it in the bin, before helping him back into his pyjama bottoms. She relished the touch of his tiny hand steadying himself on her forearm as she kneeled beside him. The toast popped as she swooped him and Ben up in a quick good-morning hug, kissing them on their heads. Hastily she buttered the toast and grabbed for the Vegemite. In the lounge room, she rummaged through a small mountain of washing that was piled on the couch to find Ben's uniform. She set the little dark blue shorts and a light blue polo shirt in front of the kitchen woodstove, running her fingers over the emblem of the Bendoorin primary school, a mountain eagle, embroidered above the heart. It was only then she remembered it was Anzac Day. A public holiday. There was no school today.

She covered her eyes with the palm of her hand and felt the tears burn inside her closed eyelids, the emotion rising like hands about her throat, constricting her breath. Was she going mad?

As she thought this, Charlie sauntered in, tossing an oily machinery part on the kitchen table amidst the tumble of plates, toys, Textas and unopened mail. Busy with what she was doing, she didn't turn to face him. Instead she felt his presence behind her. Like a sniper's.

'Bearing's gone. Bloody brand-new plough. You going to town?'

'It's a public holiday,' she said, wanting to add 'dipstick' to the end of her sentence but refraining, bitterly laughing inwardly at her own joke, mostly pointed at herself.

Archie sent up a bloodcurdling scream as Ben accidentally jammed his little brother's fingers in the toy box. The sounds of cartoons burbled happily, skippily in the background from the forgotten TV in the corner. Charlie didn't move to help, instead picking up the paper. As Rebecca went to Archie to comfort him, she shot Charlie a look. He sat amidst the kerfuffle of morning activity sipping coffee, absently spooning porridge into his mouth, reading the paper, as if the farm business depended on it for the day. Rebecca had long given up asking him to wipe down a benchtop or make a sandwich. The days when he helped in the house were long gone.

As she scooped up Archie and inspected his reddened fingers, kissing them better, and as Ben clung to her, saying over and over, 'I didn't mean to, Mummy. It was an accident,' she cast Charlie another dark look.

'For god's sake, Charlie, take them for a moment. Please. I need a rest.'

'A rest? From what?' Charlie said. He must have seen she was about to cry. He threw the paper down in a huff and stood abruptly. 'Get your coats,' he said to the children.

'But they're not dressed yet.'

'And?'

She watched, her body shaking, as Charlie dragged the coats on over their pyjamas and jammed little footy beanies onto their heads, taking them out into the misty morning via the verandah doors and jamming on their boots.

When they were gone, Rebecca silenced the morning cartoons with a flick of the remote and went back to the sink. But as she felt the giant space of aloneness in the big old grimy house, she suddenly felt violently ill. She ran outside to the mudroom toilet, banging open the door and promptly throwing up in the bowl. She had been like this after Tom's death. She knew her body gave way to stress via her stomach. At least, she thought wryly, I'll lose weight feeling like this. As she bent, catching her breath over the bowl, she winced at the fresh and crusted splatters from Charlie's morning crap. Why did his mother not teach him to use a toilet brush? she thought angrily. His mother could bloody well have him back. She thought of Mrs Lewis in her house frock and sensible old-lady shoes. The way she served the Lewis men on the expansive wheat property in the west, silently meeting their every need. Providing them with ironed underpants, cream buns fresh made for smoko, baked dinners and crisp clean sheets. Really, Rebecca wondered, what was the point when the men, if left to it, would live like animals in their own grime and survive on chops, beer, white bread and tinned baked beans.

She shut her eyes and felt another swell of nausea, her body giving way to the stress and grief she had endured.

At the washroom tub she splashed cold water over her face and tried to look at the paddock beyond, but the morning fog impaired her view. The horse paddock outside looked like a gas-filled battleground as the gentle morning sun edged its way up into the sky. A faint morning star to the west blinked weakly at her before fading beneath the cap of a mountain. Swiping a dirty hand towel over the grubby washroom window, she heard the rumble of Charlie's tractor in the machinery shed.

He was hell bent on ploughing again. She left one sink for another, going from the washroom back to the kitchen. She plunged her hands into the kitchen sink. 'Chained to it' was the expression. She certainly felt that way.

She had felt this slow rusting of a marriage. A seizing-up of love. Was she just numb from busyness or motherhood? Or had it all been her own convenient lie right from the outset? Were the farming men of her generation just not advanced enough to let go for a woman? Too many questions. Too many days alone. She had shut herself off from Yazzie and even Gabs, and now she was regretting it. She felt utterly bereft.

She cleaned the kitchen window with a tea towel so she could see a view of the property. This vista looked as barren as the one from the washroom. It wasn't a case of 'if only it would rain'. It was more a case of 'if only Charlie would take on the grazing management systems I've been studying'. That way the morning dew would have all been captured by long vibrant living grasses instead of landing on barren and bare overgrazed soil.

She held the thought of what was going wrong with the farm so tightly within herself that every sinew and muscle in her body hurt with the tension of highly strung wire. She was tired, but sleep never seemed to make amends for the years of living that, at times, seemed so pointless on Waters Meeting when the bills kept coming in and money was always so tight. She still thought often of the messages on her phone. The handset sat on the kitchen dresser now on top of a painting Archie had done at mothers' group last week. Even though Rebecca had erased the voice mail, the memory haunted her.

As she stacked Archie's Winnie the Pooh plate in the drainer, her eyes caught sight of the horses lifting their heads. They baulked, trotted and snorted, mist escaping their nostrils like dragons. Bec frowned, knowing the old nags rarely shied at anything these days ... not even the tarp flapping loose from the ute as it sped by or the sheets cracking in a gale on the clothesline. Something was up.

Walking outside, she rounded the side path. There she could see the young black heifers rampaging about, some of them gaining speed to a gallop, heads low, tails carried high. Some kicked fat hocks in the air. Squinting, Bec strained to see what the commotion was about. She glanced back to the machinery shed. Charlie was in the tractor, and she could just make out Ben playing with a stick in the water trough near the horse yard. But where was Archie?

'Charlie! Where's Archie?' she called, but she knew he wouldn't hear her. He had the new sound system blaring with AC/DC. In front of her, the young cattle fizzed in excitement. But why?

Bec jogged to the front of the old two-storey homestead and looked down over the bank that fell away to the river flats. And then she saw it. The gate jutted open like a piece of puzzle that had been missing but was now found. The older Angus cows and their one-tonne masculine companion had escaped and were galloping fast at a frightening freight-train pace towards the mob of equally stirry heifers in the neighbouring paddock. And there, between the two herds, stood her little boy Archie looking like a small pebble about to be swept away by a massive tide.

'Archie!' she called, desperately reining in a scream, vaulting the fence. Her wrist caught on a piece of jutting wire and was instantly etched deeply with bright blood. 'Stay still!' She tried to keep the panic out of her voice.

The little boy looked up to see the cattle bearing towards him. They were thundering, flowing around him. He looked beyond them to his mother, his face white, his eyes fearful.

Rebecca sprinted, not registering the pain as the soles of her socked feet met with the sharp corners of rocks that the plough had spewed up from the soil last summer.

She tried to keep a calm expression on her face as she bolted towards Archie, to not let him see the terror that coursed through her. He was so tiny and the cattle so massive and in that vast expanse of riverside paddock there was no trench, no ditch, no tree in which to seek refuge from the crazed herd.

Archie began to run towards her.

'Stay still, Archie!' she screamed again. There was terror on his face as he battled over the hoof-pugged black soil flats with his little legs and tiny farm boots.

Just as she was about to reach him, the young Poll bull bore down on Archie. The bull's head cast low. Then came the sickening thud as the hard black dome of the bull's head collected with Archie's body. Like a rag doll, before her eyes, Rebecca's son was flung into the air. She saw the shocked expression on his face morph into one of passivity as the life and the breath were pummelled from his body.

# Eighteen

The giant city children's hospital was made of the stuff of nightmares. No amount of cheery decor could soften the horrors that shell-shocked parents had to endure. White-faced, Rebecca watched the progression of sick and broken children as they were shuffled in with their parents and sorted by the hospital staff at the registration desk.

She could feel she was caught in the vortex of a busy, cold system spinning her down a path that led to entire worlds of tragedy. Who could tell what the damage was to Archie's little body from the impact of the bull's skull? Since arriving, he had been whisked away to theatre in some other part of the hospital, and now all they could do was wait.

Desperately Rebecca tried to keep the demons of terror and panic at bay. She tried to tell herself to hold onto hope. That things would be fine. But the peaks and troughs of fear seethed inside her as she looked at the haunted, fearful faces of the other parents who passed her by, a terrifying reflection of her own self. Still wearing the old work clothes she had dragged on this morning, Rebecca suddenly realised how exhausted she was.

The exceedingly long day had been a blur. The triple-zero call. The bush ambulance. The roaring engine of the Flying Doctor's light aircraft at Bendoorin. Archie's terrifyingly still little body and white face as he lay on the trolley and the Angel Flight doctors spoke quickly into their headset radios to the waiting surgeons in the city hospital.

Something about a splenic rupture and pneumothorax trauma. Rebecca had to look away when the nurse told her they were going to have to insert an emergency chest tube to keep him breathing. The last thing Rebecca recalled vividly was the stillness of Archie's tiny rib cage and his white, white skin. Then the nurse was urgently asking what blood type he was. Rebecca had felt like the worst mother in the world. She didn't know. All she knew was that he was her flesh and blood. The knotted feeling of terror caught in her throat that her little boy, her little angel, could die. Bec had held his limp little hand when the medicos would let her near him, and somewhere in the fog of it all she could hear Dr Patkin's voice from the Bendoorin hospital on the radio as he gave details from Archie's health file.

And now as she waited in the emergency room for news, Bec hung onto the words the dour surgeon had left her with.

'He should make it,' the surgeon had said.

'*Should?*'

She hugged Ben to her, wishing her mother, Frankie, who lived not far from here, would answer her phone and come to collect him. It was typical. So caught up in her world of vet science. Even her second husband, the bumble-footed Labrador of a bloke, Peter, still had to leave messages for Frankie at the front desk. She barely had time for him either.

Between the rows of waiting-room seats, Charlie paced, still wearing his farm work clothes too. Rebecca felt like throttling him. It was because of him they were here. It was because of him she could lose her little Archie. She'd never wanted him to buy that stirry line of cattle. She'd argued with him over it, saying they should stick to a line they knew. But those cattle, Charlie had argued, were cheap. Bec felt the guilt grip her again. She had just wanted a moment's peace from the boys. And now look. She should never have sent them out with their father.

Rebecca pulled Ben even closer to her. Eventually Charlie came to sit beside her in a chair, his fingers laced together, one knee jiggling up and down, eyes staring at the wall. He kept glancing at his phone to see the time. A minute in this place felt to him like a week.

'Stop doing that,' Rebecca snapped.

'What?' Charlie turned to look at her. A look of defensiveness. She shut her eyes.

'*What?*' he repeated.

Bec just shook her head. She was too tired of everything and too scared.

He glanced about the hospital, assessing how many people were in earshot. 'You're blaming me for this, aren't you?' he hissed. 'You think *I* did this.'

Rebecca turned her face to him. In this moment, she could scream at him. Tell him to leave. Tell him, *yes*, it was his fault. She knew she ought to. She knew it was over. But instead she watched herself, as if hovering above her own shoulders, as she reached out to squeeze his hand. She thought of the time when she believed he had loved her, when he'd given her such solace and comfort after Tom's suicide. She looked into his eyes, tears welling.

'Please, just don't let him die, Charlie,' she said. 'That's all I care about. Please.'

And the next thing, Charlie was crying too, his arms encircling both her and Ben, and he whispered over and over again, 'I'm sorry, Bec. I'm sorry. I'm sorry. I love you.'

As she held him back, Rebecca vowed that if Archie lived, she would make everything right again.

# Nineteen

Rebecca's mother swept into the waiting room, bringing with her the waft of the outside world of cities and petrol and pollution. Her hazel eyes were lively with concern and her auburn hair, as always a riot of waves, framed her elegant face. She was now greying more than slightly at the temples, always too busy with after-hours emergency work to keep hair appointments.

'I'm so, so sorry, I was in surgery. The phone was off.'

She stooped and kissed Bec on the cheek, Rebecca catching the familiar imprinted scent of the veterinary hospital that lingered on the fabric of her clothing. Charlie rose to meet his mother-in-law and delivered a perfunctory kiss.

Rebecca tried to search for comfort in the fact that Frankie had arrived, but she couldn't help feeling the familiar bubble of resentment rise up in her. She watched Frankie shrug off her coat, revealing the grey uniform shirt with its vet-surgery logo embroidered on it. The uniform prompted a rush of memories for Rebecca. Her struggle at boarding school, the times she had come searching for comfort over her father, only to find her mother called away to an emergency. The weeks of Tom's slow demise when Rebecca wished her mother had just downed tools and done more for him.

And now nothing had changed. It wasn't unusual for Rebecca not to hear from her mother for weeks on end. Even with her grandchildren there, she was still a rare visitor to the farm. It was no surprise today that Rebecca hadn't been able to reach her, despite the urgency.

'Any word from the doctors?' Frankie asked.

Rebecca shook her head.

From where he snuggled in Rebecca's arms, Ben slowly woke and blinked at the realisation that his grandmother was standing before him. He slid from Rebecca's knee and went over to hug her.

'Hello, pumpkin,' Frankie said to Ben, cuddling him back.

Rebecca felt another tug. She remembered from the fog of her childhood past that it was the nickname Frankie had used for Tom when they were little.

'I called Mick and Trudy,' her mother said, still holding onto Ben's little hand. 'They'll be here soon.'

Rebecca flashed her a look. 'What for?'

'They can help. Trudy is good in a crisis.'

Suddenly anger reared in Rebecca. 'My son could be *dying* and you are calling this a crisis and treating it like some kind of family gathering!' Her voice was loud and tense like a wire about to snap. 'What is this to you? A family shindig? I only asked you to pick up Ben,' she said through gritted teeth. 'That's all I needed, Mum. Not frigging Turdy Trudy coming in here and blowing hot air out of her self-important arse.'

'Bec,' Charlie soothed, laying a hand on her shoulder.

She shook off his touch aggressively. Frankie looked momentarily hurt, her angular cheeks flaming red. Instantly Rebecca felt guilty for her outburst. Though, in the last crisis, hadn't her mother left them all? Left Mick, Tom and Bec at Waters Meeting to struggle under the weight of their father, while she had got on with her career?

The hurt of the past swamped her, and the possibility of Archie dying further drowned her. Rebecca felt something inside her give way and her whole body began to shake.

'Come here,' said Frankie, and she swept her up in a hug and held her closely. 'I'm sure everything will be OK.' Bec let herself be held, but her body was still rigid, every sinew taut, ready to snap.

'Mum. I'm scared. What if —?'

'Shh …'

At that moment an earnest, young-looking doctor sailed in, his hair swept forwards, trendy-boy style. He came to stand before Rebecca. She looked up at his face, trying to read every nuance of his expression before he spoke.

'Mrs Lewis?' Rebecca nodded. 'I'm Paul Cartwright, the emergency surgeon. Dr Thompson sent me in to let you know we've operated. Your son has had a serious splenic rupture, along with six broken ribs. The imaging is showing there's no major head trauma. So the gods were on our side there. For now, we've done what we can,' he said, looking more at his clipboard than Rebecca's eyes. The anger bubbled again.

'Is he going to be all right?'

Paul, the surgeon, didn't give a straight answer. 'We are keeping him under for a little longer until he stabilises. All we can do is wait.'

His string of clichéd answers caused the anger to spark within her again, lifting her fury to a roaring furnace deep inside her. Did he not understand that her little boy was her whole universe? 'Tell me! Is he going to live?' There was hysteria in her voice and she felt Frankie and Charlie hovering near her.

'All we can do is wait,' the surgeon said again tiredly.

'Where is he? I have to see him.'

Paul Cartwright put a hand on her shoulder, and she felt the pulse of his weary energy and saw the exhaustion in his eyes. 'They're still settling him into a ward. If all goes well, you can see him soon — maybe an hour or so.'

A mix of gratitude and guilt mingled within her and she nodded her head, tears spilling over and rolling down her cheeks, the room wavering around her as the surgeon quietly left.

Ben moved over to her and slid his hand into hers. 'Don't cry, Mummy. He'll be OK,' he said.

Rebecca looked down at her eldest son and stooped to hold him tightly. 'You think so?' she said.

Ben nodded, opening up his tiny clenched fist. 'Look,' he said. In his palm lay the two crystals he and Archie had been given by Evie. 'These magic stones will protect him.'

Rebecca felt a wave of laughter bubble up along with tears. She hugged Ben tighter and looked into his sincere brown eyes.

'Mummy. He'll be fine,' he said with conviction, a tiny serious frown marking his forehead. Bec wiped her eyes with the sleeve of her shirt, then her mum stepped forwards and took Ben by the shoulder.

'That's nice, dear,' Frankie said matter-of-factly, completely missing the moment. 'Now once Auntie Trudy and Uncle Mick get here, how about you and I go find an ice-cream?'

He shook his head. 'I want to stay here.'

Rebecca's heart lurched. She knew he should not be witness to this trauma. Frankie should take him home. But part of her wanted him here.

'I'm not leaving,' Ben said.

Before they could reason with him, Trudy and Mick arrived. Trudy was wafting expensive scent; giant orbs of silver were strung about her neck with matching earrings. Her hair was styled in a chignon and she was swathed in a pashmina of tasteful chocolate hues that mirrored the colour of high boots from which her skinny legs emerged in black leggings. Behind her bumbled in Mick.

Rebecca almost gasped when she saw the size of him. No amount of expensive giant-man's RM Williams clothing could hide the fact he had been in a very good paddock. As usual, he was plugging text messages into his phone.

'Oh, my sweet!' Trudy said, stepping forwards and putting both perfectly manicured hands on Rebecca's shoulders, then drawing her into a hug. She pressed a cold cheek to Rebecca's. 'I'm so, so sorry!' She swung about to pull from her handbag a brown paper bag. 'I brought some grapes.'

Dumbfounded, Rebecca took them, her eyes darting over the people before her. People who were her family, but who now felt like strangers to her.

Charlie stepped forwards, a smile on his face. He took Mick's hand warmly and shook it. 'Thanks for coming, mate,' he said. 'How have you been?'

Mick shrugged, tucking the phone into his sagging back pocket. 'Property development! Who needs it?'

At that moment Rebecca felt yet another wave of anger, this time mixed with nausea so strong she thought she would have to use Trudy's recently gifted grape bag to vomit into. 'Oh, for god's sake!' she yelled. 'This is not a fucking family Christmas! My son is in there busted up by a bull because this stupid bastard thinks only of himself!' She flung a hand out to indicate Charlie as the others stood and gawped.

'We are only trying to help,' Trudy said, forcing a smile, revealing polished teeth corrected recently by braces.

'Mummy said a rude word,' Ben said.

Another wave of nausea and Rebecca's hand flew to her mouth. She fled from the room and ran the length of the corridor, turning the corner where a statue of a weeping Mary seemed to be keeping quiet vigil of all the sufferings.

'What are you looking at? A little help right now would be good,' Rebecca muttered at the statue as she passed.

In the toilets, she heaved over the bowl. It felt as if a million fingers were clawing inside her gut. Rebecca realised she hadn't eaten all day. She at last stood, her hands and body shaking from the effort of vomiting up nothing. She swung open the cubicle door and stooped to splash water on her face. When she straightened, she gave a start and cried out. Evie was standing over her right shoulder in the mirror's reflection.

'Holy shit!' Bec said. 'You scared the crap out of me!'

'Lucky you're in a dunny then.' Evie smiled. Bec turned to face her, the old woman's arms already opening up to hug her.

'What are you doing here?'

'Getting you out of here.'

# Twenty

It was peak hour in the city when Rebecca and Evie stepped onto the street. The dazzle of the outside world in the bright evening light stirred a feeling of vertigo in Bec. She shouldn't be outside the hospital. I need to be with Archie, she thought, panicked. As if reading her mind, Evie turned to her and laid a warm hand on her forearm.

'He'll be fine. Ben too. You do know that? If you don't, you best start affirming it. Now, you need something to eat and drink before you go to see him. You must be balanced, calm and strong for his sake. We won't be long.'

Like a terrified horse, Rebecca felt the calm of Evie's touch and gradually she began to relax a little.

Evie led Rebecca across a set of traffic lights and ushered her into the den of a quiet café, the owner of which clearly liked collecting Betty Boop memorabilia, judging from the posters on the wall and the giant plastic figure that stood, big-eyed, beside the counter with a tray held aloft. Evie pulled out a chair beside the window and indicated for Rebecca to sit.

Barely present as Evie gave their order, Rebecca didn't even take in the trendy-looking waitress's blunt-cut dark fringe and black square-framed glasses. Instead she turned her face to the window. All she could see were horrible scenes of the past day that swirled in her mind. How could life turn so suddenly like that? But it had, and now here she was, feeling as if she had been suddenly swallowed by a hungry city and was starting to dissolve. To crumble away altogether.

'Isn't that bizarre?' Evie said, nodding to where Rebecca was gazing.

'What?'

'That … those people.'

Rebecca dragged her vision into focus and looked at the people who were traipsing along the pavement in the peak-hour rush. They were like a huge seemingly endless mob of sheep, thirsty and walking desperately on to water in the evening light.

'They are unconscious,' Evie said.

'Huh?'

'Look at them. Really look at them. They are unconscious.'

'No. It's Archie who is unconscious,' Rebecca said, emotion straining her voice.

'Archie is fine,' Evie said comfortingly. 'His unconsciousness is necessary right now for his healing. Who knows what he and his Higher Self are up to out there in the ethers? But don't worry, Rebecca, he will come back down to planet earth. He, like you, has so much good to do in the world. I think the angels want him here. I know it.'

Rebecca looked into the kindly green eyes of the old woman before her and felt her gut unknot a little.

Evie reached out and took her hand. 'My girl,' she said gently, 'one day you will look back on this dark and awful time as the best thing that ever happened to you. It will grow you and be the making of Archie — and connect you as family. It will show each of you your inner strengths.'

Rebecca squeezed Evie's hand and clung to what she had just said, especially the conviction in her words that Archie would be all right. That life would move on from now.

'Watch,' Evie said, looking at the commuters outside the window. 'It's programmed behaviour. Bizarre indeed. They are unaware they exist as one. Instead of flowing with life energetically, they are fighting like fish in a dying stream. They are led by those things.' Evie pointed to the television flashing images into the restaurant. A man being led from a courtroom, a woman with big blonde hair smiling from a news desk as the words *toddler eaten by crocodile* slid across the screen, followed by news of stabbings and stock-market plummets.

'They are tortured and terrified by their own thoughts, thoughts that they feed with that black box in the corner. Black boxes that have grown to take up entire walls in houses.'

Both women looked again at the café television. A funeral-plan ad flicked away to be replaced by a woman smiling at her new car with such love, as if she had birthed it herself.

'That thing feeds their thoughts,' Evie said. 'They are scared of not having enough money, scared of cancers, scared of broken hearts, scared of not being "someone famous". Instead they could choose to wake up and smile at all they really have. But many of them don't until a great tragedy hits them and tears their world apart. Then they wake up to the universe and the great beauty of it. The world and other people aren't scary once you know the eternity of life. So don't look where everyone else is looking. Look to Archie being well. And you, my dear, being safe and happy with your children.'

Bec looked at the passersby who marched on at their urgent pace. Some had cords dangling from their ears on the way to the train stations and bus depots, plugged into iPods and iPhones. Most were well dressed for offices, high heels swapped for runners by the older women. Some looked rough and undernourished, the pallor of their cheeks like grey-brown fungi, which never saw the sun. And each of them wore a frown. As if fear was guiding them home.

Bec heard in Evie's words a lesson being delivered in a roundabout way to her. She knew the woman was trying to tell her it was time for this tragedy to wake her up and stir her into action. Into getting onto the path of who she truly was.

The café door opened and a woman came in. Bec could hear the rumble of the city, the rumble of humanity, busy and oblivious like ants. The outside air that wafted in felt tepid, coating her skin in a kind of amphibian-like film. The sudden roar of the coffee machine was making her head buzz and the juicer was rattling her nerves.

'I really must be getting back to the hospital,' she said.

'Trust me. Archie is fine.'

Again Rebecca felt a confidence build in her from Evie's presence and definitive stance on Archie's condition. 'Why did you come? Why are you here, helping me through this? What about your shop?' Bec's blue eyes settled on the still pretty face of the elderly Evie, a frown underscoring her question.

'You know what small towns are like,' Evie said, shrugging and fiddling with the sugar sachets that sat in red polka-dot cups. 'I heard your boy was injured. Larissa offered to mind the shop. She's just next door and there's an internal door between the two, so it's easy for her. Plus Gabs insisted I come to you. Yazzie insisted. Doreen insisted. As did Sol and Candy and every other person in that town. I was coming to the city anyway. And you need someone. Someone with a bit of sense. I used to work in the outback as a nurse. In a past life. I know what trauma is like. So I came and I brought with me all that love from the rest of the people in Bendoorin and round about. I think you've forgotten, Rebecca, how much you and the boys are loved.'

When they were done eating, Evie and Rebecca stepped out onto the street. Rebecca caught sight of a gash of blue sky between the towering buildings. The failing sunlight was glancing off the tops of the high-rises in triangular slices of golden light.

'Ten more minutes before you go back,' Evie said. Before Rebecca could argue, she was pressing the button on the traffic lights and they were crossing the street to an overwatered square of lawn that lolled out the front of a giant office building.

'Take off your boots,' Evie said, slipping off her own shoes, 'and put your feet on the earth. Let the soil ground you.'

Rebecca looked at Evie as if she was queer.

'Try it.'

She shrugged, removed her boots, then peeled off her socks. The grass felt cool on the soles of her feet, which were tender and bruised still from the river-paddock stones. Together they sat down, side by side, and watched as people passed on the street, to be swallowed up by the dark cavern of a giant railway station.

'Can you feel the vibrational energy under you?'

Bec shook her head.

'Everything has vibrations. It's quantum physics. The life in the soil does. You do. To get through life it is wonderful to learn to sit outside yourself and observe life flow past you as pure energy. It's even fun to try it.'

Prior to meeting Evie, Rebecca had only been used to straight conversations about sheep and cattle-stocking rates and grazing methods and what the footy teams might do on the weekend. But now she was being opened up to a whole new way of seeing the world. It was a relief to have such things shown to her through Evie's comfort and kindness.

'If you know that everyone is vibrational energy, you can stop yourself from getting caught up in other people's stuff if it isn't aligned to your own.'

Rebecca thought of the mornings she woke when before she could grasp any kind of thought about the day ahead, she would simply float in a sleepy bliss, opening her eyes to the beautiful mountains that basked in morning sun beyond the upstairs bull-nose verandah of their bedroom.

Then she would hear Charlie, clumping about in the bathroom. Muttering to himself. Telling her to get up. Hacking up a cough from too many bummed cigarettes and beers. His energy like a lead-weight sinker. She would feel suddenly tangled in his line and those first happy moments of waking would slide past her as she was being dragged under in a sludge pond.

'Is that why I feel so angry around Charlie all the time? I know I should make the marriage work —'

Evie cut her off. 'If you force something, it will never come to you. If it makes you feel good, do it.'

'So that's why he had an affair? Because it felt good?' Rebecca was embarrassed she had blurted out her anger over Charlie's infidelities, but she could feel something in her wanting to unravel the tangled mess that her emotions seemed to be. She plucked at the grass, wanting nothing more than to go to Archie's bedside and take him out of that hospital and back to being the healthy boy he was, grabbing Ben away too, leaving her husband and her dysfunctional family behind. She hoped Evie would offer some advice. She was tired of living with such anger towards Charlie's actions.

'We are all on a solo journey,' Evie said. 'We come into the world alone, we go out alone. Once you open up, wake up and transition into being more aware, people you may have lived with for a long time can vibrate out of your path. That's all it is. There is no right and wrong. It just simply is. Married or not. We journey along solo and sometimes we choose to hang out with others. Humanity has made it all so complicated and fraught, with impossible "rules".'

'Are you suggesting Charlie and I will separate?'

'You have been separate all along. Your choice is, do you want to journey with him still or journey apart from him? You already have children together so how you travel from here is completely dependent on your beliefs and attitudes, not his. Remember, we make our own reality with our thoughts.'

Rebecca got to her feet. 'I didn't choose to have Archie hit by a bull! Look, I'm sorry, I have to be getting back.' She tugged on her socks and boots.

'Don't be afraid,' Evie said, laying her cool palm on Rebecca's forearm. The old woman began to get up stiffly from the ground and Rebecca felt a jab of guilt. Her frayed nerves were causing her to be snappy with someone who had shown her only kindness.

She reached down and took Evie's elbow, gently helping her up, then looked deep into her emerald-green eyes. 'Sorry,' she said quietly.

'I know you are terrified of losing your boy. But you will never lose him, no matter what. Love is eternal and the energy in us is eternal. That's another flawed premise of this planet that is perpetuated by the masses … that death is the end. There is no end. We've all been sent to this planet to hang out in these meatbags so we might as well make the most of it, no matter what life throws at us. The true Archie is not his body. It's his energy. He is eternal, no matter what. And so is your love for him.'

Rebecca stooped to hug Evie. Despite the old woman's small frame, she felt the power of her peaceful life force and at last felt calm.

When Rebecca walked back into the hospital and the room where her family had been waiting, she was relieved to find they had all gone. Frankie had finally taken Ben back to her flat and Mick and Trudy had left too.

She was met with an angry bark from Charlie. 'Where have you been? What if something had happened?'

'You've got a phone. You know how to use it,' she said sarcastically.

'Well, it's my turn to get out of here. I'm going for a beer,' he said.

'Do you have to go boozing?' she said, horrified.

He scowled at her. 'I need to get out of here. You were gone for ages.'

Rebecca watched him tug down his jumper and walk from the hospital. This time she felt strangely unaffected and removed from him.

Rebecca was dozing when the surgeon arrived and gently coughed, waking her. She opened her eyes and instantly saw the look on his face. Before he had even spoken, relief swept through her body. In his hands, he held a big envelope of Archie's scans.

'He's a strong little man. It's all looking good. Very good. He'll certainly make it. We'll start to allow him to come round in his own time. Would you like to come and sit beside his bed?'

It was then Rebecca felt the pulse of gratitude and love as strong as the pull of the moon travel through her very being. She looked upwards to the panelled white ceiling of the hospital. 'Thank you,' she cried out to the surgeon, and, 'Oh, thank you, god, thank you, the universe, whoever you are,' she said, addressing the invisible force that was turning the planet and turning her days. With tears in her eyes and gratitude in her heart, she began to follow the surgeon, in search of her son.

# Twenty-one

Gabs slammed the car door a little too hard, then grinned at Rebecca. 'It's shut.' She dragged on her seat belt, then rummaged around in a shopping bag.

'Don't tell me you brought me fancy dress for the drive home,' Bec joked.

'Oh, that would've been a great idea. We could've dressed as roadkill.'

'Oh, you're a shocker, Gabrielle! But seriously, thanks for offering to come with me,' Bec said.

'Are you nuts? I'm not doing it for you, you slag. I'm doing it for my own bit of extra kid-free time. God, what a hangover! Two days' worth! Drank the whole trip down from Bendoorin, then Frank took me to some Italian place last night. Too much vino. So today Gabs was super-organised and got you a roadie, and me, hair of the dog,' she said, sitting a can of beer in the console and fizzing her own can open, then grinning at Bec. 'Man, I feel crook!' She burped loudly.

'Aw pwor!' said Bec, waving the air in front of her. 'That stinks!'

'I know, bloody garlic bread and linguine with garlic cream sauce.'

'Yuck.'

'You think yuck now; wait till it reaches my other end,' she said.

Bec shook her head. 'God, four hours in the car with Gabs and her gut, that's going to be fun, isn't it?' she said, looking in the rear-vision mirror at Ben, who sat in a booster seat, grinning at his mother's funny friend.

'Let's rock and roll,' Gabs said, swivelling round to look at Ben. 'All set to go, numb nuts?'

Ben waggled his legs up and down excitedly. 'Yes, stinky bum,' he said.

'Oi!' cautioned Bec, glaring at him. 'Don't let her steer you off track! Mind your manners, Ben.'

Rebecca pulled out into the city traffic, a mix of emotions swirling in her. She'd endured this city an entire six weeks. Six weeks of hell; but every day she reminded herself that what she endured was nothing compared to what little Archie had been through. He'd been in pain almost the whole time, and sick from the medication to boot. He'd had his fifth birthday in a hospital ward with tubes in him and no little friends. At least the hospital had arranged a volunteer clown and a slobbery Labrador.

At last they were on the road home.

Bec turned left into another busy street and double-parked near an ambulance bay. There, the driver of a patient transport vehicle was already waiting for them and he flashed his lights, motioning to her to follow. Through the vehicle window, she could see the shape of Charlie as he settled himself into the rear passenger seat for the drive with Archie back to Bendoorin.

Rebecca knew her little Archie was safely bedded down in the rear of the transfer vehicle with the kindest red-faced male nurse the hospital could muster. Archie still had a little way to go on his recovery so it had been decided that rather than bump him over the remote roads to Bendoorin, they would shuttle him there in comfort.

It was a relief for Bec too, who had watched him struggle for weeks in the city, away from the farm. Archie would only need to spend another two weeks max in the Bendoorin hospital until he came home. Bec tried not to think about what she may face with Charlie there.

Even though Archie was doing extremely well, Bec was still yet to recover from the shock of it all. Every day she had awoken at her mother's city flat with a leaden tiredness. A queasiness and uneasiness sat with her most of the time. All she wanted to do was sleep.

It had been Evie who had been Rebecca's rock. Somehow, on some level, the strength and peace that Evie brought had got them through. Rebecca and the boys were now accustomed to her gentle, loving but weird ways and words. The array of creams, tonics, crystals and affirmations that she brought to the hospital had all helped. Evie had been there on the first long, painful nights … and in her non-invasive way seemed to guide them all onto a path of healing, inside and out. Except for Charlie, who dismissed her as a 'nosey hippy nong'.

Rebecca could now barely stand to be in Charlie's presence. On the nights following the accident, they had all crammed into Frankie's city apartment, Ben and her sleeping on the fold-out couch, Charlie sleeping on the trundle. The tension between them was like an ugly ghoul in the room. The days blurred into weeks. Her mother coming and going. Peter cheerfully dishing up beautiful meals only to have them ruined by the sourness between Rebecca and Charlie.

Despite Charlie's declaration of apology and of his love for her on the day of the accident, Rebecca had felt him slip away from her. The familiar hostility and bitterness returned as soon as Archie was clear of danger.

As the time in the city dragged on, she no longer believed she could bring their marriage back to life. Nor did she want to.

Then, without warning, Charlie had announced he was going to see his parents, and had revved away with the family four-wheel drive, leaving Bec without transport in the city, not saying when he would be back.

The job of caring for the livestock on Waters Meeting was now down to the goodwill of Frank and Gabs, Dennis and Doreen and the Rivermont crew helping out.

Each day without the vehicle, Rebecca was forced to take public transport to the hospital. She felt numb and haunted, sitting on the concertina-like bus. It was like being inside a giant piano accordion and just as noisy. She looked around at the faces of the people on the bus: they were blank, sad. Energetically dead. She felt bombarded by billboards, news bulletins, iPods, newspapers, sex scandals. She baulked at the intensity of the negativity — even in the sinister advertising intentions of the pretty models plastered metres high on buildings, making her feel bedraggled and less than perfect. She longed for Waters Meeting and the stillness.

But then she realised even if she was in her home environment, her mind would still be in turmoil.

Since the first day in the hospital when Evie had come to visit, she had begun to truly listen to the voice inside her head. As she kept reminding herself to pay attention to her thoughts, she realised it was no wonder life was on the slide for her. If what Evie had said so often was true — 'that thoughts and words create your world' — then no wonder she was in the shit. Her thoughts were shitty. They stank!

In that moment on the crowded bus, she realised she was dwelling on the sorrows outside herself. The fact that the city was an ugly concrete jungle where no one in society seemed to care. How no one would offer a seat to women with young children or the elderly any more.

But with her revelation, she had figured out all she had to do was to look away from the negatives around her and grasp onto any kind of good that she could find. No matter how small that good was.

On those journeys on the bus, as the weeks rolled by, Rebecca began to practise looking for the good. She leaned into Ben's body and breathed in the shampoo scent of his hair and noticed the cute dimpled knuckles on his hand as he held the metal rail of the seat in front. She began to visualise Archie happy and well and reunited with them. She began to tell herself to 'let go' and to 'trust'. Right now Rebecca realised she needed trust. And above all, to laugh.

And it wasn't hard for her to laugh right now. All she had to do was to look to her left, where Gabs sat with her white owl-eyes Chemmart sunnies, her white-socked feet up on the dash, with her best town navy shorts and hot pink polo shirt. Her short dark hair raked at all angles. Her brand-new Kmart runners kicked off on the floor of the vehicle.

'You are one stylish unit,' Rebecca said to her mate.

Gabs turned, pulled her sunnies down, looked blandly at Bec and fizzed the pull on another beer. She lowered her voice so Ben couldn't hear. 'Tell me about it. I am a goddess! Frank can't get enough of me. He had me in the hotel shower. I put Nair on his nuts and all over. He's as smooth and as fast as Usain Bolt.'

'Nice. Really nice.'

Gabs grinned and began to open up the glovebox. 'Might as well make the most of this little road trip. You got any tunes in this Mummymobile?'

'Most of my CDs got covered in Thomas the Tank Engine yoghurt, compliments of someone in the back.' Bec glanced at Ben and smiled at him. 'You might find one under the seat.'

Gabs sat up after her search and proudly held up the Esther and Jerry CD as if she had caught a good-sized trout.

'Ta-da! Oh?' she said, looking at the cover. '*Attracting the life you want*,' she read. 'Not exactly the kind of listening I had in mind, but it sounds good. Mmm, what kind of life *do* I want though? Have you ever really thought about it? What you want?'

Rebecca pulled an 'I dunno' face. 'What I want? I want good health. Mostly for my children. And to be happy.'

'Not specific enough,' Gabs said.

'Forget me. What about you, Gabs? What do you want?'

'I've always thought I'd want a million dollars, but if I got it, I sure as hell wouldn't know what to do with it,' Gabs said.

'Well, I know where it would all go,' Rebecca said. 'It would be like my life. It would all go into the farm. You know, if you and Frank sold your place, you'd get a few million. You could retire and get into homemaking and topiary.'

'Eff off,' Gabs said. 'I'd not make a good lady of the town house.' She belched.

Rebecca gazed ahead at the traffic.

'So what would you truly want?' Gabs asked again.

Rebecca glanced around and saw Ben had drifted off to sleep, his sweet face tilted back, mouth open. She turned back to her friend. 'I think I would want this whole business with Janine and Charlie to go away. That's what I'd want.'

Gabs turned towards her. 'But it won't. I seriously can't see why you're still letting him stay as if nothing happened. If Frank did that to me and the kids, I'd be gone. I mean, haven't you dragged it on enough? Can't you see it's not getting any better? *He's* not getting any better.'

Bec swallowed.

Gabs swigged her beer. 'And as for that Janine Turner: pffft! She's had more cocks than a second-hand air rifle. It's not as if Charlie's going to fall in love with her and run off. He was just after a bit of sex on the side.'

'But why? Why do it to the kids? And to me? Why risk the farm?' Bec asked in hushed tones, glancing at the sleeping Ben, her teeth gritted.

Gabs shrugged. 'You need to think about yourself. What is it that you want from this moment now?'

'I don't know! I don't know. Just not to feel so fucking angry all the time?'

Rebecca took a swig of beer from Gabs's can, and in an instant she was braking, flinging the door open and vomiting. When she was done, Gabs offered her a KFC serviette, the smell of which made her want to retch again.

'Bec, you can't keep going on like this. The stress will kill you.'

Rebecca shut her eyes and clenched her jaw. 'That's it,' she said quietly so the sleeping Ben wouldn't hear. 'This week I'm going to tell Charlie. He has to leave.'

At the bush hospital in Bendoorin, Rebecca set the bag of toys down beside Archie's bed as Gabs busied herself by packing his clothing into a cupboard. Rebecca smiled gently, watching him sleep, drifting the backs of her fingers over his arm, taking in the rise and fall of his narrow chest. Each breath she witnessed brought with it an overwhelming sense of gratitude that he was here, almost home. Out of the city.

Her boy, although battered and broken, was alive. The bruising across his chest was now less angry and ugly, and colour was returning slowly to his pale cheeks. The scar from the emergency tubing was healing in a puckered red line. The surgery scars were neater, but still shocking. Still, he was so thin. The doctor had said, though, that he would just need a couple more weeks for rehabilitation, then life could get back to normal. It wasn't yet known if there would be any long-term impact from the injuries, but each day Rebecca was grateful and each day Archie seemed better.

From the window, both women could see Frank wrestling with Charlie on the hospital lawn, Ben standing nearby, watching, laughing.

'Will you look at the big dumb kids?' Gabs said. 'I'd better take them home now.' She slung an arm around Bec's neck and rubbed her knuckles on the crown of her head. 'Take care of yourself, knuckle head.'

'You sure you're OK to give the wandering stallion a lift home for me?'

They both turned their gaze to Charlie, who was puffing now from the exertion of wrestling with Gabs's husband. He was scratching his belly and standing with a big idiot grin on his face.

'Him a stallion? Look at him. Time to trade him in,' Gabs said as she grabbed her bag. 'Least that's my opinion. He jumped the fence; you didn't. But it's your call. You're a good woman. Too good to waste your life on someone who doesn't appreciate you.'

Rebecca blinked back emotion. 'Get going,' she said to Gabs. 'You'll make me cry. Tell Charlie and Ben I'll be along soon. Just as soon as Archie has had his dinner.'

'You sure you don't want me to bring some clothes in to the motel for you?'

'Nah. I'd better go home. Check the farm — god knows what he's done in the weeks I've been away. I can pick up my stuff then.'

Gabs walked out the door, stifling a deep beer burp, and Rebecca could hear her say 'excuse me' to someone in the hallway.

In the room, silent save for Archie's breathing, Bec watched from the window as Gabs, Ben, Charlie and Frank piled into Frank's crew-cab ute and motored away down the main street of Bendoorin.

Bec turned to begin arranging Archie's toys beside his bed. She wanted them all to be there when he woke up. Her plan was to spend the evening with him, then when he went to sleep she would camp at the motel until the nurse called in the morning. She thought about the striking conversation in the city hospital she'd had with Archie, not long after he'd regained consciousness. As she had stooped to kiss him good night, she had asked, 'Are you sure you're OK with Mummy leaving now? You won't be lonely? You know the nurses are here?'

'And Uncle Tom.'

Rebecca froze. 'Pardon?'

'Uncle Tom. He's here,' Archie said, his little face serious, his blond curls still wet from the bed-bath Bec had given him. 'He's been here since the bull got me. He keeps telling me to be brave.'

Rebecca had felt a wave of emotion wash through her. She held back tears as she stroked her son's beautiful, clear-skinned forehead. 'Does he?'

'Can't you hear him, Mummy?'

'Yes, I can,' she had lied.

Now in the Bendoorin hospital, as she stooped to gather Buzz Lightyear up, she tried to foster the notion that Tom was here in the room too, but suddenly another urge to throw up hit her. Grabbing for a steel bowl, Bec began gagging into it. Eyes watering, the reflex action tearing at her throat. But no food came. She saw her morphed image reflected back at her in the bowl. A blonde weirdo with a stomach ulcer, she thought. Just as her gut contracted again with another violent retch, Dr Patkin swept past the door, then reversed. He dragged his glasses down over his nose and surveyed her as she gagged and gagged again.

'You, my dear,' he said, beckoning her, 'come with me ...'

Not long afterwards in Dr Patkin's office, Rebecca sat staring at him with wide blue disbelieving eyes.

'Six weeks along, I'd say,' he said.

'How could I be? I throw up at the drop of a hat. Always have done. HSC exams. My brother's death. The stress of shearing time ... And with Charlie ...' Her voice trailed off.

Dr Patkin tossed the pregnancy test stick and urine sample in the bin, then, flipping out the tails of his white coat, slowly sat down.

'I can't be. He's had a vasectomy,' Rebecca said.

Dr Patkin set his elbows on his desk, clasped his hands together, pushed the glasses up the bridge of his fine English nose and said, 'It is feasible. There are several cases of women falling pregnant to their partners after the men have had vasectomies.'

'But it's impossible.'

'My dear, I'm telling you exactly the opposite. It is possible.'

'But I can't be.'

'But you are.'

'But my husband and I never have sex.'

'I see. Or,' he said cautiously, 'perhaps there was another partner?'

Bec's eyes widened in shock and she shook her head vehemently. 'No! There was this one night with Charlie … the night before Anzac Day … I …'

Dr Patkin held up both hands to ease her distress. 'I understand. If Charlie has an issue, send him to me.'

'Oh, he'll have an issue,' Bec said quietly. 'He'll kill me.' She looked down at her lap. 'How could I have not known? I put the skipped periods down to stress.'

Suddenly she wondered if she should tell Dr Patkin of the trauma, generated by Charlie's affair.

'Now you are pregnant, you will need to watch your stress levels. Go get yourself a good cup of tea at the café.'

'But Archie —'

Dr Patkin held up his hands. 'Sister and I will keep an eye out for Archie. Just take half an hour off. Have a think about your news.'

'Thank you,' Rebecca said, standing up and reaching for her handbag; there was nothing she could do to stop her hands from shaking.

# Twenty-two

Larissa's coffee shop was closed so instead Rebecca found herself wandering in a daze into the Heaven is Here! hippy shop. She couldn't help but roll the word 'pregnant' around and around in her head. Half of her was overjoyed at the prospect of another child, the other half devastated in light of her situation. Mostly she worried about what Charlie would say.

As she stepped into the shop, the peaceful vibe of the room and the scent of sandalwood instantly soothed Bec's jangled nerves.

She looked about. Ornate umbrellas bejewelled and bright in pink and green silks hung from the ceiling. They reminded Rebecca of Indian brides riding to weddings on elephants. The shelves were cluttered with Balinese-style ornaments while stained-glass decorations and crystals adorned the windows. Candles and hearts clustered together on tables and gentle flute music drifted throughout the store.

'Hello?' called Bec as she poked her head around a shelf.

'Crikey!' Evie said with a start from where she sat behind the counter. 'You scared the crap out of me.' She stood up. 'Hah! You got me back from scaring you in the hospital! It's funny, I should expect customers, shouldn't I?'

Bec laughed just as Evie's Jack Russell started up suddenly from his deep sleep, like a machine gun with a round of rat-a-tat barking.

'Jesus! Jesus Christ! Sit!'

The Russell wagged his whole body in greeting at Rebecca, then, as she reached to let him sniff her hand, he curled his lip.

'Oh, for god's sake, Jesus,' Evie said, looking down at the dog, then back up at Bec. 'Good to see you back in town. How is Archie? I was going to bring Jesus Christ in as a "Pets as Therapy" dog, but five minutes with him and you bloody well need therapy. Cuppa?' Evie held up a blue-and-white Chinese-design teapot.

Bec nodded. 'Love one. Archie's fine. Why did you call your dog Jesus Christ?'

'Partly because I kept hearing myself say it every time he piddled inside as a pup and partly because it's funny, and Jesus was a funny bloke. The church has us thinking He was all about suffering, but I reckon He was all about laughter and living life to the full.'

'I'm not really into religion. I don't believe in all that god stuff that they tried to ram down our throats at school.'

'I don't blame you. God is really only a word for the life force of energy that runs through everything. But we've mixed it up so much, it's hard to swallow, particularly if you are a woman.' Evie disappeared into a back room and Bec heard her running a tap and putting on a kettle. She reappeared, setting out two handleless cups beside the teapot. 'If I was born in another time, I would've been burned for being a witch.'

'Me too, I think,' Bec said. 'The way I want to farm Waters Meeting, I'd be called a witch as well, I reckon.'

'I've got a good book here if you like,' Evie said.

'Um. I haven't read the last one I got here,' Bec said a little guiltily. 'Or listened to the CD.'

'You mustn't be ready to hear it yet. But I tell you now, there is someone knocking loudly on your door. For your own health and sanity you must let them in.'

'What do you mean?'

'I see an extra energy around you. Another aura. As colourful as a painting.'

Rebecca felt goose bumps shimmer across her skin when Evie said the word 'painting'.

The old woman left the room again, returning with the steaming kettle. 'He's trying to tell you something. You're holding yourself in such resistance and he wants you to let go. To paint your world how *you* want it to be, using your feelings to guide you.'

Rebecca watched Evie pour the water into the teapot and thought about the words Archie had spoken in the hospital about Tom. 'My brother used to paint.'

'Well, the energy has a male feeling to me. You weren't aware?'

'Aware of what?'

'That you carry two auras with you. One is your own and there is this bright other. What was his name?'

'Tom.'

'And what do you think he's waiting for you to hear?'

'I don't know.'

'Do you think he put that book and CD in your hands?'

Rebecca lifted her shoulders in a shrug.

'Do you think he protected Archie in some way? Archie could feel him in the hospital with you. Would he be happy for you about this new pregnancy?'

Rebecca's mouth fell open, and Evie almost squealed.

'How did you know?' Bec narrowed her eyes. 'Have you been spying through Dr Patkin's windows?'

Evie laughed. 'No. It's just me. I can see a third energy with you. One that is yet to physically manifest. Plus your tits have got so massive since the last time I saw you, you'd *have* to be up the duff.'

Rebecca looked down to her cleavage, which was indeed bursting out of a cowgirl shirt that had once been fairly loose on her bust.

'You say some weird stuff, Evie.' Bec snorted as Evie handed her a cup. 'You know that?'

'Ah, yes, weird to you, and yes, "out there" to many others. But the world is changing. My weird is becoming the new kind of normal. It just hasn't reached most of you at Bendoorin yet.'

'How do you know all this stuff?'

'Because I spent the first third of my life doing what you've been doing: doing what others *expected* me to do. Then I spent the next section of my life inviting bad things into it by being careless with my thoughts and words. Watching all that frightening stuff on the news about what is wrong with the world and then in the advertising breaks watching what diseases would kill me — and what I needed to buy to feel better. Then I got sick. Really sick. And then I found myself. Bit by bit, I read, I studied, I opened my mind and I began to create my own future.'

Bec listened with interest. In all the time spent together during Archie's hospital stay, Evie had never much mentioned her past. No family. No husband. She wanted to hear more, but her friend paused, topped up their tea and leaned closer. 'So tell me, what is it that you want to create in your future?'

'Well, apparently I'm creating a baby. That's my future.' Rebecca felt the tears well. She had always longed for a little girl, but the thought of going through a pregnancy again in the midst of a marriage break-up filled her with despair. 'Oh, I don't know. It's all too hard.'

'If you tell yourself life is hard, that's the life you will create for yourself,' Evie said, settling back onto her chair. 'If we train our minds to believe life is joyful and flows easily, then we can deal with whatever life throws at us with a sense of inner peace. Affirm that all is well, even if most of it isn't. Look for the good bits.'

'I know, Yoda,' Bec said, swiping her eyes with the sleeve of her shirt. 'I've been practising.'

'I know you have, darling,' Evie said. 'You've been remarkable. Now, smile.'

Rebecca frowned at her.

'Smile! Or I'll set Jesus onto you.'

At last Rebecca smiled and Evie gathered her up in the warmest of hugs. Both women jumped when Jesus Christ suddenly cranked up with his barking again.

'*Jesus!* Who needs a shop bell when I've got that? Can I help?' Evie asked, squinting towards the blinding light of the bright day outside. Into the warmth of the shop stepped Sol Stanton.

'Hola, Evie,' he said in his deep baritone voice, stooping to bestow a kiss on the old lady's cheek. 'Rebecca. Lovely as always to see you. You look well. Delicioso.'

Rebecca looked up at him, drinking in his good looks, wondering why she felt so flushed and flustered that he was suddenly here before her. He still offered the same waft of expensive cologne and had just enough dark stubble on his jawline to make him look as if he could advertise yachts or diving watches or BMWs. 'Back again from Europe?' she said, cringing that she had just stated the obvious.

'Sí, I know the Bendoorin Show is still a long time away, but I've been perfecting my recipe and my design for the inaugural Man Cake competition. It's a long flight to Australia, so there was plenty of time to work on it.'

'Your father hasn't been keeping you busy enough, Sol,' Evie said.

'Maybe. And nowadays I have no girlfriend.' He shrugged his shoulders. 'Such a sad, lonely man. Lamentable.' He pouted at Rebecca, then turned to Evie. 'I came to see if my CDs were in? I could use a distraction. Papá is back from Europe too and he will flog me harder than the jockeys run the horses.'

'They are in. Indeed. Out the back. I'll just be a moment.'

When Evie was gone, Sol squatted down beside Rebecca and looked levelly into her eyes with his dark passionate gaze. 'Yazzie told me about your Archie.' He patted her hand. 'I'm so glad to hear he's on the mend. Buena noticia!'

'Thank you, Sol.'

'So, can we, you know, catch up for a chat? A coffee at Larissa's one time? It would be nice, yes? I have thought about you a lot while I have been away.'

'Coffee?' she said, caught off guard. 'Yes. Sure. One time. That would be nice.' And with her heart and mind racing, she rose from her chair and almost ran out the door, back towards the bush hospital.

Half an hour later, after settling Archie, Rebecca jabbed her finger at the car stereo button as the panic roared through her. Another baby? And a crush on Sol Stanton? Her mind screamed. Another baby! And a crush on an unobtainable man? The American voice of a man sounding like a Muppet filled the stuffy space. 'Hello, I'm Jerry H—' he said.

'Fuck off,' Rebecca said, jabbing the off button. That bloody CD! It was haunting her. 'No — apparently it's you haunting me, Tom, isn't it?' She looked to the empty passenger seat. 'So go on: show yourself, brother!'

She shook off the idea of Tom's ghost manifesting in her car, and started the engine. As she trundled out of town, she tried to sort through her whirl of thoughts. Her conversation with Evie had both reassured her and rattled her. She had always felt Tom with her, but it was something she carried as a notion in her head. Not a reality. The fact both Archie and Evie had spoken about 'an energy' around her had brought the reality of Tom's presence rushing at her.

Now, just before dusk, climbing down around the curve of the valley, Rebecca took in the breathtaking sight of Waters Meeting and pulled the hope of Tom's presence about her. The farm hugged the two tributaries where they met to form the one majestic Rebecca River that wound, silver, through fertile black-and-red volcanic soil flats.

She could see from up on high the cultivated paddocks suffering under the weight of a haphazard grazing regime and Charlie's 'improved pasture' sowing program. The farm resembled a patchwork quilt that had faded with age to the point of perishing and tearing.

At the mailbox Rebecca stopped and got out. Charlie often neglected to check the mail bag, so it was no surprise to find a bundle of bills and catalogues still neatly contained in the rubber band that Candy would have put on at the Bendoorin store.

Normally Rebecca would just toss the whole bundle on the office desk for Charlie to sort, but it felt like an opportunity to take back the reins of the farm and her life, so she flipped through. A bill for seed and fertiliser, a bill for stock lick, a bill for drench, a bill for diesel, a bill for groceries from Candy. Then a letter. From the bank.

As Rebecca tore open the envelope and her eyes scanned the message contained within, she felt heat rise to her face. Rebecca gleaned that this was not the first letter from the bank, but the *third*. The tone was harsh. Apparently they had defaulted on their loan repayments for the third month in a row and a banking officer would be in touch shortly. She looked at the giant fees that had been charged for missed payments on the farm debt and clenched the paper until her knuckles grew white.

Charlie hadn't told her! Not only was he having an affair, he was failing to disclose the truth about the farm finances! *Her* farm finances! The bank was about to foreclose on them!

Another wave of nausea. Rebecca tumbled from the car. Bent over, she heaved up nothing but her troubles and her misery. Crying, she slung her leg through the plain wire fence and climbed through.

Normally when she was upset, she would head to the river,

with her old dog in tow, but Charlie had taken even that away from her. She began to run uphill. Jogging, stumbling upwards, climbing so that her breath was ragged and her ribs tore with exertion. There at the top of a stony rise she found herself at a rock cairn that she and Tom had once built. Above it was a sagging fence where they had attempted to grow trees. The trees had all but died, but the fence had at least stopped the stock from eating the vegetation on the north-facing hilltop. She remembered the rock where she and Tom had sat after they'd dug the strainer posts.

'Shithouse fencing job, Tom,' she said as she easily slipped through the slack wire. 'But then again, you were only sixteen and I was tagging along to give you the shits.'

As she entered the patch of grassland, she noticed grasshoppers, spiders, beetles, ants and moths all nestled in their tiny worlds amidst a variety of grasses, sags, forbs and poas. Her hands ran over the tops of tall seed heads and with excitement she recognised the native grass species Andrew had taught her. There, thriving, were kangaroo grass, wallaby grass, weeping grass. Each with its own wispy native beauty.

She found a spot on the rock and ran her hands over the lichen, coarse under her palms. A skink making the most of the last of the day's sunshine slipped away from her presence into a crack in the rock. She looked out beyond the fence. The land looked bleak. There was a cold wind blowing the far-off bellowing of cows to her. Gentle evening sunshine eased the chill only a little.

For the first time in her life, she saw the land with a clear vision. This continent was a hot, dry place that was thirty million years old. A place that existed with ancient grasses feeding its deep rich soil. Grasses that surrounded her now. Grasses that had built soil here on this rocky knoll. She could feel the life teeming under her feet in the soil beside the rock. Billions of microbes. A whole universe of life beneath her soles. Threads of fungi billions of kilometres long vibrating with energy underneath her.

She saw in her mind's eye how in her grandfather's day, the first rubber-tyred tractor had ousted his father's horses from the sheds. Over time the tractors had laid the soil to waste. It'd been nuked and napalmed with chemicals left over from the wars. She looked out before her. The homestead, where her garden grew green and the vegetables were mulched and cared for with not a spray needed — the chooks were allowed in every now and then to scratch up the pests. Her oasis of chemical- and plough-free soil, that stood apart from the surrounding farm, where man was at war with nature. Charlie.

She took in the beauty and delicacy of the grasses around her. There was a fragility, like old lace, to the structure of each seed head. She saw that such interwoven nature held within it a resilience. Rebecca knew if she could get the whole of Waters Meeting looking like this patch of grassland, she would not only stop the farm bleeding to death from drought, but also she could find the money the bank was demanding — the farm costs could be cut by thousands. Suddenly energised and excited by her place, no longer daunted by its challenges, she stood and looked out across the valley.

She remembered something Evie had said the first time they met about reaching to find good thoughts. 'I am going to follow my bliss,' she said out loud. Then she asked herself what her bliss would be. And the answers began to roll out of her.

'My bliss would be a baby girl,' she said to the wind, gently at first. 'My bliss would be to stop spreading superphosphate fertiliser. My bliss would be time-control grazing so we grow a landscape just like this. My bliss is to have a grassland, not a farm. My bliss is to have stock on pasture as diverse as this spot here. My bliss is to teach my sons and unborn child how to pasture-crop and build soil. My bliss is that they never see a sod turned again in their lifetime.' Her voice began to build, her pace quicken, her heart beat faster. Rebecca yelled, 'My bliss is to build ground cover on this place. My bliss is to have soil that is one hundred per cent covered by plants, one hundred per cent of the time. My bliss is to celebrate the seasons with my family, not fight them. My bliss, regardless of this new baby, is to *not* spend my life with you, Charlie Lewis. To *not* spend my life with you! A man who refuses to listen to the land!'

Tears streaming down her face, Rebecca sat back down and hugged her knees to her chest. She buried her face and sobbed. 'Oh, Tom. I *miss* you.'

In the windswept dusk, she heard her dead brother's voice on the breeze. 'You forgot, Bec. Your bliss is to get a new dog and a new horse. It's about bloody time you got back in the saddle. *Life needs you.*'

# Twenty-three

Driving over the cattle grid with a whirr towards the homestead, Rebecca could see Charlie had the back-hoe out. It sat with its crooked elbow bent, giant metal scoop resting on the bare ground. The old yellow dozer, now faded to a pale butter-cream and etched with rust, had also been fired up, and it too was parked at the machinery shed.

Rebecca narrowed her eyes. For years, Charlie had been talking about making silage to feed to the cattle in winter, despite her scepticism on the subject. Now, looking at the giant mechanical beasts that sat dormant in the farmyard, she knew exactly what he was up to.

While Rebecca had been away in the city with Archie, Charlie had been left to his own devices, first to visit his family and then during the short time he'd had alone on Waters Meeting; and he was clearly making the most of it. Rebecca wondered bitterly if he'd made the most of his time alone with Janine too? She shoved the thought away. That was only going to unsettle her. That horse had bolted.

'Fucking oath,' she said when she drove around the old split-timber barn and saw the giant hummocks of upturned black soil. Charlie had put the silage pit exactly where she didn't want it. Looking like the beginnings of a dodgy swimming pool, it was on the other side of the fence from her vegetable garden. Her oasis.

Rebecca knew the yard would bog up at the pit with the big wheels of the tractor, the stench of fermenting summer grass permeating the bliss of her garden. The pungent smell of yeast, mould and sugars would waft over the washing line and drift through the kitchen as Charlie scooped the spongey fodder up with the bucket on the tractor.

With the letter from the bank shoved angrily on the dash, Rebecca wondered in exasperation what her husband was even *thinking*! Silage cost a lot of money to make and as Andrew said, 'Why cut the grass in your paddock, take it all the way to your shed or silage pit, only to have to cart it back out again come winter? It's an English farming concept that doesn't work here. Why not leave the hay out in the paddocks for the animals to eat as standing dry matter?'

Andrew was always questioning why farmers were still copying the British systems of farming that had so clearly failed here. Now, after sitting amidst the ancient pastures in Tom's reserve, Rebecca could really, genuinely see it — she'd believed her teacher, but now she'd really understood the truth for herself. The native grasses, if allowed to return, had just as much nutritional and health value when compared to the silage — if not more. The native pastures certainly wouldn't create the gut problems the cattle would suffer when adjusting to a rich diet of silage only.

Rebecca drove into a skillion shed that was sagging from the weight of an old-lady rambling rose that in summer flowered in delicate white. For a moment she sat in the car, not wanting to face the rest of what was to come.

'What is it you want me to hear, Tom?' she asked. She flicked on the CD and the voice of the American spiritual teacher filled the car. Randomly she flicked through tracks. She settled on a segment where a woman was talking. Esther Hicks, the author, she presumed. The woman had an odd mix of an accent somewhere between maybe Spanish and American, a bit like Sol's. It was a kind voice. She was saying that our lives are meant to be joyful.

'Joyful? Really?' Bec said, thinking of the depths of despair Tom had sunk to when he had committed suicide not far from the spot where Rebecca now sat.

Esther was telling her audience that there was no death and that everyone was an eternal being. It was the same concept Evie had spoken about when they were in the city, when Archie's life had hung in the balance. The woman, like Evie, said most humans had forgotten this fact. The fact there was no death. Rebecca twisted the ignition off, silencing the woman. If there was no death, why was Tom not still here? But then she thought again of Evie's words in the shop and at the hospital. Goose bumps shivered across her skin and tears surprised her. A smile drifted across her face. Tom *was* still here.

'OK, Tom, I'm up for listening now. I'm sorry it's taken so long.' She felt a warmth wrap around her like an embrace. Suddenly feeling strong enough to go inside, Rebecca got out of the car.

Walking through the garden gate, she could hear the sounds of 'Black Betty' blaring from the stereo in the kitchen. She frowned, looking at her watch. It was past dinnertime for Ben and he ought to be winding down for bed. She noticed Murray's ute was parked haphazardly on the lawn. His shearer's toolbox was on the back, as was his telltale giant blue Esky, with its lid wide open. There was a cricket set scattered under the clothesline and a pile of empty beer cans mounded up like a modern-day midden. Tangled around the clothesline, sleeping and shivering, was a tiny little black-and-tan Kelpie pup. It opened its eyes as she approached and sleepily got to its feet. She talked softly to it as she untangled its lead, taking in the little tan paws and the pulse of fear and uncertainty that ran through its body. She scooped it up: it was a female, she noted, and beautifully bred too. The pup snuggled into her arms.

As Bec entered the homestead, she could hear the sounds of Charlie and Murray hollering and laughing. Then came high-pitched peals of Ben's laughter. She glanced at the grandfather clock in the old hallway, annoyed at the time. It was a school night. Ben's first day back tomorrow after a long stint away.

Pushing open the kitchen door, Bec found the men, and Ben standing small before them, mirroring their stance. His eyes were bright and he was holding onto a small black plastic remote-control box. Every now and then Ben would press a button and laugh hysterically as Charlie convulsed around the kitchen, yelling and jerking, reaching for his throat.

'Turn it down, you little bastard!' Charlie screamed, although laughing at the same time. 'Stop, Ben!'

'Try it on three! Set it on three!' yelled Murray to Ben above the music. 'Up him!'

On the kitchen bench, Bec saw the opened box of an electric dog-collar kit. She marched over and turned the stereo off with an angry jab.

'What the *hell*?' said Charlie suddenly when he saw the fury on Rebecca's face.

During the awkward gaping silence, Ben hit the button again. Charlie leaped. 'Argh! Turn it off *now*, Ben! Mum's home.' This time the play was gone from his voice.

Rebecca looked at the box and to Charlie again. He knew she was dead against electric collars. She maintained they tortured dogs, not trained them. It wasn't the dogs' fault Charlie couldn't become a better animal handler. How could he inflict such a regime on his poor old dog, Stripes? And possibly this new pup, if that's what his intention was? He knew that Bec had lobbied hard to ban companies from exhibiting the collars at the local Bendoorin Show — she had inspired the show committee to invite dog-handling expert and former shearer Ian O'Connell to give humane training advice.

Suddenly she'd had enough of Charlie's cruelty and dominance and the way he trampled over her every belief — not to mention him encouraging Ben on the same path. Where was his empathy? Where were his humility and kindness? He was unwilling to take responsibility for his attitudes and actions. Not just to the animals, and not just to her, but to the land as well. She felt a power within her rise up. Like the wings of an angel at her back.

She grabbed the electric collar's remote from Ben, opened up the woodstove that was quietly smouldering and threw it in. Stooped over, with the pup under one arm, she struggled to shut the old unhinged door.

'God, I wish you would fix this stupid thing,' she said when she gave the door a furious shove and it closed with a clunk and a cloud of ash.

'That collar cost me a hundred and fifty bucks!' Charlie said. 'And I'll need it for the pup!'

'I don't give a fat rats!' Rebecca said. 'You don't deserve to have a dog in your life, the way you treat them! The way you shot mine without even talking to me about it!'

'I think you'd better go, Muzz,' Charlie growled as he began undoing the electric collar from his neck. 'I'm about to get a bollocking.'

Rebecca narrowed her eyes.

'Right-e-ho,' Muzz said, rubbing his hands together. 'See you then.' And he was out the door as fast as a shorn wether out the gate.

'Ben, it's bedtime,' Rebecca said quietly. 'Upstairs. Quick sticks. I'll be along to tuck you in soon. Here, here's some jarmies.' She tugged some flannel PJs from the old wooden clotheshorse that was still in the same place as it had been the day of Archie's accident and passed them to him.

'Aw! But, Mu—' he began, coming over to stroke the pup's ears.

She raised an index finger at him, bent down and looked him in the eye. 'Stop! No buts. Just *do it*, thank you.'

Ben sulked out of the kitchen, but she knew he'd climb the creaking stairs and make his way to the other end of the big old house to his room. She knew he didn't really want to stay up to see his parents fight.

Rebecca sat at the kitchen table with her head in her hands, the pup on her lap. Behind her a tap dripped into a sink that was laden with dirty dishes from Charlie's days of batching. She saw the pot she'd been washing on the day of Archie's accident, still crusted with old beef stew.

'We were just having a bit of fun, Rebecca! Or is that something that you've forgotten?' he said.

'For god's sake, Charlie. You're drunk. Again. And to teach Ben that shit. Electric collars. I mean, come on. Can you not see I've had enough?'

'What do you mean?'

'I have had *enough*! Of you. Of me. Of us.'

'It's only a dog collar, Bec.'

'It's not only a dog collar. It's everything. *Everything!* I mean, look, out there! The silage pit. The ploughed paddocks. You don't listen to a goddamn word I say! And you know what else? You have no respect for me!'

'I think you'll find you don't have any respect for me! Why do you think we're in the shit like this? It's because of you. You're permanently in bitch mode.'

Rebecca tried to ignore his jab. She breathed in deeply, then delivered the words that had been caught in her heart for so long. 'It's time for you to leave, Charlie. Go back to your family. Get off Waters Meeting. Go!'

She detected a flinch in him, then he stood straighter, his voice louder. 'I won't leave. I've invested too much into this place.'

'Invested? Is that what I am to you? *An investment?* Fuck off, Charlie.'

He stood before her, fists clenched, brows pulled down over his green eyes. She could tell he was trying not to waver from the dozens of beers he and Muzz must have put away.

'For fuck's sake, Charlie, it's up to you to work out why there's such a void inside you. Stop blaming me for the crap in your life. You've ignored me for years. You edged me out as soon as the boys came along. You spend thousands and thousands on toys for yourself and cut up sick when Ben needs something for school. You shat in your own nest. With that Janine. Now go build a fucking silage pit on your father's farm.'

Charlie was clearly at a loss — he'd been used to Rebecca's silence. For years she'd zipped her lips, not saying much beyond some whingey protests. Now here she was, howling like a wrung-out feral cat, trying to kick him out.

'I won't go. You want changes around here? I'll make changes. I've already dug a grave for those sad-arse old horses you've had hanging on here, costing us a fortune.'

She felt a jolt through her body as if she herself had been shot.

*'You've shot my horses?'* she said, her voice barely audible, her body shutting down from shock. She kicked a chair out of the way, put the pup on the kitchen floor and ran to the window to look for Hank and Ink Jet in the paddock. It was dark outside, the last faint glow of the sun hidden by the pitched peak of the western mountain, so her gaze was met with blackness.

Charlie stood behind her, defiant, drunk. 'Bugger all meat on them for the dog. Should've done it years ago and sold them to the knackery.'

Bec let out a muffled cry.

'While I'm at it, shall I dig a grave for the past, Rebecca? Because that's all you hold onto, the past and your days with Tom. I can't compete with a dead man! I've tried, but I'll never be like him. I'll never be sensitive or artistic or forever young like him.'

'You leave Tom out of it!'

'It's true! I'm just here as your whipping boy. Nag, nag, nag. Never good enough. You just want to control me. I might as well leave the fucking collar on and you can zap me each and every time you want to have a shot at me about what I have or haven't done.'

'Well, I know what you *have* done. You've not only had an affair, and killed all my animals, but you've also got me pregnant!'

Charlie's mouth fell open at the revelation. He paused as he took in the news. She could swear she saw his eyes roll from so much alcohol. He was really blind.

'Woah!' he said, holding up both hands, a look of confusion clouding his face. 'I *what*?'

Rebecca took a deep breath and blew air from her lungs. She sat down and spread her hands out on the table before her. 'I'm pregnant, Charlie,' she said tiredly.

Charlie's frown deepened even further. 'But how?'

'How do you reckon?' she said sarcastically.

'I'm cut and we never have sex.'

Rebecca almost burst out with frustrated laughter. 'It was that one night. The night before Archie's accident. Anzac eve. Not that you'd remember much. You'd been on the beer again. You were supposed to be joining the ewes and rams. Not me. It was pretty crap sex. It felt to me as if *she* was in the bed with us too. But up the duff I am, like it or not, Charlie.'

'Bullshit. Tell me the truth. Who are you pregnant to?'

'Don't be a dick. With *you*.'

'But I can't get you pregnant. You had me cut.'

'The doctor says it happens. And it's happened.'

'Bullshit!'

'It's not.'

'You're lying!'

Rebecca saw fury flash in his eyes. His cheeks flamed red. With a violent burst, he knocked a wooden chair back against the slate floor. Its old spindle frame shattered into shards. The pup whimpered and crawled under the kitchen dresser. Nerves jolted in Rebecca.

'Who else have you been screwing?' he yelled.

'Oh, that's fine coming from you! No one!'

'Liar!'

'Dr Patkin said he'd see you. To explain,' Bec said, trying to keep her voice calm.

'Explain?! Oh, so it was him? Dr Patkin? You've been doing him behind my back.'

'Charlie! Are you for real?'

'It's that Andrew bloke, isn't it? Or maybe that wog Stanton? How could you, Rebecca? How *could* you?'

'How could I? It's *your* baby, Charlie.' She searched his eyes, but there was not a flicker of belief within them. She gave up. 'What about you?' she said, matching the harshness of his energy. 'What about you and that toffy-nosed scrag of yours? I've had enough, Charlie. Enough! I've done nothing but love and nothing but give! And be a faithful fucking farmer's wife! Fuck you!'

Charlie was towering over her now.

'You're lying. Just to fuck with my head. Aren't you?' He hauled her up by her wrists and began to shake her. 'Aren't you?' he repeated through gritted teeth. Her head whiplashed as he raged at her. 'Who was it? Who have you been screwing? Tell me!'

'Let me go!' She tried to wrestle free of him, but he was too strong. His jealousy was fuelling some deep-seated anger, buried far within his being.

Next Charlie had her by the upper arms and was slamming her into the cupboard. 'Bitch!'

The doorknobs pounded painfully into her back. The air was knocked from her lungs. She could smell the grog on his breath. In his face, she saw madness. The madness of a cuckold. And a drunk. He dragged her forwards and swung her about.

'You had me cut so we could do it more often! But you never fucking want it! You want some of it now? Do you? Huh?' Charlie had her by the hair now and was forcing her to bend over the kitchen table, her swollen breasts pressed painfully to the wooden surface. Behind her, she could feel him reaching to unbuckle his jeans.

Crying, with no breath, she felt his weight on top of her back and his rough grab for her belt buckle. She heard him grunt as he grappled to drag her jeans down, the fabric burning her skin, leaving it welted and reddened. The strength of him was terrifying. The anger of him paralysing. As he was about to thrust violently into her, Rebecca swivelled around under the press of his angry weight. She saw flesh exposed by his rolled-up sleeves. Then she bit.

Like a Jack Russell, she bit and she hung on as he roared and howled.

Drawing her up, Charlie raised his hand. The blow was both a relief and a devastation. A relief because it was an ending, but a devastation because this man was the father of her children and the husband who was supposed to provide for and protect her. As Charlie's fist hit, Rebecca's head snapped sideways and her body careened across the kitchen, her skull hitting the cupboard door solidly.

There she lay. Her mouth bleeding. Looking up through blurred vision to the man she no longer knew. 'Get out!' she said through already swelling lips. 'Get out.'

There was no murmured 'sorry'. There was no stooping to collect her up. After he had stood over her for a time, Charlie left the kitchen, puffing from exertion, taking the stairs two at a time. She knew in the bedroom he'd be violently shoving his clothes into a PVC rodeo bag. After a short time, the slam of the door and the rev of the Hilux, followed by the angry stillness of the house, told Rebecca he had gone.

The puppy crawled out from under the dresser, sniffing cautiously. Then she came to settle next to Rebecca, leaning her little warm body against Bec's stomach. She began to stroke the pup and cry. Eventually she crawled to the table and hauled herself up. Groggily she dragged herself along the wall of the hallway and stood outside on the verandah. She imagined Charlie's tail-lights blinking red in the night as he drove away, far up high on the mountainside, along the curving lengthy drive away from Waters Meeting.

Holding onto the old wooden banister, Rebecca clutched her way upstairs, wincing at the twinges in her ribs and spine. She held the pup in her free arm, gaining comfort from her warm presence. She looked into their marital bedroom, where all the drawers and cupboard doors were flung open. Charlie's energy still fuelled the chaos of the room.

She continued along the hall to Ben's room. A globe within the globe, Ben's nightlight of planet earth was glowing in the darkness, the American continents turned towards her son. She could see her poor little man had already fallen asleep, the pillow shoved over his head to block out the sounds of his parents' shouting downstairs. Rebecca settled the pup onto her son's bed and sat for a time stroking Ben's dark hair, crying. Thinking of Archie in the Bendoorin hospital and placing her hand on her abdomen where her new baby was growing, she shut her eyes and told herself to breathe.

'I'll make things right,' she whispered. 'I will make things right.'

Silently, in a daze, she stood, walked downstairs, pulled on her coat and boots and went out into the black night. The stars dusted the sky and she felt the chill against her face. She tried to breathe in the crisp night air, but the tug of torn sinews and bruised muscles caused her to flinch. Instinctively she walked towards the kennels where once her three Kelpies had danced in welcome. As she approached, she saw in the shadows a lump on the ground.

'Stripes?' she called. Then she noticed the gleam of chain in the dust. Charlie had taken him. But what was the dark mound on the ground? As she neared, her hand flew to her mouth in horror. A sound escaped her, like that of a muffled wail.

There on the ground lay the hacked-off limb of a horse. She could see the rigid back hoof sticking out at an odd angle, the chestnut hide of her brother Tom's horse, Hank. She realised Charlie had left the leg there on purpose. Her knees buckled beneath her. She sank to the ground and retched and retched. She held her throbbing head in her hands and pulled on her hair, crying. Feeling the suffering of the horse, who had been shot at last. Dropped in the yard by gunshot, then dragged by a tractor and chain to the pit Charlie had dug with the back-hoe. The way he must've used the sheep-killing knives to roughly hack off the limb, dragging it in the dust over to the kennels. Stripes, like a lion, feasting until he was sick.

As her sobs lessened and her normal breathing returned, she remembered the night, years before, when in a craze she had chainsawed, bulldozed and burned the giant old pines that had kept the house in shadow. She had been deranged by the death of her brother and in a rage against her parents back then. Particularly her father.

For a time there had been some relief from the letting go of the madness the eerie sound of the pines caused, but soon the shadows came back, despite the cutting of the pines and the burning of the shed where Tom's lifeless body had hung. After she had raged and burned the old away to dust, sunshine had poured in for a time, but the house and garden always, even on summer days, felt broody. For her, even now, there were still shadows about the place and a darkness that seemed more sinister than blackness. And now Charlie's shooting of her dog, his butchering of her horses and finally the beating and attempted rape reinjected that sense of foreboding. She saw that she blamed no one else for the darkness, the darkness she herself had allowed in. She had chosen him. It was her own fear. A fear of her own power and freedom. A fear that had been passed down through the ages from woman to woman.

She was still allowing herself to be brutalised by the past. By her father's coldness and negativity, which hung over the entire landscape. She thought of the haughty look of disdain in her father's eyes that she had endured as a child and young woman and realised now, devastatingly, that Charlie had been a carbon copy of him. She had married her father. Or a version of him.

A spark fired in her. A fury was lit. She was repeating a pattern decades later, but she knew when done this one last time, it would be the breaking of the past. The mending of the past. The letting go. A moving forwards to a new way of following her bliss. Not for the men in her life. But for herself. She would reclaim herself this night.

No man could make her cower on the kitchen floor or yell her into a corner with put-downs ever again. Tonight she decided she would no longer be a farmer's wife. She refused to be. She would be a *farmer*. She would again be a woman with a dream of making her life count. For herself, for her children, for her land — and for all women who had been brutalised or oppressed. She would do this for the women through the ages who were burned at the stake or stoned, or beaten with sticks, or crushed by words of derision. She heard their screams and smelled the torturous scent of hair as it frizzled to smoke and skin bubbling from beauty to ash. And what had these women — the healers, the wise women, midwives and Wiccans — been persecuted for? For having the power of birthing life. For living by the guidance of love. For healing with natural plants. For worshipping Mother Nature. For reading with their intuition the cycles of life and the seasons.

At that moment, under the dome of the starlit sky, Rebecca realised she had grown up. She would face the passed-down fear of the ages. She pushed the physical pain aside, summoned Evie's energy in to help her and stood. Then she trudged over to the back-hoe, climbed into the cab and started the engine. She drove over towards the silage pit and set the scoop down, leaving the machine to idle.

Next, in the glow from the machinery-shed floodlight, Rebecca stooped at the dozer, looking for the pilot motor crank start in the toolbox on the side of the machine. It had been a few years since she had driven the old dozer, let alone started it. When she wrapped her hand around the cold steel, she felt a jolt. A bar of metal once held by her grandfather, her father, her husband. As she clutched the crank lever, she vowed she would no longer allow herself to be beaten by their steel and hardness. The land too needed that same protection.

She found the fuel tap, ran petrol through the lines, then cranked the motor over. The kickback from the crank spun savagely, collecting her painfully on the wrist. She cried out, but with gritted teeth she gave the pilot motor another turn. With a rumble, it gave in and started. She set the choke and hauled herself up onto the dozer. The seat felt cold, seeping through her jeans, and the gear and clutch levers in the palms of her hands almost burned from the chill.

'C'mon,' she said as she waited for the oil to creep through the system. Then at last, as she pressed the starter button, the old beast chugged, coughed and at last roared, and diesel plumes puffed into the night air. She put on earmuffs, then toyed with the steering brakes and levers, hoping the memory of how to drive the thing would come back to her. Fuelled not so much by anger as by determination, Rebecca put the dozer in gear and, with the blade lowered, she chugged towards the gleaming new yellow disc plough that was Charlie's pride and joy.

She felt her body jar on impact as metal hit metal. There was a shudder, a screeching of blade upon steel. Then the offset discs began to give way to the force of the dozer. The plough lurched a little to the side so Rebecca upped the throttle, skidding along the dry soil towards the silage pit.

At this moment she didn't care that they owed the bank thousands for the new bloody plough. At this moment that piece of machinery represented everything that had hurt her and hurt her land. She hated the sight of it. The revs high, Rebecca cried out with a mix of determined freedom and reclaimed power as the plough tumbled into its dark grave.

'Fuck you, arseholes!' she yelled through her clenched jaw as she saw the circular discs glinting in the lights from the dozer, upturned like the hooves of a slayed beast.

Jumping down from the dozer, she made her way to the backhoe. There she lifted the scoop and began to drag black soil back into the giant pit Charlie had dug. She looked up to the stars and smiled at Tom. She felt so good to be burying the hideous plough and with it her old life.

# Twenty-four

Rebecca awoke with a new energy. She pushed aside all thoughts of the pain that wracked her body from the night before. She barely paid any heed to her image in the mirror. She knew that the woman there with the fat lip and swollen brow was a woman of her past. Today was a new day. The relief of knowing Charlie's energy had dissipated and he had gone from the place soothed her. There was no panic at being left alone on the farm, as she had thought there might be.

She knew deep down she was being falsely brave and her choices would lead her down a path that would be exceedingly difficult, but today she had the chance to make a new start.

In the shower, the cuts had stung, along with the reality of her situation, but she was determined to wash away all the grubby feelings she had about the ugly scenes of her life before this day. She towel-dried her hair and took the time to wind it into two pretty braids. She tried to smile reassurance to the image in the foggy mirror, telling herself she would never, ever allow herself to be in a situation like that with a man again.

Then she pulled on clean work clothes, knotting her shirt at the front of her jeans, cowgirl style. Ben wandered sleepily into her room, dragging his teddy bear behind him, the pup trotting along at his heels. She knew he wouldn't ask, 'Where's Dad?' The boys were used to Dad not being in the house.

'What are we doing today, Mummy?' he asked, clambering up onto the high cast-iron bed and snuggling under the quilt. The pup sniffed gingerly about the room.

'Um.' Rebecca thought for a minute, then said, 'No school for starters. Not today. We're thinking up a name for our new Kelpie and taking her outside to do a wee, then doing a bit of sheep work, then we're off to see Archie. Then we'll see what the rest of the day brings.'

She turned to him, and when he saw the state of her face, a look of fascination briefly came to him, then a frown of concern settled on his brow.

'Mummy! What happened? Did you fall off the ute?'

She touched her fingertips to her face and smiled, rolling her eyes. 'No. Mummy had an accident in the kitchen. You know what I'm like, splashing water out of the sink. My socks got all slippery and I came a cropper. Silly Mummy. Now come on, let's get this day happening.' It was only then she felt the first sting of tears that she held within, but instead of succumbing, she took Ben by the hand, cuddled the puppy close and guided them down the stairs and out to sit on the verandah for a moment and watch the sun bring the new day alive.

In the blustering winter wind, as the sun rose prettily above the Waters Meeting mountains, Rebecca pushed her shell-shocked feeling away and instead tried to focus on right now. The old LandCruiser chugged and thudded its way over the paddocks like a Meccano-kit truck with square wheels. Each bump brought new pain and the same mix of both relief and devastation. Also came the thoughts of the baby growing within, thoughts which prompted both a comfort and an uncertainty. But she remembered what the woman on the CD had imparted: choose your thoughts, choose your life. By forcing herself to be in the very moment, the pain and uncertainty would leave and she would be struck with the clarity, and even the beauty, of the now. It at least gave her relief from the feeling that everything she knew was unravelling. She told herself to breathe.

Rebecca made herself notice the beauty of the millions of healthy gum leaves glistening in the slanting morning light. Each gatepost was an artwork of intricate patterns of lichen and lines, and each tree trunk a visual gift brushed with golden and silver hues. She breathed slowly in and slowly out. It had been years since she'd let herself just 'be'. She saw now how she'd forced busyness and duty upon herself. She had let herself be spun so fast in life by the work on the farm and motherhood that she had forgotten to truly see her surroundings. And to truly see herself.

She cast Ben a smile as he sat with the pup on his lap, so grateful she had him with her and that her other little man was tucked up safe in hospital with Evie by his bedside, ready for when he woke. It gave her all the time in the world to soak in the farm. Just her, Ben, the new pup and an unborn energy within.

Together, Ben and Rebecca made funny 'erring' noises each and every bump so that soon they were laughing and giggling at each other. She stroked the back of Ben's beautiful little head.

He looked up at her with his big brown eyes, caught too in the moment. 'I love you *so* much, Mummy.'

'And I love you too, sweetheart. Do you reckon you could open the gate for me?'

He nodded and passed her the pup.

She stroked the little Kelpie's head. 'Well, you just landed in my lap, didn't you?' she said to her. 'Ask, allow, and you shall receive. Tom helped manifest you so quickly. I wonder what else he can help manifest for us?' She breathed in the delicious scent of the puppy as she watched Ben's sturdy legs run to the gate. She smiled at the way his tongue popped out of the corner of his mouth in concentration as he reached up and unhooked the chain. With determination, he half swung, half dragged the farm gate so his mother could pass. Bec set a goal to have every gate on the place swinging nicely before next winter. She drove a little way into the paddock and waited for Ben to climb back in.

'What are we going to call her?' Rebecca asked.

Ben bit his lip and took the pup. He giggled as she licked the air near his face. 'She's funny.'

'She is funny.'

'Yes, well then, she's funny,' said Ben, 'so that means her name is Funny.'

'Hah! That's really funny,' Bec said, then she pointed to the pup. 'That's Funny!' And they both laughed. In her laughter, she still felt the tug of sadness as she remembered the dogs she had lost, but this funny little pup would forever symbolise a new start for her and the boys. With a name like Funny, the little Kelpie would forever remind Bec to see the funny side of life. Always.

'She's a little bit small yet to do any work, so we may have to do a fair bit of walking and driving to get the sheep, but we'll be right. Won't we?'

Ben nodded, then glanced at his mother. 'Why didn't we bring Stripes?'

Rebecca caught her own look of uncertainty in the rear-vision mirror, then looked across at her son. 'Daddy's gone to visit Grandpa and Grandma on their farm, and Stripes has gone with him to help,' she said, hoping that what she was relaying was the truth. After the disruption to their lives since Archie's accident, Ben seemed satisfied with the answer, said, 'Oh,' and simply continued to look out the window.

Bec followed his gaze to the tree line, where the ewes were already turning their white faces towards them. At the top of the run, she opened the gate into the next paddock, then drove clockwise out wide around the mob, hoping that the sheep would drift eventually in the other direction towards the top gate. Without a dog, she thought it would be a challenge, but she soon had the girls mobbed and moving well with her and Ben in the vehicle.

They made their way slowly over the lumpy, rock-scattered paddock, with Bec occasionally tooting the horn or banging the side of the vehicle, but not putting too much pressure on the sheep. At the gate, Bec watched with satisfaction as the leaders of the mob cast their ears forwards and walked willingly through towards a big mob of wethers, who were already gathering up as they watched the ewes.

'What are you doing, Mummy?' Ben asked, frowning, knowing it was a farming sin to box mobs together like they were now.

'Mummy is trying something different. You know that show we watched, with the zebras and gazelles in Africa? How they all wandered around together? We could do something like that too — we're going to run the blokey wethers and steers with the girlie ewes and cows and have big, big herds to move about our paddocks. That way, the grasses and the soils get a longer rest by the time the animals have come back to graze there. Just like the antelope, buffalo, zebra and wildebeest do on the big plains. It'll also give the rivers and hills a longer rest from animals using those areas too much. You see?'

Ben nodded and twisted his little-boy mouth to one side. 'I think so. And the rams will know the girl sheep from the boy sheep when we put them in with the wethers, won't they?'

Rebecca laughed. 'Yes, they will. And we're going to stop spraying all the weeds in the paddocks. If you don't tell the animals that some of the plants are weeds, they won't know. They actually nibble at the weeds for medicine. So you see, Bennie, it's all good. The land and the animals will like it better this way.'

After boxing three mobs in together and moving the cattle in with the sheep, Rebecca watched in satisfaction as the animals all settled down to graze in one big sweep of the paddock. 'See, Ben, they'll behave differently now they're all in together and in a big mob. They'll manure all of the paddock, not just where they camp. And manure is the best fertiliser for the soil you can get! Somehow we've all forgotten that. We won't have to buy fertiliser much now and the banks will like that and so will Mummy.'

Ben's little dark eyes were wide with excitement. 'So we'll have a farm that's like Africa!'

'Yes,' said Bec, 'kind of. Healthy land and healthy soils and happy healthy animals and when rain falls it stays because of the plants. It doesn't just blow away or dry up with the sun.'

'Can I help?' Ben asked.

'You sure can!'

Rebecca felt joy swell: she was imparting a new way forwards in farming to her son. It felt so right. She wondered briefly where Charlie might be, but pushed the thought aside. He had left her and Waters Meeting long ago, emotionally and spiritually. His trips to the pub and the footy and cricket clubs and then of course Janine told her that. She wondered what he might push for in terms of the farm in the future, but again she pushed the thought away. For now she told herself that everything was all right. It would all be OK.

As Funny nestled against her thigh, curled up and sighed, Bec smiled. She knew spring growth would kick in at the end of winter so by the time she had rotated the stock off this pasture, she would have fairly good banks of feed ahead for the large mob to be moved onto. She would dig out the plans she'd drawn up that divided the larger paddocks with temporary solar electric fencing. It would mean she could rest the more fragile areas longer. She felt a warmth run through her knowing that this was the very start of the healing, for Waters Meeting and for herself. With that thought in her mind and with the animals grazing peacefully on the fertile river flats, she drove out of the paddock and back to the homestead. It was time to visit little Archie in hospital.

As she and Ben drove up the mountain pass, her back to the spectacular view of Waters Meeting below, her phone beeped a message as she came into range. She stopped the vehicle and grabbed up the phone from the dash, half hoping it was word from Charlie, for the sake of the boys. She dialled message bank and waited for the voice to come on the line.

'Hello. This is Cory Mendleton from the Agribiz Bank. Your husband has referred me onto you regarding your property overdraft. We need to talk, Mrs Lewis. Please call me urgently. Thank you.'

The man's tone was clipped. Rebecca felt her world rewind. The banks were on her back again, as they had been after her father's mismanagement of Waters Meeting years before. Now she was faced with Charlie's mismanagement. Or was it in truth her own mismanagement, of herself, which in turn had damaged the richness of her life on all levels? Suddenly looking out across the swathe of farmland and wilderness, she saw yet another pattern in her life that she knew she had to change.

# Twenty-five

There was no answer at the giant front door of the Rivermont homestead so Rebecca grabbed Ben's hand and led him over the white pebble driveway and through the stone archway to the stables. All was quiet there too, save for the trickling fountain and the snorts of the horses happily tugging on hay bags. There was no one in the smoko room so they left the stable courtyard and walked to the fodder shed. Opening the door, she and Ben stepped in. The warmth inside compared to the mountain chill outside was a welcome relief. The gentle gushing of the reticulated water in the tanks met her senses and soothed her.

Her stress over the call from the bank this morning had been softened when she'd found Evie and Archie playing happily around the hospital bed with a big soft ball. Archie was making such progress and Bec realised it would be no time until he was discharged and she could take him home. She was sure Evie had been helping her boy in a way that the doctors in the hospital couldn't. All the medical staff had been amazed by his recovery.

Archie's face had lit up when Rebecca and Ben entered the ward. It was the same expression he wore each time Evie came to visit too, when she brought him all kinds of magical things, like river stones, books on unicorns and paint sets with giant sheets of paper. When Archie was with Evie, Rebecca felt it was the most content she had ever seen her little boy. He was so much like her brother Tom, and sometimes retreated from a world which at times seemed too busy and harsh for him to bear. Watching them together, Rebecca realised that Evie was giving Archie tools for living at peace with himself, no matter what life threw at him — they were the same lessons Evie had imparted to her.

As she'd come to stand by the bed, Rebecca had tried to appear bright, singing out 'hello', but when Archie and Evie saw Rebecca's bruised face, clouds of concern had passed over their expressions.

'He's gone,' she had whispered to Evie, who had instantly stepped forwards to hug her. 'And the banks are onto me.'

'Good and good,' Evie had simply said. 'It's time.'

Rebecca, with gratitude, had allowed Evie to coach her in phoning Cory Mendleton straight back. Sitting on a bench outside the hospital, with the boys happily playing with Funny on the lawn, Bec had told Cory the truth about what was going on with Waters Meeting and her and Charlie. Quietly and calmly she'd explained about her work with Andrew and her plans for the property and how she could turn things around financially. Especially if she worked off the farm part-time.

As she spoke, she had felt Evie standing peacefully nearby as if she was in some way sending arcs of energy down the phone to the banker. To her surprise, Cory had happily concluded the call with an extended interest repayment time and good wishes, so by the time she had hung up the phone, her world was filled with hope and excitement for the future once more.

As she stood in the fodder shed now, she sent out another round of thanks to Evie. She hadn't noticed him at first so Rebecca jumped when she sensed movement in the shed. She turned and saw Sol Stanton standing before a computer system wired to the wall.

When she called out a tentative 'hello', he spun around.

'Hola, Rebecca!' he said in a deep and cheery voice; his smile opened up like a sunbeam when he saw it was her.

'It's quiet round here.'

'Big race meet. We have a dozen horses away with a big crew. And the rest off with the flu.'

Letting go of her hand, Ben stepped forwards to look into the larger room of the shed. The boy let out an audible gasp when he spied the rich green grass that overflowed from the hydroponic trays.

Sol came towards them, rubbing his elegant hands on a rag. His expression changed when he saw the fresh wounds on Rebecca's face.

'You need some help, sí?' His dark eyes flashed with enquiry.

'I'm sorry to trouble you,' Rebecca said. 'But …' She paused and sighed. 'I need a job. I came to see if I could work for you.'

He moved close to her, took her gently by the shoulders and spun her softly towards the light, surveying her bruised and already scabbing face. Her eyes slid away, her resolve to be cheery and strong slipping too under the gentleness of his touch.

He made soft noises of concern, searching her eyes with genuine care. 'Are you all right?'

She shook her head quickly, unable to speak. He drew her into his arms and she felt the vibration of his chest as he spoke, his Spanish accent and glamour making her feel as if she was in some kind of movie scene.

'Tell me. What has happened?'

She couldn't speak.

Sol eased his embrace and turned his focus to Ben. 'Hey, Ben? You like the green grass? Go take a look.'

Ben hesitated, clearly fascinated with what he saw inside the giant shed.

'Go on,' Sol urged and the boy stepped forwards and began to walk down the centre aisle.

With the little one out of earshot, Sol turned back to Rebecca. He gestured to her face. 'A farm accident? Yes? I hope so.'

Ashamed, Rebecca shook her head and looked to the ground.

'Your husband?'

She nodded; she felt his body stiffen and heard him sigh angrily.

'El bastardo.'

'He's gone now,' she said, 'I think.'

'And you? What do you need? What can I do?'

'It's the bank. There was a letter … and I spoke to the manager …' She looked up at him, realising how she must sound, and quickly added, 'Don't get me wrong! I'm not here asking for money! God no! I came to ask for a job. That's all.'

The panic inside her began to tumble out. She talked on with urgency. 'You see if I can earn a little off-farm income now, I can make it work. I've got it figured. I'm going to shift Waters Meeting management over to no-kill, no-till cropping, like you're doing here. I've already begun Andrew's grazing regime, this morning. I'll save a truckload of money that way. And I'll arrange an online machinery sale. There's thousands invested in all Charlie's fancy-pants machinery. But just for now I need a start. Just to tide me over. I know Archie will be with me because he's not school-age yet, but I can find a babysitter. Evie's already helping. He's doing so well he'll be out of hospital in the next little while. So can I work here?'

'Shh, shh, calmar,' Sol said, drawing her to him again. 'Calm yourself. Take it steady.'

She felt the pain of her tense and bruised muscles as his fingers ran up her back. She was grateful his touch was not sexual. It was one of care. She allowed herself to be soothed by him.

'Slow it down, Rebecca.' She felt the tone in his voice, the same tone she had heard him use when he was talking to the horses in the stables. She let herself settle against his chest, soaking up his compassion and gentle kindness, and he held her there, with his big arms around her. Again she smelled that lovely fancy men's fragrance and the underlying scent of his masculinity. She inhaled deeply, drinking him in. And Sol kept on holding her while her quiet tears came. She felt him stroke the back of her head, which made her cry more.

'It will be OK,' he whispered to her. 'Everything will be fine. You just need to steady yourself. Take things quietly. Yazzie and I will help you. And of course you can work here. Don't even dream of babysitters. We'd love to have little Archie about on your shifts. Everyone would love that, particularly Yazzie. This is a child-friendly place.'

His words prompted further tears, tears that had been buried deep within her over the years. Rebecca realised no man had ever shown her such compassion. She'd never experienced such softness from anyone, really, and certainly not a bloke.

She began to pull back to express her gratitude to him, but when she looked up into his face, she saw within his eyes something beyond pity or empathy for her. Instead she saw passion. It shocked her, but at the same time thrilled her. She looked harder, trying to be sure what Sol felt, but before she could find out, Ben was running to her.

'Mummy!'

Rebecca pulled away from Sol.

'This place is *amazing*! How does the grass grow in those trays? Can I eat it?'

The moment was gone. The next time she looked at the tall man's face it was shut down again. She followed him into the growing room and watched Ben running his fingers over the long green leaves of the barley, setting tiny half-orbs of moisture free from lush blades of grass. She knew the moment had been fleeting, but she was certain she had seen desire in his eyes. Her head spun from the notion.

'It *is* amazing,' Ben said.

'It sure is,' she said absently.

As Sol ushered Rebecca and Ben outside, her mind began to shatter the moment and unravel what she had felt. It was not possible. He was just being kind.

'Stop frowning,' Sol said as they walked towards the fountain, around to the front of the house where Rebecca had parked. 'Allow this to happen.'

'What to happen?' she asked, uncentred.

'To let people help you. To let life take you where you need to go. Stop resisting,' Sol said. He squeezed her hand and delivered her a shy smile, which, Rebecca thought, offered friendship and nothing more.

'You sound like bloody Evie,' she said.

'Good,' he answered.

The evening sun was lighting up the Rivermont garden, casting a golden glow over the big bare limbs of the deciduous trees and lighting up the unseasonably early buds of daffodils and winter roses.

As Ben excitedly ran to the turning circle to dip his fingertips in the soft sprays of the fountain that held a bronze horse at its heart, Bec turned to face Sol.

'But why help me? Why us?'

Sol smiled gently down at her. 'I think you might ask Evie that question. She has been showing me many truths about myself and helping me to see how much the power of helping others positively can transcend all of us.'

Rebecca frowned. 'So I'm potentially a single-mum charity to you?'

He didn't falter at her defensive tone, but instead threw back his head and laughed. 'No. I see you as strength. There are very few women like you. I travel the world and I know there are few like you. And you are awakening too, like I am. That is why your husband is gone. And that is why you and I have been brought together.'

'Sol!' Ben called out. 'Want to see my new pup?'

Bec was reeling from what he said. Brought together? What did he mean by that?

'Ben, we have to go!' Bec called, confusion causing her mind to spin.

She wanted to push him further on what he meant, but Sol was already following Ben to Rebecca's four-wheel drive, where the pup was curled up on one of Hank's old horse rugs in the back.

'Oh, she is beautiful,' said Sol, taking her gently from Ben and squatting down next to him. 'What is her name?' he asked, stroking the sleepy pup as she yawned and shook her head.

'Funny.'

'Funny? That's a funny name.'

'I know, it's funny,' said Ben, giggling.

Sol laughed too and Rebecca smiled.

'Take her for a widdle please, Benno, before you put her back in the car,' she said.

As Ben ran with Funny on the Rivermont lawn, Sol turned to her again. 'Shall we say your shifts start at the fodder shed after the morning school-bus time? Then you can finish up when Ben gets off the bus in the afternoon. You name the number of days you can cope with.'

Rebecca felt gratitude wash through her. 'Oh, Sol! That's perfect. Thank you.'

'Bueno.'

She smiled up at him, her cute nose wrinkling with an expression of enquiry. 'How did you get to be so kind?'

Sol looked out to Ben, who was now lying on the grass giggling as the puppy leaped on him and danced around him, wagging her tail and play-bouncing.

'It began the day we lost the twins.'

'Twins?'

'Yazzie's babies.' Sol's expression darkened. 'She won't talk about it. But she sees in you the same strength I see, and she needs you. I know you think it is the other way around and you need us in your life. But Yazzie has welcomed you in for a reason. It is you and your beautiful little boys who have brought light to Yazzie. We need you just as much as you need us. She needs a friend like you. Of course she has Evie. Evie was the one who kept Yazzie going. Kept her living. But she needs someone her own age. Like you.' He opened the car door and gestured for her to get in.

Shocked by the knowledge that Yazzie had lost two children, Rebecca's thoughts rushed to the bright, vibrant and beautiful woman. Externally the world would never know she had endured such pain. She was so giving. So happy. But her past must have been so shockingly painful. Rebecca's heart tore for her. A mother losing her babies. It was unthinkable. Unbearable. She wanted to ask how, but felt Sol closing down on the subject and also on her.

Not knowing what to do, she reached out and took his hand in a handshake. He stooped and kissed her European style on both cheeks, with a serious expression on his face. As he shut the door, she could tell he was shutting the subject closed too.

# *Twenty-six*

Rebecca had to blink twice to come to terms with the fact that she was sailing through the western New South Wales sky on a giant ferris wheel at the Deniliquin Ute Muster. Beside her, Gabs was waving a metre-long salami at the stars. She had bought it on a drunken whim from a smallgoods stall that sat between the country-music CDs tent and a marquee stocked with ute stickers.

'Frank! Frank!' Gabs called to her husband, who waited for them below in the crowd with Yazzie. 'Check out Hans, my new boyfriend! He's no *small*goods!'

Good-naturedly, Frank gave Gabs the double thumbs-up, then Gabs slumped back in her seat. Her eyes were shining and her hair stuck up at all angles, compliments of the tomato sauce that Frank had spiked through it earlier at the hot-chips food van. Bec could tell from the way Gabs slurred her words that she was shitfaced. She muttered to Rebecca behind her hand, 'It's more than I can say for his tiny todger.'

Gabs ran her palm suggestively up and down the salami. 'To think we wasted all that money on Doreen's Horny Little Devils vibrators and dildos when we could've just bought a couple of giant chilli and garlic salamis between us. But to be honest, I'd say smaller is better. Less means more friction action. You know what I'm sayin'? Bigger isn't better — bigger means a John Wayne walk in the morning. Smaller means get up and go again!'

'Oh, Gabs! You always do that!'

'Do what?'

'Talk about dicks when you're drunk.'

Gabs began running her tongue along the plastic covering of the salami.

'Oh, you two, get a room,' Bec said, scrunching up her face.

'Don't be boring,' said Gabs, who swung the salami and whacked Rebecca hard on the shoulder.

'Ouch!'

'You vil getz zee senze of humour back,' chanted Gabs several times over in a bad German accent. 'Haans vil make you come viz lafink!'

Rebecca snorted a laugh as she looked up to the bright pinpoints of the Southern Cross, then turned her gaze over to where the big bands were rocking from the back of a giant stage to a mass of hats and blue singlets. The crowd was floodlit by giant lights on the flat, black soil plains. All were gearing up for the big acts of the night when Lee Kernaghan, The Sunny Cowgirls and The Wolfe Brothers would make their way to the stage at midnight.

The Deniliquin Ute Muster had been on Rebecca's wishlist for a long time, but with the farm and babies she had never managed to make it. How she had come to be here was a blur, but tonight, for just one night, she had decided she would reclaim herself.

It was springtime and she was now five months along in what had been an easy pregnancy so far. She'd allowed herself just one sip of rum and a swig of red, but she was happy to roll sober and preggers and watch the fun unfold around her. She looked down from the dizzy heights of the wheel to the people who milled about as small as mice far below them.

On the drive here, the girls celebrated the fact Bec could be designated driver for the next few months, as they chose other country events to attend.

For the two hundred Ks before they rolled into the entrance of the muster, Gabs had sat in the passenger seat beside her, downing pre-mix vodka cans. Yazzie had sat in the back, sipping on a bottle of red wine, pulling faces with each swig: for Yazzie, a red bought from a bottle-o in some random town was a bit rough. Frank, next to her, buried under luggage, was happily choofing through a six-pack of beer, grateful to be away from the kids and the farm for a weekend.

In front of them, a blue Holden plastered in stickers throbbed. It speared the wide sky with aerials of every thickness and length.

'Geez, check out the aerials,' Gabs had said. 'You could probe Uranus with that thing.'

'Is that an invitation?' Frank said from the back. His question was answered with an empty can tossed at him by Gabs.

'Are we going ferals camp or shall we go old ladies and pregnant women camp?' Bec had asked as they joined the queue of utes.

'What do you reckon, Bec?' Yazzie said, sounding offended. 'You may be preggers, but we're not old ladies.'

'You are all kind of on the cusp,' said Frank.

'Shut up, Frank,' they all chorused for the fiftieth time that drive.

'What a load of rot,' Yazzie had said defiantly. 'Old ladies, my pert little arse! And who cares if you're pregnant. It's not a disease!' She reached into the front and grabbed the steering wheel. Surprising Rebecca, her strong tug on the wheel veered them off onto the dirt track that led to the main entrance of the ute muster.

'Hey!' said Rebecca, trying to reclaim the wheel, braking slightly.

'Ferals camp,' Yazzie said with finality.

Rebecca had glanced at her in the rear-vision mirror, taking in her golden blonde hair and pretty white shirt. 'You're gunna fit right in there! You'll be food dyed in five seconds, Princess Barbie.'

'Bring it on! It was you being the princess this morning! It was a battle just to get you here, you wimp!'

Rebecca thought back to that morning when she had been working at Rivermont in the fodder shed. She had heard snickering coming from behind the racks.

'What's going on here?' Bec had called out. After several months working shifts at Rivermont, she was used to random jokes from Yazzie and the sometimes raucous staff. It wasn't unusual to go out to her vehicle and turn the ignition on to find every single dial on her ute turned full blast, so that the radio blared, the heater fan roared and the windscreen wipers swiped back and forth flat-out in a dry screech. Or she would go to the fridge for milk for her morning coffee and grimace at the taste, only to find Joey had substituted mare's milk into the container for a laugh.

She'd stalked along the rows of the shed, following the giggling, and had seen a couple of pairs of legs in cowgirl boots behind the racks. As she neared, she heard a spluttering. She rounded the fodder bay to see figures who could only have been Gabs and Yazzie, standing holding onto each other, with buckets on their heads.

'You idiots! What are you doing here?' Rebecca had asked, smiling. She tipped off both buckets, their faces red from trying to hold in their laughter.

'Kidnapping you,' Gabs had said, and with that they'd grabbed her, gripping her under each arm. Gabs shoved a bucket on her head and both girls dragged her outside.

'Hey! What are you doing?'

'You've been working far too hard on the farm. Farms! It's playtime!' Gabs said.

When they'd removed the bucket from her head, Rebecca had found herself looking at her vehicle all loaded up. Frank was standing there with a grin, as were Evie, Archie and Ben.

'What?!'

'Well, we couldn't take the Rivermont vehicles. They're too flash. The ferals trash them. So we're taking your shit heap,' Yazzie had said.

'Taking it where?' Bec asked, wondering what on earth was going on.

'It's time for you to give Archie some space,' Yazzie said, moving over to him. 'He's completely well. Aren't you, Arch? And he wants to live it up a little here at Rivermont for the weekend with Ben, Funny and Evie. Don't you, mate?'

Archie had nodded. 'Yes, go away please, Mummy,' he said and they all laughed except for Rebecca.

'Where are you kidnapping me to?' she asked with narrowed eyes.

Gabs and Yazzie had looked at each other and remained silent for a time.

'Does several thousand utes and several thousand blue singlets ring any bells?' Gabs said at last.

When Rebecca heard that they had planned the trip to the Deniliquin Ute Muster from the outset, she felt both overwhelmed by their caring and offended. How could she even consider a trip away right now? Didn't they realise the pressure she was under? With the farm? The debt? The pregnancy? The silence from Charlie, who barely called his boys?

'No. I'm not going,' she'd said. 'I can't! I have to move a mob back home.'

Frank reefed open the door. 'Get in. Dennis Groggan has our farms covered.'

'You are simply in resistance,' Evie said. 'Now get in.'

'I've packed your bags. I called in this morning,' Gabs said.

'And I've revamped your wardrobe,' Yazzie said. 'Candy and I did some internet shopping for you.'

'Now get in!' Gabs said.

In the end, it had been Ben who convinced her to go.

'You are the best mummy,' he had said. 'But you have to go. I want a bluey singlet. And you've been grumpy lately. Go fix up your thoughts.'

Again they laughed as Rebecca hugged her little men. 'You know what? I think you've been Evie'd,' she said to Ben, looking up at the old woman and pulling a face.

Evie had smiled at her. 'Yazzie needs some time out too,' she said. 'This place will be crazy before the race and breeding season completely kicks in. So get going.'

There had been an undertone to Evie's voice. Rebecca sensed it. It must be nearing the anniversary of the twins' death perhaps? So, with that in mind, Bec had climbed into the driver's seat and shouted, 'So? What are you all waiting for?'

Now, several hours later, here Bec was feeling like she'd been beamed down from a different planet.

'Geez, I'm going to piss myself if I don't get off this thing soon,' Gabs said as the ferris wheel took another pass and rose again. Then she listed sideways onto Rebecca's shoulder, snuggling her salami to her chest. 'Yaknow I loveya,' she mumbled.

Rebecca wondered if Gabs was talking to her or the salami, but before she could ask, she realised the mad drunkard was asleep. Rebecca looked down at her friend, who stank of tomato sauce and spilled rum, and smiled. Settling back with Gabs's weight on her, she let the ferris wheel take her round and round in the inky night sky as more memories of the last couple of months on Waters Meeting and life without Charlie — just her and the boys — unfolded in her mind. At last she felt equilibrium was found beneath the star-dusted sky.

Soon the ferris wheel was drawing to a stop and the attendant was opening the white wire cages to let them out.

Gabs was suddenly startled awake and, without missing a beat, she was on her feet and clambering into Frank's waiting arms on the platform, dragging Hans with her.

'Tattoos!' she said, holding up the salami. 'Hans here is going to get a tattoo!'

'You have got to be joking!' Frank said, but Gabs was off, Yazzie and Bec following in her wake.

'They're only temporary,' Gabs said in all seriousness, as she plonked down inside the tattooist's tent with her one-metre salami dangling between her legs. 'I reckon we get a butterfly on him. That'll impress the chicks. Let 'em know he's the sensitive type.'

Rebecca smiled, suddenly utterly grateful she had come.

Just then her phone buzzed in her pocket. A text from Charlie: *Heard you went to the muster. What kind of mother goes boozing and leaves her kids behind, especially with one just out of hospital?*

Rebecca felt stung. It was late at night and here he was texting. She knew he'd be at the local pub, drink-driving back to his mother and father's farm like he used to in the old days. It was the first time she'd heard from him in weeks. Either Muzz or Janine must have blabbed. Bloody gossipy district. She pressed delete on the phone and shoved it back in her pocket.

'Bugger it. I'm going to get a tattoo too,' Bec said. 'Barbed wire. Coz I feel so friggin' fenced in.'

'Oh no you won't,' Yazzie said, grabbing her arm. 'That was him on the phone, wasn't it? Don't you dare slip into old patterns. This weekend we're both flying over fences! Here,' she said, jabbing her finger at the display board, 'get a horse. They're a symbol of freedom! And I'm getting those two birds with the "Eternity" heart. You know it's their birthday today. They'd be turning five, same as Archie.'

Bec shut her eyes, suddenly hit by the moment. Yazzie had endured so much too. There was no point being angry over Charlie. She stood up straight and smiled at Yazzie. 'OK. Freedom it is for me. Eternal love for you.'

'And you are going on a negativity diet! No more from this moment!'

'That's a deal,' Bec said.

'The night is but young,' Yazzie said, giving Rebecca a wink, 'and I have a feeling your life is about to begin!'

# Twenty-seven

As midnight approached at the Deni Ute Muster, people in their hundreds converged in front of a giant stage where Tassie country rock band The Wolfe Brothers was causing the best kind of scene. Yazzie, who had been badgered by so many boys all evening because of her blonde pretty-doll looks, had taken herself off to the campsite alone, but before going she had urged Rebecca to stay on.

'Keep playing on the plains, Bec!' she had said, her eyes gleaming under the big lights. 'Make the most of it! I don't have my children to face with a hangover and battle scars. I can party any time, but you'll be back to reality tomorrow, so live for this moment, now.'

Bec had watched Yazzie weave her way past the Bundy Bar and the mechanical bull, the blunt-cut ends of her straight hair shining against the black jacket she was wearing. She looked so elegant and petite in this rough-and-ready place. Rebecca felt a surge of gratitude towards her and also the swell of grief that it was her twins' birthday. Tonight was the first time she'd even mentioned them. Bec knew it was a big moment for Yazzie letting her in, getting close. Her friend hid her scars by making everyone else the focal point.

Throughout the night, Yazzie had been like a makeup artist, stopping from time to time to gloss Rebecca's lips and fluff the blonde wavy hair that fell prettily from beneath her hat.

The night was warm so she had traded the cute little brown top Yazzie had bought her for a hot pink Deni Ute Muster singlet that she'd bought from the merchandise truck. She no longer felt lumpy, mumsy and self-conscious about her body. The work on Waters Meeting and in the fodder shed meant her arms were toned and strong again. Her baby belly was barely showing over the top of her leather belt. She looked a little thick in the waist, but that was it. She was in good shape and her cleavage was something to gasp at, rounded with pregnancy hormones. Her verve and energy, generated by her new thoughts and changed lifestyle, meant she looked fit and gorgeous — and she was getting plenty of attention for it.

Some pimple-faced young clown had passed her, saying, 'Nice rack.' Then another: 'Howsabout it, blondie?'

She was enjoying being in the pulse of fun-loving, daggy and unpretentious energy that was unique to a country crowd. Then suddenly Gabs was leaping on her back, flogging her with the salami as if riding her home in the Melbourne Cup. Laughing, Bec found herself drawn like a moth to the bright lights at the front of the stage in a crush of boozy bodies, where the music was rocking out. There she danced with Frank and Gabs.

Soon, though, she lost them in the crush. She didn't really care; she was enjoying the music thrumming out from the giant speakers. She gazed up to the stage, where Nick Wolfe was looking virtually edible in a cowboy hat, worn jeans and boots, complete with his guitar. His brother, Tom, wearing a checked shirt and a cheeky grin, was wielding his guitar like a weapon. As they cranked into their hit song 'Hi Vis Anthem', drummer Casey and guitarist Brodie made the most of their Tassie talents, stirring the crowd to fever pitch. And Rebecca was soon lost to herself. Dancing beneath the old Akubra hat that she wore pulled down low over her brow, she felt eighteen again. And pregnant. And free. With a stick-on tattoo. How funny the world turned, she thought.

As she danced now to the music, she felt someone tap her on the shoulder. Spinning about, she was met by the sight of a Rivermont trackrider, Joey, smiling at her.

'Hi!' Feeling a little high on life and reckless, she reached up and hugged him, taking in his manly scent of bloke's deodorant. Joey picked her up and held her aloft in the tight squash of the crowd. Then he set her back down and leaned close to speak to her.

'I've been looking all day for my beautiful cougar, and here you are! Yazzie said I'd find ya up front!' he yelled.

The band was so loud his words were lost on Rebecca, so she just nodded and smiled. She waved to the cluster of Rivermont staff: Daisy, Kealy, Steph and another trackrider, Ken. Then, as if it was the most natural thing in the world, she let Joey take her hand and together, smiling into each other's eyes, like long-lost reunited friends, they began to dance. There were no words exchanged. Just a knowledge that they were from the same mountain, worked on the same place and hanging out together was a given.

She could see from the grin revealed under the brim of Joey's hat that he was genuinely pleased to see her. She also began to notice how sensual his soft lips looked, opening up to a wide white-toothed smile. So what if he was a good ten years younger or more than her and had an ego the size of Texas. He was good to be with and could dance like a dream. He had become one of her best mates at work and she was entitled to a little fun.

She let herself feel his hands on her as he gyrated his hips and spun her about. He was flirty ahead of sleazy and funny ahead of a tosser. She knew from the Rivermont staff that he was a womaniser, but tonight, for this moment, she didn't care.

In between songs, he pulled her nearer and asked, 'Where's Gabs and Frank?'

Bec shrugged her shoulders. Just at that moment a cheer went up when a silhouette of the giant metre-long salami was marched across the big screen that flanked the stage. Bec could make out Gabs's head in shadow as she larked in front of the stage camera.

'Ah. I think I've just found Gabs. And Hans.'

'Who the flock is Hans?' asked Joey.

Rebecca could only laugh and roll her eyes as she took him by the hand and led him through the crush of people. By the time they had made it out to where the stage camera was set up, Gabs and Frank were long gone, probably ushered away by security.

As she glanced about the people who milled in the semi-darkness of the venue, Joey fished into his pockets and pulled out some drink tickets.

'You and me? Bundy Bar, mademoiselle?'

Bec grinned and nodded. She didn't at all feel like a drink, but she certainly felt like staying near Joey. She hadn't forgotten their first meeting at Sol's stables. She had found him interesting and attractive then. And it was kind of cute to see the way he swam with self-confidence. Bec was happy to find that the world had not yet knocked him out of shape and bent his ways. He reminded her of herself when she was younger.

'You move your hips well, woman,' he said as he passed her a can of rum and raised his eyebrows at the same time he raised his can.

'How old are you?' Rebecca asked as she took a small swig, conscious of the baby.

'How old are you?'

'Too old for you.'

'Perfect,' Joey said, stepping forwards and leaning in so their hat brims touched. 'I love older women. You know I'm going to swag you tonight.'

'Cocky and cute,' she said, flirting back. 'But no, you won't.'

'It's true,' he said, staggering a little, his drunk eyes blinking slowly.

She shook her head. 'Not possible. I'm married. I'm the mother of two small children. And you have your beer goggles on.' She left out the fact she was pregnant. Only Yazzie, Gabs, Frank and Evie knew that.

Next Joey leaned so close she could feel his warm breath on her neck. 'You and I will see the sun come up, mark my words. And I am going to make love to you under the stars.' She could smell the booze on his breath and the bad-boy scent of cigarettes that caused a heady mix of temptation. She felt the nearness of his divine body, then the brush of his lips against hers in the lightest of lingering kisses.

It was then Rebecca felt the world give way beneath her feet. She drew back, looked at his handsome drunken face and bit her lip, trying to hold herself back from the rush of desire that swept through her. She was being shown an open door and she wasn't just ready to walk through it, she was ready to bolt!

# Twenty-eight

As she lay in Joey's swag and began to settle under the foreign touch of his hands, the sound of the drunks careening back to camp dissolved away, her mind became still and for the first time in many months she was lost in the moment. The Wolfe Brothers had finished playing, leaving room for a sprinkling of ute revs to throb out in the now chilly night air.

Occasionally stock whips and whoops from some of the die-hard party animals shattered the stillness, but mostly thousands of campers fell silent in sleep. Now all Rebecca could hear was the desire in their breath and the rustle of the canvas of the heavy swag that was pulled over them.

Just lying beside him, Rebecca felt transformed by his youth. He was mesmerising. Unlike the landscape of Charlie's body, his had a smoothness to it, and yet a youthful hardness ran beneath his skin. His muscles, taut from years of trackriding since his early teens. The fullness of his plush lips and the passion in his kiss were things she'd never thought she would experience again. But here he was, laid out for her to drink in, under the night sky of Deniliquin. Dead drunk though he was, he was beautiful.

His were lips she couldn't help but kiss. And his face was

one to gaze at, gently lit as it was by the dim light of a faraway generator that thrummed on the corner of the tent city. Bec's eyes travelled to his mouth repeatedly and she ran her fingertips over it, backwards and forwards.

As she bent towards where he lay, his kiss sparked a primeval desire in her body, a desire that had lain dormant for what felt like an eternity. It was the bliss of one kiss. She was drunk, not on alcohol, but on the life that pulsed around her at the muster. It was the excitement of carrying a baby within. The completeness and power of being a woman.

And Joey was part of that energy. He, young and alive, as they lay in a landscape so ancient and beautiful.

She felt his hands roam up and over the curves of her body, cupping her singlet-clad breasts. She felt the warmth run to the crotch of her jeans, beneath the little swelling of her belly where her baby lay. Hungrily she pressed her pelvis closer to him. His hands slipped down the front of her jeans, his fingers sliding inside her, making her feel so, so good. Her hands found their way under his shirt where her touch was met by a scatter of tiny pimples, a reminder that this man was still so close to being a boy.

Suddenly she panicked at his youth, thinking of her own boys and how it would be for her if they bedded a woman so much older? And for some reason, Sol came to her mind. What would he think? The farmer's wife from Waters Meeting sleeping with one of his trackriders?

She pulled away from him, muttering that they had to stop. But she felt Joey's hand reach around the back of her head urgently and he drew her into another long and sensual kiss. Evie's words came to her: 'If it feels good and you aren't hurting anyone, do it.' And this felt so good. And so natural, when she shut out the thoughts that were now rampaging through her head.

But *was* she hurting people? Surely she and Charlie were separated for good now? Surely he knew the inevitability of their situation?

She looked back into Joey's eyes, which were lit with passion but also, she realised now, a depth of drunkenness that was causing them to half close. Despite this, his hands were gently guiding her to lie on top of him. She did so, feeling the delicious warmth of his body along her torso. Slowly she began to unbuckle his jeans, desperately wanting to find pleasure from him. But as her hand slid under the elastic of his underpants, she was shocked to find his penis was flaccid. Not a single stirring of passion.

'I'm sorry,' he said, reaching for her hand and pulling it away. 'Had a few too many,' he slurred. 'The old Foster's Flop. We can have another crack a bit later.' She could tell he wasn't embarrassed, just utterly tanked. Bec laughed at the irony, kissed him on the temple and rolled off, snuggling beside him.

'I don't mind a bit,' she lied.

Rebecca settled into his arms and looked up to the sweep of the Milky Way. As she took in the darkness of the sky and the wash of stars, she realised life was all made up. All of it. From the stock market, to retirement funds, to the institution of marriage — they were all human creations from the rampage of human thought. And here she was a part of that creation. She realised if she didn't let others' made-up beliefs constrain her, life was now hers to savour.

It was entirely up to her to create a life where she felt happy and free. That her life could start again. Joey, even though they hadn't made love, had unlocked a current of passion in her, and she would refuse to feel any guilt in spending time enjoying his warmth against her in his swag. Instead she would feel reinvigorated by youth and by the wonder of life itself.

She pressed her face against his chest and fell in line with his breathing, and soon she was deep asleep.

Not long after, dawn light was creeping over the flat Deniliquin plains horizon. Campfires were smouldering sleepily and slowly people were stirring for another day on the booze.

As the sun rose slowly, Joey stirred and rolled over. Rebecca had her back to him and she felt him put his strong arm around her and drag her close, spooning her from behind.

'Sun's coming up,' he murmured, nestling his face into her neck. She could feel the scrape of his stubble and it dragged goose bumps across her skin.

'Do you know what it means when the sun comes up?' he asked, kissing her lightly on the neck and running his hand around the front of her shirt to where the pearl press-studs of her Western shirt were already undone, exposing her pink Deni singlet and the tanned domed crests of her large breasts.

'No,' she said, 'what does it mean?'

'It means my cock's about to crow,' he said, pressing the hardness of his morning erection contained within boxer shorts against her buttocks.

She laughed a little. 'You idiot.'

'You love it,' he said, pressing against her harder and running his hand up and under her singlet. 'Hello, baby.'

Rebecca giggled at the irony. If only he knew there was a baby. She felt a little guilty. He might not find her so desirable if he did know.

She felt Joey nuzzle into her neck again. 'You are so sexy,' he said. She never thought she'd let another man near her body after she had married Charlie. Up until now, she thought she would only ever share her post-baby body and the stretch marks that lined her skin with the man who had fathered her children. To her, the scars of motherhood belonged to both her and Charlie. But now, as she felt the breath in her come quickly, she decided she just didn't care, as Joey's kisses on her neck became harder and his hands firmer as he searched out the buckle of her jeans.

Just then, in the avenue of campers, a giant truck rumbled beside them and let out a noisy whoosh of airbrakes.

'Geez,' said Joey, ceasing his kissing. 'What the fuck?'

Out of the truck came two scraggy, dumpy men in high-vis

vests, looking as if they belonged in underground houses in New Zealand on a *Hobbit* set. They had thick gloves on to combat the early morning cold and the fact that they were about to pump the shit out of the portable toilets parked on a semi-trailer tray a little along from where Joey and Rebecca lay.

'You picked a good spot to camp!' Bec said, chuckling.

The men dragged concertina hoses across the short tufted grass, turned giant couplings, yanked levers, cranked over a pump and, with a roar and a giant waft of shit fumes, began draining the results of the previous night's festivities and feasts from the sewerage tank of the toilets. The stench made its way across to Joey's swag and drifted up to sit thickly in Bec's nostrils.

'Shit!' she said, watching the men in disbelief.

'Shit is right,' said Joey, who lay on his back, laughing. 'Bit of a mood killer.' As the pump continued to thrum and the foetid stench draped itself across their swag, Bec thought back to the B&S ball where she had first kissed Charlie. Their first exquisite river kiss on day two of the partying, Charlie back then looking every bit as delicious as Joey did now. But then, as Bec recalled, the kiss of her life had been interrupted by a floating poo laid by some drunk joker upstream.

Their first poo kiss had been a tale retold many times in the early years of their relationship. But now, lying here with Joey, Bec began to see the universe was showing her patterns. It was history repeating — and could the message be any clearer? This time, with Joey, the kiss of her mid-life was being interrupted by an entire poo truck. She looked at the men rolling the giant rings off the underplumbing of the truck, the seepage of smell as the valves released, conjuring a reek like the sewers of Ye Olde London Town.

'I think I'd better go.'

Joey groaned. 'I think I'm gunna chuck.'

'Well, I'll leave you to it.' She kissed him fondly on the head and rummaged her fingertips through his hair, feeling oddly maternal with the gesture.

'OK,' he said, burying his face into his grimy swag pillow. 'See you back at the ranch, babe,' he muffled.

As Bec pulled on her boots, she noted the thin spread of stubble on the side of his face. God! she thought. He really is young! As she stood, she felt a sense of vertigo. It wasn't illness, or tiredness: it was the realisation that she had her life back. In whatever way she created it.

Eventually amidst the thousands of campers, she found the sagging tent she and Yazzie had set up so hastily next to Frank and Gabs's. She crawled in and Yazzie greeted her sleepily. She fell face first onto her swag and groaned.

'So?' Yazzie said after a time.

'You don't want to know.'

Yazzie smiled at her. 'You sexy minx.'

'Nah. No sexy time. He got the Foster's Flop on me, then this morning, you wouldn't believe … Well, it all turned to shit.'

'That's still worth a high five,' Yazzie said, holding up her hand for Rebecca to slap. 'At least you scored a night of pashing. You are braver than I.'

'Braver or stupider? I *am* married and Charlie could still chuck a big ugly legal case at me. Especially if he found out.'

'You are not married. You are separated, destined for divorce and you know it. You just haven't faced it yet. You can't go back to him, Bec. Not after all he's done. Add it up: Janine, the accident with Archie, your dog, your horses. Walking out on you and the boys without a word. And I mean, c'mon. He hit you. That's plain wrong. It's time to move on.' A small frown was lining Yazzie's brow and there was concern and sincerity in her eyes.

'I know,' Bec said quietly.

'I know you know. So who was he?'

'That, you really don't want to know!' Bec said. 'But you were right. My new life after last night has begun!'

Part Three

# Twenty-nine

The Rivermont fodder shed held a peace that Rebecca loved. The sound of water being gently stirred in the nutrient tanks welcomed her as she stepped into the climate-controlled interior. Today she would have to work fast. It was Bendoorin Show day and Ben and Archie were itching to get going so they could enjoy their share of fairy floss and mechanical-bull rides with their little mates. They had already dressed Funny in a kids' bluey singlet teamed with a red-and-navy bandana for the Pet Parade. She was sitting dolefully in the smoko room, looking utterly humiliated and humourless in regards to her attire.

Rebecca sighed as she put on a waterproof apron and tied it at her back. She laughed as her pregnant stomach pushed the stiff heavy apron out, a little like a fat butcher's belly. She was five and a half months along and she was grateful to have been working here throughout the winter and now into spring. The unborn child's presence seemed to be pushing her into a growth phase, like a bulb pushing up towards the sun. She couldn't help but feel the baby ground her and move her forwards at the same time, the unseeable but knowable forces of nature taking her with them. But there was something else that had prompted the feeling of such vitality.

Bec realised it was Evie's teachings and the books and CDs she fed to her that had helped the shift. Rebecca found that instead of focusing on the aches heavy farm work had inflicted on her body, she now disciplined herself to be grateful for every day given and for her health.

She banned herself from moaning, groaning and complaining. Every ache she combated with breathing, the way Evie had shown Archie in the hospital, and every negative thought she ducked like a martial arts master, willing herself to put in place a new thought — an affirmation that supported herself.

The shed and eccentric work family of the Rivermont staff kept her buoyant too, and was a brilliant outlet for her from the relentless work of house and farm. And for the boys the bustle and fun of the Rivermont staff seemed to shelter them a little from the fact that Charlie rarely called. Sometimes Charlie's mother rang, on a Sunday evening, and would pass the phone onto Charlie 'for a word with the boys'. Bec made sure Ben and Archie sent him letters and paintings, not so much for Charlie's sake, but so the boys fostered some kind of connectedness to their dad. She had often sent him text messages, asking for at least some kind of financial support, but the messages remained unanswered. His silence spoke loudly of his stingeyness with money and his lack of care.

Thankfully the Bendoorin girls had rallied around their little family of three: Gabs dropping meals in weekly to stock the freezer; Doreen coming to clean and do washing; and Evie zipping out in her little car at a moment's notice to mind the boys so Bec could get on with the stock work. And when heavy jobs challenged Rebecca, Frank and Dennis were happy to lend a hand, using the time with her to discuss how the new grazing and cropping methods were transforming their own properties and farm businesses. Even Cory, the bank manager, had been supportive via email, knowing money would soon come in for Charlie's machinery. Tonka Jones, the dealer, had already given him an estimate and was scheduling the sale of the items. Cory too was curious to see first hand how Andrew Travis's methods could revive a farm business on the brink. The positivity on the place seemed to feed into her boys too. They were energised and full of life, particularly with Funny by their side night and day.

As Rebecca picked up a fodder harvest knife, she smiled, knowing her two little guys were happily playing Lego in the Rivermont stables smoko room. Yazzie would be in there with them, getting on with the racing paperwork, her dogs Wesley and Ruby cast down at her feet in rabbit-chase dreamland, while Funny sulked, waiting impatiently for the older dogs to wake up and play. Bec also knew the infectious and flirtatious Joey would soon be buzzing in after his trackwork to stir the boys up and swing them around in a boyish rumble. And she knew that Joey would swagger over to the shed, reef the door open and call, 'Time for a cuppa, you sexy bitch!', delivering his words with his cheeky crooked grin.

The night at the Deni Ute Muster sat between them like a giggly teenage secret, and she could see a glint in his eye sometimes when he spoke to her. When he had heard on the grapevine Bec was having a baby, he had rushed up to her shouting and skylarking with her.

'That was quick! I'm going to be a dad! What are we going to name him?'

Both of them had laughed, knowing their one-nighter was a delightful secret and a treasured memory between them. His attentions didn't spark guilt, nor prompt her to feel like some desperate ageing housewife; instead Joey's flirty comments made her zing. They felt legitimate. It was nice to feel more than just someone's wife or mother after all this time, but neither of them had mentioned the drunken encounter, that had quite literally ended in a flop, to anyone. He acted the same way with her as he had always done. Bec was relieved. She knew she was too messed up to pursue anything with Joey — and that he was not the right kind of man for her, even leaving aside their age difference. She took his joking attempts at seducing her as amusement only and he seemed happy with that. Working here was vastly different from the serious, weighty atmosphere of Waters Meeting that she and Charlie had seemed to endure, Rebecca concluded.

She found the repetitive nature of daily sowing grain into the trays and then harvesting the eight-day-old root mats of lush green fodder like a meditation. Another satisfaction was watching the racehorses, and broodmares and foals, trot along the fences, whickering for the green sprouts. Bec loved to watch them devour the juicy nutrient-rich leaves first, followed by the moist slices of white barley roots and split grain husks. Some of the more clever horses held each slab of fodder steady with a hoof as they ate. Rebecca knew, no matter what its style of eating, each horse would eventually consume every last skerrick.

When in the shed, she had often wondered what her old horses Hank and Ink Jet would have done on the daily ration of fodder. When she thought of them, she felt a twinge of sadness. Rebecca longed for another horse that she could ride, but the more she number-crunched on the computer in the old Waters Meeting farm office, the more she realised she would have to put that dream on hold. Even though the bank had given her a generous extension on the outstanding loan payments, she could barely afford *Horse Deals*, let alone a horse, even if it was for stock work as well as pleasure! Rebecca scooped the soaked barley grain into a plastic jug and tipped it rhythmically into the trays that were racked nearly as high as the roof. As she picked up a plastic spatula to slide the grain into even slabs for growing, she thought back over the past few months.

Life after Charlie leaving had felt like a storm-fed waterfall and her days seemed to tumble in a rush. Without his weighty, dark energy stalking her in the night, she found she awoke with a clear mind and, despite the huge list of tasks, an enthusiasm for her day. Even excitement. Things were happening so fast around her that on days she resisted the flow, life felt impossible. But if she let go and went with the flow, as Evie suggested, and *trusted*, she not only 'got by', but discovered previously unnoticed beauty in the world.

Every night as she collapsed into bed, exhausted but satisfied, she read and listened to the books and CDs Evie offered her. Sometimes when sowing grain, she listened on her iPhone to the wisdom from various inspiring audio books. That, and the atmosphere of the shed, helped her control her thoughts.

There were dark times of suffering too. In the gloomy Waters Meeting homestead, during that devastatingly lonely hour of four am, she sometimes awoke with her heart pounding and in a sweat, feeling completely undone and utterly alone, smothering in a veil of fear and disappointment. But if she breathed deeply and began to read or listen to one of Evie's meditations, she found she could still her mind and once again reach for the trust that the old woman was nurturing so carefully in her. Then her belief would come again with the dawn, that she wasn't on her own. She had a team around her who cared.

Evie had made it her business to come out to Waters Meeting often after school to deliver takeaway from Larissa's store and so give Bec a night off from the kitchen altogether, and to help with things like the vegetable garden and Ben's school reading. She'd also sit with Bec and guide her through a relaxation once the boys were asleep. Once realigned by Evie, Bec would feel the river of her self gain speed. She could feel the ineffable tumble of life. Now she had jumped off the cliff, Rebecca realised things weren't as bad as she'd imagined them to be.

In the fodder shed, as she focused on the tiny golden seeds that would, within several hours, begin to shoot white-tipped barley stems, Rebecca thought of the latest book Evie had given her, *The Four Agreements*, which was all about making a pact with yourself and setting beliefs to live by. She realised she was not only sowing the grain in this shed — with every thought, she was sowing her future, for her life and her land. She was also growing the seed of her baby within, and if she thought good thoughts about that, she now knew the journey would be smoother. Already her life was smoother, just from practising better thoughts.

Plants needed air, water, sunshine and space for growth and, as she gently pressed the seeds in the trays, Rebecca realised she needed the very same things. After reading *The Four Agreements* and learning the first agreement, she was now more mindful of her words, and the sacredness of the breath she took in order to speak them. She no longer talked herself or her life down. And if she did, she was quick to take the toxic words back and change them to something better.

The second agreement was to not take things personally. In the same way plants needed water to flow over them and within them, Rebecca resolved to allow other people's resentments or harsh words to wash off her like water off a duck's back.

The sudden change to her marital situation had generated a mixed bag of reactions from the people around her and words had recently stung. Some people in Bendoorin were short with her. Particularly the men, with some muttering that she'd 'kicked the old man out'. Even Amanda at the pub had been oddly short with her, saying she 'ought to sort it out with Charlie for the sake of the kids', citing that she herself had endured years of Dutchy's crap for her own children. Amanda's comments had hurt, but Rebecca now knew it was her friend's own stuff with Dutchy that was driving the words so Rebecca chose to let it wash away.

At that moment the shed's automatic irrigation system started and Rebecca heard the pump kick in and the gush of water in the pipes. The little black nozzles began to trickle water and nutrients into the growing trays. Rebecca used it as an opportunity to check the flow rates in the racks of growing grass, so left her sowing for the moment.

She turned the taps off for the seven-day-old grass that she would harvest today. She found it amazing that the tiny seeds held enough energy to grow grass that was so vibrantly green and so long that it draped over the sides of the trays. Rebecca knew over a longer period of time, the plants would begin to turn a sickly yellow if they did not find sunshine to continue their growth.

She thought of the third agreement, which was not to assume things. Rebecca now knew not to assume the sun would always shine in life. She thought about her 'failed' marriage. Her life had turned a sudden and shocking corner in an area she assumed would always be OK. She would never again assume people thought or behaved the same way she did. Her marriage hadn't failed. It had just grown and moved on.

The final agreement was to always do your best. Rebecca knew that if she kept telling herself that she was doing her best, then she would not beat herself up for the end of her marriage. And if she wasn't beating herself up, she had room to grow. Like the plants, Rebecca could feel growth within herself each and every time she read one of Evie's books. Each day there was an 'ah-hah' moment where she saw herself more and more clearly.

She still had times when she felt guilt that she hadn't worked harder at keeping Charlie in her children's lives, but she knew the path she had chosen for herself and her boys was the best one. They had only complained a couple of times that they missed their dad. It made Rebecca realise she had been the centre of their world anyway, and Charlie had always, in some way, been absent from them. Self-absorbed. After Archie's journey to near-death, she'd witnessed a wisdom in the boy that was as old as the stars. With his bravery in the hospital, she had truly seen he wasn't *just* a child. He was a remarkable human being, as was Ben, who had been so philosophical when realising their father was unlikely to return.

'If Daddy is here and unhappy, that is badder than him being *away* and happy. So then it's good he's gone,' he'd said one morning with the definitive logic of a child.

In watching the boys deal with their challenges so maturely, Rebecca had the realisation that age wasn't a number. It was a state of mind. She could see now she had been conforming to her beliefs of how society *expected* her to behave. She was living how she thought a farmer's wife *should* behave 'at her age'. Instead of listening to her heart and doing what she wanted. Maybe Charlie had been living the same way? Under a cloud of conformity. Fenced in by fear. Patterns and beliefs programmed into him by his parents, by his peers, by the wider world. No wonder he was unhappy. No wonder they had both been unhappy.

The grain racks sown, Bec walked to the other end of the shed, picked up a knife and began to slice the chunks of fodder in half-metre slabs. As her thoughts turned to Sol, she felt a resistance pull in around her. The day before she'd gone to the muster, Sol's father had called him away on business to Sydney. She couldn't understand why she felt a faint disappointment that he was no longer close by on Rivermont, but then, to her surprise, on the night she'd returned from the muster, he had called late on her mobile to see how she was getting on.

Gratefully Rebecca called him back and found Sol's willingness to simply talk staved off the isolation she felt inside. He wasn't flirtatious on the phone, but he was funny. That first conversation, they talked for an hour and a half on the pasture-cropping and grazing plans for Rivermont and how Bec could do the same for Waters Meeting. When he called again a few nights later, Rebecca found herself smiling. Over several such calls, he became a sounding board for her regarding her progress with the books Evie had given her — ones he had read himself. He asked about the awakening of her life as a single mother. He shared some of the changes he'd gone through since receiving Evie's gentle teachings and the doors they had opened for him. By the time they both finished talking, it was often well after midnight. When Bec hung up the phone, she found herself reliving the embrace they'd shared. It was as if Sol had awakened a sleeping lioness within her. After his phone calls, for the first time in what felt like an age, she longed for not just sex but to experience a type of connection with a man that was something otherworldly. To lose herself. Not just the predictable, heartless and unspiritual couplings she'd endured of latter years with Charlie.

The night she had spent with Joey and the day Sol had held her here in this very shed, she had tasted the delicious physicality of being a woman again. And now she craved it. While she loved the flirtatiousness of Joey, part of her felt exhilarated and comforted that Sol had arrived back here on Rivermont with his steady deep aura of strength. She shared most things with Yazzie, but she hadn't told her or Gabs about Sol's frequent phone calls and their growing friendship. It was something private for her. And it held a sacredness to it, as if, should the rest of the world know, it would all blow away.

This morning when Bec had first arrived, Yazzie had mentioned in passing that Sol was home and would soon turn the kitchen upside down while he frantically created his Man Cake for the Home Industries section of the show. Rebecca already knew. Sol had called her the morning before, from his and Yazzie's father's Point Piper waterside mansion. Bec had wanted to rush up the grand staircase in the airy Rivermont entranceway and wake Sol with a bear hug. But of course she held back. Their friendship was by phone. Still formal. They were talking mostly of the safe topics of pasture-cropping and soil rehabilitation. Maybe she had just been Sol's fix for the homesickness brought on by the drabness of the city, uppity people in his work and crowded cafés.

Her thoughts were interrupted by the now predictable call of Joey into the fodder shed. 'Cuppa, you sexy bitch!'

He stood framed by the open door, a picture of physical vitality and youth. Morning sunlight and shadows played on the defined muscles of his bare arms, and the fine hairs that were raised in goose bumps from the cold were picked up by the surreal light, giving him a gentle golden aura. Despite the early morning chill, he was in short sleeves, his lean torso confined in a rider's protective vest. His face was mud-splattered from galloping the racehorses up a big, grassed hillside, the chinstrap of his jockey's helmet dangling beneath his stubble-shaded chin. He stepped inside.

'How is my sexy cougar today?' he asked, eyes twinkling.

'Just fine, Joey,' Bec answered as she heaped the last slab of grass onto the trailer parked in the open section of the shed.

He whacked her on the bum with his riding whip. 'Howsabout we give it a go in your grass? You and me, eh?' He wiggled his eyebrows at her.

Rebecca laughed. 'I'll get a wet arse.'

'That's not all that'll get wet, darlin'.'

Rebecca rolled her eyes and smiled broadly as she swung her leg over the four-wheeler bike and fired it up. 'As we both know, you're all talk, Joey,' she teased good-naturedly.

'That's a relief. I thought that was mine,' he joked as he gestured to her swelling belly. 'But seriously, how can you resist this?' He reefed the Velcro on either side of his vest in a loud tear and pulled up his T-shirt, revealing a six-pack stomach and a subtle trail of hair down to a big silver rodeo buckle. His brown leather belt sat on his slim rider's hips.

She couldn't help it. Rebecca's eyes slid over his torso and she felt her mouth begin to water. She had to admit he and his body were delicious.

'Unleash those raging preggers hormones on me. C'mon, you know you want me!'

'Maybe later, lamb chop. You've got other things to ride today, Joey. Like the Rivermont horses. Get the sliding door for me, will you?'

As Joey pushed open the big sliding door, he said, 'You think you're too old for me, don't you? You are my MILF and I am going to have you again.'

'Ah!' she said. 'Technically, you didn't have me the first time, remember?' She saw amusement cross Joey's face.

'It was pretty shitty,' he said. 'I don't remember much. Just that truck.'

'There's nothing to remember, Joey. Just two mates from home sharing a swag.' But she did remember. The sweep of the Milky Way, the beauty of his warm, sleeping form, even though he was drunk as a skunk. The realisation that life was still hers to taste and to revel in, no matter what her age or stage. She winked at him. 'I'm going to get my cuppa after I've fed out. You keep dreamin', darlin',' and with a grin to match his she revved the bike and fodder cart out into the bright sunshine of what had turned into a beautifully still and sunny spring day.

As soon as the horses heard the bike and the rumble of the fodder-shed doors open and close, a chain of neighing set off from the nearest day yards and flowed like a Mexican wave to the stables. She waited for Joey to get on, swinging his leg over the back of the bike and pressing his torso against hers.

'You know I want a piece of your arse in the stables,' he said, sitting his chin on her shoulder, bumping her head a little with his riding helmet.

'Well, I want a piece of cake in the smoko room, so let's get going.'

Despite the fact she knew Joey was only teasing her to make his work morning go faster, she surprised herself by how much she relished the feel of his tight young male body against her back. She caught the scent of his bloke's deodorant on the breeze and felt an almost animalistic desire run through her body. Her mind was firing. What was going on with her? Men were the last thing she wanted in her space. Yet here they were appearing everywhere! Calling her on the phone at night! Kissing her! Pressing up against her! Holding her! Flirting with her mercilessly. And while she was pregnant too? Could she really be attractive to them after all these lost motherhood and farmer's wife years? She still had her doubts.

As Bec buzzed under the stone archway to the stable courtyard, she glanced across to the big house. She knew Sol would be in the kitchen. She felt self-conscious sitting so close to Joey on the bike. She dismissed the thought as ridiculous. Sol would know they were just mates.

Parking the bike outside the smoko room, she waited as Joey got off. He held out his hand and helped her step from the bike. Stooping in a bow, he took her hand majestically, looking both foolish and handsome in his rider's helmet, which was covered in red and white silks with a pompom on top. His striking blue eyes looked up into hers as he kissed the back of her hand. Then he laughed as she shoved him away.

'Will you give it a rest, you dickhead?' Rebecca said.

'You love it,' he said before winking, turning and striding into the smoko room. As she followed, Bec allowed herself to take in the perfection of his backside and she felt her cheeks flush red. She was turning into a perve.

'How are we all getting on?' she asked, shaking off her teenage crush as she entered the smoko room.

Yazzie looked up from her paperwork and smiled. 'Marvellous!'

On the floor, the boys had constructed a large Lego wall. 'Hello, Mum,' they chorused and the dogs all stood and wagged their tails in greeting.

Joey stood above the boys, his hands on his hips and an expression of mock indignation. 'Huh! You say hi to Mum. But not me! What am I? What is Joey to you? Chopped liver?'

Getting in on what was now a regular joke, Ben and Archie said in sing-song voices, 'Hel-lo, Jo-ey,' as if addressing a boring teacher. He then swooped upon them, causing them to squeal.

'Behaving?' Bec asked Yazzie.

'Perfectly. Until Joey arrived. Have you been behaving? You took too much time in that shed with her, Joey,' Yazzie said playfully. She beamed a beautiful smile.

'I missed out,' Joey said, putting Archie down and giving a theatrical pout and a 'darn it' click of his fingers. 'She won't take me seriously.'

'Keep onto her,' Yazzie stirred. 'She could do with some defrosting. Separated women take a while.'

'Oi!' cautioned Rebecca. 'I am actually in the room!'

Yazzie, who sat slinging a long jean-clad leg onto the desk, revealing fancywork leather cowgirl boots with worn Cuban heels, tapped her perfect teeth with a pen. She looked from Bec to Joey with narrowed eyes. 'I reckon she'd give you a run, Joey! Like all the other girls round here have.'

'Except for you, boss lady,' Joey said. 'You're just jealous I haven't put my offer in yet!'

Yazzie burst out laughing. Rebecca laughed too, but her eyes slid to behind where her friend sat. On the wall was the photo of the beautiful woman and her babies in their double pram. Rebecca felt a twinge of pain on her behalf. Knowing the depth of Yazzie's suffering in life, Rebecca was filled with even more admiration for this strong woman before her.

Just then a racehorse nearby let out a roar of frustration and kicked the stable wall.

'I get the hint!' Rebecca called out to the horses, then turned to Yazzie. 'I'll keep going then, shall I? I'll get this lot fed.' She stooped to kiss her boys, who were once again caught up in their own child's world of Lego building.

'And while you do that, I'll make you a cuppa, my sweet Princess Pure,' Joey said. 'But hurry along. I'm going to win you a big teddy bear at the show today to gain your sweet favours.'

'Oh, Joey, please! That's laying it on a bit thick,' Yazzie said. 'But yes, we'd all better hurry. We can't be late. Sol's been faffing in the kitchen since he stepped in the door. He's more excited about the Man Cake comp than he is about being invited to audition in Paris for the coming orchestra season.'

Rebecca flinched a little. So he'd be going overseas again? She realised the impossibility of even thinking about a future with Sol. Then she laughed. 'He is one odd bod!'

As she began to feed the fodder to the horses in the stables, she caught sight of Sol's dark head in the kitchen window, bent intently over his cake decorating. She tore her gaze away from him. What was she thinking? His European ways and his extreme wealth were utterly foreign to her. She could never be interested in a man like that; and surely he would find her too coarse after all the beautiful, refined women he must work with in the orchestra.

She was used to harsh brusqueness in men. Right from the outset, when she had met Sol on the roadside, she had felt more masculine than he. He was all sophistication and she was all farm girl. Her solid physical way in the world made her feel clumpy around him. Yet he seemed so kind and open. And gentle. Not rough and closed, like Charlie.

She stooped to pick up another heavy slab of feed and dropped it into the stall to a gleaming bay called Too Many Reds, or nicknamed by the staff as Tommy.

As her thoughts slid to Charlie again and his horrible leaving, she recalled the one phone call he'd made directly to her since driving off Waters Meeting.

It had felt oddly surreal to hear his voice. And to feel nothing but a void. No anger. No sadness. No longing. Just an empty space between him on the flat plain country and her in the mountains, hundreds of kilometres apart.

When Rebecca had asked him if he wanted to see the boys, he had replied, 'Only if you drive them out here.'

'OK. I will,' she'd said.

'But if you are pregnant, as you say, then I don't want to see you,' Charlie had added. 'You're too old to be pregnant. And too old to be tarting about. It's disgusting.'

She tried to believe his words no longer bit, but the sting had been too great. When she'd pressed the end button on the mobile, a heaviness had settled about her for days afterwards, like a grubby city smog.

As she made her way around the day yards to feed out the second trailer-load of fodder, she pictured Charlie at his mother's old Laminex kitchen table with its slightly rusted silver legs. After all the reading and listening she had done, Rebecca could now see Mrs Lewis as clearly as she saw herself. They were both women who were prisoners only unto themselves. If Rebecca owned up and faced the truth, she now saw she had allowed the men to hunt her from the farm into the kitchen. She had so wanted to make good as a farmer's wife. To undo the way her mother had unravelled their lives by leaving. Bec now saw she had been no better than Mrs Lewis. Disempowering herself because she had an ingrained belief system that she should serve the men. Not out of a sense of love for them, but out of a duty that she wore like an itchy heavy garment. She had been behaving as she thought she 'should' ahead of being aligned to her true self. But what was her true self? It had been buried under the demands and silent emotional blackmail of her father, the constant disapproval of her mother.

She imagined Mrs Lewis now, lifting Charlie's coffee cup and wiping the surface beneath while sighing about her family's burdens that she dearly made her own. Rebecca could visualise Charlie's father as he sat with his glasses well down the bridge of his nose, peering at farming bills and grain results, muttering that the costs were too high and the wheat payments too low. Rebecca knew not much would've changed since the days she had stayed there before their marriage. And therefore the land would be on that gentle slide into barren lifelessness.

Charlie's parents were now older, fatter and even more rusted up with angry habits that they would never bother to face and unlock. It was easier to see the world as being full of people doing wrong to them than to look within. Rebecca knew Mr and Mrs Lewis would be killing the fatted calf because their eldest son had come home, but at the same time slicing him with knives of judgement for, first of all, leaving them for her and Waters Meeting, then coming back home with his tail between his legs.

His mother would be dishing up meals to him that were peppered with 'I told you so' and 'I knew this would happen'.

Rebecca almost felt sorry for him. She slung the last slab into the day yard for the yearlings to eat and high-tailed it back to the stables. Turning off the bike, she was met with the sight of Joey on one side of the courtyard, coming towards her with a cup of coffee and a big slice of chocolate cake.

'What took you, Princess MILF?' he sang out to her. 'My hard-on's gone and it's time to go to the show. We'll have to aim for a quickie in the stables on your next shift.'

On the other side of the courtyard, as Joey finished speaking, she saw Sol walking towards her from the kitchen, holding his Man Cake entry. In keeping with the Prime Lamb feature theme of the show, Sol had created a cake in the shape of a giant pink chop, complete with white icing that served as chop fat. Stuck in the meaty middle of the cake was an Aussie flag adorned with the words, *We Love Our Lamb*.

She could tell it was going to be his 'ta-da' moment. His cake was hilarious and brilliant, but a brief cloud had crossed his face and he was looking at Joey with a closed-off expression.

Surely not? Bec wondered. He must know what Joey is like and that what he'd just said was all in jest? She was about to go over to make a fuss of his cake when her mobile rang.

It was Charlie.

'Hello?' she said tentatively, turning her back on both men in the stableyard, walking away, her shoulders hunched.

'I want a divorce,' Charlie barked down the phone.

She absorbed his words like a sudden surprising punch.

When she didn't reply, he continued, 'A lawyer will be in touch about what I get out of the farm.'

Winded from his words, Rebecca took a moment to speak. 'Just like that?' she asked in a voice barely audible.

'Just like that,' came his cold reply. Then he hung up.

# Thirty

The Bendoorin Show was buzzing with small-town country-fair activity. An array of utes was lined up for judging, some polished to gleaming, others mud-splattered and dinted beyond belief. A handful were flying huge Bundy Bear and CAT flags, the tailgates so coated in stickers it was hard to see the paintwork.

Rebecca, Yazzie and the boys walked past the line-up, and Bec smiled as she thought of her own long-carked-it Subaru she'd had when she was a teenager, which had been towed to the wreckers after the second engine blew. Ute comps hadn't been around much in her day, but she was sure she could've won the 'old bomb ute' section several times over. She missed that ute.

Up until recently she would've told herself she missed her youth too and that she herself was now 'an old bomb'. Lately she'd started to feel the energy that she'd enjoyed when she was a young girl. But after receiving the call from Charlie this morning, Bec felt her old demeanour and fear slipping back into her very being. She felt plagued by questions about what he and his solicitors might do.

Bec looked over to Yazzie, who was almost skipping beside her, a lit-up smile on her face. It always intrigued her that her friend was only a few years younger than her. She seemed so much younger! Rebecca realised she had allowed herself to become old before her time. The way she dressed and walked about in the world was so staid, compared with Yazzie's behaviour. She seemed to have no boundaries and great freedom ... not just because of her wealth, which was certainly a factor, but also because of her attitude to life. Bec had come to see her as an almost obsessively perfectionist workaholic with the horses, but always she seemed to cope with the workload and find joy in the smallest of things.

Today, for example, in the car driving to the show, Yazzie couldn't contain her excitement and was bouncier than the kids, bursting with the joy of the simple fact that she was going to the Bendoorin Show. Rebecca had puzzled at her. It was *only* the Bendoorin Show. Yazzie was vivacious now as she fussed over Funny in Ben's arms, adjusting the little costume they'd put on the puppy for the Pet Parade. Bec wondered if Yazzie's exuberance was a mask on her grief, but when she looked at Evie, she saw the same inner control.

Evie, who must've been ancient, still held a youthful way about her and seemed to have made friends with the entire town, including the sullen teenagers who normally hung outside the store, smoking, spitting and swearing. Evie was still playful and had a wicked twinkle in her eye. And not once did she ever complain about the age that must surely be settling into her bones. Instead she could be found offering the spotty, sweaty kids free angel-card readings and the occasional home-made 'herb' cheese biscuit. These had nothing more exotic in them than dried thyme, but the country kids thought the joke was pretty cool, like Evie.

Rebecca recognised that Sol shared the same zest too. She wondered if it was because the Stantons didn't have money troubles that they were able to be so carefree. But then maybe it was the other way around? Maybe it was their positivity that kept money flowing to them? Their utter belief that they *could* have all the good things in life. Sol and Yazzie were the hardest-working pair she'd known, but they made the work look effortless and they seemed to love every nuance of life — even when it came to day-to-day chores. Bec decided to try for the Stanton attitude and pushed her worries about Charlie and the looming divorce and property settlement aside.

'Hiya!' said Yazzie, waving at Candy, who was selling salad rolls at the footy-club tent. She turned to Bec. 'I've been wanting to catch up with her. I'll see you soon.'

'No probs.'

Rebecca helped Archie and Ben lead Funny past the coffee and hot-chips caravan. She managed to coax them quickly past the small array of sideshows and children's rides, until they entered a small ring cordoned off with hay bales, where other kids and their pets were already gathering. Behind them on a larger field, beautiful horses sailed over jumps and danced on collected reins so their necks arched, their riders turned out neatly in jodhpurs and dark tailored jackets.

Rebecca let go of Archie's hand and ruffled his blond locks, then squatted to stroke Funny. In the line-up of children's pets, the pup had discovered a cat, a lop-eared rabbit and a chook, and was now sniffing at the air with curiosity and caution. She's the sweetest little pup, Rebecca thought. She sometimes wondered if Murray or Charlie might ask for the Kelpie back, but she pushed the thought away. She wouldn't part with her now, nor would the boys, no matter what.

The 'celebrity' judge was a local radio announcer from a larger town a hundred Ks away. He began booming everyone awake on the PA system as he spruiked his station and commenced the event. He was clad in denim and leather that barely made it over his portly body. He cast his eye over the array of animals, which included a blindingly white goat that had clearly been washed in Napisan, some worms in an ice-cream container and even a moth on death's door in a jar.

Rebecca stooped to straighten Funny's shearer's singlet and red-and-navy bandana.

'What's your pup's name, son?' asked the DJ in a 'shock-jock' voice.

'It's Funny,' said Ben.

'That's a funny name,' the DJ laughed, his voice joining a crackle followed by a whine over the public-address system that had been borrowed from the local hall committee for a gold coin donation.

As he moved off down the line to interrogate and sometimes terrorise more small children about their pets, Rebecca looked about.

A little way off she noticed Yazzie leaning on a rail watching the jumping, her blonde hair swept up in her classy pony tail, whipped by a gust of wind. Unusually she was alone. Rebecca wondered how she so graciously survived what must have been the worst possible life event, ever. How could any mother be so well after losing two children? Yazzie was amazing.

Rebecca thought of the time in the hospital when she hadn't known if she would ever hold little Archie again. It had almost undone her and she still shuddered from the mere memory of those hours when his life hung in the balance. Rebecca now knew, thanks to her nightly talks to Sol, that it was in those dark days of fresh raw grief after Yazzie lost her twins that the Stantons had first met Evie.

Evie had been running meditation classes and doing healing work in Sydney's inner city and Sol, in desperation, had sought her out to help Yazzie through. Rebecca had pieced together a couple of the puzzles through conversation with Sol, and she now knew that the tragic event had been an accident on the way to a show-jump event: a semi had lost its load onto the Stantons' horse float and four-wheel drive, which Yazzie was driving.

Yazzie's then-husband, a Sydney businessman, hadn't coped. Sol had, in very few words, intimated that after three months of trying to keep the surviving twin — a boy — alive on life support, Yazzie had discovered payments from their joint account to a high-class Sydney brothel. One particular transaction was dated the night of the show-jump event and accident.

'Her life had completely fallen apart,' Sol said to Bec, one night on the phone. 'I didn't know how to bring her back. That was when I found Evie to help us. Bit by bit Yazzie rebuilt her world.' The sorrow in Sol's tone was palpable. It had opened Rebecca up enough to talk about Tom with him.

Rebecca knew grief would still be moving slowly through Yazzie like an ice-cold glacier and that it always would. Sol had said in return for Evie's gift of wisdom and kindness in helping Yazzie through the worst of the storms, the Stantons had offered to move Evie to Bendoorin and set her up in her shop. She had been tired of Sydney and missed the bush.

Bec knew Evie was still hovering near for Yazzie's sake. If the grief did show in areas of her friend's life, Bec knew it was on the subject of both men and horses. Yazzie never mentioned men in reference to herself. And Rebecca had noticed she worked extremely hard training her show jumpers out on Rivermont, yet she never, ever competed. She suspected that the show jumping, the death of her babies and her solo status despite her beauty were now shockingly and inextricably linked.

Yet still Yazzie radiated such love and vibrant energy it was impossible to know what went on in the quiet times when her loss returned to haunt her. It was also wrong to feel pity for her. Rebecca knew that did not honour the woman she was.

She held onto Archie's hand and Ben crouched at her boots, soothing the hesitant Kelpie pup. It didn't matter that Charlie wanted to remain away on his family farm, nor that he wanted a divorce and settlement so suddenly. All that mattered was that she was here now with her boys and her baby within. All that there was, was this moment, *now*. It was Bendoorin Show day! That in itself was the greatest thing! It was time to have fun!

# Thirty-one

Shelves of perfectly preserved fruit, frilly-capped jars of raspberry, blackberry and apricot jam, and exquisite cakes and slices all crowded the display areas in the Home Industries shed at the Bendoorin Show. Some jars wore blue ribbons and rosettes with gold lettering, others wore red ones, with third-place getters in white. The organisers, made up of the new wave of rather sexy thirty-something Country Women's Association members in winter long boots, black tights and short skirts, teamed with colourful 'Best in Show' aprons, were overseeing the whole affair.

The general public peered at the photo competition display boards, admiring the winners, picking their own favourites and promising themselves they'd put in an entry next year. Others strolled past the flower arranging, knitting and crocheting sections. But it was obvious where the main attention was, judging by the hub of people clustered around the exhibit of the inaugural Man Cake competition. Clearly farming men had gone to a lot of trouble. Some had borrowed recipes from their wives for the more traditional fruitcake, or a difficult chocolate cake. Others, bravely, had tackled the extremely complex but impressive sponge cake, made all the more yellow by free-range, farm-fresh eggs. But only a few had taken on the Aussie lamb promotion theme for the competition as inspiration for decoration.

Sol's 'chop cake' was a stand-out in the humorous category with its pink icing and swirls of white 'fat' and toothpick Aussie flag. It was getting a lot of laughs from the crowd drifting through the shed. Next to Sol's entry was Frank's cake: a giant rectangle of bright green icing, fenced off with plastic farm rails, inside which plastic sheep grazed. Candy's husband, Brian Brown from the store, had iced his cake as the Australian flag and had set barbecue tongs on top, while Doreen's husband, Dennis Groggan, had borrowed his granddaughter's Barbie doll and placed her in a cake skirt. Barbie was decked out in a striped butcher's apron, holding up a plasticine chop and a mini spatula. Rebecca and the boys laughed. All in all, the category was causing quite a sensation. A film crew from a Sydney cooking show was already bustling in and parting the crowds like Moses's waters with their bright lights and cameras.

The show committee had spent every last cent of their budget to ship Sam Kekovich of 'We love our lamb' fame in to judge the event, so they would be well pleased with the coverage, and now next year there'd be enough in the budget to invite country-boy cricketer Glenn McGrath, who most of the women on the committee had a thing for.

Later that night, Sam Kekovich would be guest speaker at the wool growers' fashion parade and cocktail party. There was an excited buzz in the crowd as they watched Sam pass with the film crew in tow. His Man Cake duty done, he was already being whisked away by the ladies to the luncheon room, where the CWA was dishing him up soup, sandwiches and richly thick cups of tea out of a gigantic metal teapot that looked as if it had arrived with the First Fleet.

Sam had awarded first place to Dennis Groggan's Barbie cake, which Rebecca was sure Doreen had made. Sol's 'chop cake', the funniest and most artistic of all the entries, had received not just second place, but also the special People's Choice Award.

Rebecca knew Sol would get more of a thrill out of this award than some of his father's high-pressure, adrenaline-generating business dealings, or from the orchestra applause that smattered like rain around Parisian concert halls. Earlier that week on the phone, Sol had animatedly said how the competition was *'Ingenious!'* and would help spark a new era for the local Bendoorin Show and CWA.

'It shows such Australian rural cultural cleverness!' he'd said. 'That's what I love about being raised in Spain, but having an Australian father — I am distant enough from it to *see* the uniqueness of it! And the madness! Es locura!'

Rebecca had smiled sleepily as she lay in bed listening to Sol's voice, the tones of Spain making her swoon, telling herself to keep her feet on the ground. 'We do love to take the piss out of ourselves,' she agreed.

'Yes, that's what I love so much about you. And the team in our stables, and living at Rivermont. The cities across the world are far too Americanised. I see it in the corporate people who work for my father. Especially the women. They think they must look a certain way, because they see the American glamour on the TV. They think that is the benchmark for beauty. But it's women like you, bonita, earthwoman, that make the world rich.'

Rebecca had shifted a little uncomfortably and brushed his praises away. She knew she was too rough and basic for him. In Sydney, in Paris, in Madrid, in his mother's artistic circles, he was surrounded by all those sleek beauties. She'd begun to feel a little insecure and inadequate, but what did it matter? Sol was just a friend. And that's all it could be. It was all she would allow it to be. Oblivious to Bec's thoughts running riot, Sol had kept on talking.

'A man cooking a cake wouldn't have the same undertones in the city, as being a foodie is a trend here,' Sol went on, 'but in Bendoorin, your people live in the heart of conservative farming culture. The Man Cake is a giant pun. I love it.'

Rebecca knew Amanda Arnott from the pub and Candy from the store, who had come up with the idea, were just as pleased. They were crossing the conventions of all the Country Women's Association Home Industry sections, but also breathing new life into what was a dying section of the show. Entries were up across all areas. And there was a resurgence in Home Industries across the board, as if the world was waking up to the benefits of simple country-style living. The CWA was back and basking in its renaissance. The media were lapping it up.

Just as she looked more closely at the cake, someone nudged her shoulder.

'Isn't it magnífico?' Sol was looking at her, smiling warmly. He was utterly out of place here at the country show, in his charcoal denim pants, tight black woollen skivvy with groovy silver zip at the neck and pointy Italian shoes. His black hair, which was greying slightly at the sides, was flopping over the excited shine in his dark chocolate eyes. Rebecca couldn't help but beam back at him as the kids squealed in delight to see him.

'People's Choice!' he said, indicating the ribbon. 'That is better than getting first!'

He was so lit up. It's as if he's won some prestigious orchestral music award, Bec thought, amused. 'Yes, I saw. Brilliant!'

He bear-hugged the kids, then turned so he looked directly into Bec's eyes. 'I have missed you so much, mi amigo especial.'

Rebecca baulked for a moment, glancing around the crowd. The way he delivered the words so passionately and intensely was like a performance from an Antonio Banderas love scene in a movie. His manner caught her off guard.

He pointed to his cheek. 'You must give a congratulatory kiss, for this Man Cake man, sí?' he said in his sexy accent.

Rebecca's eyes darted around the Home Industries pavilion. Should she be kissing him in this small-town public space with her boys right next to her and so soon after her husband had left? She hesitated for a little too long, uncertainty flashing on her face. Sol caught her hesitation. A look of hurt momentarily passed across his face. He narrowed his eyes at her wariness. Gently he moved the boys out of his space and back to stand beside their mother. He leaned towards her and, in a frustrated whisper, said, 'You are worried that there is more than just cake judging going on?'

His expression was that of challenge. Rebecca felt her cheeks flush from his nearness, but she still could not shake the feeling that all the other women were watching. And yes, judging. Before she could think of anything to say, the film crew was moving over, asking Sol for a quick comment about his cake and the People's Choice Award.

'Excuse me,' he said. 'My cake commitments call.' He bent and gave her a kiss anyway, and Rebecca was left standing there, wondering why she felt as if the earth had tilted suddenly and the room had just spun full circle.

Later that afternoon, eating hot chips with tomato sauce, Rebecca, Archie and Ben sat high on the grandstand watching sheep being paraded onto vibrant green lawn-look carpet for the Merino ram supreme championship ribbon of the show. Rebecca remembered the years when it was a massively prestigious event and the pavilion was packed with studs vying for the big ribbon. Nowadays, since the wool industry had taken a slide and many of the producers had switched to meat sheep production, the show had a 'has been' feel to it.

The remaining exhibitors were the true stayers of the industry. Even the younger men, in their twenties, were dressed as though they were from another era. Rebecca knew their faith and passion in the production of wool was sometimes the only thing that kept them going. Other times it was their stubborn clinging to the past and traditions. Still, the sheep that were turned out today *were* spectacular animals. The rams were standing tall and proud with curled horns; they were groomed to perfection. And, for Rebecca, there was nothing like wool and the whole process of growing it — it was the ultimate natural fibre. She had begged Charlie to keep a core mob of Merino ewes for wool instead of swapping all their enterprises over to meat sheep.

'I like that one the best,' said Ben, pointing to the ram on the end.

'He's my pick too. Take note which stud he's from. You can take on the ram buying for Mummy if you like.'

Ben looked up at her with surprise. 'But I'm too little to buy a ram!'

'Nah! If you're keen on something, it doesn't matter what age you are. I'll help you buy him if you like.'

'But Daddy wouldn't let us.'

'Oh, Daddy-schmaddy. He's not here to say what we can and can't do. Times have changed, Ben. I want you boys to make your own way on Waters Meeting if you want. It'll be all different from now on. It'll be fun. You'll see. You and Archie are in charge of the farm with me now.'

Ben's eyes slid back to the big ram on the end of the line-up and Rebecca could sense the thoughts in his mind flowing fast. His eyes looked alive with excitement. She felt his small hand reach for hers and he squeezed.

'Thank you, Mummy.'

Farming, she thought, it's in the blood. How often was it considered a curse? It was time to see the boys' heritage as a positive, not a negative. Then a cloud crossed her mind, the cloud of Charlie's words this morning: 'A lawyer will be in touch about what I get out of the farm.'

Could he not see the place was not his to own, but merely one to caretake for the next generation and so on? Waters Meeting didn't even belong to Rebecca. Andrew had made her see that concept clearly. They stood on a continent that was thirty million years old! How could anyone 'own' a patch of it? The land owned *them*. Surely Charlie could see that, and even in his greed would not distort what was best for his boys?

'Hello, MILFy,' came the cheeky voice of Joey in Bec's ear. He was sliding in beside Rebecca, sitting far too close to her and looking far too hot for his own good, in jeans, a long-sleeved white T-shirt and cowboy boots. His hair was all spiked with product, and he smelled like he'd not just sprayed but dowsed himself with Brut.

He elbowed her. 'You coming to the cocktail party later? We can do the wild thing on the dance floor if you like. I can show you my moves. Bit of bump and grind.' He waggled his eyebrows.

Bec pulled her eyes away from him and focused on the rams, one of which was about to be awarded the ribbon. The noise from the crowd had died a little as the anticipation of the moment built. Rebecca hoped the locals weren't watching her. Then she thought of Sol and her caution in even an innocent kiss. When would she stop worrying about what other people thought around here? It was as if she'd taken ten steps backwards being out like this in Bendoorin. She turned to Joey and smiled.

'I think Yazzie is keen for us to go. She's even lined up Evie as a babysitter and got me a party frock. So, I guess, we're on!'

'So we're on? Like as in a date?'

Bec tilted her head and wrinkled her nose. 'A date? If you don't mind, Joey, just a mate's date I think.'

Joey mirrored her quizzical head tilt and narrowed his eyes. A moment passed where a look of disappointment crossed his face, but then changed to his standard expression of a larrikin.

'Ooh!' he said, way too loudly. 'I think someone is over her toy boy. I think someone may have a crush on the boss man!'

'No, I don't!' Bec protested.

Joey began jabbing her in the ribs with his index fingers, teasing, 'Do so. Do so.'

'Do not! Don't be a git, Joey!'

Next he was standing and doing a happy dance, circling his arms about in front of his hips and wiggling his bottom. 'Rebecca's in lerve! Rebecca's in lerve! With her heart and *Sol*!' He clamped his hand to his chest.

'For god's sake, Joey, sit down and shut up,' said Rebecca, dragging at his arm as people turned to look, some in blank mild interest, others with amusement.

He waggled his eyebrows in the air. 'I reckon the feeling's mutual! He's been acting all funny since the day you turned up at Rivermont. Go on. Give him a go.'

'Joey! Shush!' Bec said, her cheeks colouring.

'That man's been like an older brother to me. I'm hotter of course, but it's your choice to go for an old man. I reckon it's great.' He gave her the double thumbs-up, then delivered her a big kiss on her cheek and gave each of the boys, who were now giggling profusely, a high five.

'You have one hot mama, kids!' he said to them, before turning to her, eyes bright. 'See you later, Princess Playgirl!' He winked, cocked a gun and fired it at his heart. 'She is one prowly, growly cougar!'

And with that he was gone, leaving Rebecca red-faced before the judge, who was glaring at her.

The judge clicked on the microphone with a loud clunk and in a formal voice proceeded to announce the supreme champion ram of the show.

# Thirty-two

Later that night in the sheep show pavilion, whippet-thin fashion models sashayed down the red carpet to pumping music, their cheekbones white under the bright lights, their hungry eyes hiding in shadowed hollows. The girls, shipped in from Sydney, were strutting the latest Merino creations from Australia's top fashion houses while many of the country men ogled from the crowd. Bec, who was standing next to Joey, watched him glance up from his beer.

'Some of 'em could do with a decent feed,' he said.

Rebecca was surprised. For all his flirtatiousness, she thought he'd be drooling with desire and making lascivious comments like the bulk of the men in the room. 'But they look gorgeous,' she said. 'Not like us fatty-boomba average women!' She tugged at her dress.

Joey shook his head. 'Genetic freaks, they are. Not my idea of a woman.'

He ran his hand along the sway of Rebecca's back as she stood in a silver figure-hugging stretchy, strapless dress Yazzie had lent her and in which she had felt oversized when her friend had drawn the zip closed with a determined yank.

'I love curves,' Joey said. 'And you, my cougar princess, are the most beautiful woman here. You look very sixties Bond girl. Well, at least like a Bond girl with a bun in the oven. Wait till the boss sees you!'

'Oh, shush you on the Sol thing!'

'You love it,' he teased.

Bec smiled at Joey, grateful for his companionship and compliments. Up until a few months ago, she had felt invisible to men, covered in a gauze of motherhood and domesticity. Maybe it was some pregnancy pheromone or something, but she definitely felt more attractive than she ever had before. With Joey leaning close, she glanced about, still a little uncomfortable that every single one of Charlie's mates would be watching her, maybe reporting to him on their phones. Was she being paranoid? They were, after all, just friends.

Just as she thought that, Murray wove past in the crowd. 'Being a good girl?' he asked with an accusing leer.

She just gave him an uncertain smile back.

'How's that pup going?' His tone had an edge to it. Definitely one of Charlie's allies. Not that she wanted to war with anyone.

'Yes and fine. Thank you, Muzz.'

She glanced apologetically at Joey, then excused herself and took herself off to the ladies', tip-toeing in Yazzie's heels away from the buzzing, noisy party-shed and into the darkness. She walked across the grass to an ugly grey showground toilet block. Inside, she looked at her reflection. Yazzie had styled her hair up in what she thought was a rather over-the-top pony tail — yet, looking at it now, she did think it was rather wildly sexy. She remembered what Evie had said once, about trying to be an 'observer of herself', so that life didn't just sweep her along.

As she looked at her reflection, she decided to stand outside herself and see Rebecca Saunders from that viewpoint. It was there, beneath the flickering fluoro light, with a tap dripping into a rust-stained sink, that Bec discovered, for the first time in her life, that she was beautiful.

Her inner critic had never allowed herself to see it. She had never wanted to see it. All her life she had so badly tried to fit into the world of rough, dusty farm work with the men, to be equal to her brothers, to get the same kind of recognition from her father.

That way of being, she realised now, had made her hard. Shut her down. She saw she didn't have to be so defensive and steely. It was possible to be feminine in that farming world. Memories of the star-dusted night sky at Deni came back to her. What had Joey seen in her that night that she had failed to see?

Sure she was blonde, and thanks to the farm work her pecs seemed to keep her breasts in the right place, unlike some of the less active women her age. Since kicking Charlie out, she had shed kilos, so she now had a waist that curved nicely inwards from broad, toned shoulders. A lifetime of walking the hills at Waters Meeting meant her legs were strong too. She stepped back so she could see more of them in the soap-smattered mirror. Her legs looked good in high heels. Really good. How strange she had never truly seen herself before this time. Just quick and critical glances in the mirror at all her flaws, like the freckles on her nose, the too big hips, the flubbery mummy tummy. But tonight she saw something utterly different. Turning sideways, she ran her hand over the belly swelling over her baby. Dr Patkin was very pleased with how she was progressing. He'd even said half a glass of wine wouldn't hurt on the odd occasion. She loved country doctors! As she headed back to the pavilion where the voices were getting more and more raucous, she thought one wouldn't hurt.

'There you are!' said Yazzie, rushing to her with wide eyes. Tonight the younger woman had put heavy eye shadow on and false eyelashes. The effect was dramatic and classy. She looked like a showstopper in her little red dress, with her long straight blonde hair caught up in a chic fishbone braid.

She grabbed Bec's arm and leaned towards her. 'I'm getting really pissed. Make sure you get me home to Evie's place in town and don't let me go snogging some old Merino bloke. What is it with me? I seem to only attract older men. Like Hugh Hefner-style older men. Depressing. And what is it with you and younger men? Joey has been tailing you all night!'

Bec laughed. 'You know what he's like. We're just good friends.'

'It looks as though he wants more! Sol is really getting shitty with him.'

Rebecca pulled a 'for real?' face. 'Sol?'

Yazzie nodded and pulled a 'you better believe it!' face. 'Never seen him like this.' She raised her champagne flute towards her and pointed an index finger at Rebecca. 'He's in love with you. That's what's up with him.'

'No, he's not.'

Yazzie nodded with a wobbly head like a dashboard dog's. 'Oh yes he is. He tells me everything. Everything. About his love life. The women. Normally he beds one of his favourites each time he goes overseas, or away. Got a string of "girlfriends",' she said, slopping champagne as she fingered the quote marks into the air. 'But not any more. Nah-uh. He's got it bad for you, girlfriend! He's been so depressed lately about not being able to fess up about his love to the vun vooman! Now he love-a you, baby! He's been celibate for months …'

Rebecca didn't know what to say. She knew their phone calls had built a connection between them, but not once did she believe Sol would fall for *her* in the way Yazzie implied. But now after tonight, and what she had seen deep within herself, she realised maybe it was possible. She deserved to be loved by the best of men. Still, standing before Yazzie, she blocked the notion.

'In love with a pregnant soon-to-be divorcee? He needs to get a life!' she said, trying to fob off what Yazzie had drunkenly confessed. 'So, where is the broody Spanish bastard anyway?' Bec asked, trying to sound distant and tough.

Yazzie shrugged. 'Probably getting as smashed as me. It's in the Stanton genes to lay low, then have a giant bender.'

With the fashion parade and formalities out of the way, the music was turned on and Ricky Martin boomed through the pavilion.

Yazzie grabbed at Bec's arm. 'Dance! C'mon, dance!'

Bec smiled and shook her head. 'No.'

'God! You're so serious!' Yazzie sulked. 'And so sober! I wish Gabs was here. I need someone to get shamelessly, titlessly shitfaced with.'

'Yazzie! That's so not like you!'

'Yeah, well, I'm a bit over it.'

'You? Why?'

Yazzie shrugged again. 'You know.'

'I know,' Bec said as she watched a cloud of grief pass through Yazzie's eyes. Even though she had never really talked about the babies, Yazzie knew Rebecca understood. There was an unmentioned thread between them. The women pulled each other into a hug and they stood there for a time, still and silent as the party swirled around them. When they pulled apart, Bec looked empathetically at Yazzie and she reflected back a sad but grateful face.

'I love you,' Yazzie said. 'You have no idea what you and the boys bring to me. No idea.'

Rebecca breathed in that very generous, heartfelt statement and smiled tearily. 'You too, babe. You too. Now!' She cleared her throat, then grabbed Yazzie by the cheeks and squeezed her lips into a fish-face. 'You're getting us both pissed and emotional! Come on. You just need a root. Let's go man-shopping,' she said, hooking her arm and sweeping her free hand out to encompass the expanse of suit-clad men in the room. 'Which one tickles your fancy?'

'It's your fancy that needs tickling!'

'But I'm up the duff. No man would want to tickle my fancy while I'm in this condition.'

'Who said?'

Bec shrugged.

'That's the best time. My ex-husband loved it when I was pregnant.'

A hundred questions flashed in Bec's mind about Yazzie's past life as a mum and married woman. 'Who was he?'

'A coward. And a bounder.' Yazzie spun on her heels, subject closed. 'C'mon, let's get this party started!' She took off, headed for the DJ.

Left alone suddenly, Bec scanned the room. There was no sign of Joey. She smiled. How strange her life felt at the moment. So many new territories to explore in her mind and in her world. Her tumble of good thoughts was momentarily halted when she caught sight of Janine in a far-too-tight, far-too-short black dress with her back to her husband, flirting loudly with the local stock agent and the eldest boy from the Clarkson Merino stud.

Bec turned away from her and spotted Candy and Doreen, who were tucking into the bruschetta platters. She was about to head over to talk to the women when she saw Sol near the show committee office. From what she could tell, he had bailed up Sam Kekovich and was waving his cake around as much as he was waving his expressive Spanish hands. Sam was clearly enjoying his beer and the entertaining drunken display by Sol. But the fact remained his car was leaving and the members of the show committee were hovering. Rebecca began to make her way towards them as Sam Kekovich was ushered away. She could now tell Sol was trying to offer his chop cake to Sam to take with him. She'd never seen him drunk before. There was something volatile about his energy.

'He does not want to teke mi ceke,' Sol said, his accent enriched by red wine. 'What is so wrong with mi ceke?'

'It's not exactly ideal carry-on luggage for a plane. Let it go, Sol. You're drunk.' She grimaced a smile at him. The Bendoorin cocktail party was renowned for once-a-year benders by the most unlikely in a crowd. This year it was the Stantons' turn to write themselves off.

'And you are flirting with that buffoon, Joey,' said Sol with a jealous flash of his dark eyes.

'I am not!' Then Rebecca began to giggle.

'What? Why you laff?'

She covered her mouth and sniggered louder, looking wide-eyed with amusement at Sol. 'You said *buffoon*.'

Sol pulled his eyebrows downwards and almost pouted. 'Here!' he said. 'You take mi pastel.'

'I don't want your cake.'

'You don't want mi ceke?'

'No. You *buffoon*.'

Their eyes met and a spark of amusement fired between them. Soon they were smiling at each other.

'I'm sorry,' he said. 'You have unbalanced me.'

'Me? I'd say it was the red wine that did that. I've done nothing.'

'Nothing but be beyond beautiful, Rebecca, and torture my mind every night,' he said, lowering his tone and stepping towards her, his eyes flaring passion. He dropped his cake onto a nearby table displaying wool and took her arm. 'Ven comigo.'

There was something intoxicating about the depth of his voice and the way he spoke. Rebecca felt goose bumps shimmy across her skin. She allowed him to lead her by the hand away from the noise of the party, out a side door of the shed. There, Sol gently spun her around and pressed her back up against the corrugated-iron wall. In the soft glow of the light that spilled from the shed, she could see the passion alive in his eyes.

'Why do you not want me?' he asked, so close his breath brushed her lips.

'I do want you,' she whispered. 'It's just that it's too soon.'

'Too soon? And what does Evie say about living for now?'

She looked up at his beautiful dark-skinned face. The manliness of him was softened by an intoxicating vulnerability.

She didn't want to fall in love. Not yet. Not now. Not when the scars hadn't healed and not with another man's baby growing inside her.

'Please, Rebecca.'

When he said her name that way, she felt her knees weaken and her resolve melt away.

She turned her face towards him and pulled him nearer. Then their lips met and Bec swam in the moment. Drunk on her desire for him. Body pressed against him. Arms about his neck, breath coming like sighs, she pulled away, a pleading expression furrowing her brow. 'This can't work.'

He took her face in his hands. 'But why? We can make it work. I will make it work.'

'I can't.'

'But why?' he murmured as he stooped to brush kisses across the taut skin of her neck.

'You know. Because of this.' She gestured to her belly. 'It's Charlie's baby.' She delivered the words to the night sky, thinking they would dispel this moment with Sol. Thinking the reminder of the reality would shut him off to her. Like shooting a cannon into the void, Bec was hoping that he would realise his drunken rationale was utterly flawed.

Sol stopped his kissing. He pulled back and looked searchingly into her face. A frown on his brow and a million thoughts running behind his dark eyes. 'Yes, you are carrying another man's baby. So? And why is this a reason?'

'What?'

He ran his hand over her belly where her baby grew. He held the palm of his hand there and Rebecca felt its heat. Slowly a smile grew on his face. 'Rebecca, do you not understand? This baby is part of you. I will love this baby too. As I love Ben and Archie.'

Rebecca looked at him, puzzled, doubt cast on her face.

Sol grabbed her gently by her shoulders and stooped to look into her eyes. 'Do you not see? After what we have been through with Abby and Nicholas, this is a gift. Why would you let this stop what the universe wants?'

It was the first time Rebecca had heard Yazzie's babies' names spoken. It fired a spark of pain in her heart and a realisation that life ought to be lived for now, as he said. Compassion for Sol and astonishment at his reaction fuelled her desire for him. She looked up into his eyes. She saw him openly, with none of her guards up, for the first time since her break-up with Charlie. Live for the moment, she told herself and the moment felt good. Unstoppable. She leaned into him and reached her hand around the back of his head, feeling the soft richness of the short dark curls on the nape of his neck. She pulled his head down gently to meet hers, their foreheads touching gently, resting on one another. Their breath hastening with passion as they pressed their mouths together.

At first the kisses were soft. The divine strong lips of a piccolo player. Rebecca felt he was breathing her alive with those lips. She kissed him harder as she slid her hand down his back, grabbing his tight backside, pulling him closer. A thrill ran through her when the weight of her own body was answered with the press of his. Rebecca ran her hand to the open neck of his shirt, where she felt the solidity of his chest rising and falling with desire. As she consumed the feeling of him, she relished Sol's touch, his hands and fingertips running over her already goose-bumped shoulders, brushing past her breast, tantalisingly, then down over the curve of her waist and thigh. He's playing me beautifully, like an instrument, she thought.

'You are cold,' he said in a whispered hoarse voice that was as sexy as the night.

'C'mon,' Bec said. 'Let's find somewhere warmer.'

She led him by the hand. In the pitch black of the night, she could see an old truck parked nearby, its bent pipe frame covered by a blue tarp. Inside there was fresh, loose, warm-smelling straw, ready and waiting for the morning, when the Merino ewes and rams would be carted away by the Clarkson stud.

She could see Sol's breath coming quickly; it was mist in

the dull sheen of the lights of the pavilion. As they leaned into one another, arms about each other's waists, they were soon swallowed by the darkness. She kicked off her high heels, raised her silver dress a little at the thighs, then with strong forearms boosted herself onto the truck tray. Turning, she offered a hand to Sol, and helped haul him up.

Pressed together, kissing all the while, they reached for each other. She unbuckling his belt and sliding down his pants, he hooking a finger along the elastic of her knickers and gently sliding them down.

He spread out his jacket for her, clasped his large hands about her waist and lifted her onto the ledge of some hay bales stacked at the front of the truck for the sheep. His mouth traced kisses from her earlobes and along the smooth plane of her neck. As he did, he reached to find the warm wetness of her and pushed a finger inside, causing her to moan and her back to arch. She threw her head back, eyes shut, but senses open to the rich smell of fresh straw and hay, the feel of his fingers deep within her and the drape of the cold night air across her skin. In that moment, she was filled with all the joys of living. She reached to find him, her hand clasping the smooth warm skin of his penis. He was decently sized and she delighted in this fact.

After more than ten years of marriage to Charlie, after so many years in the mundanity of home territory, touching Sol's body felt like the exploration of another country. Completely foreign to her, but exotic, beautiful, even dangerous. Rock hard, he entered her, and from both escaped soft moans of desire washed with relief. They pulled each other into a mutual warmth. As Sol began to thrust into her rhythmically, she answered back with gentle little noises of pleasure.

There were three of them here tonight: Sol, Rebecca and her child within. Rebecca thought it would feel grubby or inappropriate, but here, now, it felt nothing but right. It felt like pure, universal love. It felt like beauty. Her body surprised her as it rushed its way to orgasm. As Sol followed suit, she enjoyed the gentle waves of pleasure like a surfer's perfect set and she failed to stifle a giggle at her own visual cliché. Sol too let out a deep chuckle as he nuzzled into her, still breathing hard.

'Our first time,' he said. 'In a sheep truck. And afterwards you laff. This I will remember. You are so beautiful, Rebecca.' He smiled and kissed her tenderly on the lips.

Never with a man had she felt so happy and so … worshipped. They reluctantly pulled apart and began to help each other rearrange disordered clothes. When they were presentable, Sol lifted her down from the truck. His hands about her waist again felt good. She reached up towards him and laid a palm against his cheek.

'Thank you,' Bec said.

'For what?'

'It's been a long time between drinks.'

Sol laughed gently and kissed her softly on the cheek. 'I am happy I could help. There is plenty more, should you wish,' he said. 'But for now we had better get back to the party. Yazzie is messing herself up tonight. Worse than me.'

'I know.'

He took her hand and held it up, kissing the back of it, playfulness and desire still roaming in his eyes. 'You are special, my beautiful woman. Come.'

He led her back towards the shed, and for a moment Bec felt as if she was walking on air.

But suddenly in the dark, under a solitary spotlight, Janine Turner stood before them. She had her arms wrapped about her body, mascara clouding darkly beneath her eyes. Rebecca was shocked to see her there in the damp of the night, glaring at her.

'Slut,' Janine said angrily, stomping towards them. 'You made him leave me!'

Bec held up her hands as if to calm her. 'Janine, you're pissed. I don't want some ugly scrag fight with you. Let's just let it lie.'

But it was too late. Janine had been fuelling her demons with straight vodka all night. She was like a machine gun ready to fire, and Rebecca was her target at point-blank range. 'Fucking slut!' she screamed as she came rushing towards Rebecca.

'Leave her!' Sol said commandingly, as if he was addressing a dog. His words only seemed to incense her.

Janine clamoured at Rebecca, her false nails clawing at her chest and arms. Hysteria raised her voice to an ugly pitch. 'Slut! He was right! Charlie was right. Now we know where your bastard baby's come from!' she said, turning her contorted face towards Sol. 'And now Charlie's gone. All because of you, you bitch. You sent him away from me! He's gone now! All because of *you!*'

Bec grabbed Janine's arms and tried to push her away, shocked by the moment and stunned by the sudden hit, followed by the torrent of Janine's rage.

From behind, Sol was suddenly dragging her attacker away. He was shouting something aggressively to Janine in Spanish. He turned her to face him. 'Stop this! Now go!' he said forcefully. 'Go back to your husband. Stop humiliating yourself, or do I have to slap sense into you?'

'Piss off, you rich prick!' slurred the lost, drunken woman as she pushed Sol in the chest and lunged again at Rebecca. 'I'll kill her!'

Rebecca felt an energy stir within. She'd had enough. Grabbing Janine with the vice-strong grip of a farm girl, Rebecca held her at arm's length and bored her furious gaze into Janine's eyes. 'Back off, Janine!' She said the words through clenched teeth, the rage in her seething. 'Can't you see, Charlie was just using you? He's an arsehole. He screwed around on me. He'll screw around on you. He shot my animals and left, and he fucked you and left. God, Janine. Wake up to yourself! Forget about him. And leave me out of your own miserable crap!'

The words were enough to deflate Janine entirely. She wouldn't look at Bec, but she drew back from her. Sobbing, she turned and swayed away into the darkness, in drunken tragic S-bends. From a little distance away, Rebecca heard Janine shout back at them, 'I don't know why you're bothering, Mr Stanton! Charlie told me she's a dud in bed. And a dud farmer's wife!'

'Go!' Sol roared back as the flak from the encounter began to smart in Rebecca's mind.

Sol put his arm around her shoulders. 'Are you all right, my princess? Did she hurt you? Come, let me see in the light. There is blood where she has scratched you. Oh, princess.'

But Rebecca was shaking now. *Princess?* her mind roared. Just that word seemed to make her hackles rise in an instant. What was she to him? Another conquest on his world tour of women? After all she had been through on her own on Waters Meeting? After surviving all that she had? She felt herself stiffen. She wasn't any man's princess. She pushed his arm away from her, fury rising again from somewhere deep within. 'Princess? You call me a princess,' she said, the shock of Janine's ambush tumbling inside her. She shook her head in confusion, as if trying to shake all the pieces of what was going on here into place. Defiantly she chose to ignore the look of compassion on Sol's face. Instead the memory of being trodden down by the men in her life surfaced. Angrily the words came up unconsciously. 'I don't need you to protect me. And I certainly don't need you to call me princess. The last thing I want or need is a man. Now leave me alone. This can't work, Sol. Not now. *Not ever.*'

And in her silver dress, that echoed the cold distance of the stars, Rebecca began to jog away into the night, barefoot across the showgrounds towards Evie's house, the straps of her high heels hooked on her index finger, tears of anger swelling in her eyes. Berating herself for dropping her guard with Sol. Beating herself up for allowing herself to be sucked back into the complexity of that frightening world of relationships with men. All she wanted to do was to hold her Archie and Ben, and leave this mess of a night behind her. She should have known better.

# Thirty-three

Smoke from the various fires in the pub car park rose into the clear evening sky. Charlie squatted before his own smoky fire, tongs in one hand, beer in another. He loved the annual Bush Tucker Cooking Competition that the town held every year out the back of the pub. He took a swig from his can, poked at the aluminium-foil package that was nestled in the coals and looked up. 'Reckon we should turn her yet?'

He was referring to the dead wood pigeon that Grunter Davies had hit with a thunk on his way to work yesterday. Knowing it was the eve of the Bush Tucker Cooking Comp, Grunter had gleefully placed the bird in his smoko Esky, along with his lamingtons and chicken loaf sandwiches. He had set the Esky in the ute cab, then, after he had parked his substantial arse on his tractor, promptly phoned around to see who wanted to be on his cook-up team.

Charlie Lewis was an obvious choice. He never said no to a beer. But Grunter knew they needed a woman on the team. Grunter couldn't cook. He left that to the missus. And he knew old Mrs 'Pantyhose Pedantic' Lewis had done everything for Charlie out on their property, bar wipe her husband and sons' arses, so chances were Charlie couldn't cook much either.

Grunter had wracked his brain for a local woman who might know how to make a dead wood pigeon taste reasonable. A couple of rounds of the wheat field on the tractor with the spray rig and Grunter had suddenly thought of Chatelle Frost. Chatelle had moved back to town, freshly divorced, and was living in the old rectory with three rug rats under six. He'd put the calls in straight away and both Charlie and Chatelle had been keen.

Now here they were, Grunter, Charlie and Chatelle, all clustered round the fire, hoping the judges would like the taste of their 'double-smoked (roadkill) wood pigeon, wrapped in smoky prosciutto with a native pepperberry sauce'.

'Yeah, sure, Basil, toss her over,' said Grunter, scratching at his bald head under his CAT cap and draining his stubby.

'No! Not yet!' said Chatelle as she glanced at her watch. 'It needs another ten.'

'Great! That's another beer's worth.' Charlie grinned as he lobbed his empty into a nearby forty-four that was already filled to overflowing with the drinking efforts of the other master chefs of the district. 'Another beer, Grunter?'

'A man's not a camel, mate. Of course another beer.'

'And another Cougar?' Charlie asked Chatelle. She nodded, flicking a wisp of thin fair hair out of her dark brown eyes and smiling at him. She stood before him in dogger boots, skinny jeans and a padded flannelette jacket of blue check with a black scarf cast about her neck. Charlie thought again how little she had changed since primary school. She was still pretty in a local kind of way. The sleeves of her jacket were too long and her small hands looked delicate as she rattled her nearly empty can. For a moment Charlie thought of Rebecca crumpled on the floor of the Waters Meeting kitchen, blood and snot smeared across her face, her hair sticking out wild like a shrew's. He shut out the sight of her in his mind's eye and swigged his beer. All that surliness for all those years. She'd asked for it.

This Chatelle, though, she was all right. She had less of a

brain in her head than Rebecca. She'd be easier to handle, less complicated.

And with three kids to keep her occupied, she'd be less of a worry than Janine, who had nothing better to do than send him irritating 'come back to me' texts. He blocked the women of his past out of his mind. Time for another beer, he thought, and one for the little lady. She was a bit of a tiger, this one, he suspected. He felt his mood lift as he connected with Chatelle's inviting stare.

'I never say no to another drink. Thanks, Basil.' Her voice was as light as a bell. Very girlie, he thought. Nicely girlie. His childhood sweetheart was back in his sights after all these years. He remembered the kiss in the bag room in grade six after the Nativity Play … he a Wise King, she one of the sheep.

As he sauntered to the makeshift bar set-up under the fire-escape steps of the large old wooden pub, Charlie took time to stop in at the other competitors' fires. The teams of three were busy with an array of bush tucker, while bystanders stood about chatting with them and drinking.

One team was slow-roasting wombat in wine in a giant heavy black camp oven. Another was doing a wallaby fricassee on a bed of wild rice.

Most of the recipes took many hours of slow cooking, so the drinking and culinary supervision had begun early that morning as campfires were built, onions chopped, garlic crushed and coals coaxed to the right temperatures. The last team to arrive to join the comp was the Farnell family, who was cooking yabbies in a wild herb sauce. They were rather churchy non-drinkers, but didn't seem to mind the ribbing they got from the well-oiled cooking crews at their late arrival.

By dinnertime, the dishes would be laid out on trestle tables under the gleam of spotlights in the pub car park for the entire town to taste-test and vote on. They would gingerly pick at the possum and wombat, devour the roast duck and sniff at the camel and wild pig steaks.

Then most would baulk at the snake pie that Skegsie Wilson had cooked. Skegsie had shot the giant King Brown in his kitchen, blasting a hole through the floor, the sudden boom of the shotgun scaring the kids and wife more than the snake had. There was still some shot in the pie, so the dish came with a warning.

Charlie hadn't been to the boozy bush tucker event in years, but he was relishing his time back at home. Even though his mum got on his nerves, it felt so good to be back eating three square meals a day, with the flashest smoko in the district thrown in. Plus everything was in order at his mum's house. It made him feel ... more settled? More cared for? More at home? What was it about Bec and her lack of ability to keep a house? It had always grated on him. Sure she could move a mob, but she was crap at vacuuming.

Even though his mum fussed, he knew she meant well. Bec, on the other hand, hadn't given a fat rats about him. Especially since the boys had arrived. Had he merely been the sperm donor? She'd got what she'd wanted, then nagged him to turn his sperm taps off for good. Charlie sighed. It was such a relief to be home. Sure there were times when he missed the kids, a missing that on some nights caused a hollow ache in his belly. But during the day, he mostly felt anger. He wished Bec would stop sending their paintings and their scribbled letters to him. Opening them only opened up wounds he didn't even know how to begin to heal. But each time he missed them, he'd down a beer and reason with himself that he'd never seen the boys much anyway. They were Bec's domain. They didn't really need him, so it was best he came home.

His mum wasn't the only one pleased to see him. Even though his dad said little, Charlie could tell he was excited to have him back. He had laid out all the plans for the place on the kitchen table the second night when Charlie announced he was staying, possibly for good. Maps, notes, paddock plans. Mr Lewis had shown Charlie the next paddock rotation for ploughing, spraying and cropping for the cereals. It was a relief for Charlie to settle back into the comfort of the old system. It was one his dad worked like clockwork from year to year on the farm.

Even though his parents were utter squares and rarely mixed with the locals, Charlie loved the fact that the town was so near to their place. He could have Friday-night drinks with ease. Unlike the isolation of Waters Meeting, where there was only the cricket club and the Fur Trapper within a reasonable drink-driving distance. Here there was a social life on tap, whether it be golf-club functions, the RSL bar, the pub, the sports ground or pissy barbecues on other farms.

His party persona was being well received tonight and he was enjoying chatting to many of his fellow chefs en route to the bar, people he hadn't seen in years. As he did, he felt his phone in his pocket vibrate and he excused himself from the Johnsons, who were turning a hare on a spit. He fished the phone out and leaned on the steel upright of the fire escape. It was a message from Muzz. A photo was attached.

A picture of Rebecca. He recognised the place as Bendoorin Show, as he could see flowers and cakes in the background with show ribbons. In the photo, Sol Stanton was leaning into Rebecca, looking as if he was about to kiss her. It was an innocent enough shot. There were other people around them and he could see the tops of the boys' heads, standing near Sol, but what hit him hard in the stomach was the look in Rebecca's eyes. It was a look he hadn't seen in years. In her eyes, there was love. Desire.

He read Muzz's text: *Private Investigator Murray at your service. Your ex-missus playing the field here!*

Charlie cleared his throat and shut his eyes as he absorbed the image of his ex-wife gazing up at another man. Ex-wife? He wondered at what point he had started thinking of her as an ex-wife? The photo had hurt. He flinched a little, then stood up tall. Resolutely he flicked Murray a text back: *Thanks for that, mate. Keep an eye on her. She tarts about. The more dirt the better for the lawyers.*

He hated himself as he pressed the send button, but at the same time he felt a fury rise within. So Sol was the father of the baby? Rich bastard. If that was the case, Charlie vowed bitterly, he would take her for all she was worth. With determination, he strode to the bar, ordered, then, with the drinks in hand, made a beeline back to Chatelle and passed her the can of Cougar. Tonight, he promised himself, there was no backing down.

By three am the campfires were almost cold and the party at the pub had moved from the car park to the bar. Not content with the jukebox, Charlie wanted to drive the party harder. He knew he had Chatelle on a string, but she could wait. He was tanked to the eyeballs and having fun. When he had wavered outside to the pub verandah to take a piss, he found just the party prop he was looking for. With drunken determination, he grabbed the lawn mower, lugged it through the back doors and up the rickety stairs to the first floor of the hotel, where he knew the rankest orange shag-pile carpet lay. It drooped with dust and was crusted with god-only-knew what. It could do with a tidy-up, he thought wickedly, knowing his audience would follow. When the drinkers had seen Charlie Lewis was up to his tricks, when he passed the bar pushing a lawn mower, they let out a cheer.

By the time he had dragged the mower up the stairs and reefed the starter cord a few times, the people in the bar were loping up the stairs too, laughing, egging him on. As two-stroke fumes filled the upstairs pub hallway, Charlie gave a whoop and began to mow the shag pile down the length of the corridor.

'Lookin' a bit long,' he called over his shoulder, through the choking fug of dust, fumes and fibre. By the time the publican had made it upstairs to put an end to the whole scene, half the corridor had been mown.

'Basil effing Lewis!' he yelled, then shook his head. 'Cut it out!'

'Huh?' said Charlie over the droning engine.

'I said cut it!'

Charlie pointed to the carpet. 'But I am cutting it!'

The publican drew a line across his throat. 'Cut it!'

Charlie turned off the mower. 'I was doing you a favour, mate,' he said, leaning on the mower handle. 'Your carpet was getting way out of hand. I can do the edges if you like? Bit of a trim up here. Bit there.'

The publican rolled his eyes and flicked his head in the direction of the bar. 'Everyone, downstairs. *Now!* Otherwise we're shut and you're all out. Bloody oath, Charlie Lewis, who let you back in town?'

Like schoolkids, the drunken punters stomped back down the stairs, still chuckling. Except for Charlie, who stayed, leaning on the mower, his eyes locked on Chatelle. Chatelle, who had her back pressed against the crooked hallway wall, did not look away. She remained there, her eyes just as devilish as Charlie's. Both wore soft seductive smiles. Charlie moved over to one of the hotel-room doors and tried the loose brass knob, his eyes never once leaving hers. The door swung open. He glanced in and nodded.

'Yep,' he said, 'I knew it. It's a double.' He entered the room, knowing that Chatelle Frost would certainly follow.

# Thirty-four

Rebecca held up a bedraggled threadbare sock and looked down to the pile of missing pairs that lay scattered on the couch like an unsolved riddle. She couldn't help but think resentfully that Charlie's mother would be at home pairing socks for him, so he was free to play.

'What gets me is that no matter what, they always go missing,' she said to Ben and Archie, who were scoffing toast at the kitchen table and playing with two Vegemite-smeared plastic dinosaurs.

'Maybe there's a sock monster,' Ben suggested.

'And the sock monster eats them,' added Archie.

'Maybe he does,' said Bec. She threw down the sock. 'Oh, I give up. They look so sad and lonely on their own. I think I'll just start all over again.'

She gathered up the worst-looking of the single socks, stepping over the purple plastic vacuum cleaner where it lay like a sleeping Doctor Who beast on the floor. She made her way to the woodstove in the kitchen, thinking that the awful vacuum cleaner had been a Mother's Day present from Charlie and the boys. When she had opened it, she couldn't help but take offence from the gift.

Number one, it seemed to be another message from Charlie that she was not keeping the house to his liking, and number two, she hated housework. Not so much because of the work, but because of the catalogue of lack that stomped about her head when she did it. How the old house was falling down around her. How there were never enough hours in the day. What Charlie had or hadn't done out on the farm. How she was stuck inside the house in a constant round of mess that was not only created by the boys, but by them all. There was always a scattering of clutter, complete with an assortment of mismatching items like bale twine, old Icy Pole wrappers, rubber bands and cast-off dirty clothes. She knew she used the children as an excuse, but in truth, after talking at length with Evie and Yazzie about it, she realised she had a mental block. The more she focused on the mess, the more the mess came. The more negativity she allowed in, the more it came.

The women had asked Doreen Groggan to come and clean for Rebecca. Then, most importantly, Evie suggested getting Bec to think differently about the house. Bec had at first baulked at spending the money on Doreen, but was now mindful of how negative she had been. As she reefed open the old woodstove and threw the tumble of single socks into the flames as a symbolic defiant gesture, she realised she was blocking the flow of her life again. What was fifty bucks a fortnight? And what was wrong with spending money on some new socks for the kids? The agent was coming out today to finalise the value and photograph all the machinery for sale in a traders' magazine and on the net. After next week, she'd have some cash coming in.

To top it off, the weather was starting to warm and if the rains came, the rested pastures were sure to take off better than if they had been subjected to the old grazing regime. As she clunked the woodstove shut, she swore, then rolled her eyes wryly at herself. There she went again with another grumble to add to her catalogue of complaints. The fire door was *still* unhinged. Each and every time she opened it, she thought of Charlie.

'Please would you fix this?' she'd asked him over and over. But he never did. The old girl's door seals had gone and she chewed through far too much wood as a result, trickling bright orange coals occasionally out onto the hearth that would slowly blacken and eventually die out, leaving more mess for Rebecca to sweep up. To top it all off, Charlie was not at all good at getting wood. He would bring it in in dribs and drabs, not like Gabs's Frank, who cut walls of the stuff and stacked it around the house in a sweeping towering bend as if a king's army was coming to raid them.

'C'mon,' she muttered to herself. 'You're not fucking Cinderella stuck in a rut.' If things weren't right here at Waters Meeting, she no longer had Charlie to blame. She only had herself to move and shake. She reached up for a dusty old pillar candle and set it on a plate. Just then the baby kicked inside her and her hand flew to the area beneath her navel. She smiled.

'Hello,' she said, stroking the taut skin of her belly. She felt she was struggling this morning. Tears had been coming easily and she felt utterly exhausted. She wondered how on earth she would cope.

She lit the candle with a fizzing match. Ben looked up.

'What are you doing, Mum?'

'This is my housework positivity candle. Every time I look at this flame, I am going to say to myself, "I get through the housework with ease and grace and joy!"' She waved her arms about. 'I am done with being angry about everything! It's just going to get done. And I'm going to remind myself of all the good things every time I start to grumble about a bad thing. Man, this stuff takes practice!'

'I'll help you,' offered Ben excitedly, clearing his plate.

'Good man,' she said. 'I'll fill the sink. Ben, you wash. Arch, you can dry.'

Archie looked pleased that he was being given a job. He ran to get a little old milking stool to stand on.

'Mum?'

'Mmm? Yes, Arch?'

'When can we see Daddy?'

Rebecca stopped folding the washing for a moment.

'Soon. I promise. I'll call him. Maybe we can go visit Grandma and Grandpa.'

'Grandma Fuss-pants or Grandma Vet?' asked Ben.

'Grandma Fuss-pants.'

'Oh.' Ben took up the dishwashing brush and gingerly tested the water temperature. 'Why is Daddy on Grandpa's farm and not here on our farm?'

'Because Daddy's brother has married and moved away, and they now need Daddy to help out.'

Satisfied for the moment, the boys fell silent. Bec smiled sadly at them. She felt awful for them that Charlie never called. She wondered if she *should* take a trip out west so the boys could see their dad. Or would it just unsettle them? It was so hard to know what was the right thing to do for them. Rebecca sent up a silent prayer for the boys' future, hoping she could buffer them from the storm that might come with Charlie's push for a divorce and property split.

'Bus time soon, Ben. You ready to go?'

Ben nodded.

With the boys doing a very dodgy job of washing up, Rebecca left them in their happy state. She gathered up the last piles of washing to take up to the bedrooms, glancing at the candle for mental support before she tackled the stairs. As she climbed with the folded washing towering in a basket, her thoughts once again, for the umpteenth time, roamed to Sol and the night of the show and the terrible way she'd stormed away from him.

It had been a week and she hadn't had the chance to see him again. He had only called once and the conversation had been brief. Traffic noises were in the background and he'd had to shout for her to hear.

'My driver's just pulled up,' he had said, 'I have to go. I want to see you again. But if you need more time ...' Then the phone had cut out.

The following day, as she was tossing kitchen scraps to the chooks, she'd heard a vehicle coming along the winding Waters Meeting track. An express delivery van emerged. The driver spotted Rebecca at the chook shed. She raised a hand in greeting, so he swung on the wheel and the van bumped over the tufted pastures of the house paddock, pulling up before her. A short bald man as round as he was tall in high-vis orange got out and passed her a clipboard, asking her to sign. She'd wiped her hands on her jeans before she took the pen from him, frowning at this bizarre occurrence. Delivery trucks *never* made it this far unless big bucks were involved for something essential for the farming operations.

'You've come a long way,' Bec had said.

'Tell me about it.' He made his way around the side of the van. She heard the sliding door being reefed open, then slammed shut. When he emerged again, he was carrying in his arms the largest bunch of flowers Bec had ever seen. He handed them to her.

'Someone must friggin' love ya,' he'd said, before muttering something else, getting in his van, slamming the door and driving away.

Rebecca had stood breathing in the beautiful perfume of soft pink and white roses. She felt tears prickle in her eyes. How long had it been since she had been given flowers? She set down the chook bucket and reached for the note. It had been written by the florist, but it read: *Sorry. Had to dash to Paris. Orchestra work there. Back by Christmas. Thank you for a very special night. Love, Sol.*

Now, putting the clothes away, seeing her flowers softening in their vase on her dressing table, she smiled sadly. Of course he had gone again. He was never still. He was either called away by his father, or chasing his dreams with the orchestra. And away two months! *Two months!* It wasn't a long time to wait, but by the time Sol came back she would be only weeks off having the baby! Not an ideal time to be trying to foster a new love affair. She almost cried at the impossibility of it, then remembered that *she* had sent *him* away. Plus there was her pledge to herself about positivity. Until she sorted that out, there would be no room for a man in her life. Suddenly she chose to laugh at how ridiculous her mess of a life had become.

She knew she was attracted to Sol, but he was so different from any man she had ever known. His idiosyncrasies and foreign ways freaked her out a little. Not only were there the cultural differences, but he seemed so 'citified' at times. He was so genteel in his speech, mannerisms and clothing that sometimes Bec felt she was more bloke than he. And he played *piccolo* in an *orchestra*. In her earlier days, she would've taken one look at him and muttered the word 'poof'. How she had changed!

She was now feeling so much more open to the world. With Sol, a whole new unknown life could open up for her. A thrilling life that she had never even conceived as possible. Not because of the lavishness he could offer, but because it would be so different from all that she had ever known.

She recalled that on the night of the Bendoorin Show, delicious though it had been, and as tender with his words as he had been, he had been pretty drunk. When she hadn't heard from him the next day, after her grumpy exit, she thought maybe she had burned a bridge. Maybe he thought of her as too raw and damaged after a separation from a long marriage, and their encounter should merely remain as a one-night stand? But now the flowers? At great expense. But what was expense to a Stanton? She wondered if Yazzie knew what had happened between her and Sol that night. Maybe she should talk to her?

She threw Archie's and Ben's washing into a chest of drawers that was covered in stickers from her own childhood and now joined by a more modern collection of her boys'. Once she'd got Ben on the school bus, she'd call Yazzie.

Hastily she rammed the drawers shut just as she heard Funny barking in the garden below. Frowning, she looked out the window. The pup, her ears pricked, was trotting to the garden gate just as a white ute pulled up in the farmyard. Another rare surprise visitor. And typically, it was right on bus time. But who was it?

She made her way downstairs, opened the back door and was surprised to see Andrew Travis stooping to greet Funny as he opened the garden gate. Smiling, he walked along the path towards Rebecca and dropped a large canvas bag at his feet on the verandah.

'Here I am!' He held his arms out in greeting.

Rebecca didn't have time to disguise the surprise and also the delight on her face. He looked extra good, with his salt-and-pepper hair freshly trimmed, and his blue RM Williams shirt tucked neatly into his chocolate-brown workman's jeans with hips framed by a thick stockman's hobble belt.

'Hello! What brings you all the way out here?'

He rolled his eyes, eyes that beautifully mirrored the blue of his shirt. 'Typical RLM! They have me scheduled to do a series of talks and field days in the region.'

'Yes,' Bec said, 'I saw on the email you were coming.'

'But they forgot to book me into the Dingo Trapper. I turn up and Dutchy has closed all the rooms for renovations.'

'Renovations?'

'Apparently mining's on its way. Old Barry Clarkson caved in and has given up his land. Dutchy knows he'll get a tonne more business if he fixes up the old pub rooms a bit.'

'What? Mining?' Rebecca looked up at the sky. It was finally happening.

'Yep.' Andrew shook his head. 'Coal. It's a travesty.'

Rebecca felt a rumble of disquiet filter through her. She knew the mining industry was gradually creeping out into the better agricultural areas and the geos had been sniffing around for years. But now they'd got a hold here. Her blood ran cold.

In other regions, she found mining on food-producing land so upsetting that she often took the longer route to the city just to avoid looking at earth that was being carved up and tumbled through crushers and into smelters. For what? For people's insatiable need for bigger and better. For blind greed.

'Long and the short of it is,' Andrew continued, 'I've got no place to stay for the next couple of nights. I could stay in Bendoorin like I did last night, but most of the work is this side of the mountain. Would you mind?'

A smile grew on Bec's face. 'Not at all. I'd love the company.'

As she stooped to pick up his bag, he put his hand over hers and stopped her. 'Now look here, young missy, you're not carrying my bags for me! How about you let someone help you for a change? I'll carry that in and then you can show me where the kettle is and I'm going to make you a cuppa. Then you can show me where the woodpile is. There's a big cold snap coming through. It'll be cold in November, especially up here.'

'I'm afraid it's school-bus time, so my cuppa will have to wait. I've got to run Bennie to the main drag.'

'Can I take him for you? Run him out in the RLM ute?'

Rebecca looked into his eyes. His outburst of kindness sparked emotion in her. Suddenly she felt her body relax a little and when she did, she realised just how leaden with exhaustion she really was. 'That would be such a help. Yes. Please.'

Andrew saw the tears rise in her eyes. He frowned at her in sympathy. 'Looks as if you need a bit of help and a bit of a hug.'

'I'm right. Tough as old boots. And I've had so much help already.'

Andrew stooped and shook his head, searching her face. 'The truth.'

She cast her eyes downwards. 'I am a little overwhelmed. Yes,' she admitted quietly.

'Plus a baby on the way. And Charlie's gone,' he said gently.

She nodded, then the tears arrived. 'Sorry,' she said, swiping her eyes with the back of her hand, embarrassed. 'I thought I was done with bloody crying all the time! Sorry.'

'Don't be.'

And then he drew her in, folding her into his strong arms and rubbing his hand up and down her back. Rebecca stood there, feeling the beat of his heart, allowing herself to be held, grateful for the kindness from this amazing man, whom she had admired and adored for so long. It was like having someone like her brother Tom back with her again. She felt relief sweep through her whole being and again the knowing that things would turn out all right.

# Thirty-five

Later that morning, Rebecca stood drifting her palms over the tall native grasses of one of the mountain-run paddocks while Funny galoomphed her puppyish form in and out of the tussocks in loop-the-loop circles, her pink tongue hanging out, her eyes bright with excitement. Archie looked up from where he played in the tray of the ute with a bucketful of Matchbox cars that used to belong to her, Mick and Tom. Archie pointed to the pup. 'She's being Funny, Mummy.'

Rebecca threw her head back and laughed. 'She *is* Funny.'

Andrew smiled too. 'Funny name. Funny dog.'

'It's not funny when she drags the boots from the back verandah onto the lawn,' Rebecca said.

She watched Andrew drive a spade strongly into the ground to sever out a square sample of plants and soil from the earth and felt warmth run through her. It was rare she had Andrew Travis all to herself. Normally she was out in the field with a cluster of other farmers. This one-on-one time with him felt utterly precious.

She knew she was in awe of him intellectually and from a farming perspective. But she hadn't known she had relied on him and his energy so much to keep her motivated and going with

Waters Meeting until now. She admired the smooth tanned skin of the back of his neck and his squarely cut hairline as he squatted down and inspected the soil, crushing the loamy earth between his fingers, smelling it, his fingertips splaying out root systems. As she watched, Rebecca plucked a pretty kangaroo-grass seed head from a stem and rolled its bristly golden brown husks between the palms of her hands. She shut her eyes and allowed herself to soak in the peaceful energy of the land up here on the mountain and the comforting presence of Andrew.

When she opened her eyes, the view of the valley that was cast out before her stole her breath. She could *feel* it too. The pulse of the land within her and of her baby too. And she felt the presence of Tom.

'Just look at this,' Andrew said excitedly and Bec snapped out of her daydream.

She walked over to him, weaving through the tussocks and poas and stepping over a scattering of speckled, lichen-covered rocks.

'*As above, so below,*' Andrew said emphatically. He held up a freshly dug grass plant that offered up not only new shoots, but also long yellowing withering leaves. Beneath it hung an equally long, feathery root system as pretty as lace.

'This is what we're after,' he said, his fingers teasing out both ends of the plant specimen. 'The leaves that are dying will become composting leaf litter, and that's what will feed the creatures in the soil. You've done a great job, Bec. It's been years since this run has been allowed to have grasses left to grow long enough to compost down.'

'I remembered you telling me you need to give Mother Nature a chance to heal the land by herself,' Rebecca said. 'I've pushed the stock rotation out to *at least* one hundred and fifty days. Longer for the less fertile areas, so they get more rest from grazing.'

'I have taught you well, grasshopper,' Andrew said.

She smiled at him. 'You have, master,' Bec answered back,

bowing with the palms of her hands pressed together. 'My master teach me this fact: you need birth, you need growth, and you need reproduction, but equally you need *death and decay*. Plants need the four seasons. You say: we farmers always miss one of these seasons; we do not allow time for death and decay to replenish the soil. So our soil never gets fed. So I am giving the death and decay season to the soil by keeping the stock off longer and growing longer plants.'

'Velly good student,' Andrew said, then suddenly turned serious. 'That's my next push. To help everyone understand that grazing animals aren't bad for Australia. People need to realise this continent *needs* ruminant animals to cycle carbon, as much as it needs predators to cycle carbon. We, by eating meat, are part of what could be a sustainable cycle. Not like this bullshit being dished up. This "lock it up to protect the land" crap that the scientists are coming up with, and their drive to save the planet by everyone turning vegan is so damaging.' He held up the plant. 'This little baby can help the entire world, if we let it. We need to compost the whole landscape, create a canopy so we cycle water and nutrients slowly. That's not happening on most farms. But here, you've made a start.' He glanced up at her and the sun caught the glint of genuine admiration in his blue eyes.

'You really are a nerdy scientist,' she said. 'You're only masquerading as a Queensland cattle farmer, you know that?'

He laughed.

'And if only we could get those scientists who try to deny your work to come up here and see it for themselves,' she said, 'it might stop them from giving you a bollocking.' Rebecca squatted down next to him and took the plant. As she did, Funny trotted over and leaned against her leg.

She knew that many of the environmental problems the world faced could be solved in six months by grasses storing carbon in the soil — they were so much faster than trees, which took years to store carbon in their wood.

Bec knew the long root systems were now helping restore the Waters Meeting soil. She wanted everyone to see what could be achieved in a relatively short time. But she knew the work they were doing had sparked controversy.

'Money rules most,' Andrew said. 'And people will do what they do. You and I will do this work, and then along comes a mining company or a property developer and tears it all away,' he said, looking at her mildly. He gently nudged her with his shoulder. 'No point stressing over what others do.'

She smiled at him. She loved the fact he was incredibly humble and quietly spoken, so self-contained in his own skin. She watched the way he stroked Funny in long soothing pats along her back.

Even though he knew how dire the world's food-production future was, Andrew never seemed daunted by the huge task he had set himself. He simply showcased his own farm and gently warned of the situation everyone faced if nobody changed their ways. Andrew simply walked quietly among farmers and trusted that just a handful would begin to see. He knew the ones who did would no longer need so much costly fuel, or the manipulated plant varieties or the expense of artificial fertiliser. He held a vision where farmers were paid to increase carbon in the soil — and the healthier the agricultural sector, the healthier the food for people.

Rebecca, here on this hill, knew the man beside her had some big mountains to climb. The large companies were out to silence Andrew and his renegade soil-scientist friends because the corporations of genetically engineered seed companies, fertilisers and oil companies stood to lose millions of dollars if his knowledge became widespread.

'You know,' Andrew said, 'Franklin Roosevelt once said, "The nation that destroys its soil destroys itself."' He stood up, offered Bec a dirt-etched hand and pulled her up from where she squatted.

She took it and relished his steadying touch. Then Andrew dropped her hand and began to tread the sod back into the neat hole from which he had dug it.

'I wonder how long it will take for the rest of the farmers to realise that we are being fed bullshit and lies by the big companies and the scientists?' Bec said.

'It'll take as long as it takes,' Andrew said. 'Or it won't happen at all. All we can do is what we do on our own places. You're doing it now, Rebecca, and that's all that counts. Waters Meeting is singing now, thanks to you.'

Rebecca felt the rare experience of praise wash through her and for the moment she was overjoyed she was here on this hillside in the mountains with this exceptional man.

When they arrived back at the homestead, it was almost lunchtime. Rebecca was expecting the machinery valuer soon to catalogue and photograph the machines for the sale, but she asked if Andrew wanted to quickly look at an old plough frame and air seeder. She left Archie in the sandpit in the garden with Funny, both of them digging happily, and walked with Andrew over the short distance to the machinery shed. On their way, Andrew whistled and raised his eyebrows at the assortment of farm equipment.

'Your husband sure loves expensive toys!'

'Ex-husband,' Rebecca corrected, then sighed. 'Never thought I'd say that. I guess we both had such different views of how it all should be.'

'No point living with regrets,' Andrew said.

She led him around the side of the shed and indicated the metal plough that had grass growing up through it from where it sat on two old railway sleepers.

'I'm not sure, but it could be converted into a pasture-cropping seed drill, couldn't it?' Rebecca asked. 'If it could, then I would really make a start on the place. Get some oats in to help the perennial plants start to function.'

Andrew laid a palm on top of the machine and looked it over. 'It sure could be converted! It's perfect. Then you won't need any of Charlie's big machines,' he said. 'You'll simply need a tractor and this direct drill seeder, slightly modified of course. The rest you can sell.'

The prospect excited her. Charlie and his complex machines had isolated her from the day-to-day practice of farming. The newer machines were so computerised she found she never had the time to learn how to operate them and she was hopeless on breakdowns. She'd found herself resenting the constant ordering of expensive electronic parts in the office. Rather than learning to drive the technical machines, it had been easier to leave it all up to Charlie. But now, simplifying the management to just a tractor and a basic drill would mean she could do it all herself again.

Andrew stooped to inspect how he might attach the metal coulters and space out the tines on the frame. Then he stood, brushing off his hands on his jeans.

'That old Connor Shea you have round there next to the baler?' he began. 'You could use the seed box off that and mount it onto this frame and link up the existing seeder tubes. Voila! Instant direct drill.'

'That easy?'

'Yep.'

'No bank loan for new machinery?'

Andrew shook his head. 'It's perfect. There should be enough parts floating about. I can weld her up in a matter of days. May need to change a few of my flights and move a couple of things, but I'd be happy to get you started. Then you'll be up and running. You can trial some autumn sowing by drilling oats into your pastures nearby the house.'

As she listened to his words, Rebecca breathed in deeply, realising that a whole new future could come into play for Waters Meeting right from this very moment. It was much better than pairing socks! 'That's so exciting! Thank you so much.'

'It really is my pleasure,' he said, then looked at her and smiled for a time.

She could tell he was thinking and was about to say something. But the moment was shattered as Archie launched himself at the back of Andrew's legs like a monkey, Funny following suit.

'Oi!' Andrew said, his grin broadening, his arms reaching behind him to hold the small boy. 'How'd you sneak up on us?'

As Rebecca watched Andrew swing Archie onto his back, she again thanked what Evie referred to as the universe for sending her Andrew. With a bit more positivity, it seemed everything was falling into place.

# Thirty-Six

'What's that?' Andrew asked as they walked from the machinery shed back to the house. Bec saw he was pointing to the jutting steel of the buried plough that rose from the earth like a partially sunken ship.

She grinned. 'It's Charlie's silage pit.'

'Doesn't look much like a silage pit.'

Bec scrunched up her freckled nose. 'Um. Actually it's also his new beaut several-hundred-thousand-dollar plough. I buried the bastard.'

Andrew's eyes opened widely and when he saw on her face that she was telling the truth, he threw back his head and laughed loudly, then high-fived her.

'Go, girl! But you didn't think to take off the discs first to use as end assemblies for your fences? That's what I did to my plough so I was never tempted to use it again.'

'I wasn't in the frame of mind to think of that,' Bec said. 'So you don't think I was an idiot doing that? I could've got good money for it.'

'Not for a second do I think you are an idiot. I would like to bury every plough in Australia. I'm proud of you. If you had sold it, it would've been used to tear up the soil elsewhere. Mind you, you may have trouble explaining Charlie's plough to his solicitor.' Andrew set his square hands on his hips and shook his head.

'He's not going to get it, is he?'

'The farm?' asked Andrew. 'Your family farm? He wouldn't be that cruel.'

She looked up at him hopefully, then shook the worrying thoughts from her mind. 'I'm hungry. You must be too. Let's grab some lettuce out of the garden for lunch,' she said.

Rebecca pushed open the old wooden gate to the vegetable patch that bordered one side of the homestead and entered her Eden, Archie and Funny following at their heels. She instantly felt a sense of peace as she stepped along the white gravel pathway that ran between raised beds formed from thick slabs of lovely old bridge timber.

On hard days, when her babies had been really little, her vegetable garden was her one place of mental stillness and contentment. She relished the chance to get to it and would park both boys in the shade in their double pram, Ben as a toddler and Archie a baby, lethargic from the rhythmic swaying of the leafy trees and the heat. She would sink her fingers into the manure-rich soil, delighting in the feel of the cool moist haven of worms and other unseen creatures. Her old Kelpie dogs nearby, sleeping on their sides in the sunshine.

As she mulched and watered, weeded and pruned, then harvested crisp fresh vegies for the kitchen or to give away to neighbours, Bec would sometimes glance out over the fenceline to the barren, dry paddocks of Waters Meeting beyond and wonder why they couldn't manage it so the farm looked and felt the same way as her garden.

Innately she knew the answer, but she was too hesitant to form the thoughts into one ugly conclusion. Her gaze would slide to the chemical drums that were stacked up behind the machinery shed, and to the hard metallic discs of the plough. Then she'd look back to her sleeping boys, a picture of chubby baby health bundled up in the pram, their pure skin as yet unblemished by life.

There she stood, a farmer's wife and mother, in her oasis in the middle of the desert that was her family farm. It was at that moment, when she saw her garden alive and thriving and her farm struggling and dying, that she knew, for the sake of her children, she had to inspire change in the men. But it was also in that moment that her marriage began to fail. And once Andrew had arrived into her life and given her the answers, everything had shifted.

Andrew's voice woke her up from her reminiscing. 'I found some interesting research the other day,' he said. 'When I get the chance, I'll put it on some slides for my next presentation.'

As Rebecca pulled carrots from the rich soil, she listened to Andrew with interest.

'There were some American scientists who studied mineral depletion in vegetables between 1940 and 1991. I couldn't find any results post '91. I have a feeling the US government might have suppressed the findings because the depletion would be far worse these days. You know, levels would be scarily low. Anyway,' he continued, 'the studies showed a reduction of vitamins and nutrients as high as seventy-six per cent in some vegetables. And in Australia, some of our meat only has *half* as much iron as it did in the seventies. All due to lack of nutrients in the soil.'

'Not this soil,' Bec said, grabbing a handful and drifting it through her spread fingers. She could tell it was teeming with vibrant living health.

'This soil is unfortunately the exception. Did you know in Australia today it's possible to buy an orange that has zero vitamin C in it?'

'Doesn't surprise me,' she said, flicking a slug from the lettuce into the chook scrap bucket. 'You know, Charlie used to scour the papers and talk about commodity reports, inputs and returns. I think he'd forgotten agriculture is about food.'

'But when you're a mum, you don't forget. The women haven't forgotten,' Andrew said. 'Look. We blokes ought to judge our farms not by how profitable they are, but how they look. And how they *feel*. But you know, sometimes men aren't too good at letting themselves feel.' Andrew turned his gaze on her. 'I can talk all you like about soils, but when it comes to talking about how I feel, I'm hopeless,' he said, 'especially when I need to ask people for help.'

Just then a car horn sounded. It would be Tonka Jones come to see the machinery.

'He's early,' Bec said, turning away from Andrew. 'Lunch will have to wait, sorry. Come on.' She gathered up lettuce plants and carrots in her soil-stained hands.

'Afterwards, when your machinery man is done,' Andrew said as he opened the gate for her, 'we can go out in the paddock with your heifers and I'll show you how to poo score.'

Rebecca's eyes brightened. She had missed the field day that the RLM had dryly titled 'Manure assessment as a measure for stock health'.

'Poo scoring!' she said. 'Now there's an invitation a girl doesn't often get. *Yes, please!*' As she walked ahead of him, she laughed up at the sky. 'I am the luckiest woman in the world!' She smiled.

Rebecca's mouth fell open when Tonka Jones gave her a rough total value of the machinery inventory.

'Of course it's a conservative calculation,' Tonka said, leaning on the bonnet of the ute with the clipboard and paper spread out before them, a booger crusted with dust hanging from his nostril hair, unbeknownst to him.

'Conservative? It's amazing,' said Bec, swiping at her own nose, hoping Tonka would take the hint.

'Bet you didn't know the old man had that much tangled up in diesel and big wheels.'

The total on the page leaped out at her. Over a million dollars' worth.

'Bet you've never felt like a millionaire,' Tonka said as he began to flick back over the digital photos he would soon upload on the internet.

'I'll be phoning Cory at the bank straight away,' Bec said excitedly. 'Recently I have been feeling very rich. But I'm not talking money. I'm talking soil.' She smiled at Andrew and put her palm on her pregnant belly, thinking of Sol and the blessings of her children and friends around her and the future of Waters Meeting.

When they had farewelled Tonka, who had accused Bec of having hay fever due to her constant nose rubbing, Andrew and she made their way back into the kitchen.

'How about that poo-scoring lesson?' she asked Andrew a little while later after lunch. 'I've got half an hour before I have to leave for Ben's bus.'

Andrew rubbed his hands together. 'Yes. Let's go!'

Rebecca, Archie and Andrew made their way down to the lucerne flats. She hadn't been in the riverside paddocks since Archie's accident there. She felt a shiver of awful memory run through her and wondered if she should recount the events to Andrew. She opted not to. It was part of the past now, and her little boy who seemed happy trundling along with Funny didn't need reminding.

'Pretty pugged,' Andrew said, looking at the deep divots the cattle hooves had made.

'Tell me about it. Charlie would put the cattle on here in the winter. It drove me nuts. Plus we used to irrigate this paddock a lot, but then the government took our water licence away. Downstream, an entire state away, people were kicking up a fuss.'

'Probably a good thing, really,' Andrew said. 'Putting on more water the way we do is fool's gold. Look at how capped your soil is.' He expertly unhitched his pocket-knife from his leather belt and with the silver blade flipped the crusted soil over. 'The moss in between the lucerne plants shows me you are on ground zero. It's really degraded. At least the moss is soil cover, but you can feel the lifelessness under your feet. It's like concrete.'

'I know,' said Rebecca sadly, realising that what she had thought was so wonderful about irrigation ten years ago was now failing the land. 'And I don't like the look of those thistles.' She nodded towards a swathe of high scotch and variegated thistles.

'Well, my advice to you is start to like the look of them,' Andrew said. 'Let them seed. Better to have them than just moss and bare soil. Plants build soil health, not the other way round. You just need to focus on the plant species you do want and manage for them. Not manage against the species you don't want. If you get rid of those thistles, there's a million more seeds in the ground to bring more. At least their long tap roots are doing some good. Over time the thistles can't come if you generate the competition by managing annual and perennial plants together — not separately, which is how we've always farmed in this country.'

'You make it sound so simple.'

'It is. As long as your animals and your soil microbes are getting plenty of Vitamin F for food with a diverse range of plant species. "Weeds" have root systems that are as deep as the plants are tall. Your farm should look as messy as a roadside. Like it's been abandoned.'

'Is that how your farm looks?'

'It does. The neighbours think I'm nuts, but I have a full metre of topsoil, I have drought-resilient native pastures and healthy animals and any rain that does fall is held on the place due to the ground cover. But it does take a paradigm shift in thinking. Now shall we go score some poo?'

'Let's.'

They fell into silence as they trudged over the paddock to the gate into the heifer paddock. Here Bec had boxed the young sheep in with the cattle, giving them the best of the flats while the conditions remained dry.

'They look OK,' he said, eyeing the stock and walking to a fresh pat of dung. 'I'd score that about a five. Not bad. If it's not mounding like that, it means the animals don't have enough dry matter.'

He scouted about for more dung while Archie inspected a pat with a stick and Funny began to roll in some.

'Your poo is all pretty spot on. The pup likes it anyway!'

'Thanks,' said Bec, delivering a cheeky grin. 'It's great for a girl to hear that!'

Andrew laughed a little.

'It's a juggle, but I have enough feed ahead of them to maintain them. Just.'

'You'll be fine. And the baby? When is he or she due?'

Rebecca baulked a little at Andrew's question. The reality that she had Charlie's baby on the way sometimes still surprised her. She was busy enough now. What would her already packed life look like after a newborn was added to the mix?

'Another few months to go.'

'That's great.'

'It's scary. Being on my own and all.'

Andrew put an arm around her shoulder and gave her a quick squeeze. 'Everything will turn out.'

She thought Andrew would drop his arm away, but he didn't, and they stood like that looking at the heifers, young ewes and wethers that grazed calmly before them.

'My wife and I couldn't have kids,' he said, looking off to the distance. 'It's why she left me. She was angry about it. It would've been nice. To have some of our own. But now I get to enjoy other people's kids. Like yours.'

'No kids may be a meant-to-be kind of thing for you. Your work around the world is very important. Kids would limit you.'

'No, they wouldn't, and you know it. They grow you.' He turned to face her. His sadness was tangible. 'I've been wanting to ask you this for a long time, Rebecca. Since even before Charlie left. I really need your help. You're perfect for what I plan to do. I'm going to the States next year. Montana. I've teamed up with a big-wig movie producer, who has a ranch. He's passionate about the soils work. His name is Bernard Truman. He wants to facilitate a world information tour.' His voice began to quicken to one of urgency and almost pleading. 'He and I could really use someone like you on the team. You know the material back to front and you're just as passionate. You could bring the boys and the baby. Help me out while I'm away on the speaking tour in the headquarters. Bernard has a massive ranch. It's a beautiful part of the world. You'd love it!'

'Hah! Yeah, right.' Bec laughed, but her laughter faded when she saw the intensity of Andrew's look.

'I mean it. I'd love to have you and the little ones along.'

He looked so tall and so utterly rock solid standing before her. Then Rebecca realised with a flash it was here on this very same river flat she had kissed Charlie when he had first come home to Waters Meeting. They had made love in the leafy green of the lucerne crop not far from here. Now over a decade on, here she was with another man. There were no Cinderella notions running around her head now. Life had taken her on a very long journey and to a place where she realised her journey was her own to make. She didn't need to be attached to a man to live her dreams. But where were her dreams? Here on Waters Meeting? Or beyond in a bigger life contributing to such meaningful work as Andrew's? Or could her dreams lie with Sol?

She looked away from Andrew. Off in the distance on the edge of the paddock, the Rebecca River was sleeping quietly. Unlike her river namesake, Rebecca felt a torrent within her, as if she was in flood right now. There were so many possibilities. But this place was her everything. She couldn't, wouldn't, leave it. Ever. 'I can't.'

Andrew pulled a disappointed face. 'I knew it was a long shot. But I had to ask. You would be a perfect assistant to me. There is so much work to be done. However, I completely understand the time isn't right.'

Rebecca wrinkled her nose and shook her head. 'It's crazy. I'll have a baby. And the boys. And, of course, Waters Meeting.'

Andrew shrugged. 'Life's more fun when it's crazy.'

She smiled at him apologetically. 'I can't. I'm sorry.'

Andrew shrugged again. 'We'll find someone.'

Rebecca glanced at her watch. 'Ben's school bus. We'd better be getting back.'

'Come on, Ms Perfect Poos, I'll make a start on dinner,' he said fondly, and together the three of them walked back up to their homestead with the Rebecca River at their backs.

# Thirty-seven

At the back door, the boys had tumbled inside, Ben excited to be home, back with his little brother and Funny, and to find Andrew still there. Rebecca was about to kick off her boots when she heard the airbrakes of a truck hiss from behind the screen of trees up on the ridgeline. Who could this be? She hadn't ordered any stock.

'Expecting a truck?' Andrew asked, his gaze following hers.

Bec shook her head. 'I'm not buying any stock. Nor selling any.'

As the truck neared, they could see it was a horse transport vehicle. It pulled up with a loud shush of brakes and the driver got out. He waved to them where they stood on the verandah and went to drop the back ramp of the truck. By the time Bec had reached the garden gate and was walking over, the driver had already unloaded the most stunning quarter horse she had ever seen. It was the sort of horse Barbie might have, or a warrior princess on a movie.

The mare was a deep golden blend of palomino chestnut with a long flowing blonde flaxen mane. She carried her head high and looked about with her dark eyes at the hillsides as she swished

315

her full pale tail, which almost fell to the ground. She let out a small nervous whinny.

'What a stunner,' Andrew said, gawping as the mare dropped her head to sniff at the ground, her long forelock falling across her pretty face. So muscled were her hindquarters, she looked as if she could spin on a dime.

'Here you go,' the driver said, handing Rebecca the lead rope.

'But I didn't order a horse,' she said, realising how stupid she must look and sound.

'You didn't?' Andrew asked. 'So what's she doing here?'

'I think she belongs on Rivermont, the previous property to this one. You've come too far.'

The driver shrugged and handed Bec an envelope. 'Says here Waters Meeting.' He jabbed an index finger at the envelope. 'Just dropped two off at Rivermont.'

'But she doesn't belong here.'

'Paperwork says she does.'

'But —'

'Look, little lady,' the driver shot at her, 'it'll be midnight before I get home. My missus is already after my balls. I'm outta here. Do what you like with her. I was just told to deliver her to you.' And with that he climbed back into his truck and was gone.

'Happy chappy,' Andrew said, watching the truck lumber away.

'Can this get any stranger?' Bec laid her palm on the mare's neck, talking gently to her, trying to settle her a little so she could open the envelope. The mare did settle, turning her nose to sniff at Rebecca, leaning into her touch. Soon, after her long journey, she dropped her head to graze.

Ripping open the envelope, Bec first discovered the mare's papers. 'Why hello, Miss Luella,' she said to the horse, questions still racing in her mind.

'Miss Luella?' said Andrew.

'That's her name.' Bec read, in a thick Texan twang, 'Cootibar Ranch Miss Luella USA Import. Says here risin' five years of age.

But what in god's merciful name are you doin' here, Miss Luella?' she said to the horse, sounding like a character from *Green Acres*.

Next Bec flicked to the card that was stapled to the papers.

*For my beautiful farm girl (I dare not call you a princess!): you need a decent horse. This is a gift horse you can look in the mouth. She's dead quiet, but a tonne more fun if you wear spurs! All my love, Sol.*

Rebecca's mouth dropped open. Sol! First the flowers. That had felt over the top! Now this! A horse! This was too much. Was he trying to buy her? She felt a rumble of irritation, a rush of disbelief, then a quiet fear that he could have fallen for her so hard and so soon. It couldn't be true.

She breathed in sharply and turned her back on the horse, towards the mountaintops, where sunlight brushed the Waters Meeting peaks with a soft golden light.

'Are you any more enlightened after reading the card?' Andrew asked, frowning.

'Yes,' she said tensely. 'She's a gift from Sol Stanton.'

'Oh, I see,' was all Andrew said.

As Rebecca led the beautiful quarter horse into the round yard, she called over her shoulder to him, 'I ought to phone Yazzie to double-check there hasn't been a mistake.'

'Oh, there's no mistake, I'm sure,' Andrew said.

Just then they heard the boys spill out of the house with the bang of the screen door, shattering the difficult mood between them.

'Mum! What's that horse?'

As Archie and Ben fired questions about Miss Luella and hung on the rails eyeballing the mare with amazement, Rebecca moved with determined steadiness as she went about filling up the trough and getting hay for the mare. But inside her a torrent raged. What was Sol *thinking*? Giving her a horse of this calibre? She couldn't even conceive owning a horse like this. Was he nuts?

And then there was Andrew. Standing there in his quiet loneliness with his gifts to give to the world. She felt split down the middle. No. She felt split into four. Part of her was still eddying off in the turbulence of her break-up with Charlie. And the other divide was between two wonderful men who had come into her life, one as a lover, the other as a mentor to fulfilling all her farming dreams. And then there were her boys. As she looked at her kids, she felt herself drawn away from the confusion within. She had children to raise. A baby on the way. And now, she not only had a puppy to train, but a mare to get to know. The men and the pressures they placed upon her right now seemed altogether too hard.

She wanted to allow the joy to wash over her that a man would do this for her. Give her a horse. She wanted to spend hours now with her mare, to celebrate her beauty. The good fortune that life can bring such rich surprises. She wanted to run her hands over her perfect butterscotch coat and brush her luxurious mane and tail and then she wanted to pick up each perfect rock-hard hoof. And to swim in the bliss of knowing Sol would trouble himself so much to send her such a present ... but she felt herself shut down. She would not allow it to flow. Andrew was here, the boys needed feeding and deep within her Bec struggled to find the belief that she deserved any of it.

They sat, a replica of a family, at the kitchen table. Rebecca was torn that her agricultural god was at the head of her table, her husband gone and yet the presence of Sol was calling out from the yard in the form of a glorious, beautifully bred quarter horse. Not to mention the invasive memory of Joey with all his (almost) virile youth. Her head swam with all that had happened this year.

Andrew had helped her set the meals of steamed vegetables and lamb chops in front of the boys, then sat down. Rebecca remained before her own meal, not feeling at all hungry. Part of her was loving having Andrew here and knowing she was so frequently in Sol's thoughts, but the other side of her was wishing the boys were already in bed and she could take off and have time to digest the confused thoughts that tumbled in her head.

She looked at Andrew. He was beautiful. A different beauty from Sol. Within her she knew she didn't want a replacement of a husband in any form. Not now. Not yet. It was too soon. But his quiet, pleasant presence seemed to make her realise that her life could be utterly difficult and lonely once the baby came, no matter how much she practised being positive.

After the meal, Rebecca, for the first time in months, settled herself into a comfortable threadbare armchair by the woodheater. Andrew cleared away the plates while she just sat watching the flames. It was Andrew who made the journey up the creaking Waters Meeting homestead stairs to put the children to bed and to read them their story. He even settled Funny down in a cane basket in the laundry and tipped dried food into her bowl.

When he came back to Rebecca, he stood in the doorway. 'All done. All settled. They are wonderful children, the Kelpie included. A credit to you.'

'Thank you,' she said, 'I'm just so grateful for the rest.'

He moved closer and sat perched on the coffee table next to her. 'You OK?'

Rebecca shook her head. The fire whispered as he reached out and patted her hand.

'It'll be fine. You'll be fine.'

Tears came to her eyes. The road had been too long. The road had been too rough. She thought she had her life in hand again, but tonight everything was swirling and muddled. Soon the phone was ringing and she was hauling herself up from the chair. Numb. Apologising to him over and over for crying so much. She walked to the phone in the hallway and picked it up. 'Hello?' she said.

'You sound tired,' came the voice of Sol.

Bec glanced at Andrew. 'Not really. Just got the kids to bed.'

'Did you get my present?'

'Oh, Sol,' she said as if it was a trouble to her. Andrew turned his back, cleared his throat and moved away into the kitchen, realising the call from Sol would be personal.

'You sound displeased,' Sol said.

'Overwhelmed, more like.'

'She's beautiful, is she not? She is already quiet in her nature, but I've had her schooled and schooled so she is safe for you, so you can even ride her while you are pregnant. Yazzie can go with you. It will do you both good.'

'You've thought of everything, have you?' Sol didn't seem to hear the tension in her voice.

'She reminded me of you the moment I saw her.'

'It's too much, Sol.'

'Too much? No. Evie says "allow".'

'Evie said that? Good on her, but giving me a horse? An entire horse? After just one … you know.'

'Well, I would not give you half a horse? Of course I gave you an entire one!'

'Don't tease, Sol,' she said.

'Why not give you a gift?'

'There's every reason why not.'

'I can't think of one,' he said with cheekiness in his voice. 'Ahh! The lady is not used to gifts.'

He waited for her reply, but she didn't speak. Sol went on, 'Besides, Miss Luella was part of a good deal. I wanted a mount that was not a show jumper for Yazzie for Rivermont. We need working horses more suited to that country. I also wanted a stock horse for me. You can read your pastures better from a horse than a ute. And along with the holistic grazing, I want to start practising low-stress stockhandling, and I can do that with these horses. Miss Luella was part of a three-horse deal, so she really is a gift horse. So there is no reason why not. You deserve her. For what you have done for Yazzie. For what you have done for me.' When Rebecca didn't reply, he said sincerely down the line in a deep quiet voice, 'Rebecca, I miss you.'

'Sol. Don't.'

'What do you mean, *don't*?' he asked, his voice giving way

to irritation. 'Don't give you things? Like horses? Don't give you emotions? Like love?'

'Sol. It was only one night.' She felt her cheeks redden, knowing Andrew was in earshot.

'One night can last an eternity. For me it was more than one night. But obviously for you, it was not.'

'Sol,' she said sadly, 'I have to go.'

'Don't go. Talk to me.'

'Sol. I have to. I'm sorry. I just need some time. I'll talk to you later.' And she hung up. Silence filled the Waters Meeting homestead.

Eventually she turned and looked into the kitchen to Andrew. 'I'm sorry,' she said, tension firing the muscles in her body.

He smiled sadly at her. 'Don't be. He's a good guy. A great bloke.'

'I know, but ... Sol ... well ...' she began, but couldn't finish.

Andrew went over to where she stood beside the phone and shook his head. 'Come with me to the States. Take the pressure off yourself with the farm. The work is so important to the world ... and you ...'

He was interrupted by the phone's insistent ring again.

'Huh!' said Rebecca. 'Excuse me.' As she reached for the receiver, she mouthed the word 'sorry' to him again. He shrugged, then motioned to the dishes in the sink, went back into the kitchen and began to run the water. As she picked up the phone, she half hoped it was Sol again, so she could soften the blow she had just dealt him. 'Hello?'

'Sis,' came a deep voice on the line.

'Mick?'

'Yeah, well, who else?'

Bec instantly felt her hackles rise. There was another brother once. Another who would ring just for a chat, and write her letters and emails, not like this one who only called when he wanted something. It took all her resolve not to spit out angrily, *'What do you want?'*

'How are you?' she said instead, picking up a pen and flicking it end on end.

'Fine.'

'Truds? The kids?'

'Yeah, she's good,' said Mick, sounding impatient. 'Kids are good. Danny's just been expelled from the best school in the city and David's on an obesity program, but other than that they're good. Least Trudy tells me they are. I hardly ever see the little — or rather *big* — buggers. Work. Always work. You know the drill.'

'Yeah, I do.' Rebecca began to doodle on a school newsletter, etching deep sharp lines into the paper.

'So you up for a meeting then?' he asked suddenly.

She stopped drawing. 'What?'

'A meeting,' Mick repeated. 'About the farm.'

'What do you mean?'

'Well, after you and Charlie splitting up.'

'What do you mean?'

'With Dad's will and all.'

'Sorry?'

'Charlie called me about the divorce and Dad's will. Mum and I have got together and checked it out. According to Dad's wishes, Waters Meeting was only secure in your ownership so long as you were married. And now that Charlie's filed for divorce, well, you know, she's all over red rover, according to Dad's will.'

Rebecca absorbed his words and felt panic rise like a plague upon her body. She felt her skin run hot and cold.

'Didn't you know that?' Mick asked. 'Coz if you didn't, you really should have made it your business to know it, sis. I mean, *really*? You're always one for putting your head in the sand, aren't you?'

Rebecca sucked in her breath and her eyes travelled to the ceiling where cobwebs hung onto dust. She swallowed down nausea.

'Bec?'

'I'm here.'

'Well, in light of this, Charlie and I planned to come out tomorrow for a meeting with you. A Waters Meeting meeting. OK?'

Rebecca couldn't speak. She felt ambushed. By her own brother, in cohorts with her ex-husband. And even her mother. Couldn't Frankie have called her about this?

'Sis?' Mick said into the silent gap.

'Yep.'

'OK then? Tomorrow, mid-morning?'

'Sounds like I don't have a say.'

'All right then, tomorrow.' He paused. 'You OK?'

'Fuck off, Mick.'

'Don't be like that.'

'Oh, I'm not like that. But fuck off anyway.'

'OK then,' he said, adding tersely, 'So typical of you. See you tomorrow.'

Rebecca put down the phone. White-faced, she stood numbly with her back to the kitchen, where Andrew, sensing something was wrong, had turned and was surveying her from where he stood at the sink.

'Are you OK? Come here …' He stepped forwards and came out to the hallway. He moved to put his arms about her.

She raised both hands. 'No. Stop. Just leave me.'

He froze and frowned. 'OK.'

'I'm sorry,' she said, tears filling her eyes, 'I didn't mean to snap.' Her hand massaged the beginnings of a headache on her forehead. 'That was my brother. He and Charlie are on their way tomorrow. They say I have no right to the farm once I divorce.'

'But that's —'

She cut him off, not wanting to talk about it, too raw from the shock of the news. 'I have to go out, get away for a bit, to think. OK? Can I ask you to watch over the boys this evening? They shouldn't wake. I'll be back later.'

'Sure,' he said, bewilderment on his face. 'Do whatever you need to do.' And then Rebecca turned and walked out of the kitchen, grabbing her coat and beanie on her way, feeling as if her father, from the grave, had just stabbed her in the back.

# Thirty-eight

In the stables, Rebecca dragged out Ink Jet's old bridle and gathered up the worn, cracked leather stock saddle. She stooped and buckled the spurs around her boots.

The old gear stirred memories of Inky and Hank and their horrible end by Charlie's hand. She felt fresh fury rise again. She felt furious with herself. She had *trusted* her family. And now this! She gritted her teeth and strode out of the stables. She knew that saddling Miss Luella and riding her out was a lot to ask of the new horse, but she just had to get away. To clear her head. And besides, when it came to horses, Rebecca trusted Sol. She knew the mare would be near perfect. It gave her comfort knowing she had him to trust on that level.

She went to the round yard and sat the saddle on the top rail, then hung the bridle on an old bridge spike. Miss Luella seemed pleased to have some company, whickering at Rebecca in greeting and ambling over as she slipped through the rails.

In the gleam of dying daylight, she took in the mare's pretty-girl looks and fancy appearance. Bec could also sense a strong calmness and a friendly curiosity held within the animal. She seemed self-contained and confident.

The horse didn't seem to mind the feel of the strange gear when Bec threw on the saddle blanket, cinched the girth and clipped on the crupper and the breastplate. The old saddle and dirty saddlecloth looked far too grotty on such a tremendous animal. Even worse was the bridle, which looked so worn and brittle that the reins might snap at even the lightest pull.

But there was no time to fuss. Rebecca, hot-headed and flushed with a quiet anger and confusion over all that was happening, led the mare about the round yard. She flapped each stirrup leather noisily against the saddle pads to test the mare's tolerance. Standing at her shoulders, she asked the mare to flex her head around with each rein. She obeyed perfectly. And then Rebecca swung on, carefully avoiding the bulge of her pregnant belly, giving the mare a few turns of the yard in both directions, first at a walk, then a trot, then a calm lope.

Bec instantly relished in the amazing lightness of such a well-schooled creature. She was rock solid.

After a time, she side-passed to the yard gate, lifted the latch, swung the gate open and with one sound of a kiss opened the mare up to a loose-rein lope across the river flat towards the mountain that lay beneath the bright shine of a waning moon that was rising before the sun had yet set.

As she rode, the thought of her unborn child passed through her mind. She could feel that they were both safe on this mare. Sol had chosen well. She felt a gratitude rise in her and a flash of intense love … then intense guilt. As she settled at a canter, she felt joy for the fact her baby was riding with her for the first time. She had ridden often when pregnant with her first baby, Ben. Why not ride with this one?

She thought she would ride as far as the river, then turn around, but something within her made her want to keep going. How long had it been since she'd been on a horse? How long since she'd had any kind of solitude? Or how long since she'd splashed across the river and ridden the trail up the mountain to the hut?

The mare only gave one snort as she dropped her head to peer at the darkened river crossing, but then she plunged in. Bec pulled her feet from the stirrups and lifted her legs a little to avoid her boots getting wet. Ears cast forwards, the mare picked her way steadily over rocks, then eagerly climbed the bank on the other side with minimal effort. Rebecca wasn't sure where Sol had bought the mare, but she was clearly experienced and a pure joy. She ran her hand over her beautiful neck and kissed her on again.

It didn't take long to reach the first ledge. Rebecca knew she was lucky to have the moon. It was so strong it created a faint halo of light on the domes of the mountains as it rose in the blue-black sky. She pulled up for a moment and stroked the mare's neck. Should she head back down to the homestead, which she could see off in the distance? Andrew had turned on the kitchen lights and she could just make out the faint trail of white smoke from the revived woodfire.

He'll be all right alone with the boys, she thought. For the moment she just couldn't face going back there. She didn't want to lie awake in her old marital bed, with Andrew sleeping in the spare room, while all the while Sol was somewhere on the other side of the world feeling hurt by her. She didn't want the weight of the old homestead with all its ghosts and memories pressing down on her as she replayed over and over in her head the fact she was about to lose Waters Meeting at the hand of her long-dead father, her brother and her estranged husband, while her mother stood mute and watched. She didn't want to accept the devastating fact that in the months Charlie had been gone, he had not made an effort to see his boys, yet he was willing to drop everything and come to Waters Meeting with Mick if it meant sinking Rebecca on the farm.

No, she thought, I'm not going back tonight. On an impulse, she urged the mare on, up the mountain. How many times, she thought, have I run away? Like the time she'd cleared out north from her father. Or in a blind rush of disappointments felled and burned down the pines after Tom's death. And then, recently, buried the plough. She realised her patterns of reaction had to stop. If she was to transcend where and who she was in life, she had to respond differently to life's pressures. But surely she could have just one night in the hut? One night alone.

She told herself, this time, I am not running away. She was taking time out to think. She reached into her coat pocket for her phone. She knew a stump on the rock plateau on the next zig-zag up on the track that offered one bar of reception. As she neared it, she steered Miss Luella to its side and the mare stood obediently as Rebecca scrabbled from the horse and onto the stump, then sent Andrew a quick text.

*Need to camp at hut tonight. Sorry. See you first light. Please watch boys. Will be home before they wake.* She pressed the send button, then swung her leg back over the saddle.

Her phone beeped a reply text. *OK, no worries,* was all Andrew sent back.

'Good girl,' she said to the mare and again stroked her as she settled back into the saddle. 'You are magic. I think I'm falling in love with you.'

It was much darker by the time she reached the hut. The moon offered a little assistance on the trail in between the white trunks of ghostly gums and the mare was sure-footed on the track. The moonlight glinted off the corrugated-iron roof.

Charlie and Murray had replaced the old tin the summer before on one of their boozy shooting weekends. Rebecca hadn't seen it since: she hadn't been to the hut in years. Before the boys came, she would sometimes ride up with Charlie, checking the cattle on the summer runs. They would camp in the hut, throw partially defrosted chops on the barbecue, happily down a can or two of Bundy, then cuddle up in the swag. Charlie would soon be snoring, but Rebecca always lay awake in the hut, listening to the whispers of Tom who, at one time, his darkest time, had sought refuge here.

After seeing to the mare in the night yard, Rebecca dumped the saddle down on the verandah. She lifted the latch on the door, surprised to find it was new. Small touches that somehow eroded the strength of Tom's memory. She was grateful Charlie had done some work on the hut, but when she struck a match and lit a few candles, then ignited the glowing kerosene lamp, her gratitude became tainted, even tortured.

The light revealed Muzz and Charlie had plastered the hut walls with girlie pictures from pornographic magazines. A pyramid of beer cans was stacked to the roof in one corner. Charlie had made this his male domain. As she cast the lamplight around the room, Rebecca felt reduced. His reach was still so powerful into her psyche. She looked at the faces of the women, who pouted full lips, thrust out their backsides or lifted their breasts up. Some lay back in high-heeled shoes, their legs spread, their vaginas and puckered arses waxed and bleached back to childhood. She felt humiliated. She had given this man children. Given away her own body for their family … to become a mother, and this was Charlie's answer to her devotion. This was his tribute to her womanhood?

Why had Charlie had to do this to Tom's place? Why had he had to do it to her? Why did so many men not see the impact and the insult? She felt tears rise again and the baby inside her kicked. She stooped, lit the woodheater and started to tear down the images of the women, burning them one by one.

When she got to one rough-sawn post and began to rip away yet another porno page, she knew what she would find beneath. She was crying before her fingertips found what she was searching for. The initials carved deep in the wood. Her grandfather, her father, then of course the initials belonging to her and Tom.

'Help me,' she said as she leaned her forehead against the post, meeting with the indented carvings made so long ago by Tom. She began to sob, her knees giving way. She allowed her body to slide onto the cool damp floor, her back held rigid by the post. She hugged her knees to her chest and let the tears flow. As she gazed into the roaring flames of the woodheater, she saw the women burning, the corners of the pages where their images were trapped curling up in the inferno. The women were screaming, then bursting into stellar orange flames, then fading to black.

She thought of all the women in history who had been burned at the hands of men. Men who feared their power.

As the frenzy of the fire settled into a lull, Rebecca saw the face of Tom in the dark recesses of the heater. His features were a blend of shadow and fire, but as the flames leaped and danced, sometimes Rebecca found a steadier, clearer view. To her horror, she saw on his face the devastation she was feeling: he was crying too.

# Thirty-nine

Stiff from cold, Rebecca woke from a shattered night of sleep. She was glad to hear the first bird call on the edge of dawn and felt a deep longing to see her children. She got up from where she had dragged a camp-bed mattress and blanket in front of the now dead fire and stretched her aching body. Wearily she pulled on her dogger boots, tidied up a bit in the hut, then, dragging her jacket more tightly around her, went out to saddle the mare.

By the time she was heading across the mountain plain, the sunrise was well on its way and beginning to drape colour onto the treetops. Despite the turmoil of thoughts that still swam in her head, she couldn't help but feel the joy of the horse beneath her. What a sure-footed, sure-minded, magnificent creature. But then trudging through her mind came Charlie and Mick. She could feel them on their way. Charlie would've stayed the night in the city, Trudy fussing over him at dinnertime, then they would be setting off by now. Filled with camaraderie at the 'task' they had ahead of them. Was Charlie even thinking about the little boys he seemed to have abandoned to her care?

She thought of Evie and how she advocated that 'you reap what you sow'. Why was it that Rebecca felt she had only ever put forth love and a driven passion for her family and her farm, and yet here she was on the outer of it all? She felt her father's reach. It was as if he was sending his henchmen to do his dirty work. He'd never wanted her to have the farm. What would Evie advise? she thought desperately as she wove her way down the track.

The morning sun was now turning the understorey of the bush a deep silver. She suddenly recognised within herself a damaging core belief: that she didn't deserve the best in life. What if that was the very thing that kept tripping her up? The belief that she didn't *deserve*?

But hadn't Evie also said, 'There are nasty, greedy bastards in the world.' What did you do when you woke up and discovered they are not just in *your* world, they are in your very own *family*? She knew what Evie would say. It was hard to swallow. Evie would say to practise being grateful for the 'nasty bastards' and send them love anyway, for it was only through their greed and unkindness that they were showing her the way to a better life of being forgiving and loving, particularly to herself. It was a tough concept to take on board. Particularly today. She wound her fingers in the mare's flaxen mane for warmth and breathed in the sweet scent of the bush.

As the track dipped away beneath her, then rolled up another rise, Bec pressed the mare into a jog, turning Evie's philosophies around in her head. On the flat rock plateau above the valley of Waters Meeting, Rebecca sat back in the saddle and the mare abruptly stopped. Both horse and rider cast their gaze out to what was in front of them.

The valley swept off into the distance, split by two rivers like the forked tongue of a snake. When the rivers merged, they widened and the Rebecca River continued, ribboning along fertile flats. The homestead sat to the southwest and Bec watched as the sun cleared the mountain and began to illuminate the blank faces of the windows of the house. It was hard to know what decisions the men would bring to the table, but Rebecca had the feeling the property was about to slip right through her fingers. She clenched her jaw so tightly her skull felt a split of pain run up and over it. Should I have been able to remain silent in the thankless role of the farmer's wife, she thought bitterly, the property would have remained the same.

She resolved to fight them today. To make sure Waters Meeting would not be carved up and sold out from under her boys and the baby within her. She pressed the mare on and descended the track.

The dodgy old woodstove was lively and Andrew had already found his way around the kitchen. Porridge was gently geysering in a cast-iron saucepan on the edge of the stove top. A silver pot of tea was by its side. Rebecca was about to turn from the kitchen to seek him out when she heard him on the stairs. He had his bag in his hand and was looking at her with an expression of concern and also one of slight embarrassment. He came to her.

'All OK?' he asked, taking in her tired eyes and messy hair and her nose, slightly reddened from the cold of the dawn.

She nodded, but her eyes remained haunted.

'Come. Have breakfast with me. I've got to get on the road in about twenty minutes. Frank and Gabs want me to stay with them tonight so I can explain their soil tests to them.'

She felt his quiet energy as he led her to the kitchen, stood beside her and drizzled honey over her porridge. He passed her a cup of tea.

'I'm sorry this has happened,' he said.

Rebecca smiled gently. 'I should've seen it coming, but I just couldn't face it, I guess.'

'Maybe you ought to call Sol back? He could help.'

She paused before she answered. 'No. It's not his business.'

Andrew shook his head. 'I was brave enough at least to ask you for help. You need to do the same.' He moved away, dishing up his own bowl of porridge and sitting across from her at the large wooden kitchen table. 'What time do they get here?'

Rebecca shrugged.

'What will you do?'

She shrugged again.

'I opted not to change my schedule. So I didn't crowd you. But I put in some calls and got onto Gabs. Frank and Dennis will happily modify the machine for you. Frank's modified one himself, and the Groggans are doing the same, so they'll be over next week. I've also contacted Evie and Yazzie about the meeting today. I hope you don't mind. Evie's all ready to mind Archie for the day. She said you send him in on the school bus to her from time to time.'

Rebecca nodded gratefully, a little sad Andrew was leaving. 'Oh, Andrew. Thank you. You are the best!'

He looked at her sympathetically. 'I fly out to LA at the end of the week and then on to Montana. My offer still stands. You could come on board as a project manager. We'd pay you good Bernard Truman kind of money. We're searching now for someone. The speaking circuit will run for a year, then if the movie funding comes on line, we could be looking at extending to a two-year project. Your role could be carried out mostly from the Montana ranch. It's amazing. Like a village. You and your little family are welcome.'

Rebecca thought of the passports that lay in a folder in the farm office. She'd been so excited when the boys' navy-blue books had arrived with their cute little photos, trying so hard to look serious. She'd been attempting to arrange a trip away as a family. To Bali? Or Fiji? A package tour. Anything. Anywhere. But then Charlie had put the knockers on it.

The passports had been a waste of time and money.

'Impossible,' Bec said.

'Nothing's impossible.'

'I don't think so, Andrew, but thank you.'

'The Trumans would welcome you on their ranch. They have any number of houses. Saying they're not short of a dollar is an understatement. Bernard Truman and his wife are big-time movie producers. Big ideas and big Montana hearts. It'd be exciting work for you — Bernard is somewhat of a philanthropist and a Hollywood A-lister. And he's keen to get the soils message out to the world. He'd love you on board. There's even a ranch school for the kids.'

Rebecca stared down at the bowl of porridge, knowing she ought to eat, but feeling disoriented and ill. 'Thank you. But I couldn't. I can't leave this place.'

Andrew fell silent and got on with his breakfast.

A little while later, Rebecca stood outside the back gate. Andrew bent to give Funny a pat.

'Thanks for having me,' he said, glancing up at her.

'Sorry, I've been a little rattled,' she said. She reached up to hug him goodbye and he stooped and kissed her softly on the cheek.

'Good luck,' he said, 'I'm here for you. Always remember that. Call me any time. And stop apologising.'

Watching him drive away, Rebecca felt a bitter wind get up in a gust, blasting the loose strands of hair from her forehead. She wrapped her arms about herself and, frowning, went back inside the empty kitchen and began to wash up Andrew's bowl. Never had she felt so alone.

It wasn't long until Ben and Archie were thudding sleepily down the stairs and pressuring some normality into her morning. As Bec rushed to get Ben ready for school and Archie ready for a day at Evie's shop, she felt a dull panic begin to wrap itself around her. Mick and Charlie were on their way to take Waters Meeting from her.

# Forty

They arrived around eleven-thirty. Mick clambered out of a fat-cat four-wheel drive and Charlie, who had obviously put on an extra few kilos from his mother's cooking, got out too and stretched. Rebecca watched them from the kitchen window, feeling distaste and a distance of a million light years. It was odd seeing Charlie back here again, and her mother-bear hackles rose at the thought of him not seeing the boys all these months. He could've called in to see Ben at school and Archie at Evie's if he'd been interested, but clearly he was not.

Mick walked to the back door of the vehicle and dragged out a briefcase. He looked ridiculous in his crease-proof beige chino trousers, boating shoes and a big expensive navy jumper, all teamed oddly with Blues Brothers sideburns. His hair was long and wavy, receding slightly on either side of his forehead. His skin looked marshmallowish: puffy and white.

Rebecca hadn't seen Mick out on Waters Meeting since three Christmases back. He got bored here. The reception on his phone wasn't strong enough, a fact of which he often complained. It meant he missed work calls. Trudy too was always reluctant to come. She stressed over every little danger on the farm with

Danny and David and always insisted they take off home a night or so earlier than planned. The more the boys grew into surly teenagers, the less their parents liked to share car travel time with them. Rebecca turned to heave the woodstove door open and stoke up the fire. She then dropped the hissing kettle onto the hob to make them a cuppa. Isn't that what you do for family who are about to unravel your entire life? she thought sarcastically. Give them a cup of tea?

When Charlie first walked into the kitchen, he brought with him the memory of the last night she had seen him in this place. She caught her memory with a sudden gasp: slammed up against the kitchen cupboard, his spittle on her face, the taste of blood in her mouth, his fury tearing up the room and her heart. She folded her arms about her chest, noticing how his eyes slid from her face to her pregnant belly. His mouth twitched in distaste. She wanted to yell that it *was his baby*, but instead she just muttered 'hello', not able to look long at his cold expression. Mick soon bumbled in behind with a too loud, 'G'day, sis.' He put his briefcase on the table, then made a show of kissing her on the cheek and squeezing her upper arms. She wanted to punch him.

'Tea? Coffee?'

'Not for me,' said Mick.

'Me either,' said Charlie.

Both men dragged kitchen chairs out and sat down, Mick flicking open his briefcase and taking out a neat stack of manila folders. He tried to make small talk, but he could clearly tell Rebecca wasn't up for it.

'Shall we get down to it?' he asked eventually, his dark eyes only briefly looking up from his paper-shuffling. He was a businessman after all and time was money.

Rebecca pulled up a chair. 'Get down to exactly what?' she said frostily.

'Now there's no need to be like that. This is business. You know that, Rebecca.' He slid a folder over to her. 'This is your copy. In it is Dad's will and details of the estate. I've flagged the bits relevant to the divorce. Also there's a copy of the land titles for both Waters Meeting and the cattle runs up top.'

Rebecca opened the file, the typed words swimming on the page in front of her. All the clarity she had gained in saving Waters Meeting from the banks, in planning to buy out Charlie and making a life on a regenerated property with three small children began to dissipate as Mick's words fell like bombs in a blitz.

'Firstly,' Mick pointed out, 'is the clause in the will that states Waters Meeting only stays whole and in a family estate if you remain Charlie's wife.' He glanced up to see Rebecca's reaction. When she sat bolt upright at the kitchen table and remained silent, he continued on, 'If divorce occurs, then the property shall be split between the remaining children of Harry Saunders. That would be you, Rebecca, and me, Mick.' He was spelling it out to her as if she was a baby. She felt the colour in her cheeks rise. She realised now she had been stupid to not look closer at the legalities of splitting with Charlie. But she had *trusted* the men in front of her.

She stared at Charlie; his eyes flicked over her briefly. There seemed to be no guilt, only a fury within him. He reached towards Mick's pile of documents and pulled out a red folder on which he'd scribbled *Divorce Papers* in permanent marker. He virtually threw them at her. 'They're ready to sign,' he said.

Rebecca sat staring at the folder as Mick filled up the space of her silence.

'There will be plenty after the sale for you and the boys, even after you've cleared the farm debt and given Charlie his half,' Mick said, looking across at her. He tried to sound soothing, but he was looking at her as if she was an irritation.

'Sale?' Rebecca blurted out. 'You can't sell the farm? Mick?' She looked at him desperately.

He frowned. 'You can't expect Charlie to have worked so hard on this place and not get anything for it. He needs a share of the assets.'

'But to *sell* it? Can't you give me and the boys time to pay him out?'

Mick pulled a smile with his mouth, but narrowed his eyes at her. 'Surely you didn't think you could sit on all this and not share it with your family? And as if you can pay him out. This place is going down the gurgler.'

One after the other he launched words at her that battered her, cannonballs of devastation, so that when he was done, Rebecca felt her body shaking right from her very core. But somewhere within she felt the mama-bear inside her rise. She narrowed her eyes and turned her body towards him. '*Don't* patronise me, Mick,' she said sharply. 'I'm not sitting on this because it is a monetary asset. I'm here because it is my *home*, and my *children's home*!'

'I'm not patronising you,' Mick butted in, 'but realistically —'

'Realistically you don't care!' Rebecca said. 'Neither of you care. What about Ben and Archie? Charlie, your sons?'

Charlie's eyes slid away from her.

'You're such an idealist, Rebecca,' Mick said. 'What about *my* boys and their share of our inheritance? They have just as much right now the marriage is over.'

'You were paid out years ago,' Rebecca said. 'And you know it. Your boys will have plenty and you know that too. This isn't about money. Waters Meeting isn't about money. It's about the land.'

'Don't be retarded, Rebecca,' Mick shot at her. 'It's always about money.'

She felt rage rise in her and was about to explode when Funny began to bark from her basket on the verandah. Mick stood up abruptly, glancing at his watch. He gathered up his papers and tucked them under his arm. 'That'll be them.'

'Who?' Rebecca asked.

Mick looked at her. 'Just go with it, sis. We'll sort you out very well. We can't have you out here on your own up the duff like you are with a whole farm to run. It'll be right. You'll be very comfortable and extremely cashed up.' And then he walked out of the kitchen.

She was left sitting at the table, Charlie facing her at the other end. 'Charlie?' Rebecca growled. 'Who is coming here?'

He looked at her mockingly. In a victorious, sanctimonious voice, he said, 'The geos. From the mining company. They're doing exploratory work. Mick's cut them a deal.'

'Mining? Here?'

'Where the fuck else, Rebecca? That'll teach you for getting knocked up by that Stanton. You can go running off to him now,' Charlie said as he stood and walked out of the room.

Mining? Rebecca swallowed down the shock. She ran to the window. To her horror, she saw what he said was true. A convoy of four-wheel drives and utes was pulling up to park in a line outside the farm gate. On the doors were the dust-covered logos of the mining company. The doors opened and out spilled the mining men. And in that moment, Rebecca's heart sank like a stone.

# Forty-one

That afternoon, rain blew in from the south in a furious squall. It landed on the tin roof with a roar. Rebecca had to make her usual rounds of putting pots and pans under all the places that leaked. As she did, she felt sudden uncontainable sobs rise. Occasionally a rogue tear would roll from her eyes and she'd swipe it away. In a fog, she moved about the house, knowing that out there in the rain Mick was showing the geologists over Waters Meeting and knowing Charlie would be coming back in later to see her boys. Right after he had so horribly sold them out.

In Bendoorin, she knew Evie would've put Archie on the school bus and it was now time to drive to the highway to get them.

She reached for her coat, drew on her gumboots, jammed on her Rough Rider hat and ran out from under the shelter of the homestead's verandah, Funny at her heels. Just as she laid her hand on the latch of the garden gate, she heard a vehicle arriving through the wash of rain. It was Evie pulling up in her small white car.

The old woman got out, popping up an umbrella colourfully patterned with cartoon cats and dogs. Then she opened the back door, ushered Ben and Archie out of the car, and led them by the hand to the verandah.

'Thought I'd save you a trip,' she said, holding onto the boys' backpacks and glancing up at her.

'Oh, Evie,' Rebecca said, barely holding her emotions together. 'Mick and Charlie ...' she began, but couldn't finish. 'The mines ...' she started again.

'I know. Andrew had a feeling that's what was happening and told me,' Evie said.

Then Rebecca was crying and Evie was reaching out to hold her tightly.

They stood in the rain, Evie giving comfort with one arm, and with the other, holding the umbrella up to shelter them both from the pelting drops.

After a time, Rebecca pulled away. 'I'm sorry, I'm getting you all wet. Shall we go inside?'

Evie shook her head. 'You've got a four-wheel drive? Let's go see what these miner boys are doing. The kids will be interested to see.'

Rebecca looked at her, stunned, but then she saw the look in Evie's eyes. There was mischief there. A slow smile of understanding grew on her face. 'Boys!' she called. 'Let's go see your father!'

They drove down past the shearing shed and on towards the river, following the tracks left by the mining men. They forded the river, then followed the trail onto the northern track up the Rebecca River, where the clouds were tussling with sunshine. Slowing on the bumpy road, Rebecca could hear the wheels of the vehicle splash through puddles as they lumbered up and over the farm tracks. Their progress was slow in the wet and with the boys perched on Evie's lap, Funny at their feet. Jesus took centre command between them on the seat, curling his lip at the pup, who mildly wagged her tail at him each time he growled.

As Rebecca drove, in between scuds of rain, she wound down the window and took in the beauty of the bush that was bursting with springtime vitality. The rain had only enhanced the vigour of the vegetation so that every leaf shone with silver and the air was scented with moistened perfumes.

Eventually Evie and Rebecca found the men over the old wooden bridge in the upper reaches of the property, decked out now in high-vis waterproofs and hard hats, with core-sampling machines roaring from the back of their trucks that spat up soil and rocks. The rain had eased so the noise of the drills seemed to permeate the entire valley, shattering and fracturing the air itself.

The moment the door was opened Ben launched himself from where he sat on Evie's lap. 'Daddy!'

Desperately Archie reached out for Evie to help lift him down and soon both boys were running over to their father, the dogs spilling out too. Evie and Rebecca followed.

'Hi, kids,' Charlie said, his face lighting up to see them. He stooped to hug his sons, drawing them into his embrace and kissing the tops of their heads. He slapped them on their backs in a manly greeting.

'Daddy!' they chorused. Rebecca noticed tears in Charlie's eyes.

Ben pulled back and looked around him. 'What are you doing?' he asked, pointing to the sampling machines.

Charlie looked down at the boys and Rebecca closely studied his expression. She saw the warmth leave his eyes and a sternness settle once more on his face.

'Adult business. Just farm stuff.'

'But, Dad? What's that machine doing? Why are those men here?'

'Pipe down for a bit, Ben. Can't you see I'm working here with Uncle Mick?'

'What's that, Daddy?' Archie asked, looking up hopefully to his father.

Charlie rolled his eyes with impatience and looked over at Rebecca. 'Why'd you bring them here?'

'They wanted to see you,' she said coldly.

He glanced away, irritated. 'I'll catch them at the house before we go,' he said gruffly.

'But, Daddy …'

Charlie delivered a sharp look at Ben, then returned his gaze to Rebecca. 'You had to bring them here, didn't you?' he said. Mick came to stand next to him.

'I wanted them to see the truth,' she said, standing hands on her hips, her blue eyes looking openly at him.

Charlie glanced at Evie, who stood wrapping her blue waterproof about her tiny body. 'Look, if you came here to make a scene, just get on with it,' he said.

Rebecca shook her head. 'No, Charlie. You and Mick are the ones making the scene. And once all this is over and this place is sold and dug up, it's one scene your boys will remember for the rest of their lives.' Then she turned and guided her children away from the men, whistling the dogs to her, and together with Evie she drove back downstream towards the house.

That night when Rebecca pulled the quilt up over her head, she wondered if she should rage. If she ought to fight. She imagined racing to the gun cabinet the moment she saw the geologists drive onto the place. She imagined firing a rifle out over their heads, like some crazed woman from a Western. Then she imagined rising to the call, taking on the mines with a huge media campaign. Meetings at the hall, committees formed, placards and letters, press conferences and sleepless nights.

But instead she shut her eyes and breathed, feeling the stirring and turnings of her baby within. She again felt grateful for Evie's wise counsel on the drive back to the homestead. If it hadn't been for Evie, she would be raging, out of control.

'Choose the path of love,' her friend had said, and it was in that moment that Rebecca knew she had to let go of everything she had held onto so tightly. Knowing the men and their machines would not leave. It had pained her even more to see the glory of spring and the new vibrancy that she could actually feel on Waters Meeting since she'd altered the management. But for the sake of herself and her children, she had to let it go. For the sake of love.

She turned over, tucked her pillow under her head more comfortably and looked out to the blackness behind the window, where raindrops thrummed on glass. All those years of fighting. All those years of battling. Trying to prove to her father she was good enough. To prove herself to her brother Mick, then to her husband, Charlie. To fight for her beliefs in farming methods. To fight even for time off just for herself.

She thought of Tom's tortured face in the flames. Now as she lay beside the sleeping Ben, she realised she only wanted to give her precious energy and attention to her children. Not some drawn-out fight with Charlie and a ruthless mining corporation. She just wanted to be with her kids. Nothing more. She whispered to herself: 'Let go, Rebecca. Let go, let go, let go. Let it all go, just let go.' And in a state of exhaustion, she fell to sleep.

# Forty-two

'Rebecca!' came a voice in the dark. 'Rebecca!' It was a whisper, but the tones were insistent.

Rebecca didn't want to wake, but she dragged herself from sleep. 'Tom?' she murmured.

'Rebecca!'

When she did at last wake, she knew instantly something was wrong. The heavy sound of rain wasn't the only roar coming from the tin on the roof. There was also an eerie kind of screaming, a crack and another kind of roar above the rain. Also there was the unmistakeable smell of smoke. She felt an asphyxiating crush in her lungs. She was out of bed and on her feet. She tried to flick on the light, but the power was out. She roused Ben. 'Wake up! Wake up! We have to get up!'

'But …' came Ben's sleepy voice. She hauled him up and ran into the hallway. There from the stairs flames were already feathering their way up the walls, peeling away the paint and layers of old horse-hair plaster.

Terror gripped her as she ran into Archie's room. She set Ben down beside Archie's bed. Thankfully the smoke was less thick there, but still she and Ben had begun to cough.

'Ben, you have to be a big boy and crawl along the floor with Mum. I need to carry Archie.' She bundled Archie up onto her back as he sleepily protested. The smoke was becoming unbearable, stinging her eyes and crushing her lungs, and the roar of the fire rising up the stairs was growing louder.

Outside Funny barked frantically down below in the garden. Rebecca heard a sheet of roofing iron bang and buckle. Frantically she lifted both boys and together they crawled to her room at the end of the corridor, flinging open the French doors of the verandah. She glanced down to the eastern side of the house, where panes of glass had already exploded in the heat of the flames. Licking tongues were darting out into the wet night. The blast of the cold storm shocked the boys awake and soon both were whimpering in fear.

How to get down? She thought of the old rose on the far side of the verandah and the rarely used portico at the more formal front entrance of the house. She ran along the verandah, lugging both boys. She put Ben down and ordered him to stay put.

'No!'

'But Mummy can't carry you both down at the same time. I'll take Archie and come back to get you.'

'No, Mummy, no!' screamed Ben and he refused to let go of her.

'On my back then. Hold on like a possum. Don't let go.'

Silently in her mind she sent up a call of help to Tom. Then with all her strength, she gathered up the boys and began clambering over the railing and dropped down onto the roof of the portico. Both boys dragged on her body and she almost screamed with pain when her bare feet landed on the rough roof surface tarred with tiny sharp rocks. Rain lashed down. Everything looked normal from this side of the big old homestead, but Rebecca could see sparks shooting from the line of the steep pitched roof. Rain was fizzling on the flames, but the fire had taken hold and was rapidly gobbling up the tinder-dry wooden frame of the old homestead.

'Hold on,' she said to both boys. Ben was almost cutting her airway as he wrapped his arms about her neck. Archie too was clasping tightly onto her shoulder. She was so sodden now from the rain that her pyjamas were almost slipping from her body and ripping where Archie clung so tightly.

Slowly, carefully, she lowered herself down, her toes searching for a hold. Rose thorns tore at their skin and the boys cried out. She felt her pregnant belly scraping down the dry and fragile lattice. She grabbed what she could. Gnarled old branches of the rose bore their weight, but the bite of thorns pierced their skin. A metre from the ground the lattice gave way with a crack and all three of them toppled downwards, landing hard on the gravel driveway. There was silence for a time, Rebecca lying winded, unable to move, her eyes blinded by the rain that fell. The silhouette of the chimney above the kitchen was now glowing red against the pitch-dark sky. The house was roaring and groaning as it was consumed from within.

'Boys?' she called, her hands fumbling for them, trying to make out their faces in the darkness. 'Are you OK?'

Ben was whimpering and Archie had begun to build up to a loud wail.

Funny had found them and was scooting about, huffing with distress, curling her body as she nervously wagged her tail.

'My arm,' Ben was saying. 'Mummy, my arm.'

'C'mon,' Bec said, hauling herself up and reaching for them. 'It's not safe here. We have to keep going. We have to get Funny to safety, OK? You have to be brave, boys, and save your Funny dog! Come on.' Barefoot and soaked, she half dragged, half carried the crying boys across the farmyard towards the machinery shed. Now with some distance from the house, their little faces were lit with awe as they watched the Waters Meeting homestead dance and buckle with the death of flames.

Bec reefed open the back door of the LandCruiser and ushered the boys into the back, then lifted Funny in with them. She turned the key over and started the engine to give them some heat. In the dim interior light, she saw her phone lying on the dash from the bus run that morning. She pressed a button and while there was no phone service in that part of the yard, the time displayed 12.15 pm. Then she climbed into the back and kissed Ben's and Archie's faces over and over. Crying, she held them all, the pup included, as they watched the farmhouse burn. The sparks jettisoned years of memory out into the night.

Rebecca opened up the glovebox and found the boys a packet of forgotten dried old jelly beans, which she fed to them for shock. Flicking on the roo spotlight that was always stowed under the passenger seat, she looked at Ben's arm. She couldn't tell if it was broken, but she told him to cradle it to his body and showed him how to control his breathing. Once the boys were settled and staring amazed at the fire before them, she went out to the shed.

Shining the big spottie, she found some horse blankets, shook them out for spiders and returned to the LandCruiser, rugging the boys up. They were both crying and shivering. She soothed them for a time as she watched the burning house crumble in on itself. The blaze of light that had been illuminating the outbuildings was dying down to a softer glow. She backed the vehicle up to the horse float and hitched it on, then returned to open the passenger door.

'Now both of you have to be brave boys. Mummy's got stuff to do. You can't be scared or you'll scare Funny. So you look after your puppy, OK?' She kissed them on the crowns of their heads as they nodded, tears gathering again in their eyes. She watched Ben's lower lip tremor, but he held onto the pup.

Rebecca knew the livestock would be fine. They were far away from the homestead on the other side of the river. But she knew she had to get herself and the boys out of here and there was no way she was leaving Miss Luella so close to the devastation to stress all night.

Rebecca jogged over to the stables. She found a halter and went to the day paddock to where Miss Luella was standing, her nose lifted to the smell of the smoke, snorting nervously, trotting back and forth, tossing her head. The mare gratefully came over to her and dipped her head into the string halter. Rebecca hitched it at her cheekbone, took the lead rope, lifted the gate latch and led her towards the already opened float door. It was shadowy and dark inside the float. The mare bowed her head, snorted and then, with one steady hoof after the other, inched her way on, snorting again loudly and tearing nervously at the hay net.

'Good girl,' Bec said, stroking her before securing the side door and lifting up the back ramp.

When she opened the door of the LandCruiser again, her boys were asleep. The muscles under her belly were screaming now. She pushed all thoughts of the pain and her baby aside. She grabbed the matches from the glovebox and went to the shed. Tonight she had one last thing to do.

Lifting up the heavy jerry can, Rebecca threw it into the back of the LandCruiser, then inched the vehicle and float down the hill towards the shearing shed. She turned right and, in the beam from the lights, found the garden gate into her father's log cabin. At the small house, she flung open the door, flipped the lid of the jerry can and slopped petrol into the dark interior. Then she tossed petrol up the walls of the old cabin, throwing the jerry can in too. She backed out the door, striking a match. She paused for a second, then threw it, listening to the *wumpfh* as the building ignited.

As the heat and pungent smell of paint and plastic began to billow toxic black smoke, Rebecca retreated to the LandCruiser. The flames warmed her face. She was soaking wet, but the rain had stopped and steam was lifting from her clothes, drifting from her like dragon's breath. She stood transfixed, watching the flames tower higher and higher. She was about to turn and go when she saw again the face of Tom behind the dance of flames.

'Tom,' she said.

He was smiling.

She turned and drove away from Waters Meeting.

# Forty-three

From her bed, Rebecca could hear parrots making the most of the morning sun following the rain as they chattered to each other, winging their way through the Rivermont garden. She watched as they clustered in the trees, nibbling at the flowering-gum blossoms. Bec lay flanked by Ben and Archie, her arms around each boy, her hair still damp from a bath just a few hours earlier. Despite Yazzie's supply of luxury body wash and loofahs, she could still detect the faint taint of smoke that remained etched in their hair and skin. Bec looked up at the ceiling as she remembered the events of the previous day and night. She wondered what the rubble of the Waters Meeting homestead would look like now in the cold light of day and whether the cremation of her father's cabin was complete.

She had seen TV news footage of people who had lost everything in bushfires, and had felt their pain at having to start again. But this morning, instead of feeling devastated as she'd imagined she would, she felt utterly cleansed. Her boys were safe. That was all that counted. Mick and Charlie were going to sell Waters Meeting to the mines. The land was lost. To her, that was far worse than losing the homestead, which she knew now had carried so many demons and ghosts. What tore her up, though, was the fate of the land. She pushed the thoughts from her mind and kissed each of her sons.

Bec knew the fire must have started in the kitchen woodstove: the dodgy old door had been telling them for years it was time for a new firebox and seals. She also knew that fire investigators would probably discover the cabin fire was deliberately lit, but she just didn't care. It was as if the whole sorry business was meant to be.

She thought of Tom and suddenly she knew it *was* all meant to be. In some way, from where he was in the non-physical world, he was freeing her from the place. From the negative memories of himself, her father and her life as the farmer's wife.

Each time she began to catalogue what she had lost in the house fire and all the old family possessions, she would sway her thoughts back to gratitude. She had her life. She had her boys. She had her freedom. It could have been so horribly different. The thought shuddered through her. She could almost hear the screams of burning people in the night. She pulled her children closer, realising they all could have died. Thankfully it hadn't turned out that way.

Instead they had landed in the safety of Rivermont. Yazzie had met them at the door under the gleam of the porch light with a puzzled and fearful expression on her face. The sight and the smell of Rebecca, Ben and Archie, who held the shaking Kelpie pup in his arms, soon told her all she needed to know.

She had bustled them inside, escorted by the dogs Wesley and Ruby, and said only, 'I'll get Evie.'

Rebecca had felt a relief wash over her. Evie was here.

Yazzie had rushed to the guest room to wake the old woman, who, in her quiet no-fuss manner, had brought a sense of calm to the situation, giving Yazzie a chance to go out to the float to unload Miss Luella and put her in a stable.

While Evie had run the boys a bath, she had taken the time to look over their injuries. Ben's right forearm was knocked badly, but Evie concluded there were no breaks. She set out one of her creams and a bandage for him on the bathroom cabinet as she stripped him off and helped him into the giant frothing bathtub. Next she surveyed the cut on Archie's head and laid out butterfly plasters to suture it after his bath. They cried a little as the water stung the rose-thorn scratches on their bodies, but the lavender oil that orbed in the water released a soothing steam that soon settled them.

Next Yazzie was back, standing at the bathroom door. In each hand was a cute rubber ducky.

'I got these out of the cupboard,' she said as she squatted down beside the bathtub and held them out to Ben and Archie. 'Here you go. My little ones, Abby and Nicholas, loved these. You can play with them too.'

'Thank you, Yazzie,' said Ben quietly as he took the duck and passed the other to his brother.

'You're so very welcome.' On her way out of the room, she squeezed Rebecca's arm. 'I'm so glad they're OK,' she said before leaving.

Rebecca swallowed down tears as she stooped to bundle their pungent smoke-soaked clothing into her arms.

Evie moved over to her. 'Now you.'

'I'm fine.'

'You and your baby need healing,' Evie said, taking the clothes from her. 'I'll get the bath going in Yazzie's room.' She plucked a guest robe from the back of the door and passed it to her. 'Put this on and watch the boys while I'm gone. I'll call Dennis. He's the rural fire captain, isn't he? He'll sort things out for you.'

Rebecca nodded, grateful for Evie's gentle instructions and control. She could feel her muscles jump and spark from nerves and her hands had begun to tremble. By the time she had eased her scratched and sore body into the bathtub, the tears had come again. Next Evie was back with a tea and some 'tonic'.

Bec sat up, the bubbles of the bath sticking to her skin, and took the cup from Evie, the fine bone china rattling as she held the saucer. 'Oh, Evie, I can't believe Mick and Charlie —'

Evie shushed her. 'Have your bath. Sleep on it. Don't think of it again until the morning. Nothing will seem as bad then.'

And Evie had been right. To have each child folded into her arms and breathing softly on her skin this morning was enough for the moment.

But the feeling of peace was short-lived. A sharp contraction ripped through her pelvis, causing her to jump suddenly and wince. Ben and Archie both murmured and stirred, but did not wake as she slid her arms from beneath their heads.

Rebecca hauled herself up, cramped over and grimacing. Crab-like, she hulked her way to the bathroom and saw her wild-haired, wild-eyed reflection in the mirror, which sent a wave of panic through her. Another rip of pain swamped her and she gripped the marble benchtop white-knuckled and stared into her own eyes in the reflection. Fear that she could be losing her baby charged her mind. She spun away from the mirror and, clasping her abdomen beneath the swell of her belly, made her way along the hall. 'Evie?' she moaned. 'Evie!'

There was no haste or panic in Evie when she came to meet Rebecca at her bedroom door. 'Lie down on my bed,' she said as she pulled on her light green silk robe and flicked her long plait out from beneath the collar. 'Breathe.'

Evie stood over her. Her hands hovered in the air above Rebecca's body. She saw Evie shut her eyes, then felt the heat and energy radiate from the old woman's palms. Yazzie was soon at the door, looking from Evie to Rebecca with concern.

'Get the car ready, sweetheart, please,' Evie said to Yazzie without opening her eyes. 'We're going to get Rebecca to the hospital. The doctor can run some tests.'

# Forty-four

In the Bendoorin hospital, Dr Patkin peered at Rebecca with concern, his glasses sliding down the bridge of his nose as she lay on the cool sheets of the bed in a hospital gown. She was shaking uncontrollably and her teeth were chattering. She felt ice cold. The fear that her baby would come slithering, premature and dead, from her body haunted her mind. Evie clutched her hand and told her to breathe and to trust. Rebecca could tell from the way the nurses hovered and by Dr Patkin's deep frown that the situation was serious.

'Won't someone crack a joke?' Bec said, her voice choked with fear. She couldn't possibly lose her baby. Not now. Not after she had lost everything, save her children!

As Dr Patkin hooked her up to the ultrasound monitor, he said to her, 'What on earth were you doing, getting yourself into that kind of a scrape? Burning buildings! I mean, *really*.' He delivered her a phoney look of disapproval and patted her hand. But his reassurances did little to quell the dread that haunted her as they stood, waiting.

'Now let's see,' Dr Patkin said, turning to the monitor. The nursing staff who had rushed Rebecca straight in, downing the tasks of their usual early morning rounds with the elderly patients, were now watching the monitor too. She could see the worry in their eyes. By the time they'd set the sticky monitor dots on her body, and Dr Patkin had dolloped a good dose of lube on her belly, Bec realised the cramps had stopped. But still fear raged through her that she could lose the baby. The silence within her body filled her with more fear than the pain.

Dr Patkin slid the ultrasound handpiece over her belly amidst the cold jelly-like lube and for the moment all she could see was a kaleidoscope of colour on the screen.

The nurses stood still and silent. Rebecca squeezed Evie's hand.

'Look,' he said at last. He tapped the image on the monitor with his index finger. 'There she is. Right as rain. Happy as Larry, or Lara as the case may be.' He swivelled the monitor and his index finger tapped again on the image. Rebecca felt the collective sigh of relief from the staff as the tension left the room. Tears came to her eyes as she looked at the image, which reminded her of a weather satellite photo, the way the colours swirled in a kind of vortex. At the centre was a tiny little being. Joy at seeing her baby there on the screen, alive and well, rose in Rebecca, along with a sense of utter relief. Evie let go of her hand. The nurses began to drift from the room, smiles on their faces.

'She?'

'Did you want to know the sex? I kind of let it slip, sorry,' Dr Patkin said.

'She?'

'Yes, she. And all looks fine. You and she will be fine. I believe you've pulled a few muscles. That's all. And the stress of your night-time dramatics, combined with a lack of sleep, has brought on some cramping. I'll run some more tests in an hour or so, then if everything still looks OK, you'll be right to go home, I'd say. But your blood pressure's fine. You're as fit as a fiddle and the baby is too.'

Bec laughed as Evie again took up her hand and gave it a squeeze.

'Can you call Yazzie please?' Rebecca asked Evie eventually. 'Let her and the boys know it's all OK.'

An hour later, propped up in bed and halfway through a meditation on Evie's iPod, Rebecca's eyes flew open. Standing at the foot of the bed, grinning like an idiot, was Gabs, wearing a long orange paisley maxidress and Elmer Fudd-style beanie.

'What the …?' said Rebecca, tugging the earpieces from her ears.

Gabs proudly held up a brown paper bag stamped with Evie's shop name. 'Been shop lifting!' she said, then twirled about so her dress skimmed over the toes of her Blundstone boots. She rummaged in the bag and pulled out what looked like a giant purple-and-gold striped curtain with an orange sash.

'What is that?' Rebecca asked.

'Your get-out-of-hospital outfit. Like it?'

Rebecca clapped her hand to her mouth and shut her eyes.

'You're not gunna cry on me, are ya?' Gabs said. 'It's not that bad. Count yourself lucky. I've been thinking of burning my house down too. I just can't face the housework either. Especially the washing. Smart move, Bec, torching the joint. And you get a new wardrobe! Look.' She held the garment up in front of her and wiggled about, lifting her eyebrows up and down. 'Sex-y!'

Rebecca shook her head at her cheeky friend and giggled.

'Candy's store isn't open yet, but I've had my eye on a packet of super-sized beige undies in there for a while now. Reckon they could tide you over till you get more clothes.'

'Oh, Gabs,' sighed Rebecca.

'Oh, Gabs? Oh *fuck*, I'd say,' Gabs said. She also sighed, then lifted her dark eyebrows. 'Hard to believe it's all gone. House and farm!'

Bec agreed, the sombre moment settling between them.

Gabs broke the silence. 'Still, as long as you and the boys and the bub are OK. That's all that matters.'

Bec blinked away tears. 'I know,' she said quietly.

'And of course looking fabulous matters too, so c'mon, try it on!' said Gabs as she whipped the garment up in front of her, then tripped on the hem of her maxidress and tumbled over to Rebecca with the giant kaftan in her hand. As her friend landed groaning on top of her bed, with her beanie askew, dress rucked up, Bec couldn't help but feel the sense of life's ridiculousness wash through her, causing her to laugh at herself and her dear friend.

Later, Rebecca waited in the passenger seat for Evie outside the Heaven is Here! shop, wearing the bright purple-and-gold kaftan. She looked down and snickered again at the sight of herself. 'Un-bloody-believable,' she said.

Bec watched as Evie came out of her shop with Jesus tucked under her arm, locked the door, then went into Larissa's coffee shop next door. She was grateful after all that had happened she could still laugh. Rebecca looked down to her lap, her body beginning to ache from all that had gone on. She reached for her phone on the dash. She felt like calling Sol. She hadn't heard from him since she'd been so rude about Miss Luella. She knew Yazzie would've called him to tell him about the fire. He'd had plenty of time by now to call her, no matter which hemisphere of the world he was in or what time zone. Perhaps he was giving her space, or perhaps, as Rebecca hoped, he'd given up on her altogether. That would be easiest.

She scrolled through her contacts and saw Charlie's number. She thought of the baby they could have just lost, along with Ben and Archie in the fire. They were his children. He ought to know what had happened. On the spur of the moment, she dialled his number.

\*

Charlie stood in his boxer shorts on rather grotty brown carpet at the foot of Chatelle Frost's empty rumpled bed. He frowned when his phone rang and he saw it was Rebecca. He'd driven all afternoon and most of the night from Waters Meeting to manage a few hours in the sack with Chatelle, so his parents wouldn't be any wiser. They had always frowned upon him dating local girls. His mum had already been calling his phone to ask when he would be home and to find out his whereabouts. Now here was Rebecca calling, clearly to give him an earful about Waters Meeting and the mines. 'What do you want?' he barked down the phone.

Rebecca winced at the sound of his voice. 'Charlie?'

'What?'

'There was a fire,' she began slowly.

'So early in the season?' he said impatiently. 'Not likely.'

'The homestead. It's gone.'

'Gone? Whaddaya mean gone?'

'Burned down.'

Charlie ran his fingers through his thinning hair and felt fury rise to his face and his neck muscles strain. 'You lit it, didn't you? How could you? You stupid —'

'No, Charlie. I didn't,' she said. 'It was horrible. We could've lost our boys. And … and now,' she stammered, 'I've just come from the hospital. I thought we'd lost our baby. Our girl.'

Girl? Charlie thought. As he stood in silence, digesting Rebecca's news, he watched Chatelle from the bedroom window as she put washing on the line, barefoot, while two of her kids tore about in a noisy game of chasing. The third little one was plonked at her feet on a tufted patchy lawn in a too full nappy, sucking on the end of a turned-off garden hose. Charlie noticed the soft shape of Chatelle's upper thigh as she reached up in her short black-and-red negligee to clasp a peg on the washing line. He turned his back on the sight.

'*Our* baby, Rebecca? *Our* boys? For all I know, none of them are my kids. And now you've gone and done this. I'll be calling my lawyer. And the police. And I'll be putting in for my full entitlement of the insurance on the homestead.'

Rebecca felt the coldness in him. Did he not even care if his own children were safe? Did it all come down to money now? She sat in Evie's little car, staring at the road ahead of her, wondering where on earth the boy she fell in love with had gone? How had he become so lost? How had she allowed herself to be walked on this way by the man she had at one point trusted? Then she shut her eyes and felt the sting of a life she herself had created. It was little wonder given her upbringing. She thought of her aloof career-focused mother and her bitter angry father. And of her mother's disappointment in her and her father's coldness towards her. And suddenly she knew why her life had turned out this way. Never had she felt truly loved, or protected in life. Never.

She let out a deep slow breath. 'Do whatever you want when it comes to the money,' she said gently. 'And do what you like to Waters Meeting — it's on your conscience for the rest of your life. Just don't ever take my children from me.'

'That,' he said definitively, 'is one thing I will never take from you. I don't want to see you and I'm not even sure I want to see them. Not for a very long time at least.' And with that he hung up the phone.

Rebecca sat for a time slowing her breathing. In through her nose, then slowly out her mouth, closing her eyes and gently trying to bring calmness into her body. Charlie was lost to her. And for now, to the boys. But she knew, slowly, he would come back to his boys, and possibly his third child, once he saw that she was so clearly his.

Genetic traits couldn't lie.

Somewhere in the future all she could do was trust that they would all be happy as Lara, as Dr Patkin had said. Rebecca laid a hand on her belly. It was a nice name, Lara, but it was not for her baby. The memory of the name would forever be linked to the scare she'd just had in the hospital and to the fire.

Bec looked up to see Ursula Morgan trudging along the street purposefully with a big cardboard box in her arms. She walked right up to Evie's car and stood, trying to wave with the box. Bec wound the window down.

'I'll chuck this in the back, shall I?' Ursula asked, lifting the box. 'We heard about the fire and the hospital and that. So us school mums did a whip round this mornin' … got ya clothes, toys and stuff for the boys.'

Bec tilted her head, amazed at how fast word travelled in this tiny town, and surprised by Ursula's gesture of kindness.

'Really? Thank you! Thank you so much!' Bec swallowed down tears.

'The bub OK?' Ursula asked as she placed the box in the back seat of the car.

'Right as rain, thanks.'

'Good,' she said, slamming the door. 'Sing out with whatever else youse need. A new dress for one thing. That thing you're wearing sucks. But don't worry, the Parents and Friends are doing a raffle for ya.'

'Thanks. Tell them thanks,' Bec said, a little stunned.

'See ya then.' And then Ursula was gone, hitching up her shiny black tracksuit bottoms and heading to Candy's store.

Bec pressed her thumb and forefinger into her closed eyes, overcome by the sudden show of kindness from Ursula and the other mums. It was a good place, Bendoorin. She sighed and tried to find some kind of centredness after all that had happened.

Soon Evie was coming over to her with two takeaway cups in her hand, along with a bag of groceries and Jesus trotting at her heels. She opened the car door.

'It's arranged,' Evie said. 'Larissa is taking care of my shop while I help at Rivermont. We've opened the internal door between the two, like we did when Archie was in the city. Ideal. Customers can wander through. She'll just run the two tills. It's easy. I'm all yours.' As she settled the shopping bags on the back seat, she said, 'I see Ursula and the P&F ladies found you. That's good. I got the boys and me a quiche for dinner. You'll be too tired to cook for them and Yazzie will be busy with the do that's on later today.' She shut the door while Jesus pushed his way to the front and sat on Bec's lap.

'Do? What do?'

Evie got into the driver's side and began to drag the seat belt over her shoulder. 'You've forgotten?' she asked, looking at her. 'That's why I was staying at Rivermont last night. Sol's flying in for it.'

'What kind of do?' Rebecca asked, stroking the smooth white hair of Jesus.

'The bloodstock show. They used to hold it on their place at Scone … just an annual day to showcase their babies and their stallions. Fancy-pants people fly in, look at horses, sign big cheques for the yearlings or put in dibs for a service fee. It's a bit of a wank. Yazzie hates it, but does it for her dad.'

'Ah!' Rebecca said, remembering Yazzie swearing at the over-the-top invitations her father's new French wife had designed and the ridiculous number of celebrities the woman had asked, ahead of the regular clients.

'They're people who aren't even remotely interested in racing!' Yazzie had said in exasperation, eyeing her new stepmother's guest list with disgust. 'They only go for the fashions on the field once a year at the Cup and the attention of the cameras.' It was all coming back to Rebecca. The Rivermont staff had been preparing for weeks.

'That's *today*?' Rebecca asked Evie, realising she'd been an entire world away from Rivermont lately, with her focus on sorting out Waters Meeting.

'Yes. And Sol's flying in,' Evie said again.

'You mentioned that bit. Twice.'

'Did I?' said Evie with a glint in her eye. 'Must be getting senile,' and she turned over the ignition so her little white car purred. Then she locked her green eyes onto Rebecca's profile as Rebecca stared ahead at the road, trying to stifle a smile. So the old lady knew about what had gone on between her and Sol. Evie must've been his confidante. She knew it all. A sudden rush of feeling for him flooded her mind and body, but as soon as she felt it, Rebecca shut it down again. Her confidence wavered.

'Maybe I should go back to Waters Meeting. Let the chooks out to free range. Check the stock.'

Evie shook her head as she put the car in gear and pulled out onto the wide empty main street of Bendoorin. 'Not on your Nellie! There's no way I will let you go back out there. Dennis and the local firies are dealing with it. All those boozy nights in the shed with your ex-husband will pay off. They'll handle it for you. Gabs said she'd head out now to relocate your chooks at her place and Frank will check the stock. I'm out at Rivermont anyway for the next few days. You may as well make the most of a free babysitter. Take some time for yourself.'

'But the fire. The mining ...'

'It's all over now, Rebecca,' Evie said, glancing at her. 'There's not a thing you can do. Plus, even though Dr Patkin said you and the baby are perfectly fine, if you go out to Waters Meeting, you won't rest in *here*.' Evie tapped an index finger to her forehead. 'You must take your mind off that place and the plans those men have for it. It will do you no good. Stay at Rivermont where the energies and people are bright. It will stop you worrying.'

'Who said I'm worried?' Bec said, a frown on her face. She sat with her head downcast. 'I worry too much, don't I?' she said eventually. 'It's as if I've learned nothing!'

Evie laughed. 'Nonsense. You have transitioned in an amazing way. Believe in yourself. Now I'd suggest, while we're in range, that you phone your brother. Let him know about the house fire. He can take care of all of it now. The livestock. The lot. If he wants the money, he can deal with it.'

Rebecca looked at her phone on the dash. The thought of calling Mick settled like lead in her belly, but Evie was right. 'OK, I'll call him.'

Evie pulled the car over. Rebecca looked up to see the police sign. A smart-arse youth had again graffitied the sign. This time it read: *POLICE ARE NOW TARGETING FUCKWITS*. She found a chuckle. Then she looked at her phone. 'I can't. I can't call him.'

Evie made a tut-tutting noise. 'Here,' she said, 'give me your phone. I'll call the fat bastard.'

Bec chuckled again, this time at Evie. She sat and listened while her friend delivered her clipped businesslike message to Mick. She could hear his charming bluster on the other end of the line. He'd already heard from Charlie about the fire and was wondering what was going on (though apparently not about her or the boys' welfare).

Rebecca knew now that Mick would make a few calls, offer some cash and cartons of beer around, and the responsibility of the clean-up and the livestock would be palmed off to some local man. Blokes who Mick would've sunk beers with in the Fur Trapper in his youth. Mick always got his way. Bec felt the pang of longing for the sheep and cattle she had begun to connect with again. She was giving those animals over to Mick too. The thought tugged at her heart.

'Fuckwits indeed,' said Evie once she had hung up, staring at the sign. She drove on.

Rebecca watched the countryside rolling past: it seemed softer now since the rain. As they began the first climb up the mountain pass, she broke the silence and turned to Evie. 'You knew the baby was fine, didn't you? In your room at Rivermont.'

'Yes. I did,' she said.

'Then why did you take me into the hospital?'

'Because you needed to go to allay your fears. Your own belief system in energetic or self-healing is still a little blocked. Often conventional medicine reassures the mind until you learn to be in your own alignment. It's a slow process for some.'

'Particularly for dumb buggers like me,' Bec said, sipping on the takeaway hot chocolate Evie had bought her.

'Yes, especially for dumb buggers like you,' Evie said with a soft smile. 'Get control of your thoughts and you will get control of your life. And you must *allow*. Allow love in. Allow good things in. You deserve it.' And with that Jesus let loose with a toe-curling stench that sent them grappling for the window winders.

'I'm more about allowing dog farts out of my life at the moment than I am about allowing love in! *Jesus Christ!*' said Rebecca.

# Forty-five

Later that day, Rebecca felt a surge of vertigo that came from the shock of the past few days as she walked to the horse truck that was rumbling into the Rivermont car park. Over at the tack room, Joey was already sipping on a mid-morning UDL of raspberry vodka. He would set the can down in random places as he polished tack and hung the bridles and halters on the brass hooks beside the stalls. The rearing bits clanked as he washed them in buckets of steaming water. He seemed to be excited about the afternoon parade. He looked up, took in what Rebecca was wearing and burst out laughing. She was still wearing the kaftan and a borrowed pair of riding boots.

'Oh! Thanks for the sympathy!' Bec said. 'I've had a very harrowing experience.'

'You still are, by the looks of it.'

'Joey! A bit of sympathy would be nice.'

'No. No. It suits you! You look really … really … swinging seventies?'

It was clear Joey was up for a big one, as he apparently had been at every year's Stanton bloodstock parade that they'd held in Scone. This was the inaugural one for Rivermont, so Joey was putting on an extra show of excitement as he turned towards the horse transport vehicle.

'Scuba!' yelled Joey as he raised his bottle at the truck driver. 'Check out the female version of Kamahl here!'

The door opened and out jumped a lean-framed man; a little scraggy white dog wagged her tail from the driver's seat, mirroring Joey's excitement. The Rivermont dogs and Funny joined in the fray, Jesus curling his lip and growling wildly yet wagging his tail at the same time.

'Hello,' the man said to Rebecca. 'Nice frock. Did it come with a flying carpet?'

'What took you? Did you use your dick as a compass and get waylaid?' Joey asked.

'That'd be you, Joey,' came Scuba's dry reply.

Yazzie emerged from the stable office. 'What lucky straw did we draw getting you to drop the horses off?' Yazzie called when she saw which driver had transported the Rivermont gallopers back from their city stable at the racetrack. 'How are you, gorgeous?'

Scuba beamed at her and opened up his arms. 'I'm better than good! I wouldn't miss a day like this with my galloper girls! Oh, I much prefer you over my pacer girls any day! You're a far classier lot and you fight less between yourselves!' He folded Yazzie into a hug before dropping the truck's hydraulic tailgate, which acted as a rubber-coated loading ramp. With speed and efficiency, the Rivermont crew soon had the sheened horses unloaded from their angled bays and the gear unpacked from the side boxes of the truck.

'Only light duties for you,' Joey said, taking the bag of racing prize-winner rugs from Rebecca. 'There's flowers to arrange in the smoko room for the podium where Sol will speak.'

'Flower arranging? Me?'

'Go on. Get in touch with your girlie side.'

As Bec walked alongside Joey, she realised Evie was right: there was no time to dwell on the fate of Waters Meeting or the fire. She heard a fizz and next Joey was handing her a watermelon Midori that he'd grabbed up from his stash in an Esky near the stables.

'There you go, hot stuff,' Joey said with a wink.

'But I'm pregnant. I'm just out of hospital. And it's only eleven-thirty.'

'It's five o'clock somewhere and it's got fruit in it. It'll be good for the bub. Drink up, you smokin' hot mama, you!' He began to sing 'Light My Fire' and cast a stirring grin over at her.

She'd thought she would spend her day in a state of shock, exhaustion and devastation, but instead she felt utterly energised. It must be Evie's magical kaftan, she thought jokingly to herself. The complexity and tragedy of the situation over at Waters Meeting felt an entire world away as she watched Joey's and the crew's energetic efficient manner as they led horses to and from the washbay, soaping the animals' tails, gliding the scraper over their perfect coats. She had already stopped into the stable to see Miss Luella, and the mare had whickered to her and leaned her head into her chest, acting as divinely as if she was a horse from a pony-club novella for kids. Tears of shock and gratitude rose again, but Bec soon settled herself with her slowed breathing and inhaling the rich scent of her beautiful horse. Then Rebecca had returned to the smoko room, where tubs of flowers had been delivered, making the room look like an opera diva's dressing room.

'We need six big vases in all. Two for the podium, two for the buffet and two for the entrance to the parade ring,' Yazzie had instructed, looking cowgirl-chic in cut-off jeans, cowgirl boots and a white lacy top.

'Righto,' said Bec, taking in this odd world she had found herself immersed in. They're rich people doing their thing, she thought, but they're good people, somewhat still tortured by their parents, she concluded. No different from herself.

'How's your Martha Stewarting going, Smokey Bandit?' Joey called to her through the window of the tack room. As painful as Joey sometimes could be to all the staff with his occasionally over-the-top exuberance, Rebecca was grateful for his stirring jibes. She knew he was doing it out of support for her.

He'd come alive, knowing there would be more people here soon to satisfy his insatiable thirst for attention and he was keeping her buoyant too. Evie again was right: the energies of this place and its people were *brighter*, somehow.

With a vase of red and white roses clasped in her hands, Rebecca walked through the gleaming white wooden gate to the front lawn, where a marquee was being put up. The younger of the horses were already being led about by Steph, Daisy and the rest of the girls to get them used to the ring, their brushed, washed and glossed tails cut to blunt ends. Some yearlings called out, others snorted with bowed heads, wearing headstalls of leather with brass buckles of gleaming gold. Bec spotted one filly with the nearside brand of SS for Sol Stanton. It stood out in frosted white against her deep bay shoulder.

Sol will be here soon, she thought, and felt a shiver of anticipation and nerves. She looked at the kaftan that was drawn tightly over her six-month baby belly and wondered what else she could find to change into. Then she laughed at herself. What hope do I have with Sol? Look at me, she thought.

She made her way round to the front of the house, passing daffodils and boxed hedges made even more quaint by painted wooden bird houses.

The Stantons had gone all out for this event. The English oaks that stood elegantly above the homestead were waving their leafy greens to the blue sky and later, the limbs of the grand old dames would be lit by spotlights as the sun dropped beneath the horizon. The garden looked as if it was a patch of a Jilly Cooper novel transported to Australia. The roses were blooming succulently and sunlight was gliding off the flanks of the horses. In a cage near the marquee, doves were fanning their tails and cooing and flapping at each other.

Bill Hill was busy setting out plastic chairs for the small elite crowd that would soon arrive. 'Nice outfit! Where'd ya park ya camel?' he called.

Bec smiled. He gave her a sympathetic nod of his head. He too was jollying her along this morning, following what had happened at Waters Meeting. The moment she thought of the fire, Bec suddenly felt incredible tiredness wash over her.

Yazzie, speaking on her mobile, gestured to Rebecca. She placed her hand over the phone and said, 'After you've done the flowers, would you mind taking the silk rugs and dropping the correct ones outside each of the stalls for our veteran runners? The names are on them for each horse.' Bec nodded and was about to turn to go when her friend put a hand on her arm. 'You feeling OK?'

Bec smiled and mouthed 'yes'. But Yazzie shook her head. 'You're not. Go and lie down. Go see your boys, then go lie down. And take that … that … *thing* off. Honestly! Evie and her shop clothes!' She pointed to the phone. 'Don't worry, they've put me on hold. Bloody airlines.' She rolled her eyes.

'OK.' Bec made to leave again, but Yazzie came to stand before her on the perfect lawn before the perfect homestead where Rivermont was crawling with staff and activity.

'Sorry about all this,' she said, waving her arms about the scene. 'I can't stand it. But every year Dad insists on doing it. And do you know what … I hate doing it, but every year I keep saying yes to him. I keep organising it for him. For what?' She rolled her eyes again.

'It's very glam,' Bec conceded. 'A little bit … how shall I say it without being rude? Over the top?'

'I know,' Yazzie said, wrinkling her nose. 'To add insult to injury, I've just found out Dad's not even going to make it now. He and Sol are battling it out with a big company on some secret corporate deal. It's got conservation at its heart, apparently, so Sol isn't letting go of it. To top that, Dad's headed for *another* divorce by not bringing wife number three here to mix with all her fancy-pants guests! She's furious!'

Bec felt her heart sink. And Yazzie must have sensed it.

'Men,' she said. 'They go off as if it is their duty. As if they are supposed to be the big providers. And what do we women want? To have them home with us and to hear we are loved. My dad, he's never once told me. No wonder I make poor choices in partners!' She let out a breath. 'Come, I'll walk with you to the house. You, my girl, need a sleep.' They fell in step on the white gravel drive. 'Did your dad ever say he loved you?'

Bec shrugged. 'Don't recall,' she lied.

'Oh, you would if he had. All my life I've worked my guts out for Dad and his life … This is the last year I do this. I swear. I'm through.'

Bec noticed tears in Yazzie's eyes. The stress of everything was at last getting to her. 'What is it with us women, hell bent on pleasing men?' she mused. 'Men who aren't even kind to us.'

'Gawd,' Yazzie said. 'It's the whole Cinderella thing. Look at me. I was raised a princess. Blonde hair, blue eyes, small enough to blow over in a strong wind. Oh, I did the men thing. Men would want to *own* me. Treat me like some little wind-up dolly. Mum put me in ballet shoes and little silk dresses from the day I was born and *encouraged* it. It was all about meeting *the one*, getting married. Living happily ever after. What a crock that turned out to be. But I'm glad I went there. I wouldn't be who I am today.'

'But don't you want to repartner?'

Yazzie looped her arm in Rebecca's, her slender fingers resting on her forearm. 'My dad is doing enough repartnering for all of us. With wife number three chucking the hissy fits she does, it won't be long till there's a number four on the way. So after today, I am outta here. At least for a month, so Dad realises what I do for him.'

Bec glanced at her with concern, not wanting Yazzie to leave.

'Oh, don't worry! You can stay at Rivermont. As long as you like. There's room, as you know,' she said, gesturing to the house and shaking her head. 'And Sol will be back soon for a stint to keep you company. I rattle around in it by myself. Just me and the dogs.' Then she looked out hopefully to the hills. 'I'm going to stay with a family I stayed with once in Argentina. Beautiful horse place. Lovely people. Just for a month to get my thoughts right again. I'll be back in time for you and the baby though,' she said, smiling. 'In the meantime, get your head on that pillow, girl!'

The first helicopter laden with guests woke Rebecca at around one-thirty that afternoon. She got up from her bed and pulled on a robe, then picked up the purple-and-gold kaftan and made a face. She was stunned to realise that after the fire she didn't own a bra, or a set of undies, let alone any party clothes. All of her past was burned. As she stood naked beneath the bathrobe, she felt utterly cleansed. All she wanted to wear right now was a set of wings, so she could fly in life.

She smiled when she saw the pile of clothes for her to try and a little daisy set nicely on top with a note from Yazzie. *For the new you*, the note read.

Just inside the door someone had placed polished cowgirl boots turned in fancy tan and turquoise embellishments. Judging from the red rose that protruded from one boot and the bottle of fruit Midori that jutted from the other, Bec figured Joey had been on the job and he and the stable girls had got together to organise the boots.

She glanced out of the window, seeing the trees whirl about as the chopper landed. She wondered if Sol had changed his plans and would be on board. Part of her wished he had.

In the shower, she took extra care in washing her hair. There would be some fancy people out there and she didn't so much feel compelled to look her best, as she wanted to help put on a good show for Rivermont.

When she went downstairs, she found the boys, exhausted from the night before, snuggled with Evie on the couch, watching *Puss in Boots*. The sound of Puss's accent only accentuated her longing for Sol. She sat with the boys for a moment, giving each of them a cuddle.

Neither Ben nor Archie were interested in going out for the horse parade, where the guests were clustering in the marquee, bubbles in hand, women divoting the lawn with their spiked heels. Bec's boys had seen enough of the choppers and they'd had a quick tour of the setting. It was enough for them to get that this was a boring adult world and they were better off inside with Evie and the DVD.

Bec chose a fresh white linen shirt that draped nicely over her pregnant belly and pulled on faded but new denim maternity jeans, which she did up with a thick leather hobble belt beneath her belly bulge. It was down to its last notch.

As she looked in the mirror, she felt renewed. And utterly grateful for the care of the people around her. Before her stood an entirely different person. On the outside and within — not to mention that other part of her that sat high up somewhere on another plane of existence.

Bec let her hair down for a change, blonde waves brushing her shoulders and down her back. It felt odd to be putting on makeup in Yazzie's fully stocked guest bathroom, but she enjoyed what had become an unfamiliar process. She stopped and smelled the roses that Yazzie had placed in a small clear vase on the bathroom vanity. 'Delicious,' she said, allowing the scent to seep into her senses.

She went downstairs, out the main front entrance and walked towards the soirée that was gaining momentum on the Rivermont front lawn.

She could hear Yazzie on the PA system, taking over from Sol's designated role of MC and compere. She read from notes and was describing each horse that paraded the ring.

Bec could see Joey was parading himself more than the fancy stallion he was leading by wiggling his perfect, pert little backside sexily as he walked. There was no doubting Joey moved just as nicely as Shining Light, one of the most successful Rivermont stallions standing in the country.

She'd heard Sol once say the racehorses were bred to run, but not to thrive or to think. This stallion, however, looked anything but frail and flighty. He was swishing his tail faster than a cheerleader. The well-dressed men in the crowd stood shoulder to shoulder watching the horse as the manicured women watched Joey from behind big sunglasses that glinted gold. Many of the women were indeed not really there for the horses, but more for the glamour of the event, and sat looking somewhat bored in the fancy marquee with its scallop-edged trim, getting themselves quietly tiddly.

What was missed by the women but admired by Bec was Joey's expert handling: he gave just the right amount of check on the lead rope, inviting the best behaviour from the stallion. He had nailed the stallion's arrogance in the most subtle way in front of the crowd so they didn't even notice. Rebecca knew from the giant bruises the Rivermont staff sometimes wore on their eyes, their torsos or thighs, just how dangerous the iron hooves of a horse could be. They had the ability to pulverise muscle into permanent dents and to splinter bones. Bruises the size of dinner-plates were common in this world. As he walked past in his aviator sunglasses, Joey gave Bec a quick grin. She smiled back.

Bec felt herself falling into this world, tumbling into it, away from her known existence. The world of sheer hard work and Waters Meeting's daily domestic grind. It made her realise there were many entire worlds out there — any one of which she could choose if she wanted to. She was free.

When the parade of bloodstock was over, a string quartet began playing on the lawn, the musicians sitting straight-backed, all in black. Yazzie, in a pretty little dress of gold sheered with black lace, looked over to Bec and discreetly mimed putting her fingers down her throat, then grinned. She turned back to a big fat bald businessman, who was red in the cheeks and clearly drooling over her.

Not wanting to join the guests just yet, Bec headed back to the stables. She was more aligned with the worker's world and when she got there, she realised she and Sol would never fit. She couldn't be in his world. Only on the edges of it: with the farm and the horses. The rest of it held no interest for her. She felt sad at the realisation, and almost relieved Sol hadn't come so she wouldn't have to face his desire for her.

Suddenly she thought of Andrew and wondered how he was. Where he was? He would be out there, quietly revolutionising the world and helping enlighten others to care for the soil. She realised with a tug that she missed him too.

At the stables the team was tidying up and putting horses back in their stalls. The sun was lowering itself behind the mountain and a gentle glow was settling over the landscape. It wouldn't be long until the helicopters shattered the peace, taking many of the exclusive guests up and out of the valley, back to the city. The rest would be wined and dined at the homestead before being shown to their rooms in the guest wing.

Bec entered the courtyard and there sitting on the fountain, having a cigarette, was Joey. He was holding onto one split rein of Miss Luella's. She was saddled and standing quietly beside him, clearly pleased to be out of her box, looking about with curiosity.

'She's a beauty, isn't she?' Joey said, narrowing his eyes as he drew on his cigarette.

'She sure is. What are you doing with her?'

'You, my princess, need to ride her. I spent hours schooling her for you.'

'*You* did!'

'Sol said it was on my head if she put a foot wrong. So here she is, my gift to you.' He stood and held out the rein to her, along with a set of spurs hooked on his index finger. 'Take her for a ride. It's the best therapy. And don't worry about your baby falling out of you. I swear you are the bloody Virgin Mary. I'm still amazed you got up the duff by not having sex with me!'

Bec laughed at him. Then his face turned serious.

'Go on. Even if you just walk her. You need it after what you've been through.' There was a rare stillness to him. A softening. Bec took the spurs from him and stooped to strap them onto her new cowgirl boots. As she did, she could feel the nearness of Joey.

'You know you'll always be my Deni princess,' he said.

She stopped buckling the spur and looked up at him. 'Don't ever call me princess.'

He flashed a look at her. 'Get over yourself. You're gorgeous and I can call you what I like. Princesses can be strong and wear spurs too. Now get on.'

Bec took the reins and swung on. As she settled into a beautiful Western saddle that clearly belonged to the Stantons, Joey put his hand on her leg and looked up at her.

'You know you are awesome.'

Bec was touched by his rare show of seriousness. 'No.' She laughed nervously. 'No, I'm not.'

'Think what you like,' Joey said, 'but I think you are fucking awesome, Rebecca Saunders. I love you to bits.'

She smiled down at him. 'And I love you too, buddy. You really have helped me get back in the saddle again. I owe you. I'll never forget that night. It opened me up to seeing myself differently.'

'I know the timing wasn't quite right,' Joey said, his hand still on her thigh, 'and things flopped between us quite literally, and the age difference and all, but in another life, Bec, you'd be my woman.'

'Yeah?'

'Yeah,' he said. 'You would.' He looked up at her, sincerity on his face.

'Thanks, Joey. That's special.'

'So I suppose a quick fondle in the stable's out of the question then?' he shot at her, his joking demeanour suddenly firmly back in place.

Bec slapped him on his shoulder. 'In your dreams, man whore!'

Joey sank his hands in his pockets and said in mock indignation, 'Go on then, git with you. Heartless hussy.' He flicked his head in the direction of the stable archway and the hillsides beyond, rising up to steep-pitched granite mountaintops. 'They say if you love something, set it free … Now go for a ride, princess, and don't come back until you've figured yourself out.'

As she cued Miss Luella with her legs, neck-reined her round and rode away, Bec felt a great gratitude for Joey. As she rode on out the gate and along the laneway, she tried to read what her body might be telling her. She felt cautious about riding after that morning's scare, but her body felt fine. In fact, better than good. Live without fear, she decided suddenly, and she urged the mare on to a faster walk. There would be no cantering away to the mountains today. This evening she would ride at a walk and slow herself and everything about her life down. She wove her fingers into the luxurious blonde mane of the mare and smelled the air around her, which was scented with bushland in flower. Bec could feel she was sitting astride the most wonderful horse she had ever ridden. She registered the easy rhythm as Miss Luella walked freely over the long grasslands of Rivermont. She felt the freedom.

As she climbed the hill, the breeze quickened. The wind picked up the mare's tail and carried it through her hind legs and blew her mane in a dance, but still she ambled on in her calm quarter-horse gait. The well-schooled mare brought Rebecca thoughts of Joey's fun and kindness. She imagined what she could do with her riding once the baby was born and she could cue the mare with the spur. Surely she *would* spin on a dime!

Rebecca sent out a thank you to Joey and then of course to Sol.

Not only had Sol given her this amazing creature, but as she took in the freshness of the healthy landscape, she was grateful Sol had created all the health and vigour that grew about her on this farm.

She felt so lucky that both she and Sol had shared in the lifetime work of Andrew and his gift for inspiring others. Two incredible men. Two forms of answers to her prayers. But what now? What future could she choose? She had a deep love for them both in different ways, but as she sat on her horse, she reached deep down inside herself for an answer. Within, she felt something flicker. A glow. It wasn't strong, but she knew with time she could build it to a brighter flame … and that flame was to do with love. Not for men and 'finding the one' or relying on a man's stability. Nor was it the flame of love she always carried for her children. Instead it was the start of a burning candle that represented love for *herself*. For the first time in her life she could see the light within herself. She was, if she chose to see it, *magnificent*.

As she sat upon the golden horse high up on a ridge and looked out at the vast stretch of treed mountains before her, suddenly Rebecca knew for certain what she must do, for herself and for the world. She looked at the tall grasses wavering their native seed heads in the breeze.

And then, her mind made up, digging her heels gently in, she spun the mare on a dime.

# Forty-Six

The ten days following the Rivermont parade had become a flurry of packing and paperwork for Rebecca. Now, Ben and Archie waited excitedly beside an airline dog crate while Funny sat within, her face looking dour and unimpressed at the situation. The gangly young dog sniffed at the air, taking in the unfamiliar scent of the aviation gas and hunching over slightly from the noise of the busy airport. In a smaller crate, Jesus sat, worrying at the world he found himself in, letting out the occasional 'yip!' At the freight check-in desk, Rebecca passed the vet's letter and the rabies injection documents to the man at the counter.

'See you on the other side of the world, pooches,' Bec said, feeling a little sorry for the dogs, but pleased with their decision to take them. Having Funny along was as much for herself as it was for the boys.

The one major regret was leaving Miss Luella at Rivermont, but the cost of taking the horse with them to the United States was far too high. Bec knew the mare would be loved and ridden a lot by the Rivermont crew and that Joey and Daisy would spoil her.

'Oh, Funny, you'll be OK,' said Ben as he stroked the dog's ears through the wire.

Evie stooped to peer through too as she laid her hand on Ben's back. 'Funny how things turn out,' she said, then smiled.

The freight man stepped from behind the counter. 'Don't worry, folks, we'll take care of them.' He lifted the crates onto a small trailer and tagged them, passing Rebecca back the paperwork. 'All good to go.'

Before they left Funny and Jesus, Evie rummaged in her purse and sprayed something over the dogs.

'What's that?' Bec asked.

'Rescue remedy and bush-flower essences,' Evie said. 'I use it on Jesus every time we travel.'

'And it works?' Rebecca asked, raising an eyebrow.

'Nothing works on that dog! But animals are sent to teach us lessons,' she sighed.

'That makes sense. Funny has come to help me see the funny side of life, and to help the boys through a tricky time. The faithfulness and loyalty of dogs are inspirational. But what's your lesson from Jesus then?' Rebecca asked.

'To curb my swearing and blaspheming!' Evie grabbed each person's wrist and sprayed them with the remedy, just as Jesus started barking. She let out a loud sigh. 'Bloody dog. Here's to a smooth, safe journey!'

'Well, if you've got anything to do with it, it will be,' Rebecca said as she recalled the past few days. She'd been amazed by Evie's fast-talking efficiency on the phone with the various bureaucratic departments as she organised them all replacement passports, new visas and, in Rebecca's case, work clearances. In conversation, Evie used the house fire to open a door, but if a block came up in the process, she skilfully sidestepped it. Bernard Truman on the other side of the world in Montana turned out to be the same. He was very influential, pulling strings to get Rebecca there in time for the start of their grasslands documentary film project and Andrew's speaking tour.

As the travel plans all fell into place, Evie said, 'Just throw love and light onto the situation and watch the doors fly open for you.'

Rebecca watched and learned.

'Affirm to yourself that it will all flow!' Evie had said.

A year ago, Rebecca would've thought the woman was off with the fairies, but now she had seen first hand what a centred, calm mind could achieve with ease. It was giving her the courage to do what she was about to do.

'Let's flow then!' Bec said. 'Come on!'

Soon they were all piling into the Kluger and Yazzie drove them around the spaghetti bypasses of the airport to the busy kerbside at International Departures. There they joined the throngs of people unloading luggage from cars. Rebecca dragged the suitcases from the back and she, Evie and Yazzie hauled them onto the concrete kerb, ushering the children alongside them. The luggage was packed not only with their clothes, but also Australian Christmas gifts for the Truman family who they were yet to meet and, of course, Andrew. Their first white Christmas with either two kids or three, depending on when the baby arrived. The boys were excited. And with childish delight, Bec was too.

'That's it?' Yazzie asked.

'That's it.'

They stood for a moment, looking into each other's eyes.

'I'm going to miss you,' Yazzie said tearfully.

A glimmer of doubt passed through Rebecca as her baby did a tumble inside her and a nerve in her back twinged. 'Should I really be doing this?' she asked, placing the palms of her hands on her swollen belly.

'I'm sorry, I wasn't going to get mushy,' Yazzie said. 'Of course you should be doing this. Get your backside in there. Dr Patkin's written you a letter so you're clear to fly in your third trimester. Evie here has had more than a lifetime's experience delivering babies on outback stations. The Trumans have lined you up the best baby doctor money can buy and the boys are bursting to go. And finally, Miss Luella will enjoy her Rivermont stay. What on earth is there to stop you?' Then Yazzie answered her own question: 'Only yourself. You are the only block. It's the opportunity of a lifetime! Now go live it up!' Bravely she gathered Bec up in a hug and planted a kiss on her cheek. 'I won't be far behind. I'll be getting a big metal bird out of here asap to Argentina for the show-jumping season. I won't last a day at Rivermont with Wife Number Three. And especially without having you both around,' Yazzie said, turning to Evie.

She gave Evie a warm hug and Rebecca felt a stab of guilt that Evie would be leaving Yazzie to help her with the boys and the baby.

'A trip for yourself will be good for you, I'm sure,' Evie said. 'You make sure you get back on the horses over there! Along with whatever or whoever else is available to ride!'

Yazzie chuckled. 'Yes, I'll find my love interest too, I'm sure. It's time, like Bec, to get back in the saddle. We'll meet at Rivermont soon with tall tales to tell, and I may even get over to see you in Montana. All of us together, soon. I know it.'

They were about to part ways when a shrill of whooping and hollering rose up from behind them. Next they were swooped upon by Gabs, Candy and Doreen. They brought with them so much of their vibrant, colourful country energy to the city airport that people turned to stare.

'You came to see us off!' said Rebecca, beaming a smile.

'We had to make sure you *did* fuck off,' Gabs said, punching her on her arm.

'Shush, children present,' warned Evie.

'You can talk, you foul-mouthed trollop,' Gabs said.

'You didn't give us much notice!' Doreen said. 'One day house burns down, next day gone!'

'Yeah, but no more housework at least!' Bec said. 'And now, no more farm.'

The girls looked at her sympathetically, but then Candy excitedly began reaching into her bag. She pulled out a gift-wrapped present, tied with a red ribbon. 'Impromptu airport baby shower!' she said. 'Yay!'

Bec set down her backpack and unwrapped the present, smiling. Inside was an excessively colourful tie-dyed baby jumpsuit in rainbow hues. 'Wow!' she said.

'I made it myself.'

'Wow, Candy,' Bec said again, not sure what else to say.

'Geez Louise!' Gabs shouted. 'How's the baby s'posed to sleep in that? It's so bloody *loud*!'

'Shut it, Gabs!' Candy said. '*You* are so bloody loud! Don't you know that's what your life-force energy inside you looks like? Like rainbows. Doesn't it, Evie? Larissa's been reading the books in your shop. She showed me a picture.'

'Really?' Gabs said, holding up the vibrant baby suit. 'I reckon that's what I must look like inside after I've been mixing my slushie cocktails on ladies' night at the Bendoorin RSL.'

'Oh, Gabrielle. Four hours in a car with you is far too much,' said Doreen. She turned to Bec. 'I got this for you, the mother of the baby.'

'Oh, how sweet of you, thanks,' said Bec.

The women snickered as Rebecca folded back the gift paper. Their snickers unravelled to hysterics when she screamed. There in her hands were a selection of jelly butt plugs, a remote-controlled clit-stimulator, a purse vibrator and a giant rotating dildo.

'What are those things, Mummy?' asked Ben.

Bec quickly turned her back. 'Er, just lightsabers for adults,' she said, then swivelled to the women. 'You absolute buggers! How am I supposed to get through security with those things? This one could be considered a weapon!' She thumped the dildo on Gabs's shoulder.

'I'm sure you can switch them to flight mode. Mile-high solo club here you come!' said Gabs.

Laughing, they began to stash the presents in Bec's luggage, but fell suddenly silent as they looked behind her.

'Well, see ya then,' Gabs said abruptly.

'Yep, bye,' said Doreen and just as quickly as they had arrived, the women were scuttling away. Bec frowned at their behaviour.

Evie and Yazzie had also, for some unknown reason, ushered the boys to a nearby vending machine and were bent over fumbling for coins in Evie's purse, even though they'd just had a big airport hotel brunch. Rebecca puzzled at what they were up to. But when she turned to glance behind her, she knew exactly why they had all disappeared from her space.

There weaving his way through the airport crowd came Sol Stanton. He looked so good. Striking, with his dark hair messed up from the wind, his divine torso sculpted under a black tight-fitting woollen top.

'Rebecca!' he called out, intensity personified. The women had been stalling her! What did they know? But her questions faded when she took in the fact that *he was here*! Desire for him swept her up along with an eddy of pain. She felt the wash of longing for him. At last she finally acknowledged that she had been blocking him and fooling herself. She had missed him utterly.

He came to her, passion and emotion cast on his dramatic face. Then he gathered her up in his arms and held her. They stood like that for a time, just feeling each other breathe, the solidity of their bodies, the intoxicating subtle scent of the other, as the world revolved busily around them. In that moment, she knew: she loved this man.

He stooped and kissed her deeply. With love too. When he pulled away, she saw he had excitement in his eyes.

'Sol! What are —?'

'Silencio, my love! I have something to show you.' Sol reached around to his back pocket and handed her a folded-up newspaper clipping.

As she straightened the paper, Rebecca took in the headline: *Stanton Corporation Outbids Mining Giant*. Her eyes scanned the print with a mix of joy and disbelief ...

*In a dramatic last-minute deal, historic Australian property Waters Meeting was rescued from the fate of open-cut coal mining when Stanton Pty Ltd director Sol Stanton outbid mining giant Texlon. Stanton plans to rehabilitate the property and use it as a study for grassland carbon sequestration to bolster the agricultural sector and the environment.*

Rebecca looked up at Sol. His eyes were searching her face nervously for her reaction.

Her mouth dropped open in shock. Tears rose to her eyes. Her hand flew to her burning cheeks. 'You *bought* it?'

'Sí.'

She looked at him, the laughter bubbling up in her, a wide smile growing on her face. *'You bought Waters Meeting?'*

Sol laughed too. 'Sí! I did. For you, but at the same time, no, not at all for you. It was a business decision. My father and me. Could you see Rivermont next to a mine site? No way. Horroroso! And after our work with Andrew, I am committed to regeneration of land — not destruction. So yes, I love you, but I did not do this for your love. You have my love whether it comes back to me or not.'

'Sol. This ... this is ...'

'I wanted to tell you in person. I didn't want you upset that I am now the owner of what was your family farm.'

'Upset?' Rebecca said, goose bumps sprinkling her skin, her baby girl taking tumbles inside her. 'Oh, Sol. It couldn't be better! No mining on Waters Meeting! No more mines! And you will restore the soil!' She was jumping up and down now, holding his hands. Ecstasy flooded through her very soul that the beautiful property where two rivers met would now be taken care of by a man like Sol. 'This is the best news!' She reached up to hug him.

As he held her, he began to speak rapidly. 'Soon I start to build a home,' Sol said, his voice and accent thick with emotion. 'Not on the site of your old house, but on the flat rock, overlooking where the rivers merge. Comprender?'

Rebecca nodded and smiled. She knew the exact place. 'I've always thought it would be amazing to build a house there. Beautiful.'

'It will be an eco-house — made from the land, self-sufficient, comprender?'

Rebecca nodded again.

'With a big kitchen and big oven. I am going to be Bendoorin Man Cake champion for many years to come.'

Rebecca nodded, her eyes tearing up at the vision he was creating for her.

'You and your boys, and your new little girl when she arrives, are very welcome there. So you must come!'

Rebecca swallowed. The reality that she was about to get on a plane hit her. And yet here was a man she adored before her. For a moment she felt herself tugged towards him. She drew in her breath. 'That's lovely of you, Sol. But I have to go. I have to go to the States ...' Distress was entering her tone.

Sol held up his hand and smiled gently at her, shaking his head. 'Rebecca,' he said, 'of course you have to go. I would not dream of stopping you. And I will come to you and help with Andrew's project. Waters Meeting and Rivermont can be used to showcase what results can be gained. This is a long-term project ... for both of us. And we shall see what happens between us, sí? Let the stars decide.' He looked deep into her eyes, imploring her to believe what he was saying.

'Sí! Yes!' Rebecca said, nodding, laughing, as she laced her fingers into his. 'Right now I don't know if that will be my path, but we shall see. OK?'

'OK!'

She reached up and kissed him gently on the lips and held his face in the palms of her hands. 'Thank you, Sol, thank you,' she breathed, resting her forehead on his.

And as she shut her eyes, she saw the image of herself standing on a timber verandah that cast itself out over a rock ledge overlooking two tributaries, the Rebecca River flowing on from that point as one. And beyond that the land, spread out before her, the plants thriving in soils that could now sing with life. She saw them all there. Her children, Sol, her animals. She saw the ancient pulse of the land, and the celebration of the Indigenous souls who had loved the land too before her time. In her mind's eye, she saw it all. And in that moment, she knew she was already, and always would be no matter where she was, *home*.

As Rebecca tightened her seat belt and felt the massive plane taxi along the runway, she shut her eyes and felt the rush of adrenaline course through her body. The baby kicked and turned within. Beside her she could hear the boys quietly chatting, kept calm by the extraordinary, gentle presence of Evie. She pictured the new version of Waters Meeting with Sol at its heart. She breathed in deeply and thought to herself how lucky she was. How lucky to be alive. To have looked into the fire. To have had her life burned beyond recognition and to have survived.

As the jumbo's engines revved, she could feel her heart beating. It was beating for her baby within, her boys beside her. It was beating for the land. And now she knew it was beating for Sol. In her heart, she knew she had to make this journey. It was a new beginning. She had the chance to make a difference not just on a few thousand acres on one farm, but on millions of acres, across the globe.

She had seen the pictures on the internet of where she would live on the Lucky D Ranch. Dreamy photos of the pine-clad Montana hills that rose up towards mountain peaks. Summer skies swathed with streaks of pink and gold. Then a similar shot from the same angle taken in mid-winter with deep snow coating the landscape in a softness of white. In another photo, she saw the sharp-pitched red timber barn of the Lucky D Ranch where it stood in rustic beauty beside the cottage where she and the boys would live. The dwellings nestled in a cottonwood grove beside river flats where glossy quarter horses grazed lazily beneath cedars. Andrew had also emailed a picture of the office in which she would work and a snap of a jet-black mare named Loretto, the horse Andrew said she would ride, as well as the paint ponies for the boys and the little ranch schoolhouse. It was all ahead of her.

As she lay back against the headrest and felt the vortex of speed gathering and heard the plane engines roaring, she realised after all she had been through, after all life had dished up to her, she hadn't just survived — she had *thrived*. She was stronger than ever.

As the plane lifted into the blue and soared through the clouds, Bec suddenly decided she would name her baby girl Skye. For it was sky that connected her to everything. To the country she had just left behind and to the idyllic place that would soon be her home. It was sky too that linked her to the universe beyond the clouds where stars hung in nothingness. A place Evie had taught her to feel within, so the craziness of life on this one tiny planet could no longer overwhelm her.

Rebecca felt goose bumps course across her skin. There was no trace of bitterness or regret in her body. Only the zinging sensation of love. And the knowledge that she had learned and she had grown. And she was a better mother for it. A better human for it. And now, thanks to all those happenings, all those turnings of the world, the slow forming of the days and nights of her life, *after all that*, from this moment now, Rebecca knew she had a blank page on which to create.